Cry of the Cat

Kevin Bouchard

Publisher's Note:

This is a work of fiction. All names, characters, places, and events are the work of the author's imagination.

Any resemblance to real persons, places, or events is coincidental.

Photograph credit:

A New England church as photographed by Kevin Bouchard.

Solstice Publishing - www.solsticepublishing.com

Cry of the Cat

A Supernatural Thriller

Kevin Bouchard

This book is dedicated to a high school English teacher who taught me that there was so much more to a story than the story, to a college professor who told me I could write well when I wanted to, to a Pulitzer Prize Winning photo-journalist in whose rock band I was lucky enough to play drums, to my mother for encouraging me in all that I've ever attempted, to my grandfather for being a genuine presence in my life, and to my amazing wife Robin who has stood by my side for three decades and from whom I draw all my inspiration.

"Raw emotion is like an open wound and wounds can
become infected."
—Memoirs of a 'Stringer' by Chase Nathaniel Christian (as
yet unpublished)

Requiem

Chase Christian is standing in a long dark corridor built of centuries-old wood, the smell of damp and dust seeping into his flesh like a virus. There is the faint sound of wind moving through old joists, fingering its way into forgotten nooks and crannies and catching like threadbare cloth on hand-hewn rafters and rusty nails.

A sound rises up in the distance, a cat's cry echoing through the thick black air, growing louder, coming from everywhere and nowhere all at once.

Chase's spine stiffens and a gut-shriveling cold winds its way through his being. He knows he must run, get out, but before he can move a muscle he feels heat rolling past him, passing *through* him, wringing the chill from his bones. It is a white-hot tsunami from an unimaginable blast furnace, a tornado of blue flame rushing toward him. And piercing the cacophony like the screech of a dying animal is the cat's cry, its ear-shredding pitch deafening. And the unrelenting heat is searing his skin, causing his flesh to bubble and fall away, and Chase screams into the burning hell around him as he claws his way up and out of his nightmare, gasping, bathed in sweat, the sound of the cat's cry fading into nothingness. And then there is only the night and the darkness and the rain on the window.

Chapter One

"Chase Christian, you fucking 'ambulance chaser,' climb out of that Tequila bottle and talk to me!"

Chase, taken aback by the voice on the mobile phone, squinted against his suddenly all too bright surroundings, the smell of Cuervo and lime swimming around him.

It was Eloise on the line sounding anxious. This was unlike the usually cool, calm, and collected Eloise.

Chase had intended to cover a crash on the Old Cape Highway to which his police scanner had alerted him. But the endless line of stragglers returning from Cape Cod had squashed that effort by snarling every access point. When the scanner reported that the scene would be clearing soon, Chase, who was still miles away, decided to call it a night. He rarely missed such opportunities, but Gevaudan, a city of nearly two hundred thousand people, had never let him down. By Friday he'd have at least two good pieces to peddle to the local air waves as well as a few second-rate clips to pad his portfolio. Gang fights, night club brawls, car crashes, they were all fodder for Chase's lens.

"Are you there?" Eloise prompted her voice low and impatient. She was clearly on duty and taking a big risk. "I'm hanging this phone up right now if you don't—"

"I'm here," he growled. "And you can drop the 'ambulance chaser' bit. Reporter. Videographer. Stringer will do."

Chase could sense Eloise rolling her eyes at the other end of the line, ready and willing to offer up her home-grown definition of ambulance chaser as one who profits from the misfortune of others, to end his protestations. And, as usual, he would let her derogatory observation roll off his back. He'd gotten good at that, he'd had a lot of practice. Julie, Chase's ex, had made certain of it.

But, unlike Julie, Eloise usually changed her tune once Chase's efforts came to monetary fruition. Though Eloise *had* always maintained that her motivation for helping him was, at its core, a noble one—keeping the authorities honest, supporting the first amendment, these were her arguments. She'd once said that it was all related to her late father's activities back when she was a child growing up in Haiti, though she'd never elaborated on the subject. And Chase had never cared enough to risk their relationship by pressing her for details.

"Give me a minute," he insisted, reluctantly pushing the latest shot of Silver Edition away and rubbing his eyes.

The bartender, a thick ruddy Irishman whose face might have been carved from the Blarney Stone, was studying Chase from the end of the bar. Strangers receiving phone calls was apparently frowned upon by the locals. Mginty's was not Chase's usual watering hole. But Jimmy Jazz's was temporarily closed, (fucking Department of Public Health), the music of The Clash and The Sex Pistols having been replaced until further notice by that of The Pogues and U2.

"Sorry, what have you got?" he said.

"I'll be *getting* a new job if you don't clean the shit out of your ears and answer your phone," Eloise said, her voice betraying her Creole roots, as was the case when the old girl was riled.

Swing shift dispatcher for the Flint Village Division of the Gevaudan, Massachusetts PD meant Eloise was in a unique position to provide Chase with a head start on other stringers. And, on rare occasions, if fortune was with him and Eloise was feeling generous, even the cops. That's why he'd assigned her a specific ring tone: Mike Oldfield's

Tubular Bells, the theme from The Exorcist, which he'd failed to hear due to The Edge's guitar solo on *All I Want Is You* crackling through the bar's crude stereo system.

"Thought you'd be covering that wreck out on the Old Cape Highway," Eloise said.

"Didn't work out."

"Side-tracked by a bar I suppose. We need to talk about that one of these days."

"Give me the details mom," he said, brushing her comment aside.

"Thirteen Warren Street, near the Ship to Shore Bar. Watch out for the water rats. I hear they're as big as cats down there."

"It's true," Chase said. "My grandfather used to shoot them with a single-shot Daisy when he was a kid."

"Well, the Delacroix Street Boyz own that neighborhood, and they don't carry no BB guns, so watch out your ass don't get ventilated."

"Ventilated," Chase snorted, glancing warily at the bartender who was talking on the phone. Reporting to his boss about the night's profits no doubt, or else running interference for one of Mginty's regulars whose wife was looking for him. Five dollars got you a "he just left," ten, an "I haven't seen him," and twenty got you a sincere sounding "never heard of him."

"Warren Street," Chase confirmed. "Lucky number thirteen."

"You hear fine when you want to," Eloise said.

"When I'm properly motivated."

Chase knew that Warren Street was one of those waterfront neighborhoods that seemed to be rotting away like the pilings of an old pier. The area was crammed full of run-down tenements, 'triple-deckers' as the locals called them, built in the days of mill baron royalty, once crammed full of immigrant families slaving away at piece-work well into the wee hours of the morning.

Today these same tenements served as crude housing, mostly Section-Eight welfare flops for *wanna-be* hoods and gang-bangers all trying to make a buck, the bounty of the mills having petered out decades earlier.

Cotton had once been king in New England, but cheap southern labor had ended its reign. Since then the Warren Street neighborhood, which had been a dubious one to start with, had gone completely to the dogs. There was nothing happening there lately but back-alley drug deals, aging hookers seeking non-discriminating clients, and would-be wise guys rolling drunks for their wallets.

Everybody wanted to be Whitey, Chase thought. Even those who'd never heard of him.

"So what's the complaint?"

"The complaint is an anonymous one," Eloise said. "Someone calling from one of those 'burner' phones no doubt, using '67' to block the number. But Gevaudan PD appreciates its anonymous tips, so the switch board computer doesn't reject any calls. Besides, lower Warren is the sort of place where no one sees nothing, the sort of place to which the boys in blue don't rush. No point. No witnesses willing to talk so why bother?"

"So what the hell *is* there?" Chase asked, wondering if he should bother wasting his time, especially with the Cuervo beckoning.

"Nothing substantial. No gunshots, just some screaming and glass breaking. Probably a domestic, but as it's early in the week, I thought you might want to have a look. And something about this call made my *entwisyon* tingle, and you know how *that* goes."

Chase understood completely. Eloise had a kind of sixth sense for strange events. And both she and Chase had profited from her ability over the years.

"So I'm holding on the call, but you gotta' move your skinny white ass if you want this one."

"Give me fifteen."

"You've got ten."

Chase blew Eloise a kiss and ended the call.

Gathering his wits and willing the blood back into his legs, he set some cash down on the bar and slid off the stool. The bartender was still talking on the phone, but he noticed nonetheless. Guys like that always do.

He clipped the phone to his belt and bid Mginty's adieu. And, as he did, a sliver of remorse slipped into his heart. If Julie could see him now, she'd simply nod knowingly, realizing she'd been right all along.

A fleeting observation struck Chase and he realized that, since the divorce, he'd done everything possible to prove her right. It was all there, the increased drinking, the isolation and the edgy attitude. Was it self-loathing? Maybe. Or was it self-destructive? Also maybe.

The inevitable question popped into his head: had he become the victim of the proverbial 'self-fulfilling prophecy?' His own unique brand at least? But before this new-found cognizance could take root, Chase's fragile ego jettisoned it like a gut full of bad liquor. He'd never been very good at self-reflection. Or self-recrimination. Julie had convinced him of that with little effort. And the universe had backed her up with less.

But exes weren't supposed to entertain positive thoughts about the ones they'd left behind. It was strictly *verboten*. Julie was no exception. If they'd had kids maybe she would think better of him. But that was doubtful. Some things were simply not meant to be. And the high school sweetheart thing was terribly over-rated, especially the belated variety.

To put it simply he'd married the wrong woman and accepted all the blame. It had been like taking the path of least resistance, which was something else at which Julie insisted he excelled.

But enough of this fucking self-pity, he thought angrily. The night and the job were calling.

Chase fought back the thin veil of inebriation that had settled over him, walked quickly to the door and out into the warm night, the grim-looking bartender's watchful gaze dogging his steps.

***

Gevaudan's vague attempt at a skyline was coming alive, its lighted windows glistening in the evening air like prefabricated stars. It was spring and the air already felt thick with impending summer. And the meteorologists were predicting rain.

The wail of passing sirens pierced the thick air like a blade. Gevaudan was a city with an ample crime rate fueled by a transient population that was replacing the natives with the speed and efficiency of a deadly virus. And the newcomers held little regard for the city Chase had always called home. They were simply passing through, having burned bridges behind them, aiming to consume whatever resources they could before moving on once more. And Chase's job was to glean profit from the carnage they left in their wake while simultaneously feeding the dark cravings of late-night couch potatoes who simply could not get enough of the blood and violence. And Chase Christian was *very* good at his job. This then was his true love, his *soul mate*. It was little wonder his marriage and all his previous relationships had crashed and burned.

Infused with fresh purpose he crossed the street, climbed aboard his small SUV and turned the engine over. He flipped on his police scanner, tuned his ears to the crackle and gunned the engine.

Tequila sloshed around in his stomach like clothes in a washing machine. It was an unpleasant yet familiar sensation, but Chase knew it would pass. It always did. He had purpose now, and purpose always drove his demons away. At least for a time.

Chapter Two

The horizon had been reduced to a ribbon of bloody magenta, broken sporadically by the dark outlines of high-rises and tenement rooftops, as Chase set out for the waterfront. The cool sultry air of spring in New England streamed through the open window of the SUV, carrying with it the pungent odor of car exhaust and the steady drone of evening traffic. Free from winter's grip, people were out and about, the slimmest hint of summer affecting them like an effusion of pheromones.

Chase wove through the ebbing flow of cars crammed into the northern edge of the city as if on auto-pilot. Rising from the clutter of old architecture was the Night Owl Diner perched like its namesake in all its neon glory on one of the busiest corners in the city, its windows aglow with gastronomical life, its neon green owl gazing out at the tired city with glistening red eyes from atop the building's Art Deco framework. The short order cook was visible through the glass, bent over the grill, preparing Coney Island hot dogs for over-the-road truckers and local kids grabbing some food before hitting the clubs of Providence or Boston.

Chase was a Night Owl regular, every Friday night at ten (providing some newsworthy event didn't call him away). It was a ritual begun with his grandfather, a maintenance supervisor at a local mill, until the ravages of lung cancer put an end to that particular tradition shortly after Chase's fourteenth birthday.

But the memory of evenings at the Night Owl, dining on what locals called 'dogs' with the 'works' (basically steamed hot dogs lathered with Coney Island meat sauce, mustard, onions, and celery salt) as well as a 'coffee cabinet' on the side (aka a coffee ice cream frappe with some Autocrat coffee syrup) would always be there.

Tonight, however, Chase had other business. And, though his stomach grumbled, he knew food would have to wait.

And so, with a pang of reluctance he left the diner's crowded parking lot behind and veered onto Warren Street.

Static-rich voices from the police scanner broke his mental meandering. He strained to listen, but heard no mention of the address Eloise had given him. Chase would have to pack a little extra cash into Eloise's envelope this month.

One of the longest and oldest thoroughfares in Gevaudan, Warren Street sloped downward through a man-made valley of old tenements and minor businesses. A permanent cool damp darkness lay across the place. The image made Chase think of Arcade Fire's *Sprawl* with its message of creeping urban decay. He glanced to the left where, flickering intermittently between the mostly darkened triple-deckers like glistening stars promising some semblance of normalcy, were the not-so-distant lights of Mitre Square. One of those lights was in fact another one of his favorite destinations, the Mitre Square Doughnut Shop, which accurately promised twenty-four-hour service and the finest coffee in town.

He drove onward through the gloom, night settling around him like a shroud, his spine stiffening with apprehension. The tenements surrounding him had ceased to resemble houses. Ragged, heavily shadowed, desperately in need of repair, they had been transformed into misshapen ruins from an architect's nightmare.

Chase eased up on the accelerator, his heart compensating for the decreased movement of the vehicle by hitching into a higher gear. Number thirteen loomed like an ancient obelisk from the creeping mist.

Driving slowly past the big old tenement, he took cautious note of a clutch of people gathered near the front porch of a neighboring structure—Delacroix Street Boyz. He killed the headlights and pulled into an empty space diagonally across the street from the suspect dwelling and studied the scene.

"Shit." This was no good.

Chase pulled away from the curb, drifted further down the street. Maybe there was another way.

He hung a sharp left into a shadowy back-alley connector, lights still extinguished, and swung left again and started up Delacroix Street, which ran parallel to Warren. He spied an empty lot abutting the rear of number thirteen.

He drifted into the vacant lot, broken asphalt chunks crunching beneath his tires. He drew to a halt and killed the engine. He waited a moment, the engine clicking as it cooled. He wondered if this was worth the effort. Eloise had provided him with little information. But he trusted her. She would never send him into harm's way, at least not deliberately. And she *did* have an instinct for news. She would have made a good reporter, if she hadn't decided to dedicate her life to answering phones.

Chase picked up his Canon, checked to make sure it was charged, gathered up his video unit, deactivated the SUV's cabin light and climbed out into the night. He shut the door quietly, nudging it into place with his hip, pocketed the keys and set off for a waist-high fence that separated the tenement's back yard from the empty lot.

Pausing, Chase gathered his wits. An eerie stillness hung over the old neighborhood. The area reeked of low tide. There were no cars moving through this part of town, no pedestrians out for an evening stroll. The only sounds were that of the Deep Shoal Lighthouse foghorn and a freight rumbling through the rail yard where Warren Street petered out into a broad rocky delta littered with abandoned warehouses and the putrefying bones of boathouses, relics from the first part of the previous century.

Reasonably satisfied that he would not be noticed, Chase secured the Canon and video unit straps and awkwardly scaled the rotting, rickety fence, paint flakes falling around his legs like rust-colored snowflakes. Struggling for purchase, he landed on a patch of damp earth without dropping any of his gear. He kept a penlight in his pocket, but couldn't risk alerting the Delacroix Street thugs.

He crossed to the cracked concrete walkway that ran the width of the house and moved toward the alley that ran between the side of the old tenement and its nearest neighbor, a cinder block building bearing faded letters that read Chet's Auto Body.

Chase hugged the wall and peered down the alleyway. He heard voices but could detect no movement.

He returned to the back yard and headed toward the eastern edge of the property where he stumbled upon a door set into the northeast corner of the house. He tried the handle. It gave way and he slipped inside.

The entryway was rich with the cool moist smell of old granite. Closing the door, he ran his fingers along the wall, found a switch, and flipped it. A bare light bulb came alive. There were no windows, no way for the light to be seen from the yard or street.

Chase found himself on a small landing. To the right were several stone steps leading down into an earth-hewn cellar. A short flight of wood steps led up toward the front of the house. He followed these and emerged in a narrow entryway that led to a screen door that looked out onto the front porch. Here the voices were louder.

A wooden staircase that wound upward into murky oblivion was situated to the right. It smelled of mold and decades-old dust. Chase could practically hear the old wood rotting. He blew out a breath, made sure the Canon's neck strap was secure, tightened his grip on the video unit, and started his ascent.

The darkness deepened as he climbed and the smell of mold and must grew stronger. His fingers traced the curved wall, fumbling across the crudely patched horse-hair plaster, but he found no evidence of a light switch and the dim bulb in the rear entry had faded from view. He was in total darkness, but still fearful of using the penlight.

After what seemed an eternity, Chase reached a long narrow landing. Ignoring some closed padlocked doors and boarded up windows lining the corridor, he started up the next flight of stairs.

Here the darkness was palpable and the smell intolerable. Sweat trickled down his spine. He was suddenly overcome by a deep dread. Chase had seen many accidents, dead bodies, blood, severed limbs—he'd once spent an hour helping the state cops at the scene of a motorcycle accident search the side of the Old Cape Highway for the driver's severed head, his Canon poised for action in case he got lucky—it came with the job. But this was different. He felt as if something cold and evil had crawled inside him to die.

He continued to climb, finally arriving at the third-floor landing. He moved past two more padlocked doors and arrived at a door that was not only unsecured but ajar.

Chase paused, listening, his senses tingling, his stomach roiling. Silence. There was only a dull glow seeping through the crack, gathering on the floor in a dusty puddle. He pulled a nitrile glove from his pocket and slipped it over his fingers, typical stringer issue equipment. Then, gulping down a lung full of courage, he slowly nudged open the door.

Chapter Three

The kitchen to the old apartment was thick with shadows and the smell of old grease. Flies buzzed lazily through the gloom and a rickety ceiling fan wobbled tenuously. Large plastic bags stuffed to their brims with clothes were everywhere, spilling their contents down their bulging sides. Three darkened doorways were situated at odd intervals throughout the room, the nearest abutting the doorway through which Chase had entered.

Chase produced his penlight, casting the beam into each nook and cranny, scattering shadows like bats, exploring each corner in turn, searching for movement, listening for sounds, checking for evidence of a crime. Could Eloise be wrong?

He urged the beam into the nearest doorway. The light revealed a small pantry lined with grimy shelves thick with dust and cans of vegetables and beans. There was a steel sink in a corner where food-encrusted dishes were piled high. The probing light sent a contingent of cockroaches scurrying for cover.

Beyond the pantry he found a grungy bathroom, empty save for traces of black mold clinging to the exposed shower stall and dingy wet towels lying in heaps on the floor.

Chase returned to the kitchen where he considered two windows set into the outer wall. Faded beach towels with beer logos had been draped unevenly over bent aluminum rods, their tattered edges rustling like dead leaves.

A dull clunking sound seized his attention and he swung the light toward a filthy refrigerator squatting against the room's inner wall. Its compressor was making a sound like an ancient locomotive struggling up a steep incline.

Chase reached for the handle with his gloved hand, opening the thing with trepidation, visions of shelves lined with dismembered body parts dancing in his head. He was relieved to discover only a few food items stored within: some deli meats, a loaf of bread, and a few six packs of some generic-looking beer. He closed the door and moved toward the second darkened doorway.

The pen-light revealed a large four-poster bed in need of a mattress. The dingy blankets lay in heaps on the floor. The rest of the room was devoid of furniture. He panned the light across the headboard and the beam caught on tangles of cord tied to each of the bed posts. A cold gasp rattled his windpipe. Something unspeakable had happened here. Eloise had nailed this one.

Chase turned to the final doorway where he perceived a vertical sliver of light hovering ghost-like at the end of a small corridor that led from the kitchen toward the front of the house. Cautiously, he crept toward the glow, his mouth as dry as the Sahara, hundred-plus-year-old joists complaining beneath his feet.

He reached a six-panel door at the end of the corridor and peered through the illuminated crack. He had come too far to retreat, but he glanced back at the dreary but comparatively innocuous kitchen nonetheless before stepping into the Twilight Zone.

A garish light emanating from the left side of the room rendered him temporarily blind and he stumbled back against the door jamb, his hand raised defensively. But as his eyes adjusted to the glare, the full horror of what the room contained struck him like a hammer.

The room was the width of the house, each end anchored by a window with paper-thin sheers that had seen better days. It appeared that someone had attempted to make this room look quasi-acceptable.

Chase felt a gust of air coming from a spot just past the bright light and he squinted at the glare until the image swam into focus. A window had been reduced to rubble. A warm breeze drifting through the space stirred the old sheers turning them into ghosts.

He detected a thin haze of smoke in the air and a foul oddly familiar smell. The room was lined with thick green shag carpeting, the sort that had been popular in the sixties and seventies. The walls were lined with crude veneer paneling, cheap but efficient. There was no furniture in the room, only the displaced bedroom mattress lying a few feet from the ruined window. Most of the room was awash in darkness, the only source of illumination being that of a large light fixture framed by four adjustable barn doors perched atop an expensive-looking video camera which was in turn secured to a heavy-duty tripod some few feet from the mattress. The lens of the apparatus was trained on the mattress as well as the bloody body of a naked woman lying sprawled motionless at its center.

Chase struggled to shrug off the shock that had gripped him and raised the Canon. He began squeezing off shots, his hands growing steadier with each exposed frame, the professional in him taking charge of his trembling fingers.

After a few dozen stills he slung the Canon and hoisted his video unit. Activating the unit, he zoomed in on the dead woman's face and crept closer, allowing the lens to absorb everything like the gaze of a seasoned detective. The dead woman's eyes were wide open, faded gray, sunken, the white one filled with blood, her face blanched white, her mouth agape as if about to speak. Someone had cut her lovely throat, turning her pale flesh into a jumble of gnarled hamburger. Bits of yellowish cartilage from her windpipe were visible poking out of the gore. The blood had seeped onto the dingy mattress, creating a crimson pattern which nearly encircled her head like a crudely drawn halo.

Chase backed away from the bloody carnage and panned the video unit around. Where was the weapon? And where was the killer?

A fleeting chill, like the tiny feet of a mouse, scurried up his spine, making him think of eyes watching from the darkness.

Almost reluctantly he turned slowly around and trained the video unit on the darkened part of the room. The light probed deeper until the glare glinted off the missing weapon. The straight razor that housed the bloody blade was clutched in the charred hand of a darkened husk sitting upright in the corner.

Chase's stomach slithered up into his throat. He squelched the urge to run, fought to steady the video unit and aimed the light at the monstrous thing. It was dead, that much was certain. But *dead* was only the beginning.

The body looked as if it had been fed through a wood chipper and then set ablaze. The chest and stomach had been torn open and strips of what must have been a black leather vest hung across the lower abdomen and thighs like the strops of a demented barber. The man's head was wrapped in a black leather mask replete with zippers for the mouth and eyes; it was the sort Chase had seen in S and M videos and it chilled his nerves.

The top portion of the mask had been ripped away revealing the man's torn and wrenched hairline, which was hanging in a bloody flap as if he'd been scalped by some renegade Indian from a John Wayne western. But the worst part was the dead man's eyes, which seemed to be staring directly at Chase from within the leather-rimmed eye sockets making Chase think that the man might stand up at any moment and take a step toward him.

Chase panned down with the video unit. One of the corpse's legs was twisted beneath the body in an unimaginable way and the rug surrounding the man was splattered with blood. The old paneling behind him was layered in soot, some of it black, some a strange sickly yellow color.

The scene reminded Chase of one he'd come upon years earlier while covering the aftermath of an explosion at a chemical plant in the nearby town of Nazareth. But the damage there had been much more extensive. And there had been clear evidence as to the source of the explosion. The damage here had been limited somehow. It was as if the heat source had been specifically directed at the man wearing the leather mask, sparing the rest of the room. And the dead woman was not burned at all. Or eviscerated. Her only wound was the deep laceration to her throat. But in her case, that had proved more than sufficient.

Chase's amateur criminologist brain came alive and began sifting through possible explanations. But try as he might, he simply couldn't put sense to the grisly scene. It was a bizarre puzzle with several missing pieces.

One thing was certain: whoever had killed the woman had either filmed the entire event or *planned* to film it. Unless someone showed up and killed them both, or at least 'leather mask' after he'd cut the woman's throat. And perhaps called the police before fleeing into the night?

Chase studied the light and the elaborate camera. Maybe someone was making a 'snuff' film? He forced his eyes to consider the charred body in the corner. He felt Mginty's Tequila slithering around in his stomach.

The sound of sirens found the ruined window. He shut the video camera, knocked off a few more stills with the Canon and turned to the doorway. He thought better of it, and went to the window, carefully avoiding the splinters of glass. Clearly the assailant had come crashing through the window from the fire escape, which explained the element of surprise as well as the spattering of glass.

Chase elbowed the sheers aside. He thought about simply stepping through the window, but realized that he might further contaminate the scene by knocking some of the glass shards still clinging to the window frame onto the fire escape. And so he decided to poke his head through first, to check on the approaching sirens.

A gasp hissed past his lips and he stumbled backward, missing the glass shards by millimeters. He grabbed the window frame with his gloved hand in the nick of time, balancing the video unit on his thigh, gripping it with his free hand, somehow managing to avoid joining the corpse on the bloody mattress.

Confused, he backed away and made for the door.

Chase spilled into the corridor, crossed the kitchen and passed into the entry. Using the gloved hand, he closed the door until it was barely ajar, just as he'd found it. He descended the winding stairs, the old moldy house smell finding his senses, the wood complaining loudly.

He reached the first-floor entry, paused to listen to the shouts and the sound of scampering feet coming from the street as the Delacroix crew fled the arriving authorities. He killed the back-entry light and stumbled out into the back yard, the hot summer breeze tasting strangely welcome. The glow of flashing LEDs was oozing like blue fluid through the surrounding alleyways.

Chase ran to the fence and awkwardly vaulted it, landing in front of his car. He unlocked the thing, slid into the driver's seat and fumbled the key into the ignition. He sat back, gasping, his guts in turmoil, his brain racing. He watched the blue lights dancing in the spaces between the tenement and its neighbors.

He stowed his gear on the passenger-side floor and watched as flashlight beams probed the alley walls on the other side of the fence. A moment later they'd vanished; the cops had gone inside.

Chase started the car and, keeping the lights off, backed out into the street. Hoping to remain inconspicuous, he drove along Delacroix, tripping the lights only after he'd covered some distance.

He'd made it out in one piece, but the images of the dead man and woman were flashing in his brain like strobes. He could still see the blood, the dead man's exposed skull, and the woman's empty lifeless eyes. He could smell the smoldering flesh, the burned hair, and another more pungent odor he could not quite place.

And last, but certainly not least, he saw the gaping dark space beneath the smashed window where a fire-escape should have been.

Chapter Four

Connie Moncrief shook her head, rolled her tired gray eyes. It was a car wreck, a good one too. But the footage was the problem—it was bland, boring, not shocking enough for Dark Side, Connie's late-night news spot on KTX, the self-proclaimed Nocturnal Voice of South Coast New England. People staying up late during the week needed a *reason* to stay up late and Dark Side, with its shootings, stabbings, and night club brawls, provided just the right combination of blood and entertainment that the witching hour crowd craved.

It had happened a few hours earlier. Some kid, in his infinite wisdom, had decided to drive his 1968 Shelby Cobra Mustang into the ass-end of an eighteen-wheeler entering the westbound lane of the Old Cape Highway. At least the idiot had had the good sense to duck before the impact. Never even hit the brakes, just smash! It took the emergency responders more than an hour using the Jaws of Life to pry his stupid ass out of his car. Traffic had been backed up for miles. Miraculously he'd only suffered some bumps and bruises, though he was undoubtedly still lacking even the slimmest shred of common sense.

And as fate would have it along came some opportunistic 'newbie' with a video unit. But the kid was an amateur, not a pro by any stretch. Some of the footage was out of focus, some of it just plain bad. He'd clearly been more entranced with the flashing LEDs rather than the *meat and potatoes* of the scene. Everyone wanted to be fucking David Fincher.

But the Finchers and Scorseses would have shot the blood as well as the mood, nailed the carnage, the grimaces on the faces of the responders and the witnesses, someone puking for God's sake! And the kid had actually obeyed the cops and stayed *behind* the appointed line instead of ducking into the brush by the side of the highway and creeping up on the scene like a Navy Seal sniper as some other stringers Connie had known over the years would have done. *Those* were the ones to get the ratings *and* the cash. But this…

"Where's the blood?" Connie complained aloud, making her thoughts known to her staff. "Compound fractures. Crying mother. Something!"

"None of those things," Derek Ellison said shaking his head.

Derek was a good tech, young, a tad overweight, clearly gay, and ambitious. In other words, a male version of Connie. Except for the gay part. At least in the most recent sense (there were definitely some things best left in the distant past). And of course the difference in age, which was regrettable.

"The impact peeled the roof right off the fucking car," Derek observed. "The truck driver wasn't hurt, just pissed off."

"Where's the kid who shot the footage?" Connie asked.

"Gone home," Derek said. "I guess it's past his bed time. He was so excited it was almost embarrassing." Derek pursed his lips, crossed his flabby arms. "I say we run with it."

Connie chewed on nothing in particular. Derek was new, fresh out of college, the sort who figured he knew more than some fifty-something-year-old late-night producer working some third rate shit station in a market that wasn't interested in third rate shit, could *possibly* know.

"Fuck."

Gevaudan was no longer a world-renowned mill town, though it was too big to be considered a piss-ant burg either. But it *was* predominantly blue collar and most blue-collar people were either in bed by midnight or heading to the bars to throw back a few if they worked second shift.

The folks sitting on their respective couches at this hour were mom and pop pensioners, most of whom had dozed off hours ago and would awaken and crawl off to bed when the late-night commercials got too loud, barely remembering to shut the television as they went. And to get the few who were staring at their television sets with nothing better to do, nothing worth reading on hand, no one worthy to fuck nearby, one needed to grab their attention with blood, or at least the *promise* of blood. Explosions were good. A decent shark sighting off Cape Cod would often suffice. This *was* after all spring time in New England in spite of all the rain.

"Well, if it's all we've got, we'll run with it," Connie said, shaking her head with professional remorse.

Derek smiled. He actually fucking smiled! Connie shook her head again, headed for her office, the beginning of a headache starting behind her right eye.

"Ms. Moncrief."

It was Dale Blaise, calling to her from the receptionist desk which doubled as a research terminal at this hour. Another ambitious college grad, but one with good tits, Connie had noticed, which explained why the old fucks on first shift were always staying late to finish up some project-or-other. Though the dear girl seemed oblivious to her own charms as well as other facts such as the time of day and words with more than one syllable.

But these days, the Dales of the world held no appeal for Connie; that part of her life was dead and buried. And the pickings at KTX were indeed lean, especially as of late. Old men and kids, neither of which would serve her needs. And beggars couldn't be choosers and Connie's days of being a chooser had gone by the wayside many moons ago.

"Telephone," Dale said. "Line one."

Connie sat at her desk, picked up the phone and punched the blinking light.

"Yeah," she growled.

Connie Moncrief had long since stopped being polite on the phone. Besides, at this ungodly hour, to those most likely calling, a polite response was as strange a notion as the Pope shitting in the woods and then describing the event on Instagram.

"It's your favorite late-night crime fighter," Chase said.

"Where the hell have you been?" Connie said, leaning forward, a sliver of excitement finding its way into her voice. "I thought you fucking died or something. What's it been, two weeks?"

"More. It's been slow. Listen, I've got something hot; I just got it tonight. I'm checking it on my laptop. I'll wire it in, but I'll stop by too. I want to be there when you see it."

"Chase, you shit, you always come through at the eleventh hour. But not tonight," she added, slipping into negotiating mode. Always the consummate executive, at least in her own mind.

"We've got the spot sewn up," she said. "Car crash. Some asshole drove under an eighteen-wheeler out on—"

"And I've got two dead bodies leaking blood all over the cheap carpeting."

The line went silent.

"I'm listening," Connie said snapping her fingers for Dale with the good tits to come into her office. Dale obeyed, all smiles. What was it with these twenty-somethings and their fucking smiles?

"The video is practically on its way," Chase said. "Get your checkbook out."

"*I'll* fucking decide when I get my checkbook out."

Dale sat down and opened a pad of paper.

"No memo honey," Connie said her hand over the phone. "Get your ass to the control room. Tell Derek something's coming in, something hot."

Dale nodded vigorously, flipped the pad closed and vanished.

"Believe me," Chase said, "you're going to want to marry me for this."

Connie snorted. "Just send the fucking video Romeo."

She hung up, sat back in her chair and smiled. Chase was one of the best. And he wasn't afraid of the blood or getting some on his hands in the process. And he *never* stayed behind the police line.

***

Chase shut the mobile phone and went back to the laptop on the seat beside him. The video was fucking gold, some of his best work. And he'd beaten the cops to their own party, gotten the so called 'scoop' that Connie craved.

He watched as the upload bar filled. Then he kissed his palm, touched the screen and sent the footage on its way.

Chase and Connie went back years. She'd given him his first big pay day. An elderly couple had gotten themselves shot in a road rage incident and he'd come upon it strictly by accident, grabbing his mobile phone and filming the whole thing as the cops wrestled the perpetrator to the ground after he'd fired a couple of rounds at them with what turned out to be a cheap .22 caliber pistol. Everyone had survived, but *damn* it had been exhilarating.

Since then he'd managed to spread the wealth, sending clips to other stations, raking in some decent cash, making Connie jealous and keeping her hungry. But Connie always paid the best. She had a good nose for it and she was always desperate, always on the verge of being fired because the world was simply not quite as bad as the American public wanted it to be. And there *were* fringe benefits to their relationship. And that came in handy since Chase's ex, Julie, had set out for fairer waters leaving him high, dry, and very single in a time of journalistic Cholera.

Chase had tried, half-heartedly according to Julie, to make the marriage work. But nine-to-five was not something he could tolerate. Never could. He'd told her countless times over the years, but she just hadn't listened, always figured he'd come around to it. But he hadn't. Chase was nothing if not a man of his word. It was simply that his word was something Julie never wanted to hear.

Chase shook off the emotional cobwebs, checked to see that the transfer had been successful, closed the laptop and tucked it into its satchel. Then he started the SUV and drove toward KTX's satellite facility. He wanted to be there when Connie opened the file. The old bitch was going to have a stroke.

Chapter Five

Dale Blaise ran out of the station's control room, heading to the bathroom, with her slender hand plastered across her lovely mouth.

"Too fucking young," Connie said flatly, her eyes never straying from the largest of the monitors.

"Not bad," Chase said, from where he leaned against the open door jamb, his hands shoved into his pockets.

The video was far from perfect—it vacillated between moments of grainy shadow and razor-sharp clarity, but the effect seemed only to add to its sense of authenticity. And the young intern making a dash for the restroom tickled Chase's pride. He knew all too well that in the late-night world of sensational journalism a gasp was always welcome and some vomit was a plus.

A few staffers were gathered behind him in the hall, straining to see into the studio, their faces grim. A young African-American woman among them let out a gasp.

"Jimmy, shut that fucking door," Connie said and a young Asian man with long dark hair rose from his seat and closed the door.

All eyes were on the screen as the video finished with the shot of the mangled man lying in the corner. Slowly the video zoomed in on the terrible face. The dead eyes gazing out through the slits in the black leather mask created a positively chilling image, one worthy of Hitchcock at his very best.

Connie turned to Chase. "You little shit, you got there before the cops."

He smiled. "Friends in low places."

She nodded. "Let's go to my office, talk cash. You know that once this runs, the cops are going to want to talk to you *and* me. You have a story I presume?"

He nodded. "Always do."

"Good." Connie brushed past him and headed down the hall. A beat passed and Chase followed.

***

Connie flicked on the desk light; it spilled across her bare breasts. She reached across the desk, fished around for her bra and slipped it on, snapping it in place.

"Not bad for a woman my age," she said.

"I've never complained."

"Make sure you don't start."

"Blood always did work for you," Chase said as he slipped his jeans on and grabbed up his shirt from the brown leather sofa.

"Fuck you stringer," she said grinning. "Ambulance chaser. Blood means money. *That* turns me on."

"Keep telling yourself that," he said fishing his socks out from under the sofa.

"Check's on the desk," she said.

"I feel so cheap," he said, tucking the check into his pocket.

"You?"

Chase smiled wryly.

"So," Connie began, buttoning her blouse and carefully adjusting the sleeve that covered the jagged scar on her left forearm, "do you think the perp crashed through that window? Or did he come through the door? And who called the cops?"

"The Delacroix Street Boyz were hanging around next door. They wouldn't have called the cops though, even if they'd heard the commotion. Domestics are typical in that neighborhood. I'd guess one of the neighbors called the police. And folks in neighborhoods like lower Warren don't like to let on that they'd called the police; bad for neighborly relations. The back door was clear when I got there. And it was still clear when I left. Weird all around."

"How'd you get to the back door?"

"I parked in an empty lot abutting the back of the house, over on Delacroix. Hopped a fence and cut through the yard."

"I'd say that the perp came through the window," she said. "Why else would the glass be broken? It seems simple enough. Pretty ballsy crashing through the glass that way. Maybe the cops should be looking for a professional stunt man. Or Batman."

"One problem with that," Chase said, frowning. "I checked the fire escape—almost stepped right out onto the damned thing."

"That's how I figured you got out of there."

"That would have been my choice, but there *was* no fire escape. Just a big empty space and thirty dark feet to the ground."

"Mmm," Connie mused. "Killer must have come through the door then crossed the back yard, same as you. You said the apartment door was ajar. Hell, maybe the killer was hiding in the back yard as you came along. Maybe he watched you as you passed by."

"That's a comforting thought."

She laughed. "Better watch yourself out there."

"But that still doesn't explain the broken window," he said.

"Well, let the police figure it all out. I hear it's their job, not ours."

Connie slipped her shoes on and ran her fingers through her shoulder-length dyed auburn hair.

"Thank God I'm heading home soon," she said studying her face in a small mirror she'd taken from a desk drawer. "What are you going to tell the cops? They'll be along soon, maybe even tonight."

"Just driving by, officer," Chase said, trying to sound like a bumpkin. "And I got a hunch. I *am* a reporter with a nose for news. I'll tell them I heard the call on my scanner."

"Did you?"

Chase offered her a knowing look.

"Friends in low places," Connie said, waving him off. "I know, I know."

Chapter Six

The night air was still warm as Chase made his way home. He'd waited at the station for some time after the footage aired, but the police never showed. The switchboard had lit up like a Christmas tree after the piece ended though. And Connie's boss had called to congratulate her on the video and the inevitable controversy it was bound to stir up.

Late night news was one of the few places where controversy was like Viagra—it gifted its recipient with longevity and potency. KTX's call letters would be on the lips of every anchor on every station whenever Chase's footage was aired. And that could go on for days, weeks, maybe longer depending on how the police handled the whole affair. And that was good for business.

Connie had suggested using 'Night Stalker' as the lead, like the old television show with the reporter who wore the bad suit and always got in trouble with the police. The title held all sorts of promise, sequels almost definitely guaranteed. Hell, if the name caught on the cops might start using the 'Night Stalker' tag when referring to the case in an official capacity as well. The public was into names. It probably all got started with Jack the Ripper back in merry old England. People had always loved blood in copious amounts. And a good catch phrase only added to the hype.

Chase knew that things were hot in the city just now. He knew that there had been two shootings in the past few weeks, one of them fatal, and several stabbings over the past months, mostly occurring outside nightclubs in the troublesome south side of Gevaudan or in one of the numerous housing projects that littered the city. And a rookie cop had died after falling down an elevator shaft in an old mill while investigating a possible break-in.

And of course there were the typical conspiratorial rumors flying about. It was common knowledge that the political powers that be were as always abnormally preoccupied with sweeping some unpleasant business-or-other under the nearest rug at any given moment. This last was a particularly popular practice in Gevaudan, a practice designed to attract investors and businesses seeking locations essentially devoid of crime, of which Gevaudan, with the highest crime rates in the state, was not.

And then there was the competition, that *other* case, the one receiving all the headlines, all the attention, the one with the murdered kids. The police had already given *that* killer a name—he was being called the North Side Strangler. Poetic. The details of the killings were far less artistic.

Four very young children had been kidnapped, sexually assaulted, and strangled in the past few months. And with *that* sort of horrific shit happening, two dead nobodies in a run-down tenement were hardly likely to cause a ripple in the great pond of sensational journalism.

Chase pulled into the parking lot adjacent to his apartment building, slipped into a vacant space and killed the engine. He sat at the wheel for a long time, the warm breeze washing in through the open driver's side window, the sounds of distant cars and the occasional barking dog finding him in turn. His stomach had felt queasy while he was in the run-down apartment, probably the effects of the Tequila, the heat, and the reeking corpses, but the adrenaline the whole thing had infused him with had sent the butterflies packing. But now that the night had calmed down, the mixture of Tequila and dead, bloody bodies was proving to be too much and Chase ran to the nearest shrub and let loose. He stood waiting for his head to clear, the smell of freshly recycled Tequila wafting about him.

"Tough night?"

Chase raised his eyes. A woman was leaning over the rail of the second-floor balcony directly above him. A joint was smoldering between her fingers, its faint but unmistakable aroma drifting down to him, a dull light from the open slider behind her casting her in silhouette.

"Not so bad," he said dragging the back of his forearm across his mouth. "That you Dolores Kane?"

"How many Dolores Kane's do you know?"

"Only one." He managed a smile. "How's *your* night going?"

Dolores Kane was Chase's neighbor. Brown eyed. Dark-haired. Possessing what might be considered to be a husky contralto voice. Strangely aloof, she always seemed wary of the other tenants in the building, not mingling with any of them. And, based upon Chase's experience with the other tenants in the small apartment building, he completely understood.

"Cum-see, cum-sa," she said grinning. "How are the car wrecks treating you?"

He managed a grin. "My reputation proceeds me."

A siren shrieked in the distance. He glanced toward the shops across the street with their sturdy metal gratings pulled securely down across their doors.

"Dark Side," Dolores said. "I watch from time to time."

"It is what it is," he said craning his neck to see her. She had a good face, great body, but he'd never thought to pursue the situation. Besides, they were friends, or acquaintances. Neighbors sounded right. Once upon a time Chase had asked a woman who cut his hair out on a date, and when it didn't work out, he'd been forced to find himself a new stylist. It would be a shame to have to find a new place to live.

"It keeps the rent paid and provides me with a constant stream of entertainment," he added.

Dolores laughed, tossed the spent joint aside. "I heard that." She sighed, her mind switching gears. "Though I don't know how you can look at all that bad stuff and still sleep."

Chase sighed. "It happens whether I'm there or not," he said tossing out the first rationalization that popped into his tired brain. "Once or twice my footage even helped the cops."

Dolores nodded. "Well, be careful out there. Shit happens. Just make sure it doesn't happen to you."

She turned and went inside, closing the slider.

"Strange," he thought, shrugging. One more weird thing to add to his already weird night.

Chase shook it off, returned to his car, grabbed his gear and locked up.

He let himself in through the beat-up steel door and climbed the stairs to his apartment. Once inside, he made his way to the kitchen and plucked a can of Corona Light from the refrigerator, mumbling something about it being the "hair of the dog that bit him," cracked it open, bypassing the lime wedge. Then he plugged his mobile into its charger on the kitchen counter, stowed his gear in his small office, and shuffled off to bed.

Shedding his clothes and tossing them into the corner, he flipped on the flat screen, and flopped down onto the mattress. He thought of the dead girl bleeding all over a different mattress on the other side of town, though by now he knew she'd found her way to the morgue. He squinted hard against the image, trying to squeeze it out of his mind. He took a long pull of beer and set the can down on the nightstand. He struggled to focus on the flat screen, failed, and dozed off.

Chase dreamed of blood cascading down over him like a waterfall. This was not the first time he'd experienced this dream. And he figured that it wouldn't be the last. It didn't matter; when he woke he would not remember much. Forgetting had become an easy thing. Even for his subconscious. And that had bothered Julie, bothered her very much.

"How can you put those things, those terrible things you see night after night, out of your head so easily?" she'd complain. "Are you still even *human*?"

Chase sighed, rolled onto his side, falling deeper into sleep, losing himself. Sleep had become a very welcome thing these days, as had losing himself in it.

Outside, drizzle began to fall. A dog barked. Somewhere off in the night a train whistle called to the crescent moon.

Chapter Seven

The pounding at the door was insistent. Chase held the pillow over his face as long as he could, but when it became apparent that the person knocking was not going anywhere any time soon he rolled out of bed, growled "coming" and went to the door.

"Who is it," he hollered.

Beyond the living room window, rain was beginning to fall.

"Police," a female voice said.

"Shit." Connie had been right, as usual.

He opened the door.

The woman standing in the hall was tall, athletic, and neatly dressed in gray slacks, a crisp white blouse, and a thin black leather jacket. Her dark damp hair hung to her shoulders. Her eyes were steel blue. Eve Teschal was what Chase Christian and most of the people on planet Earth would consider to be attractive. It was her curt demeanor which bordered on 'iciness' that worked against her.

"Mr. Christian," Teschal said, her voice clipped and efficient.

"Detective, to what do I owe this honor?" The words left his mouth before he could coral them. Pissing off the police at this point was hardly a logical move.

"I see that you know who I am," she said, flashing and re-pocketing a badge, "so we can dispense with the formalities. I've spoken with Constance Moncrief at KTX about your video that aired last night on a show she produces called Dark Side."

Chase nodded. "Would you like to come in?" He'd wanted to ask what she'd thought of the footage, but successfully reined that wise crack in before it escaped.

"Thank you."

Her eyes began moving leisurely around the apartment, taking in the scene, lingering on the partly unpacked boxes, stray take-out food containers and pizza boxes, as well as the brimming trash can squatting near the kitchen doorway.

"Moving in or out?"

"Neither," he said, making his way to the kitchen, a dull Tequila headache starting behind his eyes. "I'll make some coffee."

"No need. This won't take long. But I *am* interested to know how you managed to videotape a crime scene, a double homicide no less, before our people could secure it."

Chase paused while rinsing the coffee pot. Luck of the Irish, he thought to say, but managed to restrain himself.

"If I didn't know better I'd say you have an inside source."

He felt something cold wriggle through his stomach.

"But that's a conversation for another time," she said, letting her suspicion hang in the air like a foul smell.

Chase stood at the kitchen counter gazing out at the strengthening rain, the coffee pot in his hand. If Teschal had found out about Eloise, she would have come right out and said so. She was after something else.

Teschal made her way to the living room window and looked out at the deluge.

"I'm more concerned that you may have contaminated a crime scene or perhaps seen something that did *not* make it onto your video and subsequently into my report."

"You got all I shot," he said, a minor sense of relief passing through him. At least she was not calling him a suspect. Thus far at least.

"I can obtain a court order if need be, seize everything in this apartment, tie up your little nocturnal business."

Chase felt his jaw clench. Feigning disinterest, he returned to the task at hand, scooping coffee from a Dunkin' Donuts bag he'd gotten from the refrigerator. Suddenly he felt eyes on his back. He set the scoop down on the counter and turned to find Teschal leaning against the kitchen doorway, her arms crossed and her eyes on him.

"Detective, Connie has all the material I shot, aside from a few stills. You are welcome to have access to those if you like, but I've barely looked at them. The video was the money."

"Money, yes."

"Detective, I'm a law-abiding citizen and I will cooperate fully with any investigation, but I am getting the feeling that there's more to your inquiry than meets the eye."

A small grin touched her lips but quickly faded. She reached into her jacket pocket and produced a business card, which she set on the counter with an audible click.

"Four o'clock this afternoon, Flint Village precinct. Bring everything you have. It should be easy for a *law-abiding citizen* like yourself."

Chase nodded slowly, the sweat trickling lazily down his spine. He'd seen Eve Teschal only once before, but he knew of her reputation. She'd made a name for herself the previous summer while working a case involving some murders connected with a fire at the abandoned state hospital in the nearby town of Wickham. It had all happened very quickly. There'd been no serial killer headlines, no known list of suspects. In the end there had been nothing but weird rumors about an animal being involved and nothing more. And just like that the case passed from the mind of the general populace with ease, and also from the surprisingly unconcerned, perhaps even stonewalled press. But Teschal *had* made serious points with all interested parties.

"My pleasure Detective."

She stared at him for a moment more and headed for the door.

"I'll have to pass on the coffee," she said. "But I look forward to our meeting. I trust that you won't forget."

Chase managed a half smile and followed her. He closed the door behind her, listened to her footsteps echo down the hall.

He went to the window overlooking the street and watched as Teschal emerged from the lobby, crossed the street and climbed aboard a large, silver SUV. She started the thing up, remained for several minutes, before driving slowly away.

"Fuck."

There came another knock at the door.

"Fuck again."

He opened the door and was taken mildly aback to find Dolores Kane standing there.

"We just met and you already have another woman?" she said with a slight grin. "Tsk, tsk, tsk."

"Not really," he said. "Coffee?"

"Love some." Dolores stepped into the living room, glanced about. "First time I've ever been invited in."

"Hope you're not a vampire," Chase said from the kitchen where he had returned to preparing the coffee. "I hear that you're never supposed to invite one of *them* into your home. Sorry, I have a thing for old movies."

"No, you're right, one can't be too careful," Dolores said as she strolled about the room. "Can't have a guest getting *too* familiar, you might never be rid of them."

She wound her way through the maze of unpacked boxes, pausing in front of a bookcase brimming with old paperbacks. She picked one up, turned it over and blew off a thin layer of dust. *Catcher in the Rye.* She nodded to herself, glanced over her shoulder at Chase, who was still in the kitchen struggling with the coffee maker, before replacing the book. She scanned the rest of the shelves, picking names off tattered spines. *The Grapes of Wrath*, *Tom Sawyer*, *Moby Dick*. All the classics. It seemed as if her host had kept all the books he'd read in school. And, judging by the dust, that was the last time he'd cracked them open.

Her gaze shifted to a baseball in a glass case nestled among the books. She leaned closer, squinting at the autographs on the battered ball's hide.

"I can't make out the signatures," she said.

"Oh, the ball," Chase called from the kitchen. "Red Sox. Manny Ramirez and Mike Lowell. They were the MVPs from the '04 and '07 World Series. If I can get David Ortiz's signature—he was the MVP from the 2013 World Series—I'll have a complete set. But he's retired and it won't be easy."

"Ambitious," she said moving to the kitchen doorway.

"My grandfather was a big Sox fan. He was born years after the Sox won the 1918 World Series. And he died before they won another."

Dolores nodded. "He was important to you."

"Yeah," Chase said softly. "He was. My father wasn't around and I didn't grow up in the best of neighborhoods. My grandfather always told me to keep the past in the past—people can change he always said." He made a 'hmph' sound. "Sounds corny as hell, but he meant it." He shrugged. "Well, *I* thought he meant it."

Dolores felt a grin touch her lips. "Maybe there's more to Mr. Christian than meets the eye."

Chase laughed. "Jury's still out."

"So," she resumed, "I gather that you got a little too close to your subject matter last night." She took a seat at the breakfast nook, pushed some Chinese food boxes aside. "Hence the official visit."

"Something like that." Chase scooped more coffee into the filter. "How'd you know...?"

"Cops give off an aura, especially the attractive ones."

"Is Eve Teschal your type?"

"Hardly. It's just part of my profession to know them when I see them."

Chase nodded, frowning. He wanted to ask her what her profession was, but decided against it. The ache in his head was developing into a throb and a deep conversation was something he wanted no part of at that moment.

"You're going to end up in the wrong place someday," she said, plucking a copy of Rangefinder from a stack of magazines on the counter behind her, leafing through it, and setting it down on the table. "Better watch yourself."

"You care," he said, his frown deepening, suddenly wondering how many scoops of coffee he'd used. "Uh—"

The telephone rang.

"Another girlfriend?" Dolores chided.

"Paranoid?" he said, offering her a grin. Was she being pushy or cute? He realized he didn't care which, he found himself liking both possibilities.

Chase scooped up his mobile from the counter.

"Hey," Connie said.

"Hey, yourself. You're up early. Or have you slept?"

"Like a baby on oxycodone," she said, the sting of sarcasm in her voice. "Things are heating up in the fevered world of late-night journalism. I'll be awake until this thing resolves itself."

"Oxycodone, huh?" Chase said with a snort. "Healthy analogy. Oh by the way, don't be jealous, but I had a little meeting with one Detective Eve Teschal this morning. Early bird, worm and all that shit. I've been asked to go downtown."

"Like I said, things are heating up."

"I briefly wondered if I was going to be arrested."

"If you *do* get arrested, don't call me for bail money," Connie said. "But I do need you to get down here, fast. We need to talk before your little date."

"That sounds ominous," he said. "What's up?"

"You need to watch the news after your piece airs from time to time," she said.

"Why? Did aliens land on the White House lawn? Did the Loch Ness monster show up at a Texas concert?"

"Just get down here."

"On my way," he said and switched off the phone.

"I guess that means no coffee?" Dolores said.

"Rain check?"

"I'll start a tally. I suspect I'll need one," she said getting to her feet and heading for the door.

"Sorry," he called after her.

Dolores waved back at him and let herself out.

Chase watched her leave with mixed feelings and headed for the bathroom to shower. The day had just started and it was going downhill fast. But at least he seemed to be rattling someone's cage and in the world of journalism that was supposed to mean something. Wasn't it?

Chapter Eight

"Early for you," Chase said, leaning back on the sofa in Connie's office, adjusting his sunglasses, which he hadn't bothered to remove—they helped keep the Tequila-throb at bay.

"Think I'd burst into flame in sunlight?" she shot back, her mood clearly sour. "Thought you might too."

"It's raining," he said. "Rain gets you a free pass. Like that old commercial with the vampires who wear Ray Bans. Or was it Maui Jims?"

"Same parent company," she said, shaking her head with minor disdain. "Must you always be so dark and edgy? It was cute at first, even sexy, but it's worn thin. And your obsession with television and movies is disconcerting."

"You still love me."

"Hmph," she said twirling a pen between her fingers.

"So, what crawled up Teschal's ass?"

"You did, basically." She leaned back in her desk chair. "And not in a good way, I might add."

"We should have kept it anonymous."

Connie shrugged. "Maybe, but the cops would have been all over us anyway. That stuff can be subpoenaed. Obstructing justice and all that happy horse shit."

"Journalistic privilege," he mumbled. "First Amendment, fourth estate, and all *that* happy horse shit."

Connie sighed heavily.

Chase removed his glasses, tossed them aside. "What is it?"

"Some factors associated with this murder, some of the bits you caught on film, rang a bell with the cops," she said, sounding grim. "A big loud bell. Teschal is their expert; anything weird comes down the pipe, she inherits it."

"So I've heard—why is that?" Chase's mind returned to the mysterious events in Wickham from the previous summer.

Connie shook her head. "No idea. Maybe she pissed off somebody. Or maybe these kinds of cases are simply up her alley."

"Anyway," she continued, "I did a little research because God knows Teschal and I are not on the best of terms and it seems that your dead bodies have a history. Surprise, surprise. Your dead man is, *was*, an underground porn director named Drake Cummings, pun most definitely intended. His real name was Anthony Lee Carver formerly of Los Angeles and Las Vegas. He did a little time for beating up some actresses who weren't, shall we say, receptive to his *artistic* take on things, as well as some check forging and a few other things involving controlled substances. The dead girl on the mattress was a local street walker. 'I'll make you a star baby'—you know."

"Yeah, all you have to do is take it up the ass while the camera is rolling," Chase added.

"Things went too far," Connie continued. "She'd been beaten. Her throat was sliced with a straight razor. The blood tests will probably reveal a cross section of the illegal drug world. Information has arisen linking Cummings to a snuff film, which explains his state-hopping. But Gevaudan? After LA and Sin City? You do the math."

"Sounds like a man on the run. Still trying to make a living whilst laying low. Maybe making a *new* snuff film."

"Maybe; the internet can be a dark secretive place." Connie studied the pen in her hand. "I'm sure Mr. Cummings had connections in all the wrong places— prostitution, probably human trafficking and sex slavery. The internet has become the new cum-stained theater. Our girl must have been hard-up to get in bed with the likes of him. No more street walking for her. Her troubles are over. While ours are just beginning."

"Empathetic," Chase said softly before wondering just how empathetic *he'd* actually felt while shooting the whole grisly scene. Exhilarated was more like it—counting the cash, keeping Connie happy, scooping the other stations *and* the cops. He'd hardly be considered for a Nobel Prize for Human Being of the Year, even on his best day. Perhaps the saddest part was that such a realization no longer bothered him.

"So, why is Teschal getting hot under the collar?" he said.

"It seems that there was a similar murder some weeks back in south Gevaudan. Local drug dealer. Nasty character. Dylan Raccine, aka D-Block. Found on the sidewalk outside his apartment building. Ol' D-Block forgot to use the stairs, just jumped through the window. Pretty grisly scene from what I hear. You'd have loved it."

"I remember hearing something about that," Chase said. "But, as you so astutely noted, I don't much watch the news unless my work is featured. So how did you get the details?"

"You're not the only one with friends in low places."

"What were the similarities?"

"Curious?"

"I've been invited to go 'downtown' to have a little chat with Teschal this afternoon. I'd like to know what I should deny."

"The gouges in the body," she said. "Like huge claw marks. The body burned. You can see the same things in *your* video. My sources tell me that the charring of the two bodies apparently has the Medical Examiner and her minions stumped."

"So," Chase began, lacing his fingers, "it seems that we may have a serial killer on the loose. Teschal doesn't suspect me! Though if I *were* a serial killer, I could film all my crimes and make a fortune."

"Don't even joke about that." Connie tossed the pen aside.

"Are we in trouble?"

"*We?*" she said, grinning. "I'm just the messenger."

"Shit."

Connie nodded slowly. "You my friend are the one who let the proverbial cat out of the proverbial bag."

Chapter Nine

The meeting didn't take place in Teschal's office, as Chase had anticipated—it took place in one of the interrogation rooms. Sparse. Uncomfortable chairs. Cinder-block walls with institutional paint. Was Teschal making some sort of statement? Probably. Intimidation went a long way in police circles. And Teschal was not known for what one might call her *cell*-side manner, but rather her bone-chilling efficiency.

No matter. He really had nothing to hide, (other than the fact that he may have compromised the scene of a double homicide and failed to report the entire incident to the proper authorities). Though the police *had* arrived just as he was vacating the scene. It wasn't as if he was *intentionally* trying to conceal anything.

And that brought him full circle back to the *nothing to hide* position. But he knew very well that prisons were chock full of people who had *nothing to hide*.

Chase had been shown to the room by a uniformed officer and left alone to ponder his predicament. He'd been briefed, as it were, by Connie, who'd made it clear that there was more here than simply a cranky police detective who was trying to put the cocky stringer in his place. And that unknown element, whether it be the other murder or not, was what was driving this whole thing, driving Teschal as well. Chase would have to be cautious in spite of his self-professed innocence.

He was studying the digital readouts he'd downloaded from his equipment to his phone, wondering if he'd be 'detained' the way reporters in old movies often were, when the door opened. Teschal and a plain clothes male officer entered. The man took up position by the door, his arms crossed. He had that lean, mean, weathered look that many cops approaching middle-age donned whether they wanted to or not. It was all in the face, the eyes, almost like a hardened prisoner's thousand-yard stare. Maybe because they'd seen too much of what society had to offer. Or maybe it was just in the genes. In any event, Teschal wore it better, though she was clearly approaching her partner's age.

"Mr. Christian, thank you for stopping by," she said.

Chase nodded. He offered no small talk. Connie had advised him not to get friendly with this one.

"You've brought your materials?"

He took a big gold envelope he'd set on the chair beside him and slid it across the table.

Teschal eyed the envelope, smiled slightly and opened it. She removed the prints Connie had made of Chase's photos, quickly perused them and tucked them back into the envelope.

"I received your video as well as a copy of the edited footage from KTX." She set the gold envelope on the table in front of her and laced her fingers on top of it. "I suppose you've had this conversation before."

"Not really."

"Well, I'll try to talk you through it," Teschal said, perhaps not trying to sound condescending, but managing to just the same.

"You photographed a crime scene prior to officers' arrival," Teschal continued. "Tracked up the place, probably contaminating evidence in the process, maybe even broke a few laws at the same time, and never bothered to invite the police on your way out. I'm sure you're acquainted with the term obstruction of justice."

She paused, waiting, watching Chase's face for any reaction, letting her words sink in.

Chase remained calm, trying not to flinch. He knew all too well that there were basically two types of people in the world: Sayers and doers. Teschal knew this too. And she was a doer. If she'd had anything concrete on him, she'd have used it and not bothered arranging a meeting. But then again, maybe he was serving some greater purpose that he had not considered. Maybe he was actually *helping* her somehow.

"We'll worry about *how* later," she said.

That was part of it; she was after his source. Eloise.

"I told you—"

"Yes, you just happened to be driving by," she said, cutting him off, starting to sound annoyed.

"I saw the Delacroix Street Boyz hanging out front, thought it all looked suspicious and went in the back way," Chase said. "I'd been driving with the windows open and thought I'd heard something. I was heading to the Ship to Shore for a night cap."

"And just how do you know of the Delacroix Street gang?"

"I've lived here all my life, grew up in Calvary Hill."

"Project kid," Teschal said.

"They have another name for the place these days— re-branding. Golgotha maybe."

"Clever," she said.

The man at the door shook his head.

"And so you thought nothing of risking an encounter with a pack of gang bangers, most of whom were probably armed, and entering a building that was obviously part of their turf."

Chase spread his hands, shrugged. "Not my best moment."

"Determined to help I suppose," Teschal said.

Chase grinned. "Concerned citizen."

"And the fact that when you realized that you'd stumbled upon a crime scene, you decided to remain and film the thing instead of getting out and, oh, I don't know, calling the police."

"I'd left my mobile in the car. Besides, I didn't know it *was* a crime scene at first," Chase said. "And I only stayed because I was in shock. And I had to check to see if anyone was still alive. And as the shock wore off and I determined that both people were deceased, I guess I figured my film could prove valuable. I planned to call the cops, I mean the police, but as I was leaving I heard the Delacroix Street gang out front. And I saw the lights of the cruisers and figured it was time to call it a night, let the authorities sort it all out. Besides, I had a deadline."

"Always the stringer." She grinned disingenuously.

"It pays the rent," Chase said, setting his jaw.

"Yes," Teschal said fingering the gold envelope on the table in front of her. "And I'll be the one to determine the value of *these*." She scooped up the envelope, handed it over her shoulder to the man standing by the door.

"I assume that a warrant will not be necessary," she continued. "This material, along with the video we received, is all you have?"

Chase nodded. "That and my statement."

"You may be subpoenaed when a suspect comes to light."

"Optimistic," Chase said, regretting it immediately.

The man at the door grinned and shook his head contemptuously.

"You doubt our resolve in this matter?" Teschal said sounding more amused than insulted.

"No, just your luck," Chase said, ploughing blindly ahead. "Besides, even if a suspect *is* apprehended, it's unlikely that you'll need my input one way or the other."

Teschal's look of amusement grew. "Why is that?"

"I did some research," he said, his eyes studying his fingernails. "The press has been busy since last night. It wasn't difficult to put two and two together."

"Enlighten us." A sliver of annoyance mingled with her amusement.

"The woman is a local street walker, but the man is some west coast pornographer who'd made enemies. Maybe big enemies. Looks like a professional hit."

"Hits involve guns Mr. Christian," she said. "We didn't find any evidence of a shooting."

"Someone made it *look* as if a psycho committed the crime," Chase said, finding Teschal's steel blue eyes.

She glanced back at the man by the door who was grinning broadly.

"You seem to know an awful lot about this case," Teschal said, her voice growing cool, the amusement fading.

Chase felt cold. He'd mouthed off too much, trying to appear smart, trying to appear unafraid, probing for information. He decided to stay quiet about the other elements he and Connie had discussed: the burns, the weird yellow char, the funny smell, and the other victim, D-Block Raccine.

"I *am* basically a reporter."

"Of course." Teschal sat back, pursing her lips.

"I mean," Chase's ego made him say, "it's not as if there's a serial killer out there."

And just like that, he'd pointed out the elephant in the room.

Teschal grinned, glanced at the man by the door. He raised his eyebrows, smirking, and then lowered his gaze.

Teschal got to her feet, pushed in her chair.

"Mr. Christian, don't take any trips out of state until further notice. And next time you reach a crime scene before our people, I expect a call or I may just go looking for your source."

Chase watched Teschal closely until she'd left the room, followed by the man in the suit, who was still smiling.

"Shit."

He had a bad feeling about all this. A bad, *sick* feeling.

After a long moment he got to his feet and headed for the door.

***

Many eyes studied Chase as he crossed the lobby of the Flint Precinct building. He walked past the dispatch center with its bullet-proof glass enclosure. A thin Asian woman he didn't recognize was taking the calls this afternoon.

He continued through the metal detectors, gathering his mobile phone as well as suspicious glances from the officers on duty before passing through the glass doors and heading out across the parking lot. By the time he reached his car, it was pouring rain.

Chapter Ten

"Fucking ambulance chaser," Detective Jude Richards spat.

He was standing beside Teschal at the duty desk watching Chase as he left the building. He'd kept quiet during the interview, but his disdain for the press in general and for stringers in particular (a disdain that had grown exponentially during his twenty-eight years as a cop), had not waned one bit. And this most recent brush with the fourth estate had not changed his views one iota.

"That Moncrief woman buys his product," Teschal said. "And she does so because the public wants to *watch* his product. It's a question of supply and demand. Mr. Christian is providing a service rather like a supermarket tabloid except with moving pictures and sound."

"When did society become so obsessed with all things morbid?"

"I don't know." She sighed. "The Romans liked the Coliseum and its blood sport. Medieval jousting. Cage fighting. Obsession with all things bloody has an extensive history. Our job isn't to fix society; our job is to deal with the aftermath. And to keep the Chase Christians of the world honest, contained if we can."

"Well," Richards said, consulting his watch, "I've got to pick up my daughter at bass guitar practice. Call me if anything falls into place." He paused, turned to Teschal. "Whatever happened to the fucking cello?"

Teschal couldn't help but grin as Richards headed off down the hall, waving a hand at her as he went.

She turned toward the elevator and the mile-high stack of paperwork that awaited her on her desk.

"Got a minute?"

A tall lean disheveled figure was approaching from the corridor that led to the interview rooms.

"Detective Collins," she said, "as I live and breathe."

Teschal knew Jack Collins, knew him to be a good cop, a seasoned cop, but a cop who'd had the unmitigated misfortune of being assigned to what the press had dubbed the North Side Strangler case. And it was a back breaker, the sort of scorched earth case that ruined careers and political ambitions alike.

The gruesome case involved the sexual assault and strangulation of four small children aged six to nine, whose lifeless bodies had subsequently turned up in the vicinity of a nearby freshwater beach, a beach that just *happened* to be the stomping ground of a local motorcycle gang known as the Ghosts. Hardly choir boys, the Ghosts had wasted no time in espousing their innocence from every available pulpit.

Verbose denials notwithstanding, the bodies could not be ignored and the Ghosts were being watched very closely by all concerned. One of the bodies had apparently washed ashore, one had turned up partly buried in the sand, one had been found gathering flies in the nearby woods, partly eaten by coyotes, and the fourth had been discovered lying in what remained of the weed-infested parking lot, having doubtless been tossed from a car traveling along the eastbound lane of Old Dominion Road, which ran along the northern edge of the Jones Beach parking lot at the top of a sandy sea-grass rich embankment like a tired all-but-forgotten Indian trail.

"I'd like you to sit in on an interview if you could," Collins said. "Mostly as a witness. You're good at reading people. I can tell what a person is *saying*, and I get hunches, but I need someone who can tell me what they're *not* saying, what they're *thinking*. And, ah, your reputation proceeds you."

"A dubious honor to be sure, but I'll do what I can. Who's the subject?"

"Lyle Chisholm."

"Lyle Chisholm, the president of the Ghosts?"

"And his mouthpiece," Collins said nodding. "Trying very hard not to let his client look guilty as sin."

"I have a few minutes," she said, even though time was running out on her case just as it was on Collins'. But a change of gears often led to new insight. And favors were usually well-received in police-land.

Teschal knew that political pressures were mounting. A candlelight vigil was planned and there was talk of a protest march if progress was not forthcoming. The specifics were unimportant; the commotion *itself* was the issue. Politicians *hated* commotion. Commotion suggested instability and that made voters feel unsafe.

The simple fact was that Collins' case was more imperative than Teschal's. Criminals ending up murdered was hardly something to be tolerated, but when it came to children turning up dead…well, that was another story entirely. And Teschal had been raised to believe that karma went a long way toward ultimate salvation and you just never knew when the favor might come back your way.

And so, armed with professional courtesy and her ancestors' beliefs, Teschal followed Collins down the hall, to the interview rooms.

Chapter Eleven

Lyle Chisholm was a living breathing caricature of what one pictured when the words 'motorcycle gang president' entered the conversation. He was stocky, gray-bearded, heavily tattooed, dressed in a torn black Rolling Stones concert T-shirt and a frayed denim vest heavily adorned with numerous patches, mostly related to veterans' organizations (nothing like a little PR for the masses). The man's ears were riddled with dangling silver crosses and skulls likening him to some old-world pirate. His hair, like his beard, was long and gray and his teeth resembled a broken picket fence in need of a good Sawyeresque white-washing.

Chisholm's lawyer, to the contrary, was lean, young, and dressed in a well-tailored charcoal gray suit. He was sitting beside his client, working hard to look as intense as he could, probably hoping to present half as much intensity as Chisholm did, but failing dismally.

"Mr. Chisholm, Attorney Doran, this is Detective Teschal," Collins said as he entered the small room. "I'd like her to sit in on our discussion if that's all right."

"Detectives," Doran said, glancing at his Rolex. "I have no objections so long as this conversation remains informal." His voice was smooth and smarmy.

Chisholm remained silent, his beefy hands spread on the table in front of him, *Fuck* and *Off!* Tattooed on his knuckles where *Love* and *Hate* were routinely inked.

"First of all," Doran began, "I would like it to be part of the record that my client has come here voluntarily because he not only seeks vindication from any possible suspicion but also wishes to provide any assistance possible to put an end to these terrible murders."

"Yeah, I get you," Collins said. "So we won't go into your client's record or the records of any of his associates, which, by the way, are extensive."

"I—" Doran began, but Collins cut him off.

"Don't worry, I'm not interested in any outstanding B and E's or any of the other shit your client and his associates have been involved in over the years. And I've done a thorough background check on all of Mr. Chisholm's so-called associates and fortunately there are no pedophiles among them and I suppose that's admirable to some degree. Now, Mr. Chisholm's statement with regard to this situation is a matter of record so I assume that his presence here means that he has further information regarding this case?"

"It means no such thing Detective—"

"I'd like your client to answer my questions," Collins said. "Your client has not been charged and has come in of his own accord so you, Mr. Doran, can keep quiet for the time being."

"Detective, I—"

"Shut up," Chisholm said in a deep gravelly voice, placing a big hand on his attorney's forearm.

Doran glanced at his client, shrugged and sat back in his chair, arms crossed.

"Mr. Chisholm," Collins began, "I spent my teenage summers working in Mayflower Cemetery here in the city, cutting grass, chopping down shrubs, and such. Once each summer all the kids working in all the parks would stand on street corners shaking tin cans, collecting money for soup kitchens, homeless shelters, things like that. It probably wasn't legal to make us do that but in those days who cared, right? And I remember standing on a corner in Mitre Square shaking my little can one July, flirting with girls driving by, getting a tan, when a big Harley with little

American flags stuck into the windscreen pulled up beside me and the president of the Ghosts at the time, Joe Larson this was, handed me a check for a thousand dollars. A thousand fucking dollars. I was told that he did that every year. Very much the philanthropist. Ingratiating the Ghosts with the community like 'Whitey' Bulger or John Gotti."

Chisholm remained silent, his dull gray eyes nearly transparent, crystalline.

"So, I hope that that same sense of civic duty continues in you," Collins said, "his successor."

"Don't blow smoke up my ass, Detective," Chisholm said abruptly. "I'll tell you all I know 'cause I got nothing to hide, neither do any of my 'sociates. We hang at that beach, work on our bikes in the old parking lot, fuck our women, get high, and have some beers. But I'm not telling you nothin' you don't already know. What I *can* tell you is this: those little kids were dumped there *after* we'd gone home. It was raining each night a kid was dumped, so we didn't have no reason to be there. Metal and chrome rust and it gets cold as a witch's tit out there. And when we found each body we called you cops and told you about it right off."

Chisholm shifted his mass in his seat; the old chair seemed to scream in protest.

"Now, if you got any fingers to point," he started back in, "you can start pointin' 'em. If not, I'll be moving on and I 'spect you'll be leavin' us be from now on, 'specially since you and your boys have let whoever this fucker is slip through your fingers. You've been watching that beach and those woods for a while now; only this guy seems to show up during shift change or maybe comes in by another route like maybe that fire road out back or even by boat. So, if I was you, Detective Collins, I'd be more worried about your boys taking naps in those squad cars then I would be about me and my 'sociates."

Collins grinned broadly, leaned forward and laced his knobby fingers on the table top.

"Listen up Mr. Chisholm, this is a murder investigation and I'll ask you any damn questions I want any time I want," he said, his fingers clenching into fists. "Now, I appreciate you coming in here and I *do* appreciate your candor about your activities at Jones Beach, but I've got four dead children lying in the morgue so don't kid yourself, the powers that be are not happy. And I aim to make them happy. Now what I'm telling you is this: if you or your associates hear or see anything suspicious out at Jones Beach, in the surrounding woods, or in your great grandmother's fucking underwear drawer, you call me immediately. You've got my number, so use it."

Chisholm was breathing heavy. Collins was getting under his skin, treating the big man like a 'nobody' instead of the demi-god his followers knew him to be.

"Why would we leave those kids on that beach?" Chisholm spat. "That's our turf. How fucking stupid do you think we are?"

"Is that a rhetorical question?" Collins asked. "And I thought that the City of Gevaudan owned that beach?"

"Detective, my client is trying to help—" Doran began.

"Your fucking client is trying to cover his fat ass by getting out in front of this investigation."

Teschal remained silent, watching, listening, and trying hard not to grin. Collins was forcing the issue, creating critical mass, trying to get Chisholm to admit to something incriminating or even just something questionable which would give Collins leave to inquire into the Ghosts' behavior more decisively. But the big man wasn't biting. Chisholm had had far too much experience being questioned by cops to lose his cool.

"I think we're done here," Doran said getting to his feet.

Glaring, Chisholm stood up as well, pushing his chair roughly back against the wall.

"I got better things to do then kill little kids," he said. "There are bigger fish to fry."

"Is that some sort of threat?" Teschal spoke up.

Chisholm glared at Teschal and turned abruptly, tore open the door and headed down the hall.

"Good day Detectives," Doran said, raising his hands defensively, before following.

Collins and Teschal waited, the sound of the Ghosts' president complaining to his lawyer fading as the pair headed for the lobby.

"Well?" Collins said.

"I think he's a piece of shit," Teschal said. "But an honest piece of shit. At least so far as your case is concerned."

"Yeah." Collins sighed. "I guess they'd be pretty stupid to dump the bodies on their own front porch. I just wanted to see if Chisholm had anything new to deny."

"So, who *is* on your short list?"

"Usual suspects. We've been checking into every registered sex offender within twenty miles. A few have piqued our interest."

"Such as?"

"Dilbert Carvalho, for one—can you imagine that fucking name? What were his parents thinking? Please come and beat the shit out of little Dilbert, please." Collins shook his head.

"Go on," Teschal said.

"Carvalho checks out, though. Alibis and all. Nurith Cross for another. Our killer leaves no sperm behind and Nurith, being a woman, prefers foreign objects, so she would be on our list except she's apparently dying of cancer at a hospital in Rhode Island."

"What goes around…"

"But we do have one candidate who makes the grade."

"Who's the lucky winner?"

"One Joseph Griece—just a diddler. Never killed anybody, so far as we know. His lawyer argued for outpatient treatment at West Woods psych facility at Greystone Prison and got it. But our dear Mr. Griece missed his last appointment with his probation officer and has been a no-show at his last known address. And his vehicle is nowhere to be found."

"Sounds promising."

"But we have tips that put him out of state," Collins said. "He has family in Maryland. We're watching them in case he turns up. APB and all. His picture is going out over the airwaves as we speak, six, ten, and eleven o'clock news. Maybe some concerned citizen will ID him, give us a call. I never realized how valuable TV could be, always heard it was a wasteland."

"I wonder what Mr. Griece's lawyer will think of his client's sudden infamy?"

"Fuck him. Fuck both of them. We're just calling him a person of interest at this point. No need to tip our hand. Hell, things are getting desperate. Politicians breathing down my neck, concerned parents flooding our call system, candlelight vigils…I can't blame them, but this fucker…" Collins shook his head slowly, ran his fingers through his thinning gray hair. "Thanks for sitting in though."

"Don't mention it." Teschal sighed, feeling Collin's pain. "Are the Feds still watching?"

"The state, the Feds," Collins said grimacing. "Supermarket tabloids. The state is interested because Jones Beach may in fact still be owned by Massachusetts. Some paper pusher in Boston is trying to find some missing documents. The Feds are waiting in the wings because the first case was considered a kidnapping. But no ransom came and the body was found the next day, so these are murders, local matters. At least for the time being. So they've been keeping their distance. But if something doesn't break soon, they'll be all over us."

The pair got to their feet, moved silently out into the hall. Chisholm was easily visible gathering his belongings from the metal detector station by the door, still complaining about being disrespected by the *nasty* detective.

"Have you considered revenge as a motive?" Teschal said as she watched Chisholm attach his wallet chain to his belt loop, a task that required some effort considering the man's girth.

"I mean, could a rival gang be killing these kids and dumping the bodies on the Ghosts' patch to set them up for some past transgression?" Teschal said.

Collins shrugged. "I'm willing to consider just about *anything* at this point. But someone would really have to have it in for the Ghosts to go that route. Planting drugs, weapons, sure. But murdered children? Hell, I just don't know. I'm about ready to call in a psychic though. Maybe even a fucking witch doctor."

"I know what you mean," Teschal said, thinking of her own case and turning in time to watch Doran and Chisholm exit the building. The last thing she noticed was the flaming grinning skull adorning the center of the big man's black leather vest as he headed out into the rain.

"I know *exactly* what you mean."

Chapter Twelve

"So how was your girlfriend?" Connie's voice over the phone was playfully sarcastic, mingling with the sound of thunder and rain.

"Vague." Chase was sitting on his sofa with his feet perched on the coffee table, a half empty mug of java in his hand.

"Is she on to your source?"

"What makes you think I have a source?"

"Fine, be evasive. But the day may come when I'm the only thing standing between you and tragedy."

"She hinted at it."

"Maybe that's what she's *really* after," Connie said. "You know, give a man a fish and he eats for a day, uncover a stringer's source and—"

"—he's out of business," Chase said, sitting up, setting the coffee mug down on the table and rubbing his eyes.

"Well, at least she didn't lock you up and throw away the key."

"Thank the stars for small favors. So, what do you know about this other murder, the one Teschal's *not* talking about."

"Probably no more than you. Give me a little time to look into it. I'll call you later."

"Sure," Chase said, frowning.

He hung up the phone, looked out the window. The world was a wet gray shroud. It occurred to him at that moment that it was *Connie* who was being evasive. There was just no *way* she hadn't checked this all out, done the research or had one of her minions do it for her. News was news and Connie was an excellent reporter.

Devious woman Connie was though, when she wanted to be; he had learned *that* much over the years. Guarded. Especially when it came to her private life.

Chase knew for instance that she'd been married, knew that her husband drank and had been less than cordial most of the time. And there was the mysterious scar on her left arm, a jagged ten-inch suture line that she did her best to hide. It was something she never spoke of, something he'd never bothered asking about for fear of putting her off. He was also aware that Connie's childhood had been a rocky one. This was also something on which she never elaborated—only vague allusions, hints at old skeletons in older closets during intimate encounters, shutting down once the lights came on again.

He sensed that happiness was a stranger to Connie, an alien notion she referred to only in passing conversation, something she had only glimpsed in books and movies. Maybe *that* was what she and Chase really had in common as opposed to the news. Maybe it was simply a mutual desire to celebrate the misfortunes of others that had driven them together, both emotionally and physically. Misery *did* love company. But why was this dawning on him at this late date? Was his conscience thawing at long last? Or did it all have something to do with Dolores Kane? Talk about experiencing things only read about in books and seen in movies!

Goddamn, he thought, sincerely hoping that he wasn't *that* far gone. He *had* begun questioning many things about his own behavior as of late. His drinking. His lack of emotion when looking through the viewfinder. His relationship with Connie. And this fresh perspective was making him damned uncomfortable.

He went out onto the deck to clear his head. The thing was narrow, but it granted a decent view of the businesses across the street: a pizza joint with good meatball subs, a Chinese restaurant, and a hair salon. And the commuter rail platform just beyond where trains rumbled past from five a.m. until around midnight heading north to Boston or veering east toward Cape Cod. And of course there was the city beyond with its lighted windows glistening faintly through the drizzle and fog.

He listened to the traffic two streets away. The city was as somber as the weather. But hadn't it always been? Hadn't the place always been brimming with things best left unseen, places best left unexplored?

Yet somehow, as the years drifted past, Chase had begun remembering the city in which he'd spent his childhood in a nostalgic, sepia-tinted light, casting the bad memories aside in favor of brighter ones. And this made him feel old. And unrealistic.

And so in the spirit of professional progress and some semblance of a good night's sleep, Chase set his melancholy musings aside. The job helped him do this, granting him an escape from the emptiness by allowing him to focus on just how bad other people's lives were. It was sad. And wrong.

His thoughts returned to the run-down apartment where he'd shot the video. He couldn't get the image of the dead man out of his head. The girl had been bad enough with her throat slit open, flicks of yellowish-colored cartilage poking out of the red muck, the blood having flown onto the worn mattress, her frozen terrified eyes gazing blindly at the water-stained ceiling. She looked to be twenty-five at the most. He wondered where her parents were, whether they'd known what had become of her. Or whether they'd care.

The man with his chest and stomach torn open was another matter. He'd been the closest thing to a monster Chase could imagine, having purportedly produced a snuff film, perhaps having been interrupted while making another, having sliced that girl's throat while filming the entire thing for profit.

Filming for profit? The words echoed in Chase's head and he shuddered.

"No." The word sounded like a primordial grunt dripping with denial. His situation was different. Wasn't it? Chase never orchestrated the events he filmed. His job was to document dispassionately the things that could qualify as news and nothing more. He and the dead man had *nothing* in common. And the way that man had died…did anyone deserve to die like that? Was that man beyond forgiveness?

These were questions philosophers had pondered over for centuries. How bad *was* bad? And at what point did *bad* cross that vague fuzzy line into the realm of what religious zealots and ambitious politicians called *evil*? And when did forgiveness cease to be an option? This last point stood above the rest. This last point struck far too close to home for comfort.

And the grisly images seared onto the video loop in Chase's brain persisted. There was something *unnatural* about that man's death, something beyond *final*.

And there it was, that nagging sense that something impossible had happened in that dingy apartment, something he was not fully prepared to conceive. That coupled with the growing suspicion that his being there had been no accident, that he'd been drawn there, *sent* there by forces beyond his control, forces beyond Eloise's control, delivered there to bear witness to it all and to ponder about what it all meant. About what it all meant for *him*.

The gravity of the situation was undeniable. He'd rounded a corner and come face to face with something incomprehensible. Something *alien*. He'd fallen into his own viewfinder and had landed *inside* the story. His intuition was telling him that he needed to solve this mystery in order to drive the images from his brain, put closure to it before it consumed him.

Leaving the rain behind, Chase went to his small cramped office, sat at his desk and shook the cordless mouse. The computer monitor came alive, an image of the Night Owl Diner at sunset in all its neon glory set as the screen saver, the glowing red auto brake light trails moving around the building like warp speed fire flies, the result of a slow shutter exposure.

But dreams fade, reality persists and life goes on. The dead girl lying on the bloody mattress knew these things all too well, came to realize them, perhaps, in the last terrible moment of her short life as the razor sank into her soft flesh.

Chase slid the cursor to the camera icon in the upper left corner, double-clicked it. The file opened, filling the screen with thumbnails, over five hundred. He guided the cursor to the most recent, the one labeled 'Night Stalker' followed by a date and clicked on it. The folder expanded and the nearly two dozen photographs he'd taken in the old apartment materialized.

He moved from one to the other studying each in turn. It was easy to see how his pictures had piqued Teschal's interest. He had captured the whole scene so effectively without ever considering the possible ramifications of his actions. He felt like a novice reporter who'd buried the lead.

Chase enlarged the first image. It was a shot of the dead woman's face staring up at him. He flipped to the next image. The woman from farther away, her complete bloody body. He pursed his lips, shook his head. Next image was of the room from a distance.

He studied the remaining shots and then switched to the video. It was a little grainy, not his best work, but after all, in this case, it was a matter of content not quality. The room, save for the glaring barn-door equipped lights, had been dark, the situation rushed, the contrast extreme, a thin haze of smoke lingering to further obscure his efforts. And a strange pungent smell the video unit was incapable of detecting. The smell had reminded Chase of something from long ago, something from his childhood. He let his mind drift down that avenue, searching. And then he found it. The smell in the room was that of the burned up engines to the model rockets he used to launch as a kid. What was that? Hydrogen sulfide. That was it. A smell of burned sulfur in the room like rotten eggs. Strange.

The image of the man lying in the corner materialized. Chase leaned closer, clicked on the enlarge button. He studied the grisly gashes in the man's chest.

He reached toward the image, drawing his fingers back before they touched the monitor. The gashes looked like claw marks with burned edges. He opened the tint panel, dropped the color, brought up the image in gray tones, watched as the gashes came more clearly into focus. They definitely looked more like claw marks than knife wounds. Unmistakable. But the space between each gash was at least two inches. What sort of animal had a span that wide? Nothing extant, that much seemed certain.

He could make out three deep gashes running from the man's upper right shoulder to his lower left abdomen. The length seemed nearly identical, the width of the gouges essentially the same.

But if the wounds had not been made by the claws of some large predator, then the weapon that was used had been designed to function *like* the claws of an animal. And who the hell would go through the trouble to create such a weapon? And what about the burns? Who would stage such a murder and, more importantly, how? And why?

Chase sat back, crossed his arms, trying to fend off a sudden chill. Outside thunder rumbled and rain pelted the screen.

Chapter Thirteen

Corrister Flynn was packing a bag, getting out of town, still unable to believe her luck, the sound of rain and the rumble of thunder creeping through her shadowy, dingy apartment, reminding her of how bad the day could have gone and how close to the edge she'd actually come. She could still hear her lawyer, a cheerless public defender wearing an ill-fitting suit, telling her how lucky she'd been, how *fucking* lucky. It wasn't every day a public defender got to say that to a client, she figured. And it sure as hell wasn't every day that a girl from the wrong side of the tracks, a girl with Corrister's record no less, managed to walk away from a second-degree murder rap. Especially when she was as guilty as sin.

This last bit was Corrister's personal observation, not that it mattered. The jury had felt differently. They'd taken pity on her, Corrister Flynn with her fabricated Irish brogue, home grown in South Boston, and her big brown eyes that wept so easily. They hadn't seen all the ink on her body, or the scabbed-over track marks between her toes or in the crooks of her elbows; she'd even managed to get her burgeoning dyskinesia under control while in the courtroom. Nor had they been with her months earlier in that dark alley behind the Past Midnight club in Gevaudan's seamy south side when she'd stuck that butterfly knife into that woman's stomach. They hadn't seen the blood, hadn't heard the gurgling sound, hadn't seen that woman's eyes turn cold and still. No one had. No one but Corrister Flynn. She couldn't even remember what the fight had been about. A spilled drink? A guy? Money?

The K-Spice she'd smoked a few hours earlier? The hit of Flaka she'd taken?

It didn't matter. It was all in the past and it was time to leave town, put some distance between her and this shit-hole city, just in case some ghost from her sordid past showed up, pointed a finger, leveled an accusation. There were still plenty of ghosts out there who'd love to do just that. No other murder raps waiting in the wings, but there had been other indiscretions: drugs that had never made it to their destination while she was *muling*, a few stray dollars that had found their way into her pockets. The list was endless. And headlines drew attention, often unwanted attention. God only knew who might come calling.

But that was Corrister Flynn, the raven-haired girl with the trademark rancid attitude. Corrister, the girl who was thanking her lucky stars for getting out of this latest in a series of jams, each of escalating intensity, this by far the worst. And then there had been the dead woman's family making a scene after the verdict had been read, the girl's sister weeping, the brother with his shaved head and impossibly intense eyes screaming obscenities as the police escorted him from the courtroom.

Corrister slammed her tattered suitcase shut on the memory, flipped the latches shut and hissed one of the few Gallic words she knew. Maybe it was time to turn over a new leaf. But who was she kidding? There *were* no leaves left to turn over, new or otherwise. In fact there was nothing in her future, at least nothing of substance.

Thunder rolled past the dirty window making a sound like an eighteen-wheeler. Night had fallen early. And with it had come the darkness. The only light in the apartment had been from the small flat screen television on the dresser, a television she'd shut abruptly when her own faced appeared on it during the Crime Desk portion of the Channel Seven News.

A sliver of panic touched the nape of her neck and she hastily felt for the ticket in her jeans pocket. There was a bus leaving from the North Main Street terminal for Boston's South Station in just over an hour. Corrister planned to be on it.

She stepped back, considered the suitcase lying on the bed. It made her think of her mother rotting away in a similarly dingy flat in Dublin, drinking Barry's tea laced with Jameson's, staring out at the night, wondering where her eldest daughter had ended up after she'd fled back to the Emerald Isle, having concluded that Southie's streets were no better than 'Scribblestown Lane,' having also realized that larceny was just as illegal in America as it was in Ireland and it was best to flee before the authorities got wise.

The memory of her mother was a grim one, but at least the woman had had the decency to wait until her daughter was old enough to fend for herself before ditching her. Corrister had always meant to thank the old bitch for that small gift; at least it had put an end to the drunken beatings.

Corrister went to the refrigerator, plucked out the last can of Budweiser, and sat down at the kitchenette table. She cracked the thing open and took a long pull. It felt as good as ever. She felt something bite at the corner of her eye and she wiped it away. She studied the glistening speck of moisture on her finger tip. A tear? What the fuck was that about?

A sound drifted through the room, drawing a frown from Corrister. She cocked her head and listened. It *couldn't* be. Not in this building. She swallowed more beer. The sound came again. Her frown deepened.

She sat up, straining to hear. The air surrounding her seemed to crackle with some strange energy. She got to her feet, went to the door. There it was again; a baby crying…or maybe a cat. That was more likely, plenty of strays around, just like her.

Corrister hesitantly unlatched the door, slowly nudged it open and peered out into the hall. Her eyes moved along the stair rail that ran nearly the length of the landing, struggling to probe the deep shadows. Was someone playing a sick game? Or was the dead girl's brother coming for her, seeking revenge, his own shiny blade in his hand, just aching to bury it in the Irish bitch's stomach? She listened intently, but the only sound was that of thunder and the rain striking the stained-glass window above the stairs.

Corrister stepped back inside, started to close the door, but paused when she heard a creak on the stairs. A gush of warm air rushed past her, stirring her dark hair, blowing the strands back, making her eyes water. No, not warm. Hot. It felt as if someone had opened a door to an oven. And there was a strange glow spilling across the landing like dull milky moonlight.

She retreated into her apartment, slammed the door, locked it, latched it with the chain and listened, her ear pressed to the old wood, her heart thudding. The floor in the hall creaked. But it was not the creak of a footfall—this sound was different somehow. Bigger. More like the sound a huge tree might make in a heavy wind, the wood bending ready to snap.

She backed away, her eyes finding the space below the door. A shadow fell across the gap. The sound came again. A cat crying someplace, lacking substance. Ethereal. Not a baby whining. No, *definitely* a cat.

But the sound was changing, *growing*. There was a sudden size to it, a mass, as if whatever was making the noise was becoming larger, more pronounced, more substantial.

Corrister laced her fingers across her mouth. The tears started. A gasp spilled from her lips, tripping over her fingertips. She was suddenly stricken with a sick inexplicable feeling, a feeling of such dread that she almost wished she'd succeeded with one of her two suicide attempts. That would have been kind, infinitely better than dealing with whatever was on the other side of the door.

"No," she mumbled, afraid to be heard, the tears streaming down her cheeks now, carrying rivulets of dark mascara with them.

There came a scratching at the door, like a stray seeking refuge. The sound seemed to creep through the very fabric of the old wood. Then a cat's cry. *Cri du chat*, Corrister thought, her mind swimming, the phrase leaping from the memory of a movie she'd once seen. It was the sound some sick babies made, babies suffering from some sort of syndrome. It was wrong, just as whatever was in the hall was *wrong*. *Cri du chat*.

The scratching stopped. A glow was oozing in from the space beneath the door.

"No," Corrister had time to say once more before the door exploded in a shower of ragged splinters.

She broke for the bedroom, feet slipping on the faded area rug. Reaching the doorway she spun around to face the intruder and tried to slam the door behind her, fingers desperately clawing at old wood, fingernails snapping off like brittle twigs. But it was no use; the heat was unearthly, impossible, coming in waves like a heat phantom tsunami. The old wood was smoldering and paint chips were melting. A deafening sound like the roar of a jet engine was in her ears. A blinding white light was pouring in through the ruined door like a molten sea. And the unbearable heat was wrapping itself around her like a burning blanket, crisping her flesh, burning away her heavily tattooed skin, ripples of searing pain and huge razors slicing into her stomach, spilling her insides into her burning hands.

Chapter Fourteen

Chase's eyes shot open. He'd dozed off on the couch. Outside it was raining and the light had fled. There was a sound in his head—an annoying sound. The telephone was ringing. Chase rolled over and scooped it up.

"Yeah," he growled.

"You're going to get me fired fuck head."

"Eloise," he said sitting up and rubbing the sleep from his eyes. He had a dull headache, the sort brought on by the rain. At least this one wasn't the result of too much Tequila. That had to be some sort of improvement.

"I shouldn't be telling you this, but I guess I must really like you, so listen up. There's something big going on in town, near Mitre Square. Lower part of Anawan Street, number three-eleven. You won't be able to miss it; from what I hear the area is lit up like a Christmas tree. You know the place?"

"Yeah," Chase said. "Bad area."

"Bad area," she agreed. "Anyway, I got it through the grapevine. Didn't come through my board, probably Central. But it's big. So the party's going strong already, but at least you can be part of it."

"Part of what El? Eloise? What *grapevine* are we talking about? You know I don't like anyone else being involved with the information you send my way. So if you're getting leads from dispatchers in other precincts or other cities, well, I just hope you're keeping my name out of it. And besides, that detective, Teschal, she's been on my ass. And my connection at KTX has been feeling the pressure too—"

"Goes with the turf," Eloise interrupted.

"Big talk from the person sitting safely behind the bullet-proof glass answering phones—"

"Enough; I'm not on duty. Just meet me at the Mitre Square Coffee Shop in thirty minutes, after you take a look. There are things you need to hear."

"El, what the hell's going on?"

"I dropped you in the middle of something last night," she said, a raw edge to her voice that Chase had never heard before. "And we need to talk. And don't worry about my *grapevine*; there are no leaks there. I guarantee it. My cronies and I go back a long way. They say blood is thicker than water. And there are some things that are even thicker than blood. Some things older than stone."

"All right, I'll meet you at the coffee shop after I do a drive by," Chase said feeling strangely cold inside, and he slowly hung up the phone. He went to his office, gathered up his gear and headed out the door.

Chapter Fifteen

The rain had eased by the time Chase reached lower Anawan.

"God," he heard himself say as the nose of his SUV breached the glare of the flashing LEDs. It was like driving into the eye of a fearsome electrical storm—there was no wind, little rain, only a barrage of electrical impulses piercing the shadows like alternating red and blue strobes.

Slowly he crept along, heading west, past the rows of brooding old tenements, the occasional police officer waving him onward. It was only a matter of time before they cordoned off the entire street. Chase was frankly surprised they hadn't already done so.

The clutter of emergency vehicles was indeed impressive. There were at least a half-dozen police cruisers parked along the sides of the street, most in the immediate vicinity of an oversized tenement building where the activity was centered. An ambulance was sitting at the curb directly in front of the tenement in question, one of the units the Medical Examiner's office had purchased expressly to transport dead bodies without attracting too much attention, the ME insignia plainly stenciled where a private vendor name had once been. And one fire engine was parked at the curb some yards past the old triple-decker, shadowy figures reloading equipment into the engine's various holding bays and compartments.

A nebulous assortment of onlookers had gathered on the front porches of other tenements lining the street, their tongues doubtless laden with theories and opinions, their faces grim in the coruscating luminosity that was flowing like rainwater across the scene. Several kids were on bicycles some yards past the fire engine, hooded-up, their rangy shapes silhouetted by the lights of Mitre Square some few hundred yards distant at the bottom of the hill.

Chase winced; there was no way in hell he was going to get near this scene. And there didn't appear to be a back way in either. And if there were, it would certainly be covered. Teschal would be taking no chances this time, and Chase knew she was here, he could see her big SUV parked near the fire engine.

He pulled up to the curb about a hundred feet beyond the tenement, well beyond the fire engine and Teschal's vehicle, near a darkened dry cleaner's store. Heavy steel doors had been pulled down and locked, securing the business, a reminder to all just how seedy parts of Gevaudan could be.

Chase slung his Canon and grabbed his video unit and climbed out onto the sidewalk. He'd wrapped the video unit in plastic to protect it from the persistent rain, leaving openings for the lens and the view panel. He raised the thing, switched it on and panned it across the chaotic scene.

After a few minutes he killed the video unit, lowered it, and climbed back aboard his SUV. This shit footage would never do; he'd have to figure some way to get closer.

He ran his fingers through his damp hair, started the car. He pulled away from the curb and drove toward Mitre Square, a once thriving section of town replete with a huge granite mill that housed a furniture store as well as a scattering of restaurants and shops. These days the place was junkie central, with cracked curbs, weed infested sidewalks and mostly vacant lots that businesses had once occupied. The only surviving businesses, other than the coffee shop, included a run-down strip mall and a muffler shop.

He waited for the light to change and crossed the square, pulling into a small parking lot. He shut the car and climbed out into the rain. Somewhere a siren shrieked. Chase studied the sky. It was thick with clouds, and the light show up the street was bathing their undersides with red. It looked as if the sky was bleeding.

He turned to the doughnut shop, peered through its glass facade. A half-dozen people were seated at the curved counter, and a waitress with dark hair was pouring coffee and talking with two men who had 'Over the Road' trucker written all over them. And there was one heavy-set black woman sitting in a booth near the back of the place, by the door to the bathrooms.

Chase grinned. Eloise. He took hold of the door handle, hauled the thing open and went inside.

Chapter Sixteen

Eloise looked up from her coffee as Chase appeared in the doughnut shop doorway. The waitress saw him too, smiled. Chase pointed to Eloise's table and crossed the shop. The waitress nodded and began searching for her order pad. One of the men at the counter, a large burly individual wearing a torn wife-beater and coveralls with the name of a plumbing firm embroidered on the back, cast him a stony glance before returning to his java. The other people at the counter never acknowledged his arrival.

Chase shook the rain from his jacket without taking it off and sat down opposite Eloise.

"*Bonswa*," he said.

"What's good about it?"

Eloise looked shaken, scared. Chase had known her for years, had met her while shooting pictures of a body a few fishermen had pulled from a reservoir outside Bridgton. They'd been so excited to get their names on the news that they never imagined that the cops were going to lay a hefty fine on them for fishing in a reservoir.

She had been renting a bungalow up the road at the time and had come over to check on the flashing lights. The two had simply gotten to talking. A year later they'd bumped into one another again when Eloise's brother had overdosed in an industrial park motel in North Bridgton. Chase had bought her a coffee and provided her with a shoulder on which to cry.

Chase had been staying at the same motel, cooling off after a row with Julie, and heard the commotion. Eloise, who'd traced Charlie, her younger brother, to the motel (which had a less-than-stellar reputation), had begun arguing with the irate night manager who'd refused to give her Charlie's room number. She'd been driving around checking the holes-in-the-wall Charlie frequented while on one of his drug-infused benders and had spied his car in the parking lot. But the manager, who was desperately trying to avoid unwanted publicity or police involvement, had stuck to his guns. Chase had intervened on Eloise's behalf, eventually calling the cops himself. Charlie's body had been found in room 107 with a syringe containing North Bridgton's finest Heroine-fentanyl mix still protruding from his arm.

That had been the only other time Chase recalled Eloise looking scared. It was clearly evident that her reason for insisting on meeting with him was deadly serious.

"Thanks for coming," she said, her eyes intense, her jaw firm.

"A lot of activity up the road. So what's so special?"

The waitress came over just then, all smiles and flirty.

"Get you something hon?"

"Just coffee," Chase said and he waited for the woman to head back to the counter before starting in again.

"Is this murder number three?"

"Five," Eloise said solemnly. "Five murders, all related. And one other that seemed to set it all in motion like dominoes. But that one was different, almost routine sad to say." Her Creole accent was thick tonight. She usually managed to set most of it aside when answering phones at the station, but it always returned with a vengeance when she was off duty.

"Why don't I know about any of this?"

"You know more than you think. It all began more than a year ago when a college student at Bridgton University was kidnapped, raped, and murdered. A local asshole named Dylan Raccine, aka D-Block, was the last person seen with the dead girl and was suspected of having done the deed. But the cops hadn't gotten around to arresting him yet. It takes time to build a case, if one can be built at all. And to add to the mix some rookie cop at the scene had fucked up the chain of evidence and the case went cold. But everyone knew this D-Block was the perp. He'd done time for stalking, assault, was a person of interest in two rape cases, one in Southie and another in Jamaica Plain, where he'd once lived."

Eloise spun her half-empty mug slowly around, tapping its rim with her brightly painted fingernails.

"I'm confused," Chase said.

"This D-Block was spotted on surveillance video leaving a college bar in Bridgton called The Devil's Fiddle seconds after the dead girl left alone. That was the last time she was seen alive. Two days later they found her floating in the West Wickham River, out behind the old state psychiatric hospital."

"I heard about him through my KTX contact. Are you suggesting there's more to the story?"

"Raccine was found lying in a puddle of blood and broken glass three stories beneath the broken window to his rat-trap apartment in south Gevaudan. He was carved up pretty bad. And he'd been burned too as if whoever'd sliced him open did it with a very hot knife. And a blow torch."

"That's what I'd heard." Chase felt something cold slither through his stomach.

"Lots of shit-heads like this D-Block wind up wearing a toe tag due to naughty things they done," Eloise said. "And sometimes the responsible party want folks to know that it *was* personal, maybe beef up their own 'street cred.' Anyway, that's pretty much what everybody at the precinct thought."

"Until last night," Chase said.

"Not exactly," Eloise said.

A siren sounded and flashing blue LEDs sped past the big windows at the front of the shop heading toward the gathering up the street.

"Several months after the college girl's murder, and one week after D-Block's death, the rookie cop, who'd fucked up the search, wound up dead as well." Eloise shook her head slowly. "Torn to pieces and burned to a crisp at the bottom of an elevator shaft in an old abandoned mill on Quarry Street. He'd called in saying he was stopping to investigate some suspicious activity, but decided not to wait for back-up. I didn't take the call. You know those old mills—great places to get laid or get high. Crash for the night, sleep off a *nod*. Gangs love to have their little orgies in places where the landlord is hardly likely to make an appearance. Homeless squatters too. Hell, you name it."

"Here you go," the waitress said and she set a cup of coffee down in front of Chase.

"Thanks," Chase said, managing a smile. The woman accepted it, offered him one of her own, and headed back to the counter.

"What are we saying here?" he said. "Are the cops suggesting that someone's out for revenge?"

"Hits happen with single shots to the head and the bodies wind up in landfills or building foundations," Eloise said grimly.

"Unless there's a message being sent or—"

"Message? Message to who?"

"Maybe this D-Block didn't act alone."

"So someone's trying to scare his associates?"

"Who had close ties to the dead girl?"

"Her mother. Dad's dead. No siblings. No close relatives in the area. No sign of impropriety on the dead girl's part, at least so far as the cops or my sources can find. No drug dealers out to collect a debt, make an example of her. No titty shots on Instagram. She was a shining star, every parent's dream child."

"Of course the cops talked to mom," Chase said.

"Of course," Eloise said, nodding. "She had an alibi, not that anyone in their right mind would suspect a 'swell' like her. She'd just gotten in from abroad. Two-and-a-half months traveling around Europe. Video camera surveillance in the parking garage at her very expensive apartment building recorded her coming home, unloading luggage and not leaving the apartment until the next afternoon."

"Strange behavior, considering her daughter had been murdered," Chase said.

Eloise shrugged. "I've seen stranger. Maybe she needed to get away, clear her head."

"Maybe provide herself with an alibi. Do the cops think that she might have hired someone?"

"They don't exactly tell me what they think, but you should ask yourself: what would *you* think?"

Chase rapped his fingers on the table, looked around. The big plumber was eyeing him again. When Chase's eyes met his, the man looked away. A middle-aged woman with a bad dye job sitting beside the man was talking to the waitress. An old man, who'd been sitting at the far end of the counter, was shuffling toward the door, buttoning up a jacket that was very well worn and far too heavy for this time of year.

"Let's bottom-line this," Chase said. "We have the murder of the college girl, then the murder of her suspected killer months later. The rookie cop you mentioned is killed shortly after that. Then the two murders last night, the hooker and the movie director."

Eloise nodded. "That makes five. And we have this fiasco up the street."

"Six in all," Chase said.

Eloise nodded again.

"Two bad guys, a hooker, and a college girl in the wrong place at the wrong time," Chase said thoughtfully. "And the rookie cop."

"The dead hooker and the college girl don't fit the pattern."

Chase frowned. "Different MO. The hooker had her throat cut and the college girl was raped and strangled. And the college girl is the murder victim who triggered it all?"

Eloise shrugged. "Seems that way. But what's the connection with the others? Did the college girl's mom hire a sadistic killer to 'off' D-Block? What happened after that? Was the guy supposed to find some connection between the cop and the dead daughter and the porn director? Did he? Or did he just get a taste for it and go off freelance, tearing people up and burning them to a crisp just for shits and giggles? And all the signs are there that whatever is happening up the street fits into the puzzle somehow."

"Maybe this is another North Side Strangler killing?" Chase said.

"No," Eloise said, shaking her head. "Those bodies have all turned up near Jones Beach. Besides, Jack Collins is running that case. He's not on the scene. Your girl Teschal is there. You can't miss that big SUV of hers."

"I saw it." Chase rubbed his jaw. Suddenly he raised his eyes. "Wait, you know what's going on up there, don't you?"

Eloise nodded briskly. "Irish girl—did some other girl in a back alley some months back. Knifed her while jacked up on Flaka. Or so the story goes. Got off just today, *beat the rap*, as they say. Where have you been? It's been all over the television for weeks. You're supposed to be a reporter? You should keep the box on after they run your pieces for a change, you might actually learn something."

"Thanks for the advice," Chase said. "So, she was acquitted?"

"Just today," Eloise affirmed. "Everyone down at the precinct knew she did it. Jurys get it wrong sometimes. Roll those doe eyes, talk in that Irish accent even though you've never been to the Emerald Isle."

Chase nodded. "That explains the fire engine."

He let out a long deep sigh. He was suddenly very tired and excited at the same time. It was like being back in college after a night of doing coke and trying to sleep. Damn. He just *had* to find a way to get a look at what had happened, get close to the scene. This could mean some decent cash. And he knew just who would be aching for the footage. But how to get a peek?

"I'm originally from Haiti," Eloise resumed, her voice low and deep. "I've told you some of this."

Chase nodded, leaned closer.

"But I never told you why we left."

"No, you never have."

"Back then, my daddy ran a small newspaper. Just local news, ads and such. Probably some political innuendo hidden between the pages. One night, late, my momma woke me up, put her hand across my mouth and told me to hush. Said we best be going fast and quiet. I listened. So did my little brother, Charlie. We climbed out the back window, no suitcases, no nothing, just the clothes on our backs. Papa Doc's Tan Tan Macout had stopped by to talk to my daddy."

Eloise paused, shook her head slowly as if struggling to dredge up the old memory from a very deep grave.

"We ran into the woods. My momma told us not to talk, just run. And don't look back." Eloise snorted softly. "I looked back. I always was the sort to look back. I guess I'm related to Lot's wife."

"And?"

"And I saw our house burning. Watched my bedroom window filling up with flames. Tried to think how it would have been if my momma hadn't waked me up. I saw shadows of men walking around with those big-brimmed hats on, watching the fire, laughing, like they just didn't care. And I saw my daddy hanging from a tree."

Chase stiffened.

Eloise raised her eyes and found his. Chips of dark ice set in darker flesh.

"I remember saying to myself that it was *somebody* who done that, burned my house, killed my daddy. *Somebody* doin' this, *somebody* who was sending a message. But over the years I've got to thinking, and it makes me think of these murders. Maybe there *was* no message. Those men, maybe they just didn't care. And maybe that's what's going on with these murders. Maybe it's someone who, I don't know, someone who just likes *doin'* this sort of thing. Likes killing in a real bad way. Maybe someone who was *born* to kill. And enjoy it. Someone *evil*. World's full of Papa Docs."

Chase felt himself nodding slowly.

"We had relatives in New Orleans. That's where we went, my momma, brother, and me. I don't remember how he and I ended up here. Trying to be independent I guess, make a life for ourselves. He was always tagging along behind me."

Chase remained silent.

"I don't know, maybe I seen too much," Eloise said softly. "Maybe I'm tired of answering that phone at the precinct. Every time I see that little red light come on I feel cold inside and I wonder, when I pick that receiver up, put it to my ear, what am I going to hear at the other end? Heard a woman choking on the line one time 'cause her husband was strangling her. She died. Heard more than one gunshot fill up that earpiece over the years. Screams. Arguments. Glass breaking. Kids screaming. No telling what's waiting for you when you pick up that phone."

"I'm sorry…"

"What I'm saying is this." She laced her fingers atop the table. "Where I come from, the way I was raised, what I do, well, it all gives you feelings, feelings I learned to trust. And I got a real bad feeling about these murders. It's like seeing that little light blinking on my switchboard. I feel the same way I felt when I looked back at my burning house that night so long ago. I get the feeling like something else is going on here, something no one, not you, not me, not Teschal and her cops, can understand. Something bigger than all of us. There are things out there, things that don't belong. Sometimes they hide inside people, make women drown their babies, make husbands strangle their wives—"

"What are you saying?"

"Nothing," she said after a beat. "I'm just an old woman who's seen too much. The whole thing is creepy; *Ki ban M' ramp yo.* That's all."

Chase started to speak, but Eloise reached across the table and took his hands in hers. Her flesh was terribly cold. She looked him in the eye and he felt the words in his mouth dry up like dead leaves.

"Just be careful," she said.

"El, we've been through a lot, seen a lot—"

"Not like this," she interrupted. "Not like this. It's like that other case, the North Side Strangler, those kids being killed…this place is dark and getting darker, cursed somehow. Like some old long-dead Indian waved a magic stick, muttered some secret words because some white asshole took his land." Eloise seemed to shiver.

"But whoever is killing those kids is just some fucked-up pedophile," she added. "They'll find him and lock his ass away, if someone don't kill him first. But this, *these* murders…"

Eloise released Chase's hands. She considered what remained of her coffee, pushed the cup aside and stared out the window in silence. Thunder rumbled in the distance and a fresh spattering of rain, like droplets of blood from the bleeding clouds, pelted the big windows at the front of the coffee shop. After a few hushed moments she got to her feet, set some money down on the table, scooped up her ample purse. She cast Chase a tired glance, squeezed his shoulder in passing and headed for the door.

Chase polished off his coffee, contributed some ones to the cash and followed her out into the rain.

Chapter Seventeen

Chase stood in the drizzle watching Eloise's tail lights join in with the countless others moving through Mitre Square. Usually crowded at this hour, traffic was three times as dense due to the light show up the road, a show that had not waned one bit since Chase had first seen it.

He considered his situation. The doughnut shop parking lot would hardly serve as an adequate vantage point. It was time to find a better one, one worthy of his skills. And his reputation.

Leaving his SUV in the lot, he set off on foot across Quarry Street, which ran north to south effectively bisecting Mitre Square's five way intersection. Ignoring the blaring horns and blinding headlights, he managed to avoid getting run over and made a beeline toward the commotion less than two blocks distant. He passed several people milling about, talking, some in English, some in Spanish and some in Portuguese. Gevaudan was a city of nearly two hundred thousand people. And like any city its size it was composed of various races, ethnicities, income brackets, religions. It seemed to Chase that all of its residents were out tonight, each hoping to catch a glimpse of the chaos.

Chase cursed under his breath when he spied the yellow sawhorses stretched across Anawan Street a mere one hundred feet from the action, and the two rain coated cops guarding them. It was bound to have happened; he'd hoped for a little more time though.

Chase began searching for an alleyway to duck into or an empty lot to cross. Cities always had those; there had been one between Delacroix and Warren Streets. But none were evident. The old tenements in this neighborhood had been built within mere feet of each other to allow for better use of land in a time before zoning laws. The old mill barons had let nothing go to waste.

Chase's mobile phone rang, ending his deliberations, and he plucked it from his belt.

"I know you're there, so why haven't I gotten your feed?" Connie said, her voice less than cordial.

"Men in blue everywhere," Chase said. "Street's blocked off. Mitre Square is gridlock."

"It's not like you to throw in the towel," Connie said. "KTX needs you—find something or we're going to get scooped on this."

"Old reporter lingo?" Chase said as his eyes lit on something.

"*Unemployed* reporter lingo," she said.

"And how did you know I was here?"

"Hell, every stringer within twenty miles is heading there. I *do* have connections of my own you know. Besides, my police scanner is working just fine."

"Hang on. I think I've found something."

"Good," she said. "You know where to find me."

Chase shut the phone and clipped it to his belt. There was an unusually large three-story tenement standing beside the house where the action was centered. The place was set back from the street and looked deserted, its doors and windows boarded up, its front yard having lost a battle with thigh-high weeds long ago.

He moved to the edge of the curb and considered the brooding structure. The building was wide, twice as wide as a typical tenement. The front door was covered in graffiti-laden plywood as were its street-side windows. But there was one of those darkened alleyways he'd been hoping for running along the western side of the building, which was abutting another tenement, one with lighted windows. Risky, yes, yet oh-so inviting.

Chase glanced back at the doughnut shop. It was too far to go back for his gear—the scene might start breaking up, or worse, tightening up. He had his phone, the newest Samsung, and it had pretty decent photo and video capabilities. And beggars couldn't be choosers.

"Fuck it!"

He crossed the street, the glare of the numerous emergency vehicles causing the wet asphalt to glisten like ice. He reached a rusted chain link fence, found a gate and slipped through. He glanced up the street at the two cops standing by the barricade. If they'd noticed him, they hadn't reacted; they were busy talking to the kids on the bicycles.

He moved stealthily down the alleyway. He heard voices, a man and a woman, coming from inside the lighted first floor apartment next door. He crouched low as he passed beneath the closest windows.

Chase reached the back yard. What remained of the lawn had gone to seed long ago. The cement walkway that ran along the back of the old house was in a similar state, rich with weeds and wild grasses of its own. A dog was barking somewhere in the distance. Chase could see the backs of the tenements in the next street; some of their windows were alight. He could hear a radio playing, a woman singing in Spanish.

He climbed the back porch's rickety steps, crossed the warped boards. The door was an imposing wood one. No plywood on it, just a few strips of one-by-two nailed in place.

Chase flipped on his penlight and panned it warily around. If anyone in the adjacent houses saw the light, they'd assume the cops were conducting a search. Hopefully.

He climbed down to the yard and began searching for something that might serve as a tool to pry the bracing from the door. There was an eight-foot-high chain link fence running the width of the back yard. He shone the light along its base, moving slowly toward the house where all the activity was centered. He was about to turn and head back the other way when the light caught on something poking out of the wet earth.

Chase stooped down and ran his fingers along the object. It was metal, a pipe of some sort. He tugged at it. It held. He wrapped his fingers tightly around the thing, pulled as hard as he could. It came up from the damp muck with a sucking sound. He studied it before the light; it looked like something from a kid's swing set, rusted, partly bent, but sturdy enough to do the job.

He returned to the porch and slid the pipe behind one of the boards. He applied pressure—the nails complained, but one end of the board popped free. Chase grabbed the wood, waited for someone to yell or a light to swing his way. Nothing. He went back to work, prying another strip of wood free, setting it on the porch. In no time he'd managed to pry all three strips of wood loose and tried the door. Locked. No surprise there.

Chase glanced around. It was too dark for anyone to see. He turned to the door, put his shoulder to it and leaned into it. The door suddenly flew inward. He managed to grab its leading edge before it crashed into the wall. It hadn't been locked, only stuck due to the wet weather and swollen wood. He stepped up into the entry and closed the door behind him.

The entry was as black as pitch. Stale moldy air swam around him. Chase panned the light around. Water had gotten in and the horse-hair walls were black with damp and mold. The light revealed a staircase to the right. Swallowing some rancid air he began to climb.

He reached the second-floor landing where the penlight revealed two padlocked doors to the right and what appeared to be a window set into the far wall facing the house next door, where the police activity was centered.

But the window was blocked by several strips of one-by-two. He proceeded to the next floor. A moment later he found himself in an identical landing with another window at the opposite end.

Chase crossed to the window, the old floor boards complaining beneath him. There was no need for slats or plywood at this height. The glass was filthy and he tried to raise the window. It moved reluctantly, opening ten inches before refusing to budge any further.

He squatted down and peered through the opening. The smell of old dust was overwhelming and he coughed into the gloom. Covering his mouth with his palm, he braced himself against the old sill. Beyond the window was another alleyway. The building across the way was a mere twenty feet distant.

The third-floor windows of the next building were lighted and alive with activity. He adjusted his position; his thighs were already starting to ache. He brought out his phone, swiped the screen and hit the camera icon, aiming it at the lighted window.

He could see people moving about, men in suits talking. He checked to make sure the flash was off and aimed the phone at the window, through the space he'd managed to create. He leaned in, snapped a shot. Then three more. Then he switched to video mode and hit the red tab on the screen.

The men stopped talking. A woman in a gray suit entered the room, Detective Eve Teschal. Chase hoped that the darkness in the entryway would render him invisible.

Teschal began speaking with the men, but her words were inaudible. Chase wished he'd brought a shotgun microphone. He adjusted his position, his thighs were on the verge of cramping. He strained vainly to hear the conversation, but came up empty.

A door suddenly opened behind the group of officers. A man in a white anti-septic suit emerged. He shook his head and removed his mask.

"Move," Chase said, urging the man to step aside in order to grant him a glimpse into the room beyond.

He steadied the phone, squinting at the image on the screen. And then Chase got his wish; the man stepped aside.

Chase felt his eyes open wide and his stomach squirm to life. He leaned into the tiny screen, struggling to see more clearly. The man in the sterile suit had gone back into the room and closed the door. But Chase had seen it. Oh yes. And he'd gotten it all on video. And some tiny faraway voice in his head told him to be careful what he wished for.

The bedroom had looked as if it had been splattered with blood.

"Jesus," he heard himself mutter.

A whining sound broke from the shadows behind him and Chase spun around, mobile phone held out in front of him at arm's length like a weapon. He listened. There was only the vague sound of distant voices and the rain striking the dirty window glass. He was alone and he'd seen enough.

He got to his feet, his knees throbbing. He shut the video app and started down the stairs, the penlight leading the way. He reached the lower landing and took a step toward the door, but paused when he heard the whining sound again. Chase glanced warily around. There was no indication of movement. Just what Eloise would call 'the creeps,' he told himself. Nothing more.

He stepped out onto the back porch and closed the door, wiping the old brass knob with the corner of his T-shirt. He gathered up the slats, forced them back into place, using the metal bar he'd found as leverage to drive the old rusted nails back into the moldy door frame. He stepped back to consider his handiwork.

Satisfied, he hopped down from the porch, tossed the metal bar into the nearest puddle, started toward the alleyway, pausing long enough to glance up at the boarded-up windows above him. There was only darkness there. He headed down the alleyway, slipping through the gate, ghostlike. He crossed the street and headed back toward Mitre Square.

***

Sitting in his car, shivering in spite of the heat, Chase scanned through his phone's contacts and hit Connie's mobile number.

"Got something for me?"

"Sure, I'm alive and in one piece," he said, his eyes still studying the commotion up the street. "Thanks for asking."

"Yes, I'm glad you're fine. Now what have you got for me?"

"Blood," Chase said flatly. "I'm sending it in, but I'll be over in a few minutes. Get your research team ready. I've got questions. Lots."

"Sounds cozy," Connie said. "I'll make cocoa. See you soon."

Chase ended the call, opened his email and set it to Connie's address. Then he attached the video he'd shot and sent it on its way. He repeated the action attaching the photos and sent those. Then he clipped the phone to his belt and started the car. He paused long enough to glance back up the street at the jumble of lights.

Strange, he thought, considering the chaotic scene from a safe distance. Somehow, he couldn't shake the sound he'd heard. He'd thought he'd been alone in the old rat-trap of a house. But some sounds were unmistakable. Somewhere in the darkness there'd been a cat.

Chapter Eighteen

Connie met Chase at KTX's back door. The drizzle had intensified and an eerie fog was slowly devouring the parking lot.

"They're processing the video you sent," she said. "It'll take a little while to wash it through the system. Not exactly hi-def. You couldn't have used your regular gear?"

"If I could have, I would have," Chase said impatiently, running his fingers through his damp hair.

"Let's go to my office."

Connie led the way down the hall past the small cramped studio which was brimming with late-night activity. Technicians, producers, and interns were all studying Chase's footage. Editing would be needed. Clearly not his best work, but as he'd understood from the start, beggars couldn't be choosers.

Connie pushed open the door to her office and introduced Kiley Ross, a bespectacled grad student from Bridgton University, who was seated at Connie's desk tapping away at her computer.

"Hi," the young woman said perkily.

Kiley's hair was short and dark, fashionably cut. She had fair skin and an athletic body; young but attractive, in a waifish sort of way. *But too young*, Chase thought. Or was he simply too old?

Chase waved back.

"What have you got?" Connie said.

"I've got the details on the first two murders," Kiley said.

"Drink?" Connie said, gesturing toward the cluster of bottles on a table in the back corner of her office.

"No thanks," Chase said after a moment's consideration.

"Suit yourself," Connie said with a shrug.

"Ready," Kiley said.

Connie and Chase moved up beside the young woman and peered over her shoulder at the computer monitor. The grainy mugshot of a man with dark hair and a sparse beard filled half the screen.

"The first murder, Dylan Raccine, aka D-Block, known drug dealer, suspected sex offender, videotaped leaving The Devil's Fiddle night club at 12:37 a.m. on the fifth of May last year, close behind this woman." Kiley tapped keys.

The image of a young woman with shoulder length dark hair, bright eyes and an engaging smile filled the screen.

"Elise Genevieve Mckenna, graduate student at Bridgton University who'd spent the evening socializing with two friends, fellow students Joseph Rubio and Carlene Smith—the two had just gotten engaged. This was the pic her mom gave the cops and the newspapers when she was still a missing person."

"So we're thinking revenge?" Connie said dubiously.

Chase shrugged.

"Raccine was the prime suspect in the Mckenna girl's murder," Kiley said. "Revenge makes sense."

"When was he charged?" Connie said.

"Charged?" Kiley said, her eyes never straying from the screen.

"For the murder of this Mckenna girl," Connie said, checking her watch; deadline was fast approaching.

"He was *never* charged," Kiley said adjusting her glasses.

"Why not?" Connie said.

"Something to do with the chain of evidence having been broken. Some rookie cop dropped the ball," Chase said, remembering Eloise's explanation for the police having failed to charge Raccine.

"Anyway, Raccine was found on the ground beneath his bedroom window three stories up," Kiley said. "Dead before impact supposedly. One witness told a reporter that it looked as if he'd been mauled by a tiger, set ablaze and thrown out the window. Raccine's apartment was locked and bolted from the inside. The conclusion was that the killer left by means of the fire escape. While searching Raccine's apartment the police found a necklace that belonged to the dead girl. St. Brigid's Cross, to be precise, also known as a Celtic Cross. Elise Mckenna was studying archeology at Bridgton University. The necklace was engraved with her initials. Her mother had given it to her for her last birthday."

"How did you get this information?" Chase said.

"I have my own sources," Connie said.

"Good to know."

"Where was the girl's body found?" Connie asked.

"West Wickham River," Chase said before Kiley could respond.

"Yes," Kiley agreed. "Behind the old psych hospital."

Connie glanced at Chase. "Friends in low places?"

"Jesus," Chase said, not qualifying Connie's comment. "Maybe it wasn't revenge. If this Raccine, this *D-Block*, wasn't charged, who could have known? Except for the police who were investigating the murder, no one *could* have known."

Connie shrugged. "Maybe the two events are unrelated."

"Unless an accomplice was tying up loose ends." Chase turned to Connie. The glow of the computer made her look like a wax figure in Madame Tussaud's museum.

"Maybe someone helped Raccine kill the girl? But then why not just shoot Raccine? You can get a stolen gun anywhere. Offer a fifty-rock to some crack-head down on Seventeenth and Agnew and you can get a stolen 'burner.' Why go through all this trouble? And who but the police suspected Raccine?"

"Maybe someone did a little snooping of their own," Kiley suggested. "And figured out that Raccine was the real killer."

"You don't suppose there's some rogue element in the Gevaudan PD behind it all?" Chase said.

"We're doing a lot of supposing here," Connie said. "To begin with, I can't even *imagine* how to investigate the renegade cop theory. But I do know that investigations— private professional investigations—cost money. Surveillance equipment. Police informants."

"Mom had money," Kiley said.

"Do we have a picture of mom?" Chase asked.

"Sure," Kiley said, tapping keys.

A woman with shoulder length dark hair and sunglasses appeared. She was standing outside the Gevaudan Superior Courthouse surrounded by suits, lawyers, and detectives, no doubt captured in the heat of despair by some aggressive reporter, a microphone shoved in her face.

"Fucking press," Connie mumbled with feigned sarcasm.

"Doesn't look like a killer," Chase said, studying the photograph. "Or the sort who'd hire a hit man to do the job for her. But I guess you just can't tell."

"You should watch one of those shows where the wife loses it and kills the husband," Kiley said. "Plenty of soccer moms hiring hit men or lacing hubby's coffee with anti-freeze."

"So you think mom hired someone to do it for her?" Connie said.

Chase shrugged. "Just theorizing."

"Big word," Connie said. "Don't hurt yourself."

Chase grinned at Connie's derision, but it was a forced grin. Everything with Connie was becoming forced lately.

"Don't judge a book by its cover," Connie added. "It takes all kinds. And a mother will do an awful lot for her children; *most* mothers, that is to say."

"What does mom do for a living?" Chase asked.

"Nurse at Mercy General over in Wickham," Kiley said. "Or at least she *used* to be a nurse."

"Mom sounds like a straight shooter," Chase said. "If she'd hired a private detective to sound things out and the PI had made good ol' D-Block as her daughter's murderer, then why wouldn't she just call the cops, point them in the right direction?"

"So revenge seems unlikely, unless someone was psychic," Connie said. "What about the cop?"

Kiley tapped keys. The face of a young man in a police officer's uniform filled the screen.

"Jason Ledeux. Not unattractive. He was at the scene when the Mckenna girl's body was discovered. He was ultimately blamed with mishandling the evidence. Rookie mistake. But it prevented the cops from moving in on old' D-Block. They might have put something together eventually, but who knows?"

"What was the evidence?" Chase asked.

"Not clear. I'll keep digging, but the police seem to have kept it under wraps. Guessing a procedural error."

"You're not paid to guess," Connie said.

"Next," Chase said.

Kiley tapped keys. "We have the man Mr. Christian found. Here he is without the mask."

The face of the dead man Chase had photographed filled the screen. With the black leather mask he'd looked formidable. Without the mask he looked positively evil. He seemed to be of Eastern European descent, maybe Russian, broad jaw with a wide nose. Dark, shadowy eyes gazing out from beneath a heavy brow. Chase considered the cruel-looking face. Seeing him now, in the flesh, Chase realized that the mask had made him look *less* frightening.

"What woman would go anywhere with this fucker?" Connie said.

"The girl had her throat cut." Kiley tapped keys and the blonde's face filled the screen. A yearbook shot probably. Young, fresh. Full of promise.

"Jessica Jill Crosston, formerly of Crandall, Massachusetts," she continued. "Photo courtesy of the Gevaudan PD. Known prostitute and petty thief. Recreational drug user. Cocaine mostly. Pot. A few arrests. One conviction."

"The word is that the apartment was full of drugs: coke, H, ruffies." Connie pursed her lips. "Maybe she wasn't on the payroll. Sort of an involuntary acting job. Reality TV."

"The MO on the girl is different than the others," Chase said. "So is Elise McKenna's; that is, if we're counting her among the victims."

"The only thing that places the Mckenna girl on the list is the fact that her supposed murderer was the first official victim," Chase said. "It's possible that there *is* no relationship."

"And the hooker was simply in the wrong place at the wrong time," Connie said. "The girl wasn't the target, the masked man was."

"Our dead porn director's career out west was a colorful one," Kiley said. "He was associated with no less than fourteen porn films, s and m, pretty hard stuff, and was suspected of making at least one snuff film—you know the ones where they really kill somebody on film?"

"We know dear," Connie said, with a patronizing tone.

"And tonight's murder?" Chase said.

"Well, the apartment on Anawan was rented to this girl." Kiley opened a new screen featuring a young dark-haired, dark eyed woman's face.

Tattooed, trailer park chic, Chase thought.

"Corrister Siobhan Flynn. Hailed from South Boston. She had a great morning, but a lousy night. She'd been acquitted of murder just this morning. Tonight she's dead. Not much available as the scene is still fresh."

"What about our friend Teschal?" Chase said. "What's her story?"

"Well, she's been around the block, so to speak," Kiley began.

"Enlighten us," Connie said.

"Eve Isla Teschal, born July 1st, 1972, Manchester, New Hampshire to mother Vadoma Ealasaid Teschal. No information on dad. Mom's from Scotland. Mom is a Romany gypsy. Inverness area. Not a lot of gypsies there, but she was originally from Glasgow. A few *thousand* gypsies there though the real numbers are probably much higher as gypsies tend to travel about and don't exactly register to vote very often."

"That's interesting," Chase said softly.

"Eve Teschal," Kiley continued, "degrees in Law Enforcement and Criminal Justice Theory, both from UNH. Moved to New York City where she became a police officer. Moved around some. 101st, Far Rockaway, then down town. 30th Precinct, Sugar Hill, 151st Street. A couple of others. Quickly promoted to sergeant then detective sergeant."

"I guess she wanted to get away from it all," Chase said.

"Or get away from the family," Connie added.

"Twelve years in NYC," Kiley continued, "but she wasn't always in town. She spent time in New Orleans, on loan, four weeks to be precise. Raleigh, North Carolina. And almost two months in Edinburgh, Scotland."

"Scotland?" Connie said. "Visiting family or in an official capacity?"

"Looks official," Kiley said. "I'll need to do more digging to gather the specifics, but her record is an intriguing one. Most recently that business in Wickham. Several people dead in less than a week. Teschal's boss, Captain Donovan, was called in to consult on that one, once it was all over that is."

"Once it was over?" Connie said.

"That's French for cover-up," Kiley said.

"Donovan," Connie said thoughtfully. "Isn't he from the Ivory Coast or someplace like that?"

"Sierra Leone. I've looked into his bio too," Kiley added with a shrug when all eyes turned to her. "His parents were killed by rebels. He was apparently one of those child soldiers for a while, until he was taken in by a missionary and his wife. They arranged for him to come to America when he was a teenager. Apparently he kept his real first name, Abasi, which means 'stern one' or something like that. But he took the couple's last name as his own, Donovan.

"He was a cop in Boston for more than twenty years. Acquired a pretty good reputation while he was there. Gevaudan must have been glad to get him.

"Here's another case Teschal was involved with in upstate New York," Kiley said. "Sketchy information. Something to do with grave robbers and bones being used in some sort of religious ceremony."

"Weirder and weirder," Chase said.

"Yes," Kiley agreed. "The case in New Orleans involved the murder of four prostitutes." She leaned back, cocked her head. "No blood in the bodies. Seemed to have been some cult involvement."

"What the hell?" Chase said.

"What is this woman," Connie said crossing her arms, "a CIA Spook or Buffy the Vampire Slayer?"

"Maybe she's Dana Sculley?" Kiley quipped.

"We've got it," someone said from the doorway.

Chase turned. It was Derek Ellison. "But—"

"Just show us," Connie said impatiently.

"All right," Derek said with a shrug and he turned away. "Follow me to the Twilight Zone."

Chapter Nineteen

The control room was crowded, young technicians at all the stations, intense expressions pasted to their faces, all focused on the largest of the screens set into the wall across from the big control panel.

"Wind that up," Derek said as he entered the room.

Chase and Connie followed, taking up position against the back wall. The big screen filled with bug fights, the speakers with static. Suddenly the image of a lighted window as seen from across an alleyway, drizzle falling between the two making the image grainy, cloudier than it should have been, materialized.

"Shit," Chase said, disillusioned with what he was seeing. "The conditions—"

"Let's see," Connie whispered, giving his arm a reassuring squeeze.

The image on the screen swam into focus and the two men Chase had seen appeared. They were clearly talking, though their words were inaudible. Then a woman entered the frame.

"The Ice Queen," Connie said.

Teschal approached the men in suits and began speaking with them. Even from across the alleyway and through the world of electronic imagery it was easy to see how grim their faces were. A moment passed and a door set into the wall behind the trio opened and a man in a sterile crime scene suit emerged. He removed his mask, shook his head and joined the conversation. Then Teschal said something to him and he stepped aside and moved out of the frame, toward some other unseen room.

"I—" Connie started to say but the words died in her throat. "Freeze that."

The image became still, slightly blurred, but clear enough to reveal a room layered in swatches of what appeared to be blood.

"Christ," Connie said, inching forward to get a better look, setting her hands on the back of one of the tech's chairs. The young female technician occupying the chair was deliberately looking away, her hand over her mouth.

"Looks like a blood-bomb went off in there," Connie said. "And those dark streaks on the wall like soot."

"There's something else," Derek said.

"Something else?" Chase said.

"Roll it," Derek said.

The video resumed and Teschal was once again talking to the other figures. The man in the sterile suit reappeared. He went back into the bloody room and closed the door behind him. Suddenly a high-pitched sound spilled from the speakers and the camera swung abruptly, the lens randomly finding the deep shadows at the other end of the third-floor entry near the top of the stairs.

"Freeze it there," Derek said.

"What was that sound?" Connie said.

"Cat," Chase said. "Heard it when I was leaving too. Must have been hiding in the house somewhere."

"What are we looking at?" Connie said, squinting.

"Zoom in," Derek said. "I noticed it first on the small monitor."

The image folded in upon itself and opened again.

"One more should do it," Derek said.

The image folded in on itself again, but this time, when it opened, one of the techs gasped.

Chase leaned forward, a chill crawling up his spine.

"What the fuck is that?" Connie said. "I thought you were alone in there?"

"I was," Chase said, his voice suddenly hoarse.

Derek moved close to the screen, pointed at the dark tangle of shadows.

"That's a face," he said, turning to address the room. "And if it's a *human* face, well, whichever bitch spat this thing out should be shot before she spits out another."

Chapter Twenty

Chase shook the glass of Don Julio, causing the ice cubes to tinkle against the sides. He'd been sitting on the sofa in Connie's office for nearly a half hour, nursing the drink, replacing the ice whenever it started to melt. Connie was at her desk, watching the final edited version of the footage Chase had shot.

"We're running the piece with an anonymous by-line," she said. "Concerned viewer. You don't need Teschal coming down on you for breaking and entering."

"Or you for running the footage," Chase added.

Connie grinned wryly, nodding.

"Let's see it again," Chase said, leaning forward, setting the glass on the coffee table.

"I've seen it enough," Connie said, swinging the laptop around and sliding it across the desk toward Chase.

He hit the Enter key. The image of the window across the alleyway filled the screen. He watched as the scene played out as if on some endless loop, first with the detectives, then with Teschal and the man in the Durex suit, and finally the bloody soot-stained room. And then came the mysterious sound gushing from the laptop speakers. A cat's cry, ethereal, haunting and oddly distant as if it were coming from some cavernous chamber far beneath the earth's surface instead of a narrow corridor in a run-down tenement.

Chase hit the pause button and leaned closer, staring at the screen, struggling to put substance where there should have been none. A face of sorts. Crooked eyes, feline, iridescent. A mouth maybe. Fangs? Definitely cat-like but with so much more mixed in. Deformed, freakish. Wrong anywhere on Earth.

"Well?" Connie said breaking the stillness.

Chase returned to the sofa, sat back down and lifted the glass of Tequila.

"Fuck," he mumbled. "I *know* there was no one in there. I'd have heard the old stairs and floor creaking."

"Were there any rooms opening off the corridor?" Connie asked.

"I thought they were all padlocked, but maybe…"

Connie shrugged. "Maybe you woke someone up, some homeless guy sleeping it off in one of the apartments, and he poked his head out at the wrong time. And the darkness and the sudden movement of your phone blurred the image."

Chase shrugged. This actually made some sense. He downed the Tequila.

"Got to go," he said getting to his feet.

"Get some sleep," Connie said. "I'll have Kiley do more research—follow up on the other murders, the woman whose daughter was killed. She's probably the most reliable voice we'll find. And maybe the dead cop's widow, if he has one."

Chase set the glass down on Connie's desk, got to his feet, stretched.

"Sleep."

"Yes, boss," he said.

He glanced down at the laptop screen and the shadowy freakish face gazing back at him with its horrible indescribable eyes. With that image burned into his head, he was hardly likely to sleep at all. Maybe never again.

Chapter Twenty-One

The ride home was a quiet one in spite of the late-night traffic. Chase kept the window cracked. The air was murky, the street lights fuzzy, everything blurring together. He hadn't even bothered to switch on the police scanner. Too much excitement for one night, a little peace and quiet was in order.

He pulled into the lot beside his apartment building, killed the engine, raised the window and climbed out into the night.

"Hey."

Dolores was sitting on her tiny balcony, huddled under the overhang, a small light on a table beside her.

"Don't you ever sleep?" Chase said, craning his neck to look up at her.

"Starting the weekend early," she said raising a glass. "Come on up for a drink."

"You don't have to ask twice."

"That's good because opportunity only knocks once."

***

Dolores' apartment was cluttered; she was not exactly what one might call a hoarder, but she was not far off. Though everything was tidy and mostly packed away neatly in large, plastic bins. A distinct improvement, nonetheless, from Chase's unpacked cardboard boxes lying everywhere. It might appear to an uninformed observer that she simply hadn't gotten around to unpacking. But Chase knew otherwise; she'd been a resident for nearly two years. He'd helped her move in, mostly out of happenstance; he'd been in the wrong place at the right time. The two had been friendly ever since. Though nothing beyond that. Connie kept things in order in that department, physically at least. Emotionally, well, that was another matter. Chase's strange hours ruled out most sorts of relationships. But Chase figured there'd be time for that, for another relationship, a *post Julie* relationship, someday.

"Hard or easy?" Dolores called from the kitchen as Chase cleared a space on the couch, moving a stack of magazines to an already overburdened coffee table.

"Easy," he said. "At least to start with."

Dolores returned with two cans of Bud Light, handed one to Chase and settled into an adjacent club chair, folding her legs beneath her.

"Bad night?"

"Hell, literally."

"I saw your piece on the Dark Side, not your best work."

"Everybody's a critic," he said holding the cold beer can against his forehead. "Couldn't get close."

"You'll have to find a new contact," she said. "Looked rough though."

"The whole police force was out along with cruisers from Bridgton, Wickham, and at least one state SUV. Did you see the blood?"

"I wasn't sure *what* I saw. Wasn't sure I *wanted* to know. What the hell is the world coming to?"

Chase shook his head, relieved that Connie had directed Derek to trim the final sequence, the part with the unearthly face in the darkened corridor. It wouldn't have made sense to the viewers anyway. Hell, it didn't make sense to him!

He sipped some beer, trying to wash the image out of his mind, but utterly failing. The beer was cold and wonderful, though. He looked at Dolores. She was attractive, beautiful even in a natural way—dark hair,

Romanesque nose, dark eyes. No make-up at this hour. No need. Good lips and teeth. *Jesus*, he thought, when had a woman's *teeth* become a priority!

A cat purred and Chase felt his gut tighten.

"Midnight," Dolores said, setting her beer on the coffee table and picking up the jet-black cat that was winding its body around her ankles. The animal rolled into a ball and settled into her lap, purring softly.

"Shit," Chase whispered as his mind warped through time and space until he found himself once more in the darkened third-floor entryway of the run-down tenement on Anawan Street. The smell of the old house's rotting guts found him, dragging him back to a dream he'd had as a boy, a dream that had stitched itself forever into the fabric of his being.

***

He'd been standing alone in the first-floor entryway of the tenement his grandparents lived in, a part of a neighborhood across town that had vanished into history when the Old Cape Highway had been extended. He remembered the sepia-tinted color of the early evening light as it leaked through the dingy lace curtains hanging over the dirty window in the upper portion of the entry door. He remembered the filthy green speckled linoleum, its edges curling up where it touched the wall, the dark almost blackened wainscoting layered beneath ages of dirt, the old creaky winding stairs that led up to the next level, the six-panel door leading to his grandparents' first-floor apartment, and the dusty, musty smell that seemed to bleed from the old wood. And he remembered the other six-panel door, the narrow one at the opposite end of the entry set into the inner wall that led down to the granite-walled basement with its boarded-up windows and spider web-riddled rafters and waist-deep shadows. And he remembered the sound of footsteps on those creaky cellar stairs, the footsteps of some unseen thing climbing up from the world below. He remembered turning and pounding on his grandparents' door, calling to them, his fists growing sore, throbbing.

But they never answered the door. He remembered trying the knob, which refused to turn in his small hand. He wanted desperately to turn to the outside door, tear it open and run off screaming into the descending gloom. But before he could flee he heard scratching on old wood and the sound of the cellar door creaking open behind him and in his dying heart young Chase knew it was too late.

And as a single floorboard creaked under some unseen thing's weight, he'd awakened, tearing at the covers, screaming, falling out of bed and landing hard on the floor, the night engulfing him like quicksand, burying him, suffocating him, his muffled screams drifting past his inebriated mother lying passed out on the living room sofa after consuming too many Friday night Vodka Martinis.

***

"Christ," Dolores said, setting the cat down on the floor and leaning forward, "you look as if you've seen a ghost."

Chase felt a minor jolt rock his body as he was suddenly thrust back into the present, the smell of old rotting wood lingering. He considered the beer in his hand as if it were an alien artifact he'd stumbled upon while out for a stroll.

"*Ghosts*," he said, correcting her. "More than one. It's funny what can dredge them up from those dark places that you forgot even existed."

He tried to laugh, but couldn't manage it.

"A little exorcism is in order, I'd say," Dolores said.

Chase managed a smile. "Hey," he said, frowning suddenly as if in deep thought, "speaking of exorcisms, would you like to take a ride?"

Chapter Twenty-Two

"Nice place to take a date," Dolores said as she studied the run-down tenement through the rain-streaked passenger-side window of Chase's SUV. "Looks haunted. Did Norman Bates live here?"

Chase snorted an amused sound. He was reaching back over the seat, sifting through an assortment of tools lying on the floor, the sound of clanging filling the car's cabin.

"Didn't see Norman Bates, but haunted…well, the jury's still out on that point."

"Good to know," Dolores said, shifting her gaze to the flashing blue lights farther up the street. "Guess that's the crime scene."

"Yep," he said, sliding back into the driver's seat, holding a small crowbar called a cat's paw in his hand.

"Oh, we're not going to—"

"It's safe," Chase said with a sliver of apprehension in his voice. It was nothing compared to the cold dread he was feeling in his gut. But a second trip into the old building seemed advisable, even necessary. It was like repeating an experiment, testing its validity. Dragging Dolores out into the rainy night to serve as witness to whatever weirdness presented itself was the point that was worrying his conscience because, at some level, Chase knew that he did not want to go back into the fucking place alone. Selfish to be sure but scientific as well. Convenient all around.

It would be all right, he thought. He'd make it up to her, buy her dinner someday. Take her to the Night Owl. Maybe.

"I'm not going to carry my video camera in there, just my mobile phone. I don't want anybody taking special notice of us." Chase gestured toward a big SUV parked beside one of the local cruisers. "See that?"

Dolores nodded.

"Belongs to a detective who'd like my body to have been the one that turned up tonight," he said checking his phone and clipping it to his belt. "Eve Teschal's her name."

"Is she the one who paid you a visit this morning?"

"That would be her."

"Also good to know."

Chase flipped the switch that deactivated the SUV's cabin light and did his best to palm the cat's paw, sliding the straight portion as far up his sleeve as was possible.

"The forensics people will be there for some time," he said. "So tonight, with the rain and the confusion, will be the best chance I'll have."

"Hey," Dolores said, wrapping her fingers around his arm. "Exactly what are we looking for?"

He paused. "I wish I knew."

"Great," she said releasing him. "You *are* a hot date."

Chase tried to smile, opened the door and slipped out into the night. Dolores did the same, closing the door quietly and waiting by the car. The nearest street light was dark, the glass globe shattered—stroke of urban luck.

"Cross that way, heading toward the square as if we live down that end of the street," Chase said.

Dolores obeyed and the pair crossed the rain-soaked street, the drizzle falling all around them, the not-so-distant coruscating blue LEDs from the cruisers catching in their eyes.

Chapter Twenty-Three

Connie sat at her desk watching the late news on her laptop nursing a cup of coffee with some Jameson's—late night tonic to help her sleep. Chase's piece was on again. Amateur. Incomplete. Was he losing his touch? Well, he'd still managed to get shots no one else had gotten. Still not afraid to cross the yellow tape when the situation warranted it.

Connie tapped keys, switched to the full loop Chase had brought for her. For her? No. For the station, for the news, for the *cash*. Chase was Chase. And for better or worse, that was oddly comforting to her. Or at least it always *had* been comforting.

"Jesus," she heard herself say.

She leaned closer. The image of Teschal and the two male detectives filled the screen. Richards was the name of the taller one, she didn't recognize the short, stocky one. Or the stiff from the Forensics lab in the Durex suit. Then the sound broke from the laptop's fairly expensive speaker system: a cat crying. It was the mournful sort of sound a cat might make late at night when it was hungry or in heat.

Then the camera swung suddenly around. It took a second for the image to stabilize, but when it did, it revealed nothing but darkness and vague outlines, doors lining the left-hand wall.

Connie hit the pause button and tapped the zoom. Once. Twice. Not too close. There were some things best kept at arm's length, even if they were just images on the screen. Besides, too much zoom and the image would blur like an impressionist painting viewed up close.

The face, if that's what it was, came into focus. Distorted, twisted like a deformed man or animal, disproportionate like the elephant man on steroids after surviving a terrible fire. Nightmarish to say the least. It was the sort of image Hollywood would reject for being too intense, too disturbing. 'Watch the movie then report directly to therapy.'

Connie shivered, sat back in her chair. It must be a mistake, some strange optical illusion, a bunch of shadows that looked like something else. Some sort of print on the wall, a stain even.

She closed the loop, sipped some Jameson's spiked coffee. Outside a train whistle howled. She closed the laptop and headed for the door, shutting the light as she left. Bed was calling. An empty, cold bed filled with memories of blood-stained walls and a twisted, shadowy face. What the hell was happening to her? She shivered again and closed and locked the door.

The station was practically set on auto-pilot for the night. No one left but a lone third shift security guard who couldn't stop a rabbit if he stepped on it and a couple of technicians researching go-nowhere stories with dreams of big time television dancing in their youthful heads.

Connie passed unseen through the back door and crossed the drizzly parking lot. She could hear traffic on the Old Cape Highway, which passed just beyond the trees and marshes that bordered the KTX parking lot. During the mill baron days those marshes had been a river, now relegated to an underground conduit. Or so she'd heard.

She hit the unlock button on her key fob and listened to the door of her ten-year-old Lexus click open. She reached for the handle but paused, her fingers brushing against the cool damp metal. Frowning, Connie glanced over her shoulder. Had she heard something? Something like a cat crying out?

Connie felt the air flee her lungs and her pulse quickened. Why the hell should a cat crying somewhere off in the night send chills down her spine and turn the contents of her bowels to water?

With fumbling fingers, she tore open the door, climbed into the car and flipped the lock shut. She peered nervously through the windshield, the side window, scanning the parking lot. There was nothing but dark trees and rivulets of water trickling down the windows and a ground fog creeping up out of the marshes.

"Christ," she whispered. "Get a fucking grip."

She started the engine and sped out of the parking lot leaving only the mist, the drizzle, and the mournful sound of a cat crying out in her wake.

Chapter Twenty-Four

Chase and Dolores reached the chain link gate and slipped quietly through.

"Down the alleyway," Chase whispered, gingerly closing the gate behind them and guiding the rusted latch back into place.

"I've got to tell you, I'm a little creeped out here," she said.

"Don't worry," he said moving past her, the cat's paw in his hand. "I'm here."

"Yeah," she said, glancing back at the rain-soaked street, then up at the grim looking tenement. "Why am I not reassured?"

Chase led the way through the back yard and up the short flight of stairs to the door. Dolores was more hesitant, glancing about warily. Chase used the cat's paw to carefully pry the strips of wood from the doorjamb. He set each piece by the porch railing and slowly urged the door open.

"The floor creaks like hell, but it's solid," he said before disappearing into the shadows.

Dolores glanced back at the trees abutting the back yard, glimpsed the lighted tenements beyond. Somewhere a House of Pain song was playing. It seemed all Gevaudan was awake this night.

She stepped up into the entry and waited for her eyes to adjust to this new degree of darkness. She sensed Chase's shadowy shape climbing the winding stairs, vanishing around the corner, the old wood creaking softly beneath his weight. She drew in a breath, tasted dust and followed with her heart racing.

Together they reached the second floor, continued on to the third, where Chase slowly crossed to the window at the far end.

"There are doors here," Dolores said, dragging her fingers hesitantly across the first of the old doorknobs.

Glancing up into the deep gloom, she spied what appeared to be an old gas sconce protruding from the space between the two doors.

"Look at that," she said, reaching up and touching the thing. Something small with many legs moved beneath her fingers and she jerked her hand away.

"Shit," she hissed, leaning back into one of the door jambs rubbing her hand. "I..." she began, but paused, cocking her head. Had she heard something stirring on the other side of the door?

"Chase," she whispered.

She could see his silhouette set against the window at the end of the landing, which was in turn lighted by the window across the alleyway.

"Forensics is hard at work," he observed, the mobile phone in his hand set to video.

Dolores turned her attention back to the closest of the apartment doors. She laid her palm against the old wood and leaned in closer. Only silence. She moved away, back toward the stairs, rubbing her arms as if chasing away a chill.

Chase turned to her, the video camera on the phone still aimed at the scene next door.

"It was right where you're standing," he observed.

"*What* was right where I'm standing?" she said, feeling her body go rigid.

"Something that showed up on the video, something I never saw. Some sort of face. One of the technicians at KTX spotted it. Right *there*," he said pointing.

"Shit," Dolores said and she moved quickly toward the outer wall, pressing her back against the old wood and plaster.

"Thanks for telling me," she said, rubbing her arms harder. "What sort of thing?"

"Could have been some kind of defect on the video I suppose," Chase said. "A trick of shadow maybe. But it gave everyone the creeps." He was about to add, "even me," to his statement, but decided against it and turned his attention back to the window and the scene unfolding across the alleyway.

Dolores crept toward Chase, leaned in and gazed through the old window. From this vantage point, she could see clearly into the apartment across the way.

"You can almost reach out and touch it," she said softly, her lips inches from Chase's ear.

"Almost," he said.

The room was vividly lit by industrial work lights that had been positioned at either end of the room. Dolores could also make out the shadows of unseen technicians moving like fleeting ghosts across the blood-stained walls of the room where the murder had apparently taken place.

Dolores's stomach began to complain and she knew that she had seen enough. She moved awkwardly away from the window, her breast brushing unintentionally against Chase's arm as she moved. The sensation was an exhilarating one. Must be the adrenaline rush, she rationalized. Heightened senses and all that. Chase didn't seem to notice.

Chase closed the video and activated the flashlight. The glow filled the long narrow landing. He panned it around. The linoleum was worn and ripped; dark patches of old stained wood were visible through the ragged seams and in the corners where it was peeling up. The wainscoting was dark and rotted, falling to pieces in places, rusted nail heads poking out here and there. The doors appeared to be sturdy, though they had clearly seen better days. The doorknobs were old and ornate, possibly brass. The two doors were padlocked shut. Chase tested each lock.

"No one came out of either of these," he said.

Chase crossed to the spot where the 'face' had manifested. He ran his palm along the wall, and then stepped back and aimed the light at the horse hair plaster. A large dark stain was visible extending from the ceiling to the wainscoting. Chase leaned in close enough to sniff the stain.

"What is it?" Dolores asked, her hands still gripping her forearms in a vain effort to fight back the lingering chill.

"Smells like...rotten eggs." Chase stepped back, aimed the light at the spot on the wall. "Hydrogen sulfide."

"It looks singed," Dolores said, her voice fading into a hoarse whisper. She sensed Chase nodding in the gloom beside her.

"Maybe we should check the doors on the second floor," Dolores said, rubbing her arms more vigorously, desperately trying to move things along.

Chase agreed and led the way back down the winding stairs, Dolores hugging his heels. They moved into the second-floor landing and found two more doors in a similar state, secured with large padlocks.

"Nothing," she said, her voice quivering.

"Hey," Chase said, taking note of her demeanor. "Are you all right?"

He saw her shrug. He aimed the light at her face; there was cold fear in her eyes.

"Hey." He moved close, wrapped his arms around her. She was trembling, but she felt good. Smelled good. She buried her face against his shoulder.

"Let's get the hell out of here," he said.

"Yes, please."

They descended to the first floor and Chase checked the doors there. Both padlocked. Then they stepped out onto the back porch and Chase closed the door.

The steamy evening air was cool and refreshing compared to the putrefying atmosphere trapped within the old tenement and they both breathed deeply.

Carefully, Chase pushed the boards back into place, forcing their partly bent nails as deep into the old jamb as he could manage using the side of the cat's paw for leverage. Then they climbed down to the yard and headed up the alleyway. Neither of them spoke.

Checking the street to see if any police were looking their way, Chase opened the gate and the couple walked toward Mitre Square.

"Let's cross a little further down. If the cops are watching they'll think that we came from the coffee shop."

"Coffee sounds good," Dolores said. "And warm."

"Sure," Chase said and he put his arm around her and together they crossed the street and made their way back toward his car. Setting the cat's paw on the back seat, he secured the vehicle and together they set off down the hill toward Mitre Square.

Chapter Twenty-Five

Chase found himself at the same table he and Eloise had occupied earlier that evening. A different waitress, this one older and far less flirtatious, took their orders and brought them coffees.

"That was the creepiest place I've ever seen," Dolores said as she blew on her java. It was clear she'd been on the verge of tears.

"That's twice for me," Chase said, reaching out and squeezing her hand while studying the footage he'd shot on his phone.

"What were you looking for in there?"

"Ghosts." Chase forced a grin.

"No, really."

"Like I said, something showed up on the video I shot, and, well, I thought maybe someone had been in the house with me, poked their head out of one of those apartment doors maybe. But those locks were rusty and old. No one's been there for some time."

"That darkened section of wall is where it showed up on the video?"

Chase nodded. "I guess that it could have been something on the video itself, some technical glitch."

Dolores nodded slowly, thoughtfully.

"Here," Chase said, offering Dolores his phone. "See for yourself. I've pulled up the video."

"I'm not sure I want to see this."

"It can't hurt you, just hit the arrow."

She reluctantly tapped the arrow. As the video played her facial expression grew gradually grim.

"Christ." She hit the pause switch several times until the video stopped.

"What do you think?" Chase accepted the phone, which Dolores nearly dropped while handing it back to him.

"I couldn't make it out too well, but, God, it sure as hell looks as if something was standing at the top of the stairs watching you." She shivered, wrapped her fingers around her coffee mug.

"Are you all right?"

She shook her head.

"I shouldn't have shown you—"

"No," she said. "I'm in this too."

"What can I do to make you feel better?"

"It, uh, felt good when you hugged me in there," she said, trying to sound demure. She began running her finger tips around the edge of her coffee cup.

"You were shivering," he said, shutting the video and clipping the phone to his belt.

She smiled a tired little smile. Not the response she'd wanted.

"It was scary," she said.

"Yes, it was," Chase agreed.

A moment passed between them. He sipped his coffee. She watched him, studying his face.

"Chase," Dolores said, changing the subject. "That name, Chase, it implies pursuit. Tell me, just what is Chase *chasing*?"

"Headlines," he said with a shrug. "A good story, decent footage."

"Okay." Dolores nodded, accepting the futility of further questions along that line. "What about Christian? That's another telling name. Maybe you're chasing religion, trying to find God. Maybe all those terrible things you've seen through your lens have left you searching for something greater, something with meaning. You just don't strike me as the religious type."

"I'm not—I've never found religion. And it's certainly never found me."

"Cynic."

"Philosopher."

"*Touché*," she said with a grin.

"Maybe I've just seen too much through my lens, like you said. I guess it gets to you after a while." He sighed, pursed his lips in deep thought. Julie had told him this countless times, but he'd never really heard her, until that moment.

"But I suppose that the universe knows what it's doing, even if we don't agree with it all the time. *Most* of the time."

"I understand that," Dolores said.

"What about you?" Chase raised his eyes and found hers. "What is Dolores Kane looking for?"

She shrugged. "Peace I suppose. Serenity. That old adage about changing what I can, accepting what I can't and finding the wisdom to know the difference."

"That's profound, maybe impossible. You *are* a philosopher."

"That's why I'm still looking." She toasted him with her mug of coffee.

A young heavily tattooed couple wearing gothic clothing entered the doughnut shop and took seats at the counter.

"You see all sorts of things at this hour," Dolores said softly, gesturing with her jaw.

Chase glanced at the clock above the doughnut cases.

"I should be getting you home," he said.

"Afraid I'll turn into a pumpkin?"

"Nothing would surprise me just now."

Dolores grinned. "You were married?" she said, out of the blue.

He nodded. He'd mentioned that before. Hadn't he? "Yes."

"Do you miss it?"

Loaded question.

"I miss the company. Going home to an empty house...*apartment*, these days." He winced. "Julie sold the house. Well, it's not too inviting, living alone."

Dolores nodded. "You should get a cat."

"I have a history of being unreliable. I'd forget to feed it."

"I could watch it for you. We *are* neighbors. We could call it Piwac, like the cat in that old Jimmy Stewart movie where his neighbor is a witch. Maybe Grimalken. I like those medieval names for cats. Midnight might like the company."

She smiled, sipped her coffee.

"Why did it take so long for you to get to know me?" she said, switching to her intended line of questioning. "It took forever for you to even set foot in my place, sort of like you'd catch something. I mean even when you helped me move in, you just left the boxes in the hall outside my door."

"You had those two moving guys unloading the truck," Chase said, clearly side-stepping the question. "I was probably in a rush."

She gave him a probing look.

"That was almost two years ago, so I couldn't say for sure. But recently, well, I've managed to keep most people at arm's length since the divorce. I guess it's easier that way. No entanglements. No complications."

"That's the easy way out. I think you're afraid that people will let you down, not the other way around."

Chase squirmed uncomfortably in the booth.

"What was the final straw?" Dolores said. "Most marriages that fail…well, usually there are a lot of little things before one final straw ends it all."

"She was cheating. Julie. I suppose I deserved it, always busy, living through my lens. Hustling. Out nights. Stringing; ambulance chasing."

"*No one* deserves it."

He raised his eyes, considered hers. They were soft brown, bedroom brown he'd have called them long ago.

"It seems that when you hand a woman a marriage certificate it's a lot like handing a ship's captain a Letter of Marque from the king. In the blink of an eye a reasonable man with perhaps a few unspoken ulterior motives becomes a privateer, a legal buccaneer, a pirate free to loot and pillage at will with no consequences."

"Ouch," Dolores said softly, taken aback.

"Sorry," Chase said with a meager smile. "Just bitter I guess. I'm sure men are no picnic."

"A picnic with fire ants." She grinned. "The key to marriage is marrying the right person. And at the very least it's my experience that good things happen when you least expect them."

"You should be a marriage counselor."

"I'll mail you my fee," she said grinning.

"What about you?"

"Never married. Almost. Mutual cold feet. He was studying psychology. My parents were always trying to kill each other—talk about needing therapy. There were issues, with my father. Bad issues. He left suddenly. My mother said she couldn't wait to be rid of him. Until she was. Then she drank herself into a nightly stupor, blamed me for his leaving. He was a bastard of the first order. I never saw him again. Except in my dreams." Dolores' eyes became cold and grim. She rubbed her arms as if the chill had followed her from the old house.

"I collect SSI these days. PTSD they call it, post-traumatic stress disorder. I work from home, on the computer. Some of it under the table. Mostly research for a few local attorneys, private investigators. I have a BS in Criminal Justice from Bridgton University. Some graduate work. I considered pursuing a law degree, but that costs an arm and a leg. So I stick to my research. I'm the number these guys call when they need background checks, information, the e-mail they send. No face. Complete anonymity. That's how I like it. That's why I don't go out much."

Chase nodded. He didn't know what to say.

"Am I scaring you?"

Chase shook his head. "I don't scare easily." He sipped his coffee. "Um, bathroom."

"Excused," Dolores said and Chase slipped out of the booth and headed for the back of the shop.

Grinning, Dolores glanced around the shop, her eyes soaking up the 1950s style décor and the odd assortment of customers sitting at the counter.

The door to the shop opened again and a middle-aged woman entered. She had blunt-cut dark hair with traces of gray at the roots. Dressed in a track suit and a stylish trench coat, she appeared disheveled, but who wouldn't at this hour? Dolores noticed that the woman's mascara was somewhat smeared, almost as if she'd been crying. But she supposed it could have been the rain.

Dolores couldn't help but watch as the woman approached the counter, ordered a large black coffee, and paid for it with cash that she drew from an expensive looking wallet, before turning on her heel and heading out the door.

Something about the woman held Dolores' gaze and she watched as she climbed aboard a well-appointed dark-colored Volvo parked at the front window. The woman remained there, sitting in her car, the light from the doughnut shop spilling across her face, revealing lines and creases in her skin that seemed terribly premature. The woman was gazing steadily at the light show up the street. She turned suddenly and her eyes found Dolores'.

Dolores felt as if a cold hand had touched her face and she almost gasped. The expression on the woman's face was one of profound sadness; it was an expression that Dolores would never forget. Then the woman turned, looked back over her right shoulder, and slowly backed out of the parking space. She spun the wheel and drove out of the lot, merging with the lessening traffic.

"You see all sorts of things at this hour," Dolores whispered to herself.

"What did I miss?" Chase said returning and sliding into the booth.

"Nothing," Dolores said raising her mug of coffee to her lips. "Nothing."

Chapter Twenty-Six

Chase opened his eyes. It was dark outside. Rain was falling hard. Music was playing softly on a radio someplace close by. INXS was performing *By My Side*. The song had reached the electric harpsichord solo. Chase had always liked that part, there was an 'old world,' ethereal quality to it.

He sighed, turned onto his side. Dolores was lying beside him, asleep, breathing softly. They'd made love. It had been good. It had been better than good. It had been fucking amazing. He remembered looking up at her shadowy form, feeling her legs snug against his hips, her breasts inches from his face, her dark hair framing her lovely face and her eyes glistening like stars. He could still hear her breathy sighs. He could still taste her lips. And the rain beyond the open sliders in the living room falling hard, thunder thrumming like an immense heartbeat in the distance, the sound of the last evening commuter train joining in, rumbling past the platform one street over.

"The lights are still there," she'd said as they'd driven out of the doughnut shop parking lot. They'd be there all night, he'd told her. Maybe for days until they'd combed every inch of the place, removed every clue, anything that might be considered evidence.

Chase rolled onto his back. The ceiling fan was turning slowly above him, shadows moving through shadows.

They'd driven through town, along Church Green Road, toward Saint Genevieve's Square, barely speaking, not needing to, the usually awkward silence anything but awkward.

"Look at that," Dolores had said, breaking the silence.

Flickering lights, candles, people, perhaps thirty or more huddled by the door of the great old church at the heart of the square.

"It's a memorial service for the murdered children, victims of the North Side Strangler," she'd said, her voice low and husky as if in reverence for the gathering of mourners.

"Sad," he had observed, meaning it.

"Should we film it?" she had asked.

"Yes," he had agreed, after a moment's thought, and he'd pulled over, climbed out onto the sidewalk, shouldered his video unit and panned it about. There had been at least two other film crews mingling with the crowd, reporters with microphones, camera men with expensive video equipment. Dolores had pointed out mobile television units parked around the corner near the vicarage, beside the old cemetery, one bearing the name of a local cable network, the other a major channel out of Providence, most likely more on the way.

Chase had joined the gathering, filmed the candle-lit faces and captured the grief, the hope, the humanity. He'd felt something shift within him at that moment, had sensed a binding force among the makeshift congregation surrounding him, enveloping him, changing some aspect of his being. It had been a subtle thing and yet it had felt as if the Earth had moved beneath his feet.

After ten minutes or so he'd shut the unit, let it drop to his side. Then he'd turned to Dolores who was standing beside him, her arms crossed, her dark eyes alive with moisture and candlelight. And the Earth had become solid again, more solid than it had ever been.

Chase had turned back to the gathering, to the solemn faces. Small gluts of people had been visible moving down the side street, approaching the gathering, flickering candles in their hands. He'd noticed several of the nuns who lived in the convent across the street mingling with the gatherers. An old priest with a shock of thinning gray hair was among the mourners. He was speaking with a well-dressed middle-aged woman with silver well-coifed hair.

"That's Father Rousseau," Dolores had said. "The parish priest. I don't recognize the woman."

Chase remembered nodding slowly, wondering if he should stop to interview the man, ask him what Connie would call 'human interest questions,' get some close-up shots of the concern that was clearly etched into his wizened face. But at that moment stopping to do an interview had been the farthest thing from his tired brain. Besides, the networks had 'scooped' him. There was nothing original here anyway, only an additional component to a story that could hardly be considered his alone. His was the 'Night Stalker' case. He'd send the footage into Connie nonetheless along with what he'd shot from the old tenement window. She'd know what to do with it.

And so slowly, wordlessly, Chase and Dolores had climbed back aboard the SUV and driven off into the night, leaving the group of mourners to their candles and despair.

Yet in spite of the palpable grief they'd left behind them, the warm comfortable silence had returned to the cab of his SUV and had remained until the couple had reached their apartment building.

"Come in," Dolores had said as Chase stood with her at her door. "I won't bite."

It was a lie—but a pleasant lie.

It was said that traumatic situations tended to drive people into each other's arms. Maybe, Chase thought that was true. Tonight had certainly been traumatic. Dolores' life had been traumatic, infinitely more intense than his life in many ways. His mother drank, his father had run out on them, but that had been all. Hell that had been enough.

And yet that was where Dolores' trauma began. And he suspected that she had only told him *some* of her story. Like an iceberg, he suspected that most of it remained hidden beneath a dark mysterious sea. SSI handouts were not as commonplace as they'd once been, you really had to earn one these days.

Chase studied Dolores' sleeping form. There was a peace about her, a peace that should not have been there, based upon what she'd told him tonight about her family, about her medical history. And about her life goals. Perhaps she'd found a slice of the peace she sought. And maybe, somehow, he'd helped her find it. And that was fine with him.

Dolores hadn't bothered turning on the lights in her apartment. She'd gone to the veranda, opened the sliders and stepped outside. She'd stood watching the rain, the streetlight casting her in silhouette. Why hadn't he seen how beautiful she was long ago? Why had he kept her at arm's length? Why had he shut everyone out since the divorce? He blamed the job, the weird hours. But that wasn't the entire truth. The truth was that he'd been afraid to get involved with any woman, afraid she'd judge him too harshly, call him an 'ambulance chaser' just like Connie and Eloise. Tell him he was less than human.

But somehow it didn't bother him when they said those things; he'd simply correct them jokingly. But Julie had said the same thing, compared him to a lawyer lurking in a dark corner at a funeral home, handing out business cards to the bereaved, drumming up business. And surprisingly, that had hurt. Was *that* it? Was it all that simple?

Connie had sensed it from the beginning and moved in for the kill. And she'd been there ever since, more than willing to relieve the pressure, be a kindred spirit. Maybe.

They were two mercenaries walking through life who had bumped into each other at just the right moment in time, two fully armed warships passing each other in the night. But if it *was* all that simple, then why had making love with Dolores felt so good, so right?

Thunder rolled past the sliders heading toward parts unknown.

Chase had come up behind Dolores on the veranda and pressed himself against her. She'd turned slightly, far enough to kiss him.

"Touch me," she'd whispered.

And he had. Now, still long before dawn, he had no urge to flee, no desire to escape. He had never wanted to stay in one place so badly. Some deep part of his being told him that at long last he'd found where he belonged.

He sighed.

"Tell me about your parents," she'd said after they'd made love, while she was lying naked in his arms.

"My father left when I was six," he'd said, casually, with little effort. "Just walked out the door." He'd said nothing about his childhood for longer than he could remember.

"My mother stayed behind to drink. When my sister ran away at fifteen, just because she couldn't take it anymore, the drunken abuse from my mother, I decided to leave too. I was nineteen by then. It was easier for me. Victoria, that's my sister, well, I never found her, never saw her again."

"Jesus," Dolores had whispered. "What about your mom?"

"Drank herself into a grave a few years back. Or so I'd heard."

"My father stayed around too long," Dolores had said. "Gotten too close. *Way* too close. My mother ignored it. I waited until I was sixteen and then left. I still have the scar on the back of my neck where my mother hit me with an iron that she threw at me as I ran out the door with a knapsack. 'Don't leave me alone with this fucker!' were her last words to me."

Chase had drawn her closer. She seemed to have melted into him. At some point, as they'd slept, she'd rolled away. But she'd remained within arm's reach, breathing quietly. It had been the best feeling he could remember.

INXS finished up and U2 started singing *One*. Outside the rain fell.

***

Connie couldn't sleep. Not that unusual these days. She simply sat in the dark nursing a rock glass filled with Scotch and ice. The CEO's drink. Big broadcasting bitch. Success story.

She picked up the mobile phone, scanned through until she found Chase's number. She waited, her thumb poised above the contact. But it was late. Very late. Too late, maybe in more ways than one.

Fuck, she thought.

Then she shut the thing, set it on the table beside the chair and went back to her Scotch. Sooner or later sleep would find her. It always did; it knew just where to look.

Chapter Twenty-Seven

Eve Teschal was pulling into her garage when her mobile phone rang. She was tired, running out of ideas fast. And the heat was building, politically as well as meteorologically. The last thing she needed at this late hour was more grief.

She slipped the big SUV into park and scooped up the phone. She swept her finger across the screen, which featured a picture of a cemetery in Inverness, Scotland, beneath a crimson-colored sunset, the place her ancestors called home.

Teschal had left Jude Richards in charge of the murder scene. A good man with a consistent record and a somewhat open mind. Richards was nearing retirement age, but he had not yet fallen into retirement mode, switched to auto-pilot as so many seasoned cops did. Richards was still making points, maybe even hoping for a late-in-life promotion. A little more cash to add to his eighty-percent.

"Anything wrong?" Teschal said. Wrong seemed to be the word of the day. Maybe even the month.

"We've had some company down here."

"Anyone significant?"

"That stringer who whores for KTX. He was with a pretty little thing, not that woman from the station though."

"Yeah, I hear he had a piece on the news tonight. Not much to show for it, but he must have gotten close somehow. Next time—if there *is* a next time—we should post guards on the neighboring houses."

"I heard that; he probably got in next door," Richards said. "Big old tenement that's boarded up. A little breaking and entering I'd say."

"We'll overlook that for now, he could prove useful," Teschal said. "But I'm wondering about his source. That stunt he pulled the other night suggests that he has someone on the inside. *That's* who I'm after."

"And there was one other visitor."

Teschal rubbed her eyes. "Enlighten me."

"You're going to love this."

Chapter Twenty-Eight

A gray rainy dawn was bleeding through the windows of Dolores' apartment. Chase rose first, feeling oddly at ease and infinitely more comfortable than he'd ever imagined he could under the circumstances. He dressed, crept out the door and went to his apartment.

He gathered up a few supplies for breakfast: eggs, some bacon he hoped had not gone bad (could bacon go bad?), and some raisin bread for toast.

He noticed the red light on his answering machine blinking and hit the play button. There were two messages, the first from Julie.

"Chase," her voice flinty and laced with exasperation, "I found another one of those boxes of yours. More CDs and DVDs; all that *import* crap you listen to and those old movies you love so much. Come and get them please. This isn't a storage facility."

Chase felt himself grinning. She was sweeping the last vestiges of him from her life. Well, that was Julie, always compartmentalizing things.

The second message was from Connie.

"Something's wrong with your mobile. Stop in this morning. I've been up all night doing research, got some things to show you. I'll be in by nine. I just love this fucking 'Night Stalker' angle. I can see the viewing shares rising as I speak."

Chase smiled sardonically, shook his head. Connie was as predictable as the tides.

He gathered up his breakfast supplies and headed back to Dolores' place. He rarely made a decent breakfast, usually coffee and eggs with toast from a shop at the corner. This would be a first, but not the *only* first this morning. He hadn't slipped out the back door in the middle of the night, as was typical. This time he'd stayed. And that was fucking amazing and *completely* unpredictable.

Dolores rolled out of bed just as Chase was scooping the scrambled eggs out of the pan and spooning them into the plates.

"Morning," he said.

Her smile was brilliant. She moved up behind him, wrapped her arms around his waist, stood on her toes and kissed his neck.

"I thought you'd be gone—would have bet on it."

"So would I," Chase said solemnly. "So would I."

They sat eating breakfast, the sound of the rain falling beyond the open sliders filling the room, providing background noise for their conversation.

"Remind me why we waited so long to do this?" she said.

Chase paused, a coffee cup poised in his hand.

"My divorce was just finalized a few weeks ago," he said. It was a lie. The divorce proceedings had ended months earlier, but the lie made him sound somehow sincere. What irony.

"Didn't want to get involved I guess."

Dolores cocked her lovely head to one side and smiled.

"Bullshit. I know you've been seeing that television producer at KTX for a while."

It was Chase's turn to smile.

"What makes you say that?" he said.

"I *am* a woman. I don't really mind. I saw her once on television, being interviewed about some anonymous source or something. First amendment. Fourth Estate. Refusing to give up the person's name. Dedicated if not somewhat self-serving."

"That's Connie."

Dolores grinned at him.

"Who have I gotten myself involved with?" Chase said.

"I told you, I *do* have a degree in criminal justice. I guess that you only *assumed* I was a complete idiot."

Chase set his coffee mug down. "I never assumed that."

He reached across the table, took her hands in his. They were warm, inviting.

"Connie, well, she was a way to…I don't know, lose myself from time to time. Forget about my ex. Forget how I screwed that whole thing up."

"I don't mind. I guess that we all do what we have to do in a given moment. But I assume that you've found yourself, maybe?" Dolores smiled mischievously.

"Promising." He gave her hands a squeeze.

Dolores' smile grew brighter and more mischievous.

"What are you thinking?" he asked.

"I was just wondering if we're the first couple to get together at a murder scene."

"I doubt it. You know I once met a woman at a suicide attempt."

"Are you serious? Were you filming it?"

"Not exactly. There was this guy out on Memorial Bridge threatening to jump. The state cops had shut the thing down and rerouted traffic. I was on my way to work. I had a part time job a few nights a week at this liquor store. I was just sitting there in traffic, not moving, realizing I was going to be late. No mobile phones then. No way to call the night manager to tell him I was going to be late. I happened to glance over at the car beside me. Big black Corvette. And there she was, staring back at me. Blonde hair, blue eyes, all smiles. It was hot and we had the windows open. I yelled, 'Are you having fun?'"

Dolores laughed. "That's a pathetic line."

"Yeah, but it worked. She said 'no' and we started talking as our cars crept along side by side. When things broke up she followed me to the store and we sat in her car for about a half hour talking. I remember the manager staring at me through the front window of the store, probably wondering what the hell I was doing. When I explained what had happened, he laughed. The guy bought me a six pack as I was heading home; I think he was proud of me."

Dolores laughed. "Men." After a moment she said, "How long did it last?"

Chase shrugged. "A few months. Trips to the beach, movies, back seat wrestling, that sort of thing."

He nodded slowly, drifting through the memory. Then he raised his eyes, found Dolores'.

"They got the guy off the bridge though."

It was Dolores' turn to nod slowly.

"Let's hope the real thing lasts longer," he said. "I mean, that woman in that tenement is dead, as dead as the two people I saw the other night. Life can be so…abrupt."

Dolores watched him closely, studying his eyes. They were surprisingly warm, she thought, that is, for the eyes of a heartless stringer.

"And your ex?" she asked with a hint of trepidation.

He studied his coffee. "Oh, Julie and I had dated in high school. We were a steady item, the proverbial high school sweethearts. Then we graduated, drifted apart. I got a degree in journalism, believe it or not. She went into education, became a guidance counselor. We bumped into each other years later at a local watering hole and it was as if no time had passed at all. We tried to pick up where we left off, but you can't do that. You can't go back. People change. Perspectives change. Neither of us could remember what we ever saw in each other. Part of me wishes we'd left it all back in high school."

"But then you'd always wonder if it could have worked."

"I suppose." Chase shrugged. "Closure."

He sipped some coffee. "You?"

"Jim was older, well off. A good guy. I was impressed. At first. Then one day we both realized I was looking for the father I never had, looking for someone to take me away from it all. Fortunately we realized it in time."

"We are survivors, you and I, escape artists," he said, raising his coffee mug. "Here's to the two founding members of the Escape Club—no relation to the band of the same name."

Dolores raised her mug of coffee and tapped it against Chase's.

"To the Escape Club."

"Hey, I've got to meet Connie. She's got some new information."

"Information? What information?"

"I'm not really sure, she says she's been doing research. That's French for one of the interns to whom she pays a pittance has been doing research. But it all amounts to the same thing."

He got to his feet, scooped up the breakfast dishes and headed for the kitchen.

"This murder, the one last night," he said, "well I guess it features the same MO as the murder the other night. And my source tells me that there have been others. Same thing. Bodies mutilated and burned."

He set the dishes in the sink.

"Leave those," Dolores said, her eyes becoming thoughtful. "You mean to say there's a serial killer out there?"

"Well, we know about the child murderer," he said, emerging from the kitchen. "That case certainly fits the serial killer definition. So, if *our* case involves a serial killer, then it's little wonder the powers-that-be are trying to keep it quiet. I mean, they don't want a panic on their hands. A few more candlelight vigils and the press will have a feeding frenzy. National news and all. But I suppose, based on the identities of most of the victims associated with Connie's 'Night Stalker,' it's easy to keep the lid on it. Not exactly stand-up citizens going toes-up."

"'Night Stalker?'"

"Connie's idea. She's trying to steal headlines from the North Side Strangler case through sensationalism. She's good at that sort of thing."

"Jesus," Dolores breathed. "'Night Stalker'. That ought to make people sleep soundly."

"That's the idea; make 'em stay up and watch the news. I'm heading down to the station to see what she's got." He headed for the door.

"See you later?" she said, raising her eyes, a hint of dejection manifesting itself there.

"Hey." Chase paused at the door and turned. "Do you want to come along?"

"Do you mean it?" she said, brightening.

"Sure. This could turn out to be a big deal, *real* reporting. I might need an assistant." Chase smiled at her. "What do you say?"

"I say, let me get some clothes on."

Chapter Twenty-Nine

The rain had eased by the time Chase and Dolores pulled into the KTX parking lot, but the storm on Connie's face when she saw Dolores could easily have surpassed anything Mother Nature might have whipped up.

"When did this become a field trip?" Connie said after opening the door to her office and getting a good look at Dolores.

"She's my assistant," he said, sensing, even anticipating Connie's hostility.

Dolores presented a half-hearted smile.

"Seriously, what do you have?" Chase said squeezing past Connie.

Dolores followed, giving Connie a wide berth.

Connie closed the door to her office, her mouth twisting into something resembling a smile.

"Okay," she said, sitting at her desk, flipping open her laptop and tapping some keys. Chase leaned over Connie's shoulder. Dolores hung back a bit, flanking Chase.

"Cozy," Connie said.

Dolores glanced at Chase. He smiled, touched her hand.

"First my people did a little research into Teschal's family background, just to satisfy my own morbid curiosity—turns out she *is* in fact descended from the Romany gypsies. Inverness, Scotland, which is at the eastern end of Loch Ness on the River Ness to be precise. It doesn't really surprise me. I guess her relatives have been swimming in the Loch for centuries. One of them makes headlines every now and again when someone takes a picture of them coming up for air."

Dolores laughed.

"Sense of humor on the girl," Connie said snippily. "Charming. Chase likes a sense of humor. And other things."

"Can we focus?" Chase said.

"Mom's a permanent guest at Long Pond Skilled Nursing Facility right here in Gevaudan. We tried to find out more about dad but came up empty. It's difficult though; gypsy bloodlines get muddled. Inbreeding is not at all uncommon. Europeans hate to see the gypsies coming, squatters and such. They start fights, live in mobile homes. It's no wonder Teschal is so tight-lipped."

"Okay," Chase said, "so Teschal's got an interesting family history and plays it close to the vest. There's not much we can do about that. Did you find out why she was loaned out to other places?"

"Most of that material is hush-hush, but my newest protégée, Kiley—you met her the other day—is in her new office doing more digging. But we did manage to trace the dead cop's fiancée, or rather his *ex*-fiancée, as she's suddenly back on the market, in demand, so to speak, living in Texas or some such place."

Dolores shook her head, grimacing.

Connie sensed the woman's disapproval and stiffened.

"If the talk's too hard for you sweetie, you can leave."

Dolores opened her mouth, but Chase cut in. "What's she doing in Texas?"

"She moved back in with her family. Austin, I think. I guess she followed the recently deceased to New England when he moved here to visit with a dying grandmother or aunt or something. That's when he landed the job with the Gevaudan PD. I guess it was always his dream to be a cop and he was on the waiting list for Austin. No shortage of men with guns in the Lone Star state."

"So, she's off the grid."

"We could track her down, call her," Dolores said. "Maybe she'll talk to us?"

"Kiley shagged a number, but it's a little early in Austin," Connie said.

"Okay, who else?" Chase said.

"The college girl who was murdered by the first victim was local. Elise Genevieve Mckenna. Her mom's still local. Dad's dead. He died in a car crash two years ago."

"And mom didn't jump out the window?" Dolores said.

"Apparently not," Connie said, her voice becoming icier. "Nice digs. Sold the house when dad died. She and Elise moved into this ritzy apartment on Tremont Street, the Daniker Building."

"Very nice neighborhood," Dolores said softly.

"The best neighborhood in all of Gevaudan. Mill Baron Hill they call it. Mansions aplenty."

"So they could look down over their mills," Dolores added. "Their domain. And all their little serfs scurrying about below."

"Is mom still working?" Chase asked.

"She doesn't need to work apparently," Connie said. "It seems dad inherited a boatload from his folks, who owned some patents on a few medical devices. He was a doctor, the research type not the turn-your-head-and-cough type. She was a nurse at Mercy General over in Wickham. She did take a big leave of absence after little Elise was killed. Toured the globe, joined the jet set."

"Strange thing to do after your daughter has been murdered," Chase said.

"Not if you needed to forget, I suppose," Dolores offered.

"A-plus for the *assistant*," Connie said.

Chase sighed. Connie's attitude was becoming tedious.

"But then she came back here, returned to Mercy General to lose herself in her work," Connie said. "For a while at least."

"It makes some sense I suppose," Chase said. "If you've got the cash."

"She doesn't work anymore. Just counts her late husband's insurance and inheritance money."

"Hey," Dolores said, frowning, "you said the first murder was that of the girl's killer, right?"

Connie nodded. "If this whole thing is accurate, yes."

"So?" Chase said, frowning.

"Well, did the first murder happen *before* or *after* mom went globe-hopping?"

"She's a bright one," Connie said, "I'll give her that."

Connie turned to Dolores, her voice surprisingly less than acidic. "The murder happened after she returned to town."

"Enough time for someone to do some reconnaissance work," Dolores said. "Prepare the scene while mom was out of town?"

"Yeah, but if mom hired someone to whack this D-Block character, this Dylan Raccine, then why not have it done while she was out of the country?" Chase added. "To throw suspicion off her entirely?"

"Hmmm," Dolores said. "I guess the timing could have gone all wrong. Maybe there was some delay in carrying out the hit."

"I guess that's possible," Chase said softly, thinking. "But when you consider the amount of traveling mom did after her daughter died, well, that's a pretty big window."

"Unless she wanted to be here when it happened," Connie said. "The murder happened immediately after she returned."

"And the police were on to this D-Block?" Dolores said.

"They were checking into him because of a video of him and little Elise leaving a club at about the same time. But our rookie cop screwed up the evidence at the scene where they found the girl's body. Additional evidence, *conclusive* evidence, was found in Raccine's place *after* his murder."

"I guess that search was the very definition of probable cause," Chase said.

"Mom probably wasn't aware," Dolores said.

"Maybe not," Chase agreed. "But they may have shown her the tape of the man leaving the club to see if she recognized him, also to confirm that it was in fact her daughter on the video. Many murders are committed by people the victim knows. And also to ask mom if she recognized any of the *other* people who might have made an appearance on the video, just in case. Then the police could check into everyone else exiting the club around the same time as the daughter. Those videos are all time-stamped."

"So mom probably got a look at the suspect," Connie said. "So, as I tend to be the suspicious type, I'd keep her file open."

"Well, if the cop who screwed the evidence up turns up dead, then we really have a case," Dolores said, shaking her head.

Connie and Chase both turned to her.

"What?" Her face blanched white. "No."

"She's a keeper, Chase," Connie said.

"What were the circumstances?" Dolores asked.

"He apparently stopped to investigate some suspicious activity at a closed-down mill over on Quarry

Street," Chase said. "He was found burned with the same lacerations."

"Just like the others," Dolores said softly.

"Just like the others."

"Body count is climbing," Connie said flatly.

"Maybe we should speak with Elise Mckenna's mom, pay her a visit," Chase said. "You have her number of course? Wouldn't want to just barge in on the woman."

"Of course," Connie said. "Not sure if she'll see you though. Maybe Del here should call her with a story about doing a piece on moms whose kids have been murdered, or some such bullshit."

"Del?" Dolores said.

"I knew a girl at BU named Dolores. We called her Del. She shagged half the rugby team under the bleachers."

Chase looked at Dolores, who appeared mildly perplexed.

Connie let a small self-amused grin touch her lips.

"Are you game?" Chase asked.

"Sure. The worst thing she can do is say no. You can be my camera man."

"Shit," Connie said, punching some keys. "I guess I could fix you up with some ID or something, make it at least *look* real. We are, after all, a genuine news source."

Chase nodded, smiled at Dolores behind Connie's back.

"There she is," Connie said as the image of Allison Mckenna walking with the reporters in front of the Gevaudan Court House materialized on the laptop's screen.

"Oh my God," Dolores said. "Chase, look."

Chase leaned forward, stared at the screen.

"What? I've seen her picture before."

"What the fuck am I missing?" Connie said, craning to look up at Chase.

"Last night…" Dolores said.

"We went back to the scene last night," Chase said, "to check on…to check on what your people found on the video."

"I thought you covered the vigil at the church last night? I figured the little bit you sent of the murder house was left over from the previous night?" Connie said, turning on Chase.

"We didn't find anything. Doors in the tenement were locked, there was no way anyone could have gotten in or out. We stopped at the Mitre Square Doughnut Shop afterward."

"And you didn't bring me anything? So?"

"That woman was there," Dolores said. "She came in sometime after midnight, bought a coffee. She looked like death warmed over."

"What the hell?" Connie said.

"Where was I?" Chase said.

"I think you were in the bathroom," Dolores said.

"That's interesting," Connie said, nodding thoughtfully.

"I guess," Chase said, "we'd *better* pay Ms. Mckenna a visit. Fast."

"Fast?" Dolores said.

"Yeah, Del, before our friend, the gypsy detective, finds out that dear old mom was cruising around a murder scene, one that bears a striking resemblance to that of her daughter's murderer. Not to mention the rookie cop who screwed up the whole investigation. Especially since there was no way in hell mom could have been aware of *either* of those things."

Chapter Thirty

"Nice building," Dolores said as her eyes perused the granite-gray facade of the Daniker Building through the constant drizzle. "Named after Josiah Daniker I presume. He owned four mill complexes in the north end."

"Connie said it was nice digs," Chase said, checking his Canon.

"What about *her*?" Dolores said.

"Allison Mckenna?"

"No, your friend Connie."

Chase sighed. "Like I said, we're friends."

"Friends with benefits."

"We were."

"I guess I'm asking officially, well, are *we* an item?"

Chase smiled, he was enjoying the attention.

"It's not funny," Dolores said, punching his arm. "She didn't act like she was finished with you, in *that* sense at least. Women can be stubborn, reluctant to let one get away. No woman wants another woman to take what she thinks is hers."

"Our relationship, Connie and me, was always…light, non-committal. I told you that."

"But after meeting her, after watching how she behaved when she saw me…well, she may feel differently about the 'lightness' of your relationship."

Chase leaned close, his smile broadening, and whispered, "We're an item, at least so far as I'm concerned. Now back to business." He shut the engine. "Do you have the routine down?"

"Conversation to be continued at a later date."

"Agreed." Chase grinned leaning in and kissing her lightly on the lips.

"All right," Dolores said. "I'm a reporter for KTX, you're my camera man."

Chase nodded, tapped his video camera with its newly affixed KTX label.

"We're doing a special on parents of slain children." Dolores cringed.

"What's wrong?"

"That sounds so harsh, can't we soften it?"

"If you think up another angle between here and Allison Mckenna's apartment, I'm open to suggestions."

Dolores nodded solemnly.

"You have the questions we came up with?"

Dolores waved a few mini-index cards and tucked them into her bra.

Chase drew a pocket recorder from his jacket pocket, checked its power light and showed it to her before slipping it back into his pocket.

"In case she lets us record the interview," he said.

Dolores nodded.

"Well, it's now or never."

"Does the fact that she hung up on us when we called play into this at all?" Dolores offered. "Or that she refused to pick up the phone on any of the half dozen subsequent tries?"

"No. Those calls were made by our producer. So far as we're concerned, we have the green light. It's like a salesman putting his foot in the door when the home owner says 'no thanks.' Just let me do the talking if she tries to give us the boot. I have a way with women."

"Oh really?"

Chase grinned.

"She might not even answer the door," Dolores said. "You didn't see her eyes last night. I understand the sadness now. It gave me the chills. Her face…she looked as if her soul had died."

"I don't believe in the soul," Chase said coolly.

Dolores looked at Chase and he lowered his eyes.

"Most of the time," he added.

"Blaise Pascal would love you."

"Pascal's Wager? God or no God? I prefer evidence."

"Topic for a different day."

"We'd better get going."

The pair climbed out into the gray, murky day and crossed the street, heading for the main entrance. They passed the pristine landscaping that encircled the building like a moat and moved beneath a long green awning bearing the word Daniker which led from the sidewalk to the main door.

Arriving at the sturdy glass and steel doors, Chase tried one of the handles. Locked. He went to the row of buzzers and ran his finger down the list of names until he found Mckenna. He hit the switch. A beat passed and he was about to try again when a woman's voice broke from the speaker.

"Yes."

Chase opened his mouth to speak, but Dolores stepped in front of him.

"Mrs. Mckenna, I'm Bree Carson from KTX."

"Bree Carson?" Chase mouthed.

Dolores shrugged.

"I told you people I had nothing to say," Allison Mckenna said from the other end of the speaker.

"I'm sorry Mrs. Mckenna, our producer said that you agreed to speak with us. I'm a little confused. It's just that your story resonated with our viewers so much that, well, we've been getting letters and calls. Everyone wants to know how you're doing, how you're feeling. How you're coping."

Chase leaned against the door jamb, crossing his arms and smiling. He blew Dolores a kiss. She grinned in return before flipping him the bird.

"You see, your piece was going to be the final segment of our special," Dolores said. "A capstone to the entire production."

She waited, bit her lip. Her eyes found Chase. He shook his head, pursed his lips. Allison Mckenna wasn't going to agree. She might even call the cops if they pressed their luck.

"Mrs.—"

"Fifteen minutes," McKenna said.

Chase's grin broadened and he clutched his chest in feigned cardiac arrest. Dolores rolled her eyes heavenward, breathed a relieved sigh. A second later the buzzer beeped and Chase opened the door.

Chapter Thirty-One

The Daniker Building lobby was beautifully appointed, simple yet elegant, lined with cherry wainscoting and a marble floor, lots of flowers in expensive-looking vases on expensive-looking tables. Small glowing chandeliers were hung every ten feet or so leading to a bank of elevators with highly-reflective brass doors.

"Who would have imagined that a place like this could exist in a city with nearly two dozen housing projects," Dolores said, spinning slowly around, her eyes soaking up the opulence.

"Lifestyles of the rich and shameless," Chase said as he reached the elevator and hit the 'up' switch. A beat passed and the elevator doors pinged open revealing a cherry wood framed compartment. The pair climbed aboard and Dolores hit the fourth-floor button. The doors silently closed and the elevator began its ascent.

"Are we nervous *Bree Carson?*" Chase said.

"I don't know. I'm shaking too much to tell. And it was a name I used when I was a child, a sort of made up persona who lived in a nice house with a nice family. Bree served me well. Didn't you have a childhood alter ego?"

"Bond," Chase said. "James Bond."

Dolores laughed a nervous little laugh.

"By the way, you did good down there rookie." He reached out and squeezed her hand gently.

"But that was me talking to a voice on a speaker; this will be up close and personal."

"That was your foot in the door. You'll do fine."

"Wish me luck," she breathed and with a muted ping, the doors parted.

The corridor beyond was as well-appointed as the lobby. There were only four doors, two on each side of the long wide corridor which ran from the elevators to an open stairwell at the opposite end above which hung a tastefully lit EXIT sign. Each door was solid and imposing. The corridor itself was stuffed with a dead silence—it was as if the walls and floor were made of some cutting-edge sound-deafening material.

"Number four," Chase said.

"It's the one in the far corner," Dolores said, pointing. "God, it must overlook the city."

"A dubious distinction."

They reached the door together and Chase raised his fist to knock. But before his knuckles could strike the rich-looking wood, the door opened a crack and a woman wearing a track suit and a faded gray bathrobe appeared.

Dolores felt the urge to step back. The face at the door was not that of a woman in her early fifties, as the information Connie had provided suggested, not that of an educated professional who'd once flirted with a modeling career before marrying a wealthy medical researcher. This was the face of a woman who'd just climbed out of the subway after a long uneven night's sleep. Deep lines creased her upper lip, crow's feet had etched themselves into the spaces around her eyes, which were lost beneath folds of dark circles, and her hair, though shoulder length and neatly trimmed, was being slowly consumed by veins of silver.

Dolores tried to speak, but her voice failed her.

"Mrs. Mckenna," Chase managed, intervening.

Allison Mckenna eyed them both suspiciously and Dolores held up the KTX press card Connie had prepared.

"The picture is you, but that's a different name," Mckenna said, her eyes narrowing.

"Bree Carson is my professional pseudonym," Dolores said forcing a nervous little grin. "Dolores just doesn't roll off the tongue."

Mckenna seemed to chew on this for a moment, then nodded, nudged the door open, and faded into her dimly lit apartment.

Chase glanced at Dolores, and she at him before stepping through the doorway. Chase followed, closing the door behind them.

The apartment, though spacious and well furnished, was in a terrible state. There were newspapers lying everywhere, on the floor, on chairs, tacked to walls like strange bits of progressive art. Each and every table was lined with empty pizza boxes or cardboard and Styrofoam food containers as well as stacks of additional newspaper clippings. The place smelled musty, as if the windows had not been opened in some time. Somewhere, Blue Oyster Cult was softly performing *Don't Fear the Reaper*. Irony on a silver platter, Chase thought.

"In here." Allison Mckenna's voice drifted through a doorway at the far end of the large gloomy living room.

Chase gestured for Dolores to lead the way and she obeyed, a bit reluctantly, Chase moving close behind her. They passed from the living room with its large dark leather sectionals and enormous flat screen television and complicated stereo system, through a dining room with a long Chippendale-styled table layered with more newspapers and stray food containers. The windows along the far wall were closed, the heavy curtains drawn.

The pair reached the doorway to a small den where deep shadows had evidently come to roost.

"Sit," Mckenna said, gesturing to a leather sofa squatting beneath a large picture window. She had taken up position in a recliner in the corner where the shadows were thickest. She reached over and tapped a switch on a CD player resting on the table beside her and Blue Oyster Cult fell silent.

"Interesting music," Chase observed as he and Dolores settled into the sofa.

"My daughter, Elise and I, we…" Mckenna cleared her throat, adjusted her position in the recliner. "She loved all sorts of music, always experimenting: punk, new wave, reggae, smooth jazz, R and B, ska, even rap." A slight grin touched her lips as the pleasant memory seemed to caress her.

"She'd just discovered seventies and eighties rock when…" The grin faded. "We'd sit and listen to CD after CD, me reading in here, Elise working on her homework at the dining room table. I'd often hear the music playing from her room as she studied at her desk. Music was always playing when she was home."

Dolores nodded slowly.

Chase quietly lifted the video unit into his lap and began adjusting the settings.

"I didn't agree to that," Mckenna said abruptly, pointing a bony finger at the video camera. "And no audio either."

Dolores gestured with her hand for Chase to lower the device. He obeyed, setting the unit on the floor by his feet. She was doing well. It had just occurred to him that a woman might be more willing to open up to another woman. This wasn't someone he could flirt with, use his charms on, as Connie often accused him of doing; this was someone who was still very much in mourning, still wrapped in deep layers of grief. And maybe something else, something darker. Perhaps even balancing on the precipice of mental illness. And it would be a test for Dolores to coax the story out of this woman.

"What exactly do you people want?" Mckenna said, settling back into the recliner, her face sinking back into the dense shadows.

"Our station, KTX, along with all the others in the area, reported the terrible events surrounding your daughter's death," Dolores said, feeling her confidence slowly returning.

"You mean murder," Mckenna spat softly. "You don't have to tip-toe around the issue. My Elise was raped and butchered by a monster, a monster that is rotting in the ground where *it* belongs."

Dolores swallowed hard. The grief and anger pouring off this woman were palpable. For a fleeting unsettling instant she imagined those emotions manifesting themselves in the center of the room in the guise of two terribly deformed children with blood red eyes.

"Maybe we could start with you telling us how you handled it," Dolores said, her voice low and still a bit jittery.

"Does it look as if I've *handled* anything?"

There was deep anger like a shard of glass embedded in Allison Mckenna's voice and Dolores was taken aback. She lowered her eyes, feeling suddenly sick. The smell of stale food filling the apartment seemed to be growing more pungent with each passing second.

It struck her that there was deep sickness here, festering in the damp shadows of the once beautiful apartment. And the source of the sickness was sitting in the recliner across from her.

Dolores' eyes fell on the Bose CD player on the table between the sofa and Allison Mckenna's chair, the one from which the tones of Blue Oyster Cult had been seeping moments earlier, and the distraction proved helpful in settling her roiling stomach.

She noted the assortment of CDs lying strewn beside it. Late seventies, early eighties rock mostly, just as Allison Mckenna had said. Classics. The Clash's *London Calling*. Fleetwood Mac's *Rumours* with an ethereal Stevie Nicks spreading her witchy cape. The Ramones. Meat

Loaf's *Bat out of Hell* with its nightmare graveyard scene. Black Sabbath. Nazareth's *Hair of the Dog* with its image of a winged Cerberus perched atop a pile of skulls in the heart of a dismal lavender-hued swamp.

"Music," Dolores said, stumbling, seeking a foothold, her hand reaching out and touching one of the discs.

"Sorry, Beethoven and Mozart have never been my taste," Mckenna said. "*Ode to Joy* would be a stretch for me just now."

"I just meant...it's a way to stay in touch with Elise, to *feel* her around you, sense her presence."

"That's it exactly." She perked up slightly, a glimmer of life returning to her sullen eyes.

Dolores risked a glance in Chase's direction. He was watching Mckenna carefully, studying her face.

"I'm sorry," Mckenna said suddenly. "Perhaps I *can* help. Perhaps I'll tell you what happened, that is what happened *after* I stopped screaming and staring at the ceiling all night long, wondering if tearing out my eyes might help. I'll tell you what I did, if that's what you really want to know."

Dolores felt herself nodding slowly.

Chase reached into his jacket pocket for a note pad and pen activating the recorder he'd hidden there in the process despite Mckenna's protestations. Connie would say he was crossing the yellow tape at the crime scene, getting the shot, capturing the gore. And, after all, that's what Chase did best. Only this time, crossing the line felt wrong somehow.

"My daughter was a graduate student at Bridgton State University," Mckenna began. "Archaeology." She reached over to the table by the chair, lifted a framed photograph that had been facing her and studied it. Then she turned it toward Chase and Dolores. The photograph was of a very attractive young woman with shoulder length dark hair and Mediterranean features; the young woman might have been Spanish, maybe Portuguese or Italian, not the Scotts-Irish the name Mckenna suggested.

"She doesn't look like you," Dolores said, immediately regretting it. "I mean the name Mckenna—"

"My husband's mother was of Italian descent. Elise inherited her looks."

Dolores nodded. "Of course."

Mckenna turned the photo around so she could stare at it. A thin smile graced her chapped lips.

"She traveled as much as she could," Mckenna said, almost dreamily, her eyes never straying from the photograph. "Most of the trips were arranged through the university. The program was affiliated with six other schools. BC, UCLA, places like that. Elise wanted to stay close to home though, other than the trips. Especially after her father, my husband Stephen, died."

Dolores felt herself nodding, acknowledging Mckenna's pain—it was the least she could do.

"She would text me and phone often. Send me pictures. She showed me how to use Facebook. We were always in touch. I even went with her on a few of the trips, but I was working at the time, so it was difficult. Parts of North Africa, Italy, Israel, the United Kingdom. *Mostly* the United Kingdom. And Ireland. She loved those places most of all—would have lived there, *might* have lived there, later, after graduate school."

She sighed deeply.

"She loved visiting the ancient ruins," she continued, "ancient religious sites. Pagan. Early Christian. Iron Age forts. Holy mounds, mountains. Cemeteries. Ley lines, blind springs, places where dowsing took place. Stonehenge. Other standing stone circles. Burial 'tumps.' She liked churches and cathedrals too. Especially because the European ones usually have some myth origin associated with them. Which king did what with who behind the rood screen, which queen commissioned which stained glass windows to commemorate her dead father, which Duke who impregnated his own daughter is secretly buried beneath which Abby. The American churches are far less interesting I suppose. St. Brigid's in Wickham is one of the exceptions. The story goes that the architect who'd designed it walked across the street when the building was nearly completed to have a look, realized that he'd made the flying buttresses too small and went home and put the barrel of a pistol in his mouth."

Mckenna shook her head slowly, turning back to the image of the girl in the photograph, touching the frame with the fingertips of her free hand.

"She wanted to be a female Indiana Jones. She even went to a few places that weren't exactly safe. Places to which Americans shouldn't be traveling, especially female Americans. I found out afterwards—little side expeditions that were not exactly sanctioned by those who'd organized the trips. I would never have let her go if I'd known."

Mckenna's face grew slowly hard again and she gently set the photograph down. "Ironic. All those dangerous places and she was killed a few miles from home."

"I'm so sorry," Dolores said.

Chase saw tears starting in Mckenna's eyes, gritted his teeth in vexation, wondering just how much more of this interrogation the woman could stand before she threw them out. And wondering if it would be enough to suit his purpose. And also feeling oddly conflicted about it all.

"So afterward, I followed in her footsteps, going to as many of the places she'd visited as I could manage. I even went to some places she'd never managed to visit, places she'd wanted to see. She'd kept a journal, books, and maps in her room, outlining all the places she hadn't gotten around to yet. She particularly liked studying religious antiquity. *She* was looking for history, I suppose *I* was looking for *her*. Or some part of her that may have survived after…"

She paused, gathering her wits as best she could.

"Do you believe in ghosts?" she said after a moment.

Taken mildly aback, Dolores glanced nervously at Chase, her lips moving around words that simply would not form.

"Jury's out," Chase said, intervening.

"Hmmm," Mckenna said, as if expecting just such a response from a journalist.

"A safe answer. When I was a little girl," she began, switching gears, "my grandmother told me that if I stayed up late enough and watched very carefully, paying close attention to the shadows, I might catch a fleeting glimpse of myself getting up in the morning. I didn't really understand what she meant. My grandmother believed in some *unseen* things, *unproven* things. Ghosts. God. But I tried it several times anyway, thinking that if I didn't go to bed, morning wouldn't come."

Slowly, a slight smile found its way onto Mckenna's face. A moment passed and it evaporated and the hardness returned.

"But morning always came," she said, her voice growing hoarse. "Reality always won out. And in all my travels I never found my little girl. Not the slightest trace."

Dolores felt her breath turning ragged. The room seemed to have grown cold.

"I mean, I had the money," she continued. "My husband had been quite wealthy and his insurance…well, money I had, but I'd have traded it all…"

More tears found their way onto Mckenna's hollow cheeks.

"That's it," she said flatly. "I sold the house shortly after my husband died; *this* place had been Elise's and mine. She loved the view of the city, the lights like stars in the sky. And now I'm alone. I don't work anymore, but I suppose I need to get out a little. Part time job maybe, something. I am...*was* an RN. Wanted to be a DON once, Director of Nursing. But that was in another life."

Mckenna gazed at Chase and Dolores through her swollen, glistening eyes.

"So, is my story what you expected? Tough mother who survived the unthinkable. Somehow feeling victorious at the end of the day if she doesn't jump out the fucking window? Will your viewers appreciate my predicament? Will they understand how grief can consume you, can take on substance like some dark shadow hovering in the corner, watching you?"

A terrible silence fell over the room. Somewhere a clock ticked. It was a dry, dead sound. Thunder rumbled past the curtained window like a ghostly freight train.

Dolores opened her mouth to speak, but Mckenna cut her off.

"I'd say you've had your fifteen minutes."

Dolores glanced at Chase, who'd been dutifully taking notes. He casually returned the note pad and pen to his jacket pocket and shut the recorder in the process.

"Thank you so much," Dolores said getting to her feet, the lump in her throat nearly causing her to choke.

Chase followed Dolores' lead and Mckenna stood as well. Slowly, the woman led Chase and Dolores out of the den and into the dining room.

"I wonder," Dolores said, breaking ranks and stepping out on a limb, "would it be all right if we had a look at your daughter's bedroom? Maybe take a photograph?"

Mckenna paused, glancing from Dolores to Chase and back again before nodding slowly. "I suppose that would be all right. This way."

Dolores considered Chase and his eyes opened wide. He set the video unit on the dining room table and took his Canon from around his shoulder. He removed the lens cap, checked the settings, glanced around at the shadows and made some adjustments. Then he followed Dolores down the long hall, into the shadowy depths of the apartment.

Chapter Thirty-Two

Allison Mckenna led Dolores and Chase deeper into her expansive apartment toward the late Elise Mckenna's bedroom. They passed a few open doors, a bathroom, what appeared to be a walk-in linen closet, a small guest bedroom, finally arriving at a heavy six panel door. Chase looked around; all the other doors were open. This one was much heavier, oak maybe, with a strange faded metallic emblem affixed to the center of the upper cruciform portion of the door. But there was something unfinished about this door as if it had been recently and hastily installed. And most curious of all, this door was equipped with a heavy lock.

"What is that symbol?" Chase asked pointing to the medallion. "I'm sure I've seen it somewhere before."

"It's a Celtic shield for luck," Mckenna said as she rummaged through the pocket of her robe, finally producing a large key which she slipped into the heavy-duty lock. "Common enough—it's hanging on a thousand necklaces."

She gently pushed the door open and stepped inside. Dolores and Chase followed.

The room was as well appointed as the rest of the apartment, only there were no newspaper clippings or empty fast food containers in sight. The room was, in fact, pristine.

A large cherry wood desk sat in front of an equally large window. It was adorned with an old style green shaded reading lamp, the sort found in libraries. There were several books all bearing titles related to archaeology stacked on one corner of the desk: Colin Renfrew's and

Paul Bahn's Archaeology, Theories, Methods and Practice, 2nd Edition; Hester's, Feder's and Shafer's Field Methods in Archaeology, 7th Edition; and other similar titles as well as a few theoretical publications including Richard Bradley's Archaeology of Natural Places and Alfred Watkins' The Old Straight Track. The center of the desk was occupied by a large all-in-one desktop computer. A laptop sat plugged in on a small table that stood beside the desk. A photograph of a man, a woman, and a young woman sat on one corner of the desk. It took little imagination to realize that the older woman in the photograph was Allison Mckenna. The younger one was no doubt Elise and the man, who bore a slight resemblance to Tom Selleck, her late father.

Dolores and Chase turned to examine the rest of the room. There was a bookcase filled with more books, thick, hard covered volumes mostly. The bed was a large four poster carved from dark cherry wood. The spread and shams were likewise of a dark color reminding Dolores of autumn. She noted that there was a surprising hint of masculinity to the room, but she guessed that that fit in with the whole 'Indiana Jones' motif. Or perhaps Hemingway.

There was also a small sitting area with a chair and a table. The table was topped by a lead glass lamp adorned with dragon flies which might very well had been dreamed up by Louis Comfort Tiffany himself. There were also several ancient looking relics lying about: arrowheads on the desk, several carved stone crosses on the book shelf, one resembling what Dolores knew to be St. Brigid's Celtic Cross, and a grinning skull on the nightstand next to an old-fashioned brass alarm clock. Its digital Bluetooth enabled cousin sat close by.

Several old framed prints resembling parchment maps adorned the walls. Dolores approached the nearest one. It was a map of ancient London. Beside it was a map of Gevaudan circa 1811. There were also several framed photographs of significant churches: Notre Dame in Paris, Canterbury Cathedral in London, St. Paul's in New York City. Even one of Saint Genevieve's here in Gevaudan, where the candlelight vigil had taken place the previous night. Beneath these, perched on a sofa table, were more books and an old-world globe, its beige-colored oceans brimming with drawings of ancient sailing craft and arcane navigation symbols as well as the occasional sea serpent; 'here there be monsters.'

"Closet," Mckenna whispered, opening a door in the corner that had attracted Dolores' attention. Dolores scanned the hanging clothes, jewel tone dresses, crisp white blouses. Plaid skirts. Lots of boots.

Mckenna closed the door as Dolores turned to consider the remaining wall, which was nearly completely adorned with a huge cork-board mounted map of contemporary Europe and Asia Minor. There were numerous pins, red and black in color, protruding from various spots on the map.

Dolores approached the map as Chase began squeezing off photographs of the room.

"The red pins indicate places Elise had already visited," Mckenna said, her voice hushed as if speaking in reverence of some unseen person. "The black ones indicate places she planned to visit. I didn't bother adding another color for the places I'd visited on my own; it just didn't seem to matter."

Dolores nodded and leaned in toward the map. Most of the red pins were in Europe, with a heavy concentration in the United Kingdom and Ireland, just as Mckenna had indicated. She reached out to touch the pin that had skewered what looked to be Dublin.

"Don't!" Mckenna barked. "I mean, please don't disturb anything." She cleared her throat, glanced about nervously. "I think that's all."

Chase quickly moved up beside Dolores and clicked off several shots of the map before recapping the Canon and slinging it over his shoulder.

Mckenna never gestured toward the door, but her unspoken directive was obvious and the couple moved out into the hall. Dolores glanced back in time to see her staring at the map. The woman reached out gingerly and brushed the map with her fingertips, touched her fingers to her lips, closing her eyes as she did so. Then she went to the door, shutting and locking it and pocketing the key.

They headed back to the dining room in silence. Chase gathered up his video unit and followed Mckenna toward the door to the foyer. Dolores hung back, taking the opportunity to pause long enough to study the newspaper clippings lining the large expensive-looking dining room table.

Dolores felt something cold slither through her lower regions when she realized that all the clippings concerned the same topic. Chilled, she raised her eyes and found herself staring at her own reflection in an expensive-looking gilded mirror hanging on the opposite wall. She gasped, clutching at her chest. It was then that she noticed a shadowy doorway that opened into what appeared to be a large bedroom beside the mirror. She glanced toward the front door—Chase and Mckenna were standing there, talking. Chase was probably telling her how sorry he was for her loss and perhaps thanking her for the chance to photograph Elise's bedroom. He caught Dolores' gaze as if signaling for her to investigate anything she wanted so long as she did it quickly while he kept their reluctant hostess occupied.

Dolores moved quickly to the bedroom doorway, peeked inside. The bed was huge, unmade, littered with more clippings, empty fast food bags, paper cups lying on the nightstand. There were also some empty bottles of liquor lining the length of the headboard, and an assortment of prescription bottles perched on the nightstand. Dolores pursed her lips, turned to leave, but froze when her gaze fell upon something odd.

She moved stealthily around the door jamb, staring at the wall opposite the foot of the big bed. It was crammed from floor to ceiling with flat screen televisions, nearly a dozen in every possible size, one fifty-plus inch model at the center.

The voices in the other room grew suddenly louder and she sensed the need to leave. Dolores moved through the bedroom doorway and quickly across the dining room and into the living room.

"Again, thank you for everything," Chase was saying.

"I only hope it helps," Mckenna said as the couple stepped out into the hall.

"We'll let you know when the spot will air," Dolores said.

Mckenna stared blankly at her; her eyes had dried some.

"Again, thank you," Chase said.

Mckenna considered the couple coolly and then she nodded and closed the door.

***

"Jesus," Chase said as he set the video camera and Canon in the back seat of the car and took the micro-recorder from his jacket pocket, "that was fucking weird."

Dolores was sitting quietly in the passenger seat gazing up at Mckenna's terrace through a rain-drenched windshield.

"I think she's watching us," she said.

"Thanks, but I've had enough chills for one lifetime," Chase said. He flipped the pocket recorder on and waited. The mechanism made a soft whirring sound.

"What the hell?" he said after a moment.

"What's wrong?" Dolores said.

"There's nothing." Chase flipped the recorder over and shut the power button. "Shit. It's never failed me before."

"Maybe the battery is dead?" she said.

"No it's running, it just didn't record anything." Chase tucked the recorder back into his jacket pocket. "Fucking weird."

"Weird is the word of the day—what's *really* weird is that she has about a dozen televisions in her bedroom," Dolores said, her eyes fixed on the apartment terrace.

Chase had reached back for the Canon and was scanning through the shots he'd taken of Elise Mckenna's bedroom on the tiny screen. "Must be a real news hound. Or a big fan of QVC."

"Anything?" Dolores said.

"Yes, the pictures look good. But I can't understand the recorder." He set the Canon on the floor in the back and turned to Dolores.

"Maybe Elise's ghost doesn't like deception?" Dolores said. "And those newspapers that were lying around everywhere—mostly clippings. All the same *types* of clippings."

"Just what sort of reading does the good Ms. Mckenna fancy?"

"Murder."

"What?"

"Every article was about murder, rape, serial killers," Dolores said softly, lowering her gaze, rubbing her arms as if the chill from the previous night had tracked her down. "Most of the articles were from American magazines and newspapers, but I saw a few from foreign countries. Ireland, Great Britain." She sighed deeply. "Chase, what the hell is going on here?"

"I'm not sure," he said starting the car.

"And what's with the locked bedroom door?"

"She replaced the original door with a heavier one."

"I noticed that, it just stood right out. Even the lock looked too big. I mean, who the hell is she expecting to go into her daughter's room?"

"I have no idea." Chase shook his head. "But she's gone through a lot of trouble to make sure no one does."

"Chase, let's get the hell out of here, this whole thing is giving me the fucking creeps."

"Yeah," Chase said softly tapping the recorder in his pocket. "I know what you mean."

He slipped the SUV into gear and drove off into the rain.

Chapter Thirty-Three

"Good day, Detective."

Teschal looked up from her busy but neatly arranged desk to find a well-dressed woman standing in her office doorway.

"Mrs. Tinsley," Teschal said, genuinely pleased. "How nice to see you. I trust things are well."

Jennifer Tinsley was in her mid-fifties, and wore it well, with dignity and grace and an air of intelligence that might prove intimidating to some. Her hair was silver, the stylish, full-bodied sort that made any woman her age look sophisticated. The expression on her slightly weathered face spoke of contentment and a strange inner peace seemed to radiate from her very being. There was a wizened quality about her, the deep dark sort acquired after some time spent gazing into the abyss, but looking away at the opportune moment before the abyss could look back, as Nietzsche himself might have advised. It was in the eyes, Teschal had always thought. That's where the soul lives, where experience presents itself to the world.

But Teschal knew all too well how any sense of peace and contentment had abandoned this woman for a time. Jennifer Tinsley had taken on the task of heading a support group that counseled the parents of murdered children. And before she'd become the group's leader, she'd been a member.

Several years earlier her twenty-year-old son, Brook, home on break from Yale, had been killed in a random drive-by shooting in south Gevaudan while standing outside a convenience store waiting for a friend who'd gone inside to buy a soda. The incident had nearly killed Jennifer. But Teschal, who'd handled the case, and successfully gotten a conviction for a gang-banger down from Boston on a weekend shooting spree, had put the woman in touch with the Survivors Healing Group, which met every Thursday night at Saint Genevieve's Catholic School in the heart of Gevaudan. It had been rough, but in the end Tinsley would be the first to admit that the group had saved her marriage, her sanity, and perhaps her life.

"Personally things are good," Tinsley said. "Quite good. Tom and I are heading to St. Barth's in the fall. We have a friend who teaches Education at Bridgton University, he's loaning us his villa for a couple of weeks. Just how a public university professor can afford a villa on St. Barth's is beyond me. I think he inherited it from a rich aunt."

"Thank goodness for wealthy relations," Teschal said. "So, what brings you down to the station?"

"That North Side Strangler business," Tinsley said, shaking her head solemnly. "I'd like to say that our little group has outlived its usefulness, but as we both know far too well, that simply isn't the case."

Teschal nodded resignedly.

"I just stopped by to talk with Detective Collins. We're putting together another candlelight vigil. The one last night at Saint Genevieve's went well, in spite of the weather. Father Rousseau was very supportive. We've been using the church basement activity room lately. Broken water pipe in the school's Community Room, should be fixed by next week. We'd like more news coverage next time though. I don't know if Jack was pleased to hear about it or not."

"He's pleased," Teschal said. "He's just feeling the pressure."

It was Tinsley's turn to nod. "I suppose it goes with the turf."

Teschal knew that citizens' groups, though usually well intended, often found themselves at odds with government. A candlelight vigil might prove to be just such an example. Such an activity, though comforting and unifying to some, might very well prove unsettling to others, mostly those occupying political and official circles. Such a newsworthy event could easily cast light, not just on grief-stricken faces, but also on the cold realization that Detective Jack Collins and the Gevaudan PD had run into a dead end with regard to the case. And such press, more often than not, weighed heavily on the powers that be, powers that were often too paranoid for their own good, powers that were often more concerned with perception rather than progress.

"Well, I'll leave you to it," Tinsley said and she turned to leave.

No comment from Tinsley regarding Teschal's case, though her involvement in it was hardly common knowledge. And as the so-called 'Night Stalker' case was an active one, Teschal would be unable to comment on it. Not surprising though—parents of murdered children were hardly likely to show concern for hardened criminals who'd been butchered by some renegade vigilante. Even those parents who'd successfully run the emotional gauntlet of therapy, moved through the steps, from shock all the way to acceptance, and managed to find their way home, could hardly be expected to shake their heads and 'tsk, tsk' such occurrences. But perhaps that was only human.

"Oh, Mrs. Tinsley," Teschal called as an idea crept into her crowded brain. "Jennifer."

"Yes?"

"I was wondering how my latest referral has worked out? Mrs. Allison Mckenna?"

Tinsley sighed, crossed her arms and leaned against the door jamb.

"Not too well, I'm sorry to say. She only came to the one meeting. Very withdrawn, which is understandable. But..." Tinsley winced, sucking air through her teeth. "There's a lot of anger there. And something else, something I couldn't quite put my finger on. I mean, it's perfectly acceptable to want revenge on the person who murdered your child, also to be withdrawn, grief-stricken. We, all the members of the group, have experienced those feelings to some degree, the anger being perhaps the most difficult part. The purpose of the group is to remind us all that it's okay to be human, to be angry. And to reassure us that we are not alone in the pain. And of course to provide support and to help us move on with our lives."

"But..." Teschal said, leading Tinsley.

"Well, it's just that Allison Mckenna seemed to feel that we gave in on the issue, surrendered our feelings and offered forgiveness too soon. It was almost as if she was *relishing* the idea of revenge, *nurturing* the notion like some, oh, I don't know, some sick memento. Like keeping the hate alive was somehow keeping her daughter's memory alive, if that makes any sense."

Teschal sighed. "I'm afraid that makes a great deal of sense."

"I mean, please don't misunderstand, I've tried to contact her several times. At first she'd just listen to me for a moment then hang up. But lately she just lets the phone ring."

"That's troubling."

"The group is not for everybody," Tinsley said. "Maybe it was too soon."

"Maybe."

"I mean, every person in our group wanted to lash out at first, have their revenge and take out their anger, myself included. But Allison Mckenna, well, her anger was more intense, more focused. No forgiveness there at all. Little acceptance."

Teschal sat back in her chair.

Tinsley shook her head, rubbed her arms.

"Would you mind if I mentioned your group to her again?"

"That would be fine," Tinsley said, a faltering grin finding her lips. "We're more than willing to work with anyone. And Allison Mckenna needs us more than some. I think her daughter was her whole world instead of just a big part of it, especially with her husband gone as well. I mean, Tom was my rock in many ways. I don't think I could have handled it alone. But what concerned me was that Mckenna didn't just act as if she wanted to kill the person who murdered her daughter—she acted as if she wanted to destroy the whole world and everyone in it."

Chapter Thirty-Four

They'd gathered in Connie's office again, Connie at her desk, Chase and Dolores on the couch. Connie was turning Chase's pocket recorder over in her hand. A low steady hissing sound like running water was seeping from the machine's tiny speaker. She finished examining the thing and tossed it to Chase.

"Faulty equipment," she said. "That's not like you."

"It wasn't faulty," Chase said defensively, his eyes scanning through the photos he'd taken in the Mckenna apartment. "I don't understand it. I'd checked it out just before we went into the building. I mean the pictures seem fine."

"So you didn't ask her about the dead rookie cop in that abandoned mill over on Quarry Street?" Connie said, changing the subject and cutting to the bone as only she could.

Chase considered her carefully, wondering how he could ever have found her attractive. *Just a shag,* was the phrase she used when referring to their relationship. She'd been joking, her way of keeping things at arm's length, he'd always figured. He suspected, perhaps for the first time, that she'd always thought more of him, of *them.* Perhaps *he* was the shallow one. Maybe it had always meant more to her, but she'd been unable or unwilling to tell him. And he'd been too self-absorbed to notice, or maybe too insecure to think it possible, to think a woman could have genuine feelings for him, having fallen hook line and sinker for Julie's...for Julie's what? Emotional abuse? Relentless efforts to make him feel less than human, insisting that he lived his life through a camera lens? Maybe the answer was 'yes' to all of the above. Maybe.

"Didn't seem prudent," Chase said, drawing a line under the idea. "Timing is everything in comedy and journalism. We couldn't risk the woman shutting down completely."

"Sure," Connie said. "Journalistic etiquette, huh? A little late to take the high road, don't you think?"

Chase shrugged, but the comment stung. But there was more happening here than simply a case of Connie being Connie. He realized that Dolores had noticed Connie's strange behavior from their very first meeting. Was it jealousy? Damned unattractive whatever it was. Annoying even. And not helping the situation one bit. Jesus, what a self-centered fool he'd been.

He adjusted his position, wincing subconsciously at his inane lack of perception, sipping some coffee Kiley had prepared for them before returning to her office. Some reporter, Chase thought, chiding himself. Burying the lead. Maybe Teschal was right. Julie too. Maybe he *was* nothing but an ambulance chaser with a video camera. A run-of-the-mill stringer.

"It was…difficult," Dolores said ringing her hands, looking uncomfortable. "The woman was a mess, the textbook definition of grief-stricken. Maybe even suicidal."

"Well, Kiley should be able to check on Ms. Mckenna's travel history—tickets, passports, all carefully monitored these days," Connie said.

Chase nodded, stepping out of his head and rejoining the world of the living. "It's a good bet Teschal will be paying Ms. Mckenna a visit soon, just for old times' sake. Especially if our wily gypsy detective caught sight of her touring the latest murder scene."

"As did we," Dolores said.

Thunder rumbled outside.

"I thought it might clear up," Dolores said. "Wishful thinking I suppose. Rain is so depressing."

"All right," Chase said, getting to his feet. "Shall we?"

"Sure," Dolores said, as if returning from someplace far away.

"If anything shakes, buzz us," Chase said.

"Us?" Connie said, her face firm, her eyes cold. "Are we an *item* then?"

"Just call," Chase said and he led Dolores through the door.

"Bye, bye Del," Connie called.

***

Chase and Dolores spent the rest of the day in and out of bed, the radio alarm clock playing softly on the dresser, the sound of rain and thunder rolling around outside the open windows, the wind gusting occasionally, making Chase think of mountain tops and craggy moors in old movies.

"She doesn't like me much," Dolores said as she lay in bed staring up at the ceiling fan's spinning blades.

"She doesn't like much of anybody," Chase said, while gazing at the same fan, his fingers laced behind his head.

Dolores rolled onto her side, willed her hand to creep across Chase's chest. "I guess she thought that whatever you two had was stronger, even if she'd never said so."

Chase turned to her, mildly amazed that she'd reached the same conclusion he had in record time. But she was proving to be a perceptive one, her mind open to the universe, conscious of the unseen and unexplained. If only he'd believed in such things.

He looked into her eyes, kissed her lightly and said, "I'm sorry." It was the only thing he could think to say.

Thelma Houston's *Don't Leave Me this Way* was playing on the radio, an 'oldies' station Dolores kept among her pre-sets.

"I remember this song," she said. "It was in that movie, the one about the teacher who cruises the New York City bars at night picking up strays."

"I prefer the Teddy P. version," Chase said. "The Communards did an interesting cover too. But I do remember the movie. Movies are a hobby of mine. Diane Keaton. Richard Gere. Tom Beringer."

"She ends up dead," Dolores said softly. "A girl has to be careful who she picks up."

"*I* could be a serial killer."

Dolores smiled. "I think you're pretty harmless."

"I think I've just been insulted," Chase said feigning indignity.

Dolores laughed. "All right, I'm in grave danger. Lesson learned—never, *ever* pick up hitch hikers, even the ones that seem harmless. But, as long as we're using movies as examples, what if one stows away and you don't know it like in *Alien*?"

"I see your point. In that case, I guess you're screwed."

"A well-chosen word," she said before kissing him hard on the lips and rolling away to consider the rain striking the window.

Chase's mobile phone rang. He scooped it up from the nightstand.

"Put on the Channel Seven news."

"Connie? What's—"

"Just put it on. Call me back if it interests *either* of you." She hung up.

"What is it?"

"She wants us to watch the news."

"Then let's watch the news," Dolores said, rolling out of bed.

She killed the radio, switched on the television on the dresser and tossed the remote to Chase, who flipped to Channel Seven.

"It seems difficult to believe," a man with a gruff appearance and an Irish accent said into a microphone that had been thrust into his face by one of several reporters encircling him. The room was dimly lit, unfamiliar logos on the microphones.

"What about the guards?" It was the voice of a woman from somewhere off camera with a similar accent.

"We're questioning everybody," the man, whom the caption at the bottom of the screen identified as Deputy Warden Clifford O'Riordan, said.

The face of a woman with long gray hair tied back in a professional-looking pony tail took O'Riordan's place. The caption identified her as Chief Detective Inspector Jacqueline Shane.

"Of course this ends this particular prosecution," Shane said, "but we are still looking into the possibility of accomplices. Seven women have been raped and murdered. Our investigation is damaged but not closed. And we *will* find any person or persons responsible for this latest atrocity. Rest assured."

The camera cut to the face of an older man sitting at a desk. Ryan Cullen was the name that appeared in the lower left corner of the screen—anchor for Channel Seven. Cullen looked grim, his gray hair and dusty moustache adding to his stern countenance.

"Once again, Irish authorities are mystified over the murder of Derek Jacobs, the man who has come to be called the 'Moonlight Killer,' a man accused of raping and murdering no less than seven women in the vicinity of the town of Cross Corner, a relatively quiet suburb of Cork City in southern Ireland. What makes the case so striking is the manner in which Jacobs met his end.

"The Irish authorities are not elaborating at this time, but information leaked earlier by unknown sources suggests that Mr. Jacobs was brutally murdered while in custody, his body mangled and burned almost beyond recognition. And the element worthy of Houdini is that Mr. Jacobs had been in solitary confinement at Clemson Prison near Shannon due to death threats he'd been receiving. Once again—"

Chase hit the mute button and punched in Connie's number.

"Jesus," he said. "What the hell is going on here?"

"Chase," Dolores practically screamed, raising her hand and pointing a trembling finger at the screen.

Chase hit the OFF button on his phone. "What?"

Dolores nodded, unable to speak. Chase turned to the television screen. It was filled with a black and white mug shot of the man formerly known as Derek Jacobs, the suspected 'Moonlight Killer.'

"Oh God," Dolores said, nearly gasping.

"What *is* it?"

"That man, the 'Moonlight Killer'…I saw a newspaper clipping about him, about his arrest."

"Well, I guess he's been in the news—"

"I saw the clipping on the kitchen table," Dolores said, "in Allison Mckenna's apartment."

Dolores nodded slowly, a tear starting in her right eye.

"I saw it," she said, her voice a breathless whisper. "I'm absolutely certain of it."

Chapter Thirty-Five

"It's impossible," Kiley Ross dared to say. She was sitting at Connie's desk, tapping keys on Connie's laptop.

"I can't believe the police in Shannon allowed that information to be leaked," Connie said, leaning over Kiley's shoulder.

"The police in Shannon are denying it all," Chase added.

"That figures," Connie said with her arms crossed. "Do they offer an alternative scenario?"

"No." Chase scrolled deeper into the article he'd found on the BBC website on his phone. "They just keep saying that the details cannot be confirmed at this time as it is an ongoing—"

"—investigation," Connie finished. "Yeah, yeah. Cops sound the same on either side of the Atlantic."

"This is crazy," Dolores said from the sofa beside Chase. "Did our killer just pack his bags and move to Ireland?"

"Some people think that Jack the Ripper came to America for a time, but this is most likely some sort of copy-cat..." Kiley said.

"Keep typing intern," Connie barked.

Chase's phone began to ring. He looked at the screen, but didn't recognize the number.

"Hold on," he said, getting to his feet and heading for the door. "I may need to take this."

"No secrets here," Connie called after him.

"Hello," Chase said as he reached the corridor.

"Can you talk?" Eloise said in her Creole accent.

"Always to you," Chase said.

"Well, that news about the suspect in Ireland being killed has sent shock waves all the way across the Atlantic, and straight through City Hall and One Police Plaza."

"I bet."

"There's a big meeting going on with Teschal, Richards, and all the other secret police. Word is out that someone from the governor's office was on the phone to the chief the minute the story broke. And it looks as if the Feds, who've been hovering in the wings about the kiddie strangler case anyway, are interested in the 'Night Stalker' case as well due to 'potential international implications.' Someone's been keeping them at bay to this point, someone packing a lot of clout. It *is* common knowledge that the mayor has friends in the state house and D.C. Big favor there. Press conference pending, too. Interested?"

"Not my taste," Chase said. "No blood for the camera."

"You haven't been to many press conferences."

"Well, a little national exposure is good for ratings. I didn't recognize the phone number; are you at work?"

"No way," Eloise said. "Way too hot there just now. I'm on one of my burner phones, won't even trust my regular mobile. Too many ears all of a sudden."

"Do they think the murders are related?"

"Obviously, if you read between the lines. But the official statement is copy-cat killer or freak coincidence, maybe even just some inaccurate information coming from the Irish press. But some of their newspapers are already working on nicknames for the killer like the 'Irish Night Stalker' and such. You know the type who like the blood?"

"Yeah, yeah," Chase said. "You cut me to the quick. Well, keep me informed."

"I will. I mean if you think about it, when that woman in Greece turned up burned to a crisp, the cops never batted an eye."

"Woman in Greece?" Chase said. "*What* woman in Greece?"

"You call yourself a reporter?"

"El—"

"This was a few weeks ago. Nikki. Aw hell, Nikki something. I can't remember. It's all Greek to me."

"Funny. What were the circumstances?"

"You really *don't* watch anything but your own pieces do you?"

"When did I ever say otherwise?"

Chapter Thirty-Six

Teschal opened the door to her office, made her way to her desk and sat down. She rubbed her eyes and didn't look up when Richards appeared in the doorway.

"Do you fucking believe this? A coincidence?"

"Coincidence?" Teschal said. "Of course not. That's for the press. And they'll be all over the chief for making just such an asinine statement. Official press release."

"Better to say we're looking into it. Leave them guessing, instead of stating anything one way or the other." He shook his head in disgust. "Oh, by the way, the chemical analysis from the Flynn girl murder scene came back. Same as the others. Not that it helps much. Just makes it all the weirder."

"Richards, gather everything we've got, set it all up in the briefing room. About seven-thirty tonight. Witness statements. Forensics. Photographs. Everything. Invite Gabriel and Jennings to join us—just them, not their teams."

"Why not right now?"

"Because I'm going to have a talk with one of our late-night visitors, ask them why they decided to stop off at a murder scene."

"I assume that you're not talking about the stringer or his girl Friday."

"No, I'm talking about Allison Mckenna," Teschal said. "I'm curious as to why she's become so interested in morbid happenings. If *my* child had recently been murdered, you wouldn't find me within a hundred miles of a murder scene." She shook her head slowly. "Something doesn't feel right about this."

"It's really not that odd, I suppose, from a psychological perspective." Richards scratched his head. "Climbing back up on the horse I guess. Maybe even some strange form of closure."

"Maybe, but my gut tells me differently. In any event, my curiosity needs to be satisfied."

"You know what they said about the curious cat?"

"We're cops, it's our job to be curious. No matter what comes of it."

"I'll tell you this—if Mckenna hadn't just returned from abroad and if she'd been aware of the particulars of our investigation or the fuck up that cost us the ball of wax, I'd place her at the top of the list of suspects."

"Stranger things have happened," Teschal said, getting to her feet. "Stranger things have happened."

Chapter Thirty-Seven

"No personal calls," Connie said as Chase returned from the corridor. "We're all friends here. Right Del?"

"Kiley," he said, ignoring Connie's quip, "I just heard about a similar case in Greece some weeks back. Can you do a search?"

Kiley frowned, began tapping keys.

"A woman; Nikki…"

"Nikki Polymus," Dolores said from the table at the back of the room where the coffee maker was finishing its most recent batch.

"Got it," Kiley said, typing with purpose.

"She was in the news," Dolores said scooping up a paper cup of coffee and taking a seat on the sofa.

"Jesus," Kiley said, grimacing at the laptop screen.

"Well, spit it out," Connie said.

"Nikki Polymus, aged forty-two. Drowned her two children in a bath tub then vanished. She'd left a note telling the police that the ghost of her late husband told her to do it."

Chase moved up behind Kiley.

"She'd been on the run for a week. Greek authorities got a tip that she was hiding out in an abandoned building on the outskirts of Athens in a town called Maroussi, one of the athletes' quarters from the 2004 Summer Olympics. The buildings were abandoned, had fallen into ruin with neglect. By the time the local police arrived, part of the structure was in flames, fire engines everywhere. The body was retrieved, she'd been burned pretty badly." Kiley read ahead silently but quickly. "But there's more here—something doesn't make sense."

"Don't leave us hanging," Connie said.

"Well, the police began asking neighbors and family about when she was last seen, about what may have happened. The usual questions. But several people interviewed told reporters that the police kept asking if Polymus owned a big dog."

"Dog?" Chase said. "Why?"

"Because," Dolores said, her voice barely audible above the torrential rain outside the office window, "her body was apparently mauled as well as burned. Just like the others."

Kiley raised her young eyes, considered Dolores.

"It's the only reason for the police to ask that question," Dolores said. "And it fits in with the Irish murder. And ours."

"She kills her kids then disappears with her dog?" Connie said.

"The neighbors told the cops that dear Nikki did not own a dog, didn't like pets at all," Kiley said.

"What the hell is going on here?" Connie said. "Do we have *two* copycat killers out there? What the hell is this, some international society of killers? SPECTRE? This *can't* be the same killer."

Chase turned to Dolores. "Did you notice any clippings in Allison Mckenna's apartment regarding this Greek woman?"

Dolores shook her head. "No. But I wasn't looking for one either. And this murder happened weeks ago."

"Clippings?" Connie said.

"Mckenna's apartment was littered with newspaper clippings associated with all sorts of gruesome topics, mostly murder suspects, including this Irish one, Jacobs," Dolores said.

"Why would it matter if Mckenna was reading up on murders?" Connie said. "What are you suggesting?"

"I'm not suggesting anything," Chase said. "Allison Mckenna was stateside for both murders. I suppose that she could have heard of this Polymus woman while traveling around Europe and this Jacobs character too. Or maybe she saw something on television. That's how *you* found out about it," he said gesturing to Dolores. "I just can't imagine what the relationship could be."

"Well," Connie began, "not much is making sense these days. But I'd suggest that we keep a collective ear to the ground, because if the police make this connection—"

"Haven't *we* made this connection?" Dolores said.

"Yes, but I'm not sure we want to tweak our gypsy detective's nose just now, Del," Connie said.

"Taking the high road?" Chase said.

"No," Connie said, her voice lacking any trace of defensiveness. "But Teschal has our number and she'll be watching us. And you two," Connie added, pointing a lean finger at Chase then Dolores, "seem to have gotten in good with Allison Mckenna. Maybe we can do better by simply watching and waiting, now that we know *who* to watch."

Chase nodded thoughtfully, pursed his lips.

"I know you," Connie said. "What are you thinking?"

"Oh, don't worry, I won't rock the boat. I was just thinking that I'd like to have a look at the scene of the rookie cop murder. Just to satisfy my own curiosity."

"Castle Outlet Mill," Kiley said before Connie could speak. "It's been closed for years—supposedly the water rat infestation got too severe. The West Wickham River flows right behind the place." The young woman glanced around. "It used to be part of the old Daniker Mill complex. It's the only extant building…" She lowered her eyes when she noticed Connie glaring at her.

"Thank you dear," Connie said tersely.

"Daniker," Dolores said, looking at Chase.

Chase nodded. "Daniker."

Chapter Thirty-Eight

Teschal started out for the Daniker Building and Allison Mckenna's upscale apartment, but decided to make one other stop first. Most of the people she worked with would consider it to be a personal visit, family business. But Teschal knew that it was more than that. Potentially *much* more.

But who amongst her brothers and sisters in blue would accept such a notion? None but one. And he was not involved at this point. Aware of what was happening to be sure, but not yet involved. He was not some insecure micro-manager. But soon he would need to make an appearance out of political necessity. Teschal wanted to have something to show him. Not because it might mean her head if she didn't manage to find something, because it just might. It was more a point of mutual faith. And faith was a powerful word to him *and* to Teschal. And a very powerful word to the person she was planning to visit.

***

Long Pond Assisted Living facility was a picturesque place perched on the shores of the body of water that bore its name, the building's glass facade providing lovely vistas of the dark waters and the lights of Gevaudan beyond. Ducks and swans meandered leisurely through the extensive gardens and along winding paths that had been designed specifically to accommodate the widest of wheelchairs. Trees lined the cobblestone paths, weeping willows, maples, wise old oaks, their branches offering shade indiscriminately to visitors and residents alike. Benches were positioned everywhere and the lanes were lined with streetlights and footlights encouraging everyone to stroll through the grounds regardless of time of day.

It was all so serene, so peaceful and so expensive. But at the end of the day, the place was just a departure gate for the hereafter, a jumping off point for death. And everyone who passed through the big automatic glass and metal doors, whether they be resident, employee, or visitor, damned well knew it. Those who called Long Pond home rarely left by the door through which they had entered. The ultimate exit was located at the rear of the building by the tastefully hidden loading dock and the view there was far less picturesque.

"Detective," a neat-looking woman at the reception desk said as Teschal entered the lobby. "How are you this evening?"

"I'm fine," Teschal said, rays of sunset piercing the dark clouds behind her, glinting off the turbid water, making the world appear sinister.

"She's had a good day," the woman said with a professional grin.

Of course she had, Teschal thought. It's all good here at the departure gate. All serene. Memories of bygone days flitted through the air like moths. And memories were what mattered most.

"That's good to hear," Teschal said politely.

Teschal had spoken to Dr. Spencer, the primary care physician at Long Pond, on the mobile while driving over. She'd been lucky to catch the woman before she headed home for the evening.

"How's the UTI?" Teschal had asked, gravely concerned about the latest bout of confusion and the infection that had triggered it.

It had, ironically, been a urinary tract infection that had started the whole ordeal more than a year earlier, that and a little vitamin B-12 deficiency coupled with a Transient Ischemic Attack that had flown in under the medical radar. And then there was the question of early onset dementia to boot, all adding to the confusion, the paranoia, the accusations of petty theft aimed at neighbors regarding items that had simply been misplaced.

A brief hospitalization with a one-to-one with input from psychologists and neurologists had been the next step. MRIs, CT scans, carotid artery scans—the whole medical bag of tricks had followed. All this had led to a respite at Long Pond that had gradually evolved into a residency, laced, of course, with intermittent bouts of 'sun downing,' trips into the land of nocturnal delusion and confusion that came on after dusk. And of course the occasional UTI which served to stir the pot, amplify the situation exponentially. The prognosis was that it would all be downhill from this point onward, a slow progression, or rather a slow regression into…into what? Oblivion? Hell?

"Well," Dr. Spencer had said, "I'd say the latest bout has eased, she's presenting much better. The sulfamethoxazole is clearing up the infection nicely based on all indications; it was not too bad this time. And the Aricept is slowing the dementia. I'd say she's nearly back to base line. She *is* still experiencing some minor confusion. And it is evening, so please bear that in mind when you see her. But, barring another set-back, I'd say she'll be out of the Acute Ward in a few days and back in her own rooms in the Memory Unit. She's had plenty of visitors from her wing too, and that's good. Many of the other residents *do* tend to see her as a bit of a sage."

No surprise there, Teschal remembered thinking. It had apparently been the same back in Scotland. And private skilled nursing-slash-assisted living was far from cheap. Yet the funds kept flowing from the old country, from private anonymous sources, tribute to the 'old gypsy witch' who was evidently still held in high regard by those who mattered in the Romani world. And who was Eve Teschal to question the enigmatic hand that sustained her mother?

Teschal had thanked Dr. Spencer and hung up. It was good news, though an all-too-brief reprieve—she understood the inevitable direction in which things were moving. The clock was ticking.

"She was in the sitting room until a few minutes ago," the woman at the reception desk said. "But I'm sure that she's back in her room by now. Probably watching the Hallmark Channel or maybe one of those game shows she loves so much."

Teschal thanked the woman and proceeded past the desk, turning right at the place where the lobby joined the first-floor corridor. She proceeded down the hall past the rooms with their shadowy occupants and their flickering televisions, the murmur of old western movies and 'golden oldies' radio stations spilling from the doorways.

She moved past the nursing station where mostly young blonde things giggled about how much they'd had to drink last weekend and whose boyfriend was the hottest, until she reached the farthest corner of the building, the 'quiet section' as the staff called it, the wing for Memory Unit residents with various acute ailments.

Teschal stood in the doorway considering the woman lying in the bed. Family Feud was on the television. An impeccably dressed Steve Harvey had just told a joke and the audience was laughing.

"Hey Mum," Teschal said as she entered the room.

"Who are you then?" Vadoma Teschal said, her accent pure Scot's Highland—decades in New England had not driven it from her.

Teschal moved into the dim glow of the lamp on the nightstand.

"*Gadji*," Vadoma Teschal said, once her eyes lit on Teschal. She twisted her head as it lay on the elevated pillow, her long silver mane rustling like straw.

"*Chey*, mum, your daughter," Teschal said, crossing to the window that overlooked the garden and the paths that ran down to the rocky edge of the big pond. "*Romani*, just like you. *Romanichal*. Not a *Gadji*, not an outsider. But I *do* live in a house. Indoor toilet. No caravan for me. Zoning prohibits them in my neighborhood."

"*Gadji*," Vadoma spat dismissively, waving an arthritic hand.

"Tough case, this is mum, I need your advice," Teschal said to the glass, trying to ignore her mother's attitude. It was something she'd grown accustomed to doing.

Beyond the glass, the dark waters looked angry.

"Well, you were always a good girl, a bit head strong is all. Who are you again?"

Teschal shrugged it off. "Nothing's making sense mum. But it's not for you to worry. I just thought maybe you could offer a little insight."

She turned to consider her mother. No response. The woman seemed to be watching the television, but who could say? Perhaps, in her mind, she was walking down the aisle of the stone church back in Inverness where she'd been married, her gypsy contingent gathered in the pews ready to cut loose as soon as the vows had been dispensed with, drink themselves into a forty-eight-hour stupor all in the name of celebration. Or perhaps she was back in New Hampshire, raising the daughter who now stood before her, never imagining how things would turn out in the end. Or maybe even slipping into one of her *spells*, the ones that granted her a glimpse into the secret unseen world she insisted existed in spite of reality's best efforts to keep it hidden away and society's best efforts to deny it.

"Worry," the woman said with a dismissive grunt. "Worrying is for the young, for those who have *time* to worry. At my age, there's nothing to worry about. Everything is certain, no questions left. Only answers. Death is the one thing that requires no thought, no effort at all."

"Morbid observation," Teschal said, sensing a moment of lucidity settling over her mother. "May I quote you?"

"Quote away," Vadoma Teschal said. "Quotes are free."

"So, are they treating you good, Gypsy woman?" Teschal said. "If not, just put a curse on them."

"Now dear, you shouldn't joke about such things. The old ways, they tend to come back just when you thought they were dead and buried. I suspect I've told you that at least once before."

How prophetic, Teschal thought before crossing back to the nightstand. The clock read five-fifteen. Plenty of time to pay Allison Mckenna a visit, ask her about her late-night sojourn to the latest murder scene. Unexpected. The best way—catch them napping. Then Richards would have the conference room set up for seven-thirty. Gathering the facts, summing things up, adding the information gathered from the Flynn girl murder to the mix.

"Mum, I wish you would try to remember some of the *old ways*," she said, sitting on the edge of the bed. "Maybe tell me one of your *Darane Svataru*, one of your ghost stories, enlighten me with your *draba*. Maybe you could point me in the right direction. You *were* a shaman, a *drabarni*."

The woman snorted, smiled, as if seeing Teschal for the first time since she'd arrived.

"Now darling," she said her voice low and soothing. She reached out and took Teschal's hand. "Once a *drabarni* always a *drabarni*. But I never really had the light, not like some others. Your grandfather was one. Oh yes. Diviner he was. He could find a blind spring during a snow storm with a bit of yew. And you my dear, *you* have the light. I've always known it. Just like him. You just haven't come to terms with it yet."

Teschal felt something rising in her throat. She choked it back, cleared her throat. "If you think of anything, *see* anything, in your dreams..."

"Don't fret dear, things happen as the universe sees fit."

Vadoma released her daughter's fingers and let her own crooked hand fall into her lap. She sighed heavily, exhaustion had come to claim her. There would be no visions tonight.

"I do remember a story I heard once, when I was a wee one, from your grandfather." The elder Teschal's voice seemed to ooze from the shadows. "I'd been fussing with my brother, Mihai, God rest his soul, for...oh I forget the reason. Children fuss a great deal.

"Anyway, your grandfather took me aside, sat me down. He told me not to give into the urge to hit my brother or anyone else for that matter unless they were seriously trying to hurt me. He said one action leads to another and pretty soon you can't remember that you have a choice, you just keep doing the thing that comes easiest to you over and over. And that thing isn't always the best thing in the end. Prisons and graveyards, he said, are full of people who took the easy way, did the *wrong* thing until it became second nature to them and they forgot how to do the right thing, *couldn't* do the right thing if their life depended upon it."

Vadoma Teschal's eyes faltered, glistening specks winking in the gloom. Sleep was creeping up on her like a stealthy predator.

"He told me a *paramicha* once, a story, to help me understand," she continued, her voice growing softer around the edges, but no less lyrical in her Scottish brogue. "He said that there were two *ruvs*, wolves, in each of us, one evil, *mizhak*, wicked, filled with malice and greed and anger, and the other one good, filled with happiness, and kindness and love. Two wolves in each of us. Fighting. Always fighting for the possession of our soul."

"Wolves, huh?" Teschal said. She went back to the window, looked out at the dark water. "Which one of them wins?"

"Why dear," Vadoma said, her voice suddenly flat and deadly serious, "the wolf that wins is the one that you feed."

Chapter Thirty-Nine

Allison Mckenna opened the door and said, "Hello, Detective," in a voice lacking any emotion whatsoever.

"Mrs. Mckenna."

"What brings you out in the rain?" Mckenna said as she faded into the obscurity of her apartment.

Teschal glanced around, stepped inside, closing the door behind her. "Can't let a little rain keep you down."

"Easier said…" Mckenna's voice faded as she moved further into the gloom.

"How are we feeling these days?"

"*We* are living the dream," Mckenna said.

Teschal glimpsed Mckenna's shadowy form moving to the kitchen. She followed, taking up position in the doorway where the dull gray light from a shaded window revealed Mckenna preparing what might be considered to be supper, peanut butter and jelly on wheat bread.

Teschal considered the empty take-out containers and pizza boxes lining the counter. A fly was hovering by the stove, making a noise like a miniature kamikaze. There was a bad smell coming from the vicinity of the trash barrel in the corner, which was spilling over with refuse. Teschal noticed a small white bag bearing the letter 'W' lying on the floor by the barrel. She picked it up, turned to Mckenna.

"The Waterfront Café," she said. "Expensive."

"I can afford it," Mckenna said as she scooped up the paper plate the sandwich rested on, leaving the jar of peanut butter and the container of jelly on the counter, uncovered, the butter knife she'd used lying between them.

"And they deliver at all hours. The people in this building probably keep them in business."

"Tell me, have you had any visitors lately?" Teschal stuffed the bag into the trash barrel.

"Visitors?" Mckenna said, settling into a bar stool at the island.

"The press." Teschal's eyes caught on the numerous newspaper clippings scattered across the island. "A little morbid research?"

Mckenna's expression turned suddenly acidic and she reached out with her free hand and swept the newspaper clippings aside. They cascaded to the floor.

"Fuck," she hissed, slamming the sandwich down into the plate.

"Have you spoken to the counselor I recommended?" Teschal said, her voice calm and professional.

Mckenna buried her face in her hands.

"And the support group we talked about? I spoke with Jennifer Tinsley—"

"Parents of murdered children," she hissed raising her eyes. "Some acronym I can't remember just now. All of those AA rejects introducing themselves and telling everyone their sad stories. The pity club. It just wasn't for me."

"And is handling it alone any better?"

"Who says I'm alone?"

The comment stuck in Teschal's brain like a burr. Allison Mckenna, she realized, was *completely* alone.

"This will pass," Teschal said, her voice low and surprisingly compassionate.

"The fuck you know!" Mckenna growled, a sob gurgling up into her throat.

"You'd be surprised what I know," Teschal said calmly but firmly.

"Any dead children?" Mckenna countered, her voice little more than a hiss.

Teschal shook her head slowly.

"Then come back when you have more experience."

"There are many types of loss. All I'm saying is that you don't have to be alone in this." She spread her hands and placed them on the island. The kamikaze fly buzzed past her face.

"Detective," Mckenna said, gathering her wits, running her hands through her unkempt hair, "I know that you mean well, but..." Her voice trailed off as a rumble of thunder rattled the panes of the window.

"Stopping off at crime scenes is unwise," Teschal said.

Mckenna's grim little smile was almost imperceptible.

"Especially when the circumstances are very similar to—"

"Get out." Her voice was frigid, the tears wet on her face.

"It might look suspicious. And it certainly isn't healthy."

"Detective, if you have something to say, then say it. Otherwise, please leave me in peace."

Teschal drew in a deep breath, let it out. She glanced around the kitchen. There was no peace to be found here. She reached into her jacket pocket and withdrew a card.

"Here." She set the thing down on the island. "A new one. If you need anything, like the number of that counselor or Jennifer Tinsley's support group, call me. Any time."

She turned to leave, but upon reaching the kitchen doorway she glanced back over her shoulder.

"And Ms. Mckenna," she said, her voice cooler than it had been, almost officious. "Stay away from any future crime scenes."

A look of what might have been mild amazement crossed Mckenna's tear-stained face.

"What makes you think there'll be more?" she managed, her voice a harsh whisper.

Teschal paused, still looking over her shoulder, but said nothing. Then she went to the door and let herself out.

Chapter Forty

"Here's the list," Kiley said, handing Connie a sheet of paper.

Connie thanked her perfunctorily and began studying the list.

"What's that?" Chase said, emerging from Connie's private bathroom.

"Destinations of the Mckenna women," Kiley said. "The cops did a thorough check on Allison Mckenna's whereabouts at the time of the first murder, that of D-Block Raccine. Passports get stamped, destinations get logged. Everything's electronic these days."

"But how did you get such an accurate itinerary?" Connie said, turning back to Kiley and cocking her head.

"I checked Elise Mckenna's Facebook page."

"What?" Chase said.

"The police haven't taken it down?" Dolores said.

"I guess not," Kiley said swinging the laptop balanced on her knees to show the others. "Maybe the police were curious to see who might visit it. Killers do things like that sometimes, don't they? Like setting a fire then staying to watch the action?"

Chase nodded. "True. And Allison Mckenna *did* mention that Elise stayed in touch with her via Facebook while she was traveling."

"Who *has* visited her page?" Dolores asked.

"Looks like some friends from Bridgton," Kiley said. "But not lately. And mom was a regular."

"Still posting on her dead daughter's time line?" Dolores said.

"Looks that way," Kiley said.

"Crazy bitch," Connie mumbled.

The Facebook page featured a photograph of Allison Mckenna looking healthy and fit, her hair full of body, and her eyes full of life. Standing beside her was a grinning woman who might have been her younger sister, her daughter, Elise Genevieve Mckenna. The two women were wearing fashionable white woven brimmed hats and matching off-white blouses. Chase thought they looked as if they'd stepped out of an old movie with Stewart Granger searching for lost diamonds in deepest darkest Africa. The world around them was sepia-tinted, photo-shopped. Behind them, rising up and out of the picture frame, were a series of stone obelisks.

"That's them," Dolores said leaning closer.

"She was a looker," Chase said.

"So sad," Dolores observed. "Such a waste."

"Allison Mckenna wasn't half bad looking either," Connie said. "Last time she was on the news she looked like death warmed over."

"How considerate," Dolores said.

"I don't get paid for my charm," Connie shot back.

No one has wasted any money, Dolores wanted to say, but she held her tongue.

"Where was that picture taken?" Chase asked, doing his best to ignore Connie's flinty disposition, which was greatly amplified since Dolores' first appearance and quickly growing tiresome.

"The caption reads, 'Greetings from Stonehenge,'" Kiley said.

Chase took the list from Connie.

"If you follow Elise's time line you'll find a complete itinerary," Kiley said. "Destinations, photographs, comments. And, as I said, mom kept on making entries, though not so much since she returned from abroad, other than to comment about how much she missed her daughter, how much she missed doing certain things with Elise, quoting song lyrics that she felt were relevant. Mostly seventies and eighties bands."

"Allison Mckenna can't seem to let go," Connie said.

"Could you?" Dolores said.

"You'd be surprised at how much I've let go," Connie said firmly.

"All right," Chase said, ending the squabbling. "So you've listed all the applicable destinations."

"I've separated the place names into categories, Elise by herself, Elise and mom together, and mom by herself, after the murder," Kiley said.

"Very thorough," Connie said.

"Mckenna must be rich all right," Kiley added. "Great hotels. Top-of-the-line rental cars, Range Rovers mostly. Mom crisscrossed Europe and parts of Asia Minor. She spent most of the time in the UK and Ireland. I even have a list of the tours that were set up by the hotels where she stayed, the attractions she visited, mostly old religious sites, churches, graveyards and such. Pretty dry stuff. But Elise did attend a few concerts while—"

Connie turned to glare at the young intern.

Kiley threw up her hands, folded her laptop, tucked it beneath her arm and headed down the hall.

"Let's go," Dolores said, grabbing the itinerary from Chase and following Kiley.

"Where are you going?" Connie called.

Dolores didn't answer.

Chase looked at Connie, shrugged impishly and followed.

"That's right, better run along," Connie called dismissively, "like a good boy."

***

"Where are we going?" Kiley asked enthusiastically from the back seat of Chase's SUV.

"Connell Library," Dolores said while scanning Allison Mckenna's travel itinerary.

"The Connell Library?" Chase said.

"Bridgton University," Kiley chimed in. "I'm taking a course there this fall. Creative writing. Don't want to be a researcher all my life. I'd like to be a reporter, cover stories. Maybe write a column for the Gevaudan Sentinel. I mean, it's a start. Eventually I'd like to write for Boston Magazine or the Boston Globe. Wouldn't that be cool?"

Chase glanced at Dolores who smiled in return.

"It *would* be cool," Dolores said.

"Haven't you two professors heard of the internet?" Chase said. "All the information in the world at your fingertips?"

"Connell has a lot of old books," Dolores said.

"Not everything has been transferred to the net," Kiley said. "Bridgton has a lot of old English and Latin texts. And books on archaeology. A lot of primary sources. And not all those texts are considered main stream enough to commit to the internet."

"All right, all right," Chase said, giving up. "But I need to make one quick stop first."

"There are bathrooms at the library," Dolores said.

"It's not that kind of stop," Chase responded.

***

"So that's the Castle Mill complex," Dolores said as Chase drove slowly along Quarry Street. "Formerly the Daniker Mill complex."

Rows of run-down tenements had gradually surrendered to huge brooding granite mills replete with boarded-up windows, each surrounded by rusted eight-foot-high chain-link fences, their once crowded parking lots devoid of cars, the once smooth asphalt riddled with cracks and choked with waist-high weeds.

"My mom used to shop here when I was a kid," Kiley said from the back seat in a soft detached voice. "School clothes, coats."

"The whole place looks haunted," Dolores said. "You're not going in there?"

Chase pulled up to the curb, slipped the SUV into park.

"Hand me the video unit."

"*Chase?*" Dolores said as Kiley handed over the equipment.

"I'll be quick."

Dolores opened her door, began to climb out.

"No," Chase said. "I'll be faster alone. And in case something goes wrong, you get the hell out of here and call the cops. This is a lousy neighborhood."

"I don't like this," Dolores said closing the door.

Chase took the video unit and crossed to the weed-infested sidewalk. "It's all right; I probably won't be able to get in anyway," he said, heading off into the drizzle.

"Does he do this sort of thing often?" Kiley said.

"I'm starting to think so," Dolores said as she climbed over the center console into the driver's seat.

***

Chase moved along the sidewalk, damp, misty air brushing against his face. He glanced warily around at the dark stone buildings and the old tenements. He heard a dog barking in the distance and cars moving along the Old Cape Highway and through nearby Mitre Square. He shouldered the video unit and switched it on, aiming it through the rusted fence at the hulking old mill. The boarded-up windows seemed to be watching him.

He slung the video unit when he reached a padlocked gate. He tested the chain, found it to be secure but slack. Forcing the gates apart, he managed to shinny through the opening. Once in the parking lot he made for the loading dock at the side of the building.

Chase mounted the stairs and crossed the concrete platform with its badly dented metal edging and disintegrating rubber bumpers. There were two big wood doors built into the side of the mill, ripped yellow Police Line tape dangling from the handles. Ignoring the tape he tried the handles and the big doors creaked open.

He slipped into the murky darkness. He raised the video unit, activated the light and moved into a long narrow corridor. The place was a mess, trash everywhere, beer cans, and ruined crates spilling excelsior, clusters of rat droppings.

Chase veered to the left where the light revealed a wider corridor with cobweb-infested rafters. He moved into this new corridor, the ancient floorboards complaining loudly. Something scurried past his foot. He aimed the light down and watched a huge rat scamper off into the shadows.

"Just fucking lovely," he whispered.

He breathed in a lung-full of musty air, choked into the crook of his elbow and moved off toward a dark opening some yards ahead.

He reached the gaping doorway, leaned into it and panned the light around. He realized with a start that he was staring down into the blackened guts of an elevator shaft. The beam of light revealed a clutter of debris piled at the bottom of the shaft—two-by-fours, metal gears, coils of steel cable. And what might have been swatches of rust-colored paint were splashed across the floor and wall at random intervals.

Chase activated the video unit, trained its lens on the gruesome scene at the bottom of the shaft.

"Blood," he whispered for the video microphone. "And soot as if there'd been a fire."

"Look what the cat dragged in," a gravelly sing-song voice called from the shadows.

Chase spun toward the sound, swinging the video unit aside and gripping the door jamb with his free hand to maintain his balance. The beam of light from the video unit found its way into a brick-lined alcove off to the left where the four filthiest human beings he'd ever seen were huddled together, staring at him, three men and one woman. Their numerous layers of clothes were ratty, torn and stained.

"You got any H?" one of the men said as he started to stand up. "Or are you a cop?"

"I'm a reporter," Chase said, barely realizing he'd spoken.

"You should do a story on us," the woman said, her voice surprisingly flirtatious. She was Caucasian, surprisingly young, not unattractive. Her shoulder-length mop of hair was dyed blue.

"He wants to know what happened to the cop," another one of the men said. African-American, heavy black beard, piercing blue eyes. He was the one with the shrill, sing-song voice. "Got all burned up, torn apart. *Riiiip*. Fell right down that *shaaaaft*," he said, these last words slow and drawn out.

"Did you see what happened?" Chase said.

"Got some Horse?" another man said. His skin was impossibly pale, his voice was deep and intense, his eyes vivid crystals. He was clearly under the influence of something.

"Shut the fuck up Reg," the woman said. "You'll scare the reporter away," she added with a very solicitous grin.

"No, we weren't here," the man with the shrill voice said flatly. He was slowly getting to his feet, as was the third man, the one who had not yet spoken. He was stocky, dull red hair, a vague gleam in one dark eye. The other pupil was milky white, the lid badly scarred.

Chase smelled urine, thought he glimpsed something shiny in the quiet man's hand.

"Maybe we should give you the full tour," sing-song said finally managing to stand up.

Fuck, Chase thought and he broke for the loading dock.

"Where ya' going?" sing-song called and then he was cackling maniacally. "Where ya' *goiiiing*?"

Chase pushed through the big metal doors, crossed the loading dock and descended the steps, nearly dropping the video unit and falling flat on his face, his feet fighting for purchase on the rain-slicked cement stairs. Glancing warily over his shoulder, Chase half-ran, half-stumbled across the lot toward the fence. He slipped awkwardly through the gate and headed up the sidewalk, his eyes never straying from the loading dock and the torn strips of yellow police tape flapping in the breeze.

He reached the car, panting, as Dolores emerged from the driver's side door and ran around to intercept him.

"What happened?" she asked, her voice laced with raw concern.

Chase's eyes had not strayed from the old mill. He turned at last to Dolores.

"Jesus," she said, placing her palms on his chest as if feeling for a heartbeat. "What the hell happened in there?"

"Rats and vagrants," Chase said. "That's all."

Dolores shook her head slowly, gripping the lapels of his jacket and gritting her teeth as if silently saying, *I told you not to go!*

"Well?" Kiley said from the back seat.

"Let's get to the library," Chase said. "I think I've had enough excitement for one night. A little research might be just what the doctor ordered."

Chase and Dolores climbed aboard the SUV. Dolores reached over and began rubbing Chase's arm, seeking perhaps to convince herself that he'd made it out of the old mill alive and was in fact seated beside her. He started the engine, glanced one last time in the direction of the old Daniker Mill. Dark clouds were moving across the scene. A sepia tinted ray of sunlight had pierced the clouds and was creeping across the old granite like a burning finger causing the stone to glow. The gusting wind sounded raw and cold.

Chase slipped the SUV into gear, pulled away from the curb and watched as the old mill receded in his rear-view mirror.

Chapter Forty-One

Bridgton College had recently evolved into Bridgton University, but many of the buildings were still being renovated in order to accommodate additional classrooms, faculty, and students. The library, which was more than one hundred years old, was among those not yet fully retrofitted. Several sections of scaffolding had been erected at various places around the vine-encrusted stone structure and layers of tarp hung here and there obscuring many of the lead-glass windows like dark-colored sheets on Salvador Dali's clothes line.

"They'll be working on this place for months," Kiley said, pointing to the building as Chase drove past. "But the new gym and science building are open. And the continuing education center. Plus two new dorms. Say," she said, suddenly frowning, "why am I here?"

"Because you're good with computers," Dolores said. "And research. And we're going to be doing lots of research. Research is a big part of reporting, especially historical research."

"Oh, cool."

"I have a question," Chase said. "If the McKenna's were so well off, why was little Elise attending Bridgton. I mean it's supposed to be a good school and all, but why not go to one of those big Ivy League schools?"

"Bridgton collaborates with many schools," Kiley volunteered. "BC, BU, Yale. The archaeology program Elise was involved with is affiliated with Cambridge College in the UK as well as Trinity in Dublin and Columbia and Cornell plus a few others out west—that's how she managed to do so much globe-hopping."

"And remember," Dolores said, "Allison Mckenna told us that Elise wanted to stay close to home since her dad died. The trips were the exceptions and mom also told us that she tagged along whenever possible. But Kiley's right about the affiliations with other schools. The Criminal Justice program I graduated from at Bridgton was tied in with one at Northeastern."

"Really?" Chase said. "Hell, I went to UMASS Boston. I didn't realize that I was hobnobbing with such an uppity crowd."

It was nearly seven-thirty and the rain had eased as Chase pulled into the day commuter's lot, which was situated behind the former gymnasium, a large brick building replete with windows that ran nearly from roof to foundation, situated across the street from the library. He found a space easily as most commuters had apparently gone for the day, and shut the engine. The thrumming of an approaching freight train could be heard in the distance.

"The train tracks are just beyond those trees," Kiley said. "They run through the campus and past Greystone Prison and down toward Cape Cod."

"Yes, I know," Dolores said.

"The computers are on the sixth floor of the library."

"I *did* go to school here," Dolores said. "I *do* know my way around."

"Oh sure." Kiley grinned. "I just figured that it had been some time since you, well—"

"Some *time*…?"

"I mean, my ID will get us into the library," Kiley said, fumbling, trying to smooth things over. "And I—"

"Let's just go," Chase said climbing out into the gray evening.

"Yeah, okay," Kiley said following suit, not completely grasping Dolores' less-than-enthused glare. "This should be fun."

Chase fell behind the two women as they crossed the lot. His mind had returned to the old mill and what he'd seen. Things were getting darker with each passing second. And a cold dread was growing inside him. He could simply not share in Kiley's enthusiasm.

"C'mon Chase," Dolores prompted.

He quickened his pace.

The freight train arrived at that moment, thundering past the far end of the commuter lot, its whistle shrieking, stirring the surrounding trees and scattering a murder of slumbering crows like autumn leaves in a gale.

Chapter Forty-Two

Richards had set up a portable projector near the far end of the briefing room's long table, its lens focused on a white board secured to the wall, the unit rigged to a nearby laptop. He'd also prepared manila folders packed with printed copies of all the pertinent facts related to the 'Night Stalker' case, beginning with Elise Mckenna's murder and culminating with Corrister Flynn's death. He'd stocked the folders with any relevant photographs, including shots from local newspapers, those taken by crime scene photographers, along with stills shot by Chase Christian, the pesky stringer, who, whether Richards was willing to admit it or not, seemed to be providing the investigatory team with a most useful photographic resource.

Richards doubted that any new conclusions would be reached, but he figured that Teschal was simply laying it all out on the table in vivid black and white for the other members of the team to view, bottom-lining the case while reminding the powers-that-be that she was on top of things, particularly in light of the most recent murder.

It all made sense, and the political pressure was reaching the boiling point. Richards was glad that he was not lead detective on this one. And if the case remained unsolved and Teschal took the rap for the failure that might just provide room for him to do a little late career climbing. Either way, Jude Richards figured he'd manage to emerge relatively unscathed.

Satisfied with his work, he took up position in the third chair from the door, closest to the laptop, beside a heavy-set man with a walrus-like moustache and directly across from a platinum-haired woman who was perusing

Richard's materials through a stylish pair of Tom Ford reading glasses.

"Sorry for the hour," Teschal said as she entered the room and sat down diagonally across from Richards.

Never the type to sit at the head of the table, Richards thought. He would never make that mistake. Always dress better than the others do and regard them with cordial aloofness. And *always* sit at the head of the table.

"I felt it best to limit the discussion to we few," Teschal said. "I don't want your respective team members feeling left out, but I think it's fair to say that we don't have much in the form of new leads available at this time—this is essentially a summing up of what we know thus far. And in light of this latest murder, it's appropriate that we reconvene."

Politically correct, Richards thought.

"Gabriel, why don't we start with the woman at the double murder scene?"

The heavy-set man began to methodically spread the contents of Richard's folder before him.

"The woman was a known freelance prostitute, a runaway. Her Name was Jill Crosston, originally of Hoboken, New Jersey, age twenty-seven, known heroine user, cocaine user, busted twice, last time two months ago. We've spoken with a few of her friends, who were obviously a little reluctant to speak with the authorities. They are known to congregate at the corner of Lexton and Season."

"South side," the woman with silver hair said. "Lexton Road project."

"It was not unusual for the girls to do porn on the side," Gabriel said. "So no one was surprised that Jill was making a film. Good pay, tolerable weirdos. Usually. And *weirdos* is, of course, a relative term."

Gabriel drew a pair of glasses from his breast pocket, set them on his thick nose and, running his equally thick finger down the page, began paraphrasing the information.

"No semen in her vaginal canal, but there were signs of internal and external blunt trauma. The dead man, Carver, probably roughed her up for the camera lens. His DNA was all over her body and her blood was on the razor found in his hand." Gabriel adjusted his position. "We found some tools in the bedroom closet: hack saw, several replacement blades, plastic storage bins, and a hatchet. He clearly intended to process the body and dispose of it, but was obviously interrupted before he could do so."

Teschal nodded as she leafed through the photographs.

Richards tapped keys on the laptop and the image of the dead girl materialized on the whiteboard in all its bloody glory. He waited for the gruesome image to soak in, tapped a few more keys, and the woman's blanched face was replaced by the black leather clad face of the late Anthony Lee Carver. The lifeless eyes seemed to be staring at everyone in the briefing room, the flap of bloody leather and scalp hanging to one side like a crimson-colored beret.

"Mr. Carver's murder was most *definitely* a different story," Gabriel said. "Approximately one fifth of the body was covered in third- and second-degree burns. There were three deep lacerations running across the front of the torso varying in depth. Judging by the apparent point of origin they ran left to right diagonally at approximately a forty-degree angle to the spinal column originating at the left shoulder and terminating near the lower quadrant of the abdomen. The specific dimensions are all listed in the autopsy report. Lots of torn muscle, lacerations to the abdominal cavity. Six broken ribs, or should I say *lacerated* ribs, as it seems that whatever sliced through the flesh sliced through the bone as well. Even nicked the aorta, the heart, one lung. Weapon as yet unknown. But the force behind it was the very definition of the word thorough."

Gabriel adjusted his glasses, and flipped to the next page.

"The tongue was nearly severed, but the victim probably did that himself by biting down on it when he was thrown against the wall."

Gabriel drew air in through his teeth.

"Scalp torn back to reveal approximately one third of the skull, the exact measurements are in the report. And that action would have proved difficult because the man was wearing a leather mask that covered his head, so the mask was torn away as well."

He ran his finger down the page and flipped to the next sheet.

"Two thoracic vertebrae, T-1 and T-2, were fractured, again most likely as a result of his having been thrown against the wall. Fractured skull, broken femur of the right leg, compound fracture of the right tibia. I could go on, but basically this individual was butchered by someone with immense physical strength. And then there are the burns which occurred in such a way as to suggest that the weapon used to inflict the injuries was ablaze."

"Like a red-hot fireplace poker?" Richards suggested.

Gabriel shook his head. "A single edged weapon could not have produced the wounds. The weapon was most likely shaped like a large claw for lack of a better description."

"Could there have been more than one attacker?" Teschal said.

"It is very likely. It would be almost impossible for someone to wield some weapon that could cause the burns and the lacerations with one hand while using the other hand to throw the man across the room into the wall with sufficient force to fracture the skull as well as two vertebrae. Carver weighed in at just over two-twenty. I can't imagine anyone capable of such an act without assistance from at least one other very strong individual."

"Was Carver alive when he was burned?" Richards asked.

Gabriel nodded. "I'd say it all happened at the same time, which only adds to the mystery. There was no evidence of any defensive wounds, so it follows that whatever transpired happened before the victim could react. The edges of the lacerations were burned, and the eviscerated flesh was essentially cauterized, which limited much of the blood loss. I can say with absolute certainty that the heat was intense, at least six hundred degrees, which defies logic because it was localized."

"Homemade weapon?" Richards said.

"That is very likely," Gabriel agreed. "I've researched contemporary weapons and I've even looked into medieval weaponry, thinking that maybe someone resurrected some ancient torture device. But thus far I've found nothing that accounts for the wounds."

"Jennings," Teschal said. "What does Forensics have to say?"

"The rug was scorched as was the wall," the woman with the silver hair said. "The nearest curtain had burned and fallen away, but there wasn't enough material to start a fire. All evidence suggests that the entry point was the shattered window, especially since all the broken glass was on the inside. But there was no evidence to suggest that anyone walked across the shards of glass, they all seemed to be relatively intact, splintering in a pattern, and there were no traces of glass in other parts of the room."

"And there was no fire escape," Richards said. "A ladder?"

Jennings held up a photograph of the fan-shaped distribution of splintered glass strewn on the carpeting, across the mattress and the dead woman's body.

"Photograph thirty-four F. Our perpetrator would need to have set the ladder in place, climb to the top-most rung, jump through the window without touching the floor, at least not for eight feet or so, because the dead woman on the mattress was less than three feet from the window, kill the man, and leave, gathering the ladder as he left, a ladder that had to be at least thirty feet long, which means an adjustable ladder." She set the photograph down.

"Anyone ever try to adjust a ladder that big alone?" Richards said, glancing slowly around. "It ain't easy. And then what do you do with the thing afterward? Carry it down the street? Load it on a waiting truck with commercial plates to avoid risking a ticket? Stash it somewhere? Ditch it altogether?"

"A garage," Teschal said.

"No private garages in the area," Jennings said. "We checked the auto-body shop next door. Chet's. We came up empty."

"The ladder theory doesn't work," Teschal said. "But what about the roof?"

"We checked that too," Jennings said, sifting through papers and holding up a photograph of the edge of the roof. "The rain gutter is hanging by a thread. There was no sign of belaying equipment having been used either. There were no rope fibers embedded anywhere that we could find, and the gutter would have made that impossible anyway. The thing would have collapsed almost immediately. The extant moorings were rusted through."

"Then the perpetrator had to come through the door," Teschal said rapping the tabletop with her finger tips.

"That is the most likely scenario. We actually considered whether the window might have been broken earlier and left un-repaired, but there was no broken glass beneath the mattress or the girl. The only logical conclusion is that the window was broken at the time of the murder. A distraction maybe. But we found no evidence of a rock or any other projectile. Unless the perpetrator took the projectile with him when he left."

"One guy outside tosses a rock three stories up through a window as his partner enters the unlocked apartment?" Richards said.

"When you eliminate the impossible…" Gabriel offered.

"What about the video camera?" Teschal said.

"Whatever heat source caused the damage," Jennings said, "was so intense that it cooked most of the video. But we did manage to salvage forty-seven seconds' worth. And there were some elements on the surviving video that prompted us to forward the film to the FBI forensics lab in Boston. I'll explain what those elements are when we watch the video."

Richards tapped some keys on the laptop. A blurry image of the murdered woman lying on the filthy mattress swam into grainy focus.

"The sequence involving the woman's murder did not survive," Jennings said.

Richards moved the cursor to the arrow at the bottom of the scene and clicked it. The image came alive, but it was terribly grainy with filaments of static moving vertically through the image like bare twigs scratching at a window. The small laptop speakers emitted only the crackling sound of static. But the scene transpiring on the whiteboard, though vague, was gripping if not terrifying.

The woman was lying on the mattress, gasping, her hands clutching at her hemorrhaging throat, her eyes darting about wildly. A shadow fell across her upper body, its source drawing her dying gaze. The shadow hovered for a long moment, as if gloating over its grisly handiwork as the woman's clutching hands slowly grew still and fell to her sides. She lay there for several seconds, motionless, the blood seeping from her ruined throat with decreasing fluidity. Then a squealing sound burst from the speakers.

"What was that?" Richards said.

"We think it's a cat," Jennings said. "That's one of the elements that piqued our interest. My people tried feeding it through the computer with hopes of determining whether it's in fact a voice, perhaps that of our killer. We had no luck so we handed it over to the FBI lab in Boston. I've given them your mobile number, Detective. You'll be the first to know if they come up with anything."

"What's that?" Teschal said.

A weird light was seeping into the frame, spilling across the dead woman's body. And with it a new sound, a growing roar that reminded Teschal of an approaching freight train. And then there came a mind-numbing shriek and glass fragments rained down over the dead woman. A blinding white light consumed the scene and the film melted away.

A dead silence filled the room.

Richards tapped a key on the laptop and turned to study the silent confused faces.

"Dear Jesus," Gabriel muttered.

"That's all we've got," Jennings said.

"Could a Molotov cocktail or some sort of incendiary device have been thrown through the window?" Teschal said.

"There was no sign of any projectile, incendiary or otherwise, at the scene," Jennings said. "And there was little evidence of heat in the area of the window except for some scorching on the mattress and on the sheers. And the damage to the dead man was too specific to have been caused by a random projectile. But something clearly came through the window. The source of the strange light, which may have been the heat source, does emanate from that direction.

"Bottom line, I don't know what shattered that window. But one thing is certain, nothing *human* came through it. Our killer *had* to come through the door. I mean, did our killer have a jet pack? Or wings?"

"Let's move on," Teschal said. "The Irish girl."

"Too soon for specifics," Gabriel said, "but the MO looks similar if not identical to the Carver murder."

"Corrister Siobhan Flynn," Richards said. "Twelve-time loser. The girl gets acquitted of murder that morning and ends up getting killed as she's packing to leave town. Sounds like revenge. We're checking into the whereabouts of the murdered girl's family, the one Flynn was accused of stabbing, particularly the brother. He was in the courtroom when the verdict was read. If looks could kill…and he has a minor record. A few fights, drunk and disorderly."

"Revenge, maybe," Teschal said, "if not for the circumstances. Revenge uses a gun. Maybe a knife. Not a blow torch."

"Unless you really want it to hurt," Richards said.

Jennings shrugged. "We're still waiting for more information from Greece, but they're suspicious of our motives and wondering why the FBI didn't contact them. The Irish too. And there are rumors about similar cases. Japan, Australia. Possibly South Africa."

"What?" Richards said.

"Christ, why aren't the Feds breathing down our necks?" Teschal said.

"You'd swear it was political," Jennings said sarcastically.

Gabriel made a snorting sound.

"Regarding the Irish," Richards said, "the details are sketchy. I think the Micks are embarrassed. When an incarcerated suspect is murdered while in solitary confinement with guards a hundred feet down the hall, well, such an event is not likely to lend itself to confidence in the local constabulary. Someone got into that cell. And someone had to *let* that someone into that cell."

"All right," Teschal said. "Let's limit the racial slurs shall we? And let's focus on our own backyard. The chief rang the 'copy-cat' bell himself, fed it to the press—so be it."

"Oh, we got the lab results on the residue back," Jennings said. "There was no sign of an accelerant, but the composition of the ash and char *was* unusual."

"How so?" Richards asked. "Char is char, right?"

Teschal raised a finger to silence Richards, leaned forward. "What was unusual about it?"

"The first thing that we noticed was the yellowish color of some of the char and of course the odor in the room, that rotten egg smell, so we ran an analysis," Jennings said, her brow furrowed. "Most char is carbon-based. *This* char had a lot of sulfur in it."

"What would account for that?" Teschal said.

"I'm not sure. Maybe there was something in the room, something the man was using for atmosphere, something the perpetrator took with him when he left. Maybe some kind of flash pot based on the weird light in the video. If not for the extreme claw-like damage to the man's body, a malfunctioning flash pot might fill the scrip. But then again there was no sign of any sulfur stored in the apartment."

"Let's see if I understand this," Richards said, sitting back and lacing his long fingers. "Our perp can fly, has claws like a lion, and carries around sulfur."

"This isn't helping," Teschal said. She was beginning to get a headache. Richards was a good detective, but his ego often got in the way. But he was here because Captain Donovan wanted him here, to ground her, be the cynic in the room. The Devil's advocate. And God knew he was doing a great job of that thus far.

"Where can someone get sulfur?" Teschal said.

Jennings shrugged. "Chemical warehouse. There's one in Bridgton, near the university. But why? And how does it figure in the fire? Sulfur burns readily when exposed to flame, but it burns like liquid, in a flow somewhat like a river of lava. It's far from the best accelerant and it leaves residue. Maybe it's a message of some sort, a threat, something *satanic* even."

"Like a cult?" Richards said, a degree of incredulity in his voice.

"Maybe," Jennings said. "I mean, sulfur, well, back in the middle-ages, it would have suggested witchcraft—it was, after all, known as brimstone.

Chapter Forty-Three

The Connell Library was a shadowy old castle with gray concrete walls, narrow parapet-like windows and an endless maze of cozy nooks and crannies where students could gather in small knots or seek solitude to study, text, or even nap following the long days of academia. The sixth floor was essentially a large square gallery lined with small research rooms and countless shelves laden with rarely used books. The large gallery opening looked down on several chairs, tables, and couches, which sat in a clearing at the center of numerous racks of books that stretched into the gloomy outer limits of the library like a dense forest one floor below.

Kiley had led Dolores and Chase past the surprisingly busy main desk, flashing her student ID as she proceeded, and up the carpeted rise-less stairs to her favorite room, number twelve, which occupied the north-west corner of the sixth floor.

"I come up here because it's quiet and no one bothers you," she said opening the heavy wood door and flicking on the light. "And it's a great place to take a date."

Chase found himself grinning. Dolores elbowed him.

The young woman took up position at the computer terminal and Chase brought over two large wooden chairs, setting them in flanking position beside Kiley, who'd begun tapping keys with a fervor, entering her university password and sailing into the internet with reckless abandon.

"So, what should I search for?"

Chase looked at Dolores.

"I'm not sure," she said.

"*You're not sure?*"

"Let's start with the circumstances of the murders," Dolores said. "*Modus Operandi,* so to speak. How about death by sudden fire."

Kiley tapped keys.

"Spontaneous Human Combustion," she said, reading the website heading. "That's a band—saw them at the university Rathskellar."

"Are we talking about witchcraft?" Chase said.

"Chase, you were there," Dolores said. "You remember the image Connie's people found on your film."

"I…it wasn't very clear, could have been anything," Chase said, his tone betraying his doubts.

"Kiley," Dolores said, "tell us about spontaneous human combustion?"

"Well, the piece talks about this woman who just went up in flames one day. There was pretty much nothing left of her except her lower legs. She'd just been sitting in her chair. One theory is that a strange chemical reaction happens within certain people, causing them to basically go up in flames."

Chase shook his head, crossed his arms and sighed.

"Take a quantum leap," Dolores said. "We may find something."

"I may find I've lost a night's sleep."

"Shhh," Dolores prompted.

"Here's a legend about a haunted sentry box at a seaside fort in Puerto Rico. Two soldiers who took the watch burned up entirely and were never seen again. I guess some witnesses heard a scream one night and saw a bright light emanating from the sentry box and then a cloud of smoke drifting out to sea. Another sentry was said to have also disappeared. No witnesses that time. The box was kind of secluded, set out on a ledge overlooking the sea. Witnesses said that the box was lined with a yellowish powder and smelled like sulfur after each disappearance. Brimstone they called it. The box is a bit of a tourist attraction these days—"

"Sulfur?" Chase said, perking up.

"That's what it says."

"What is it?" Dolores asked.

"When I was a kid I used to fly model rockets, the spent engines smelled like rotten eggs. It was the sulfur. It was a chief ingredient in them."

"So?"

"I noticed that same odor at the first murder scene. And that spot on the wall in the tenement entry smelled the same."

"That's right," Dolores whispered.

"What are we saying here?" Kiley said. "I mean, I'm getting the creeps."

"All right," Chase said, uncrossing his arms and leaning forward. "Let's keep it together. These murder victims are not completely incinerated, so I think that we can rule out spontaneous human combustion. And don't forget the lacerations. Our victims were not alone when they died."

"But the sulfur…" Dolores said.

"Let's stick to what makes sense," Chase said. "We can revisit that later. What was it Conan Doyle said about the simplest explanation being the most likely one?"

"I don't see a simple explanation anywhere on the horizon," Dolores said, "but let's continue."

"Okay." Kiley left the site behind and moved on to Google. "Let's start looking at legends associated with the places Allison Mckenna visited. How about that?"

"Legends?" Chase said.

"Yeah," Dolores said. "If we agree that Allison Mckenna is worthy of suspicion, or at least *interest*, and, after all, visiting murder scenes in the wee hours of the night *is* pretty strange, well, maybe she got an idea while she was traveling. Maybe some ritualistic killings associated with one of these ancient places got her thinking."

"Like human sacrifices?" Kiley said.

"Who knows?" Dolores said with a shrug.

"All right," Chase agreed. "You're starting to think like a reporter. Where did she go first?"

"She went to places that her daughter either visited or wanted to visit," Dolores said.

"Most places were in the UK and Ireland," Kiley said.

"Well, why don't we cross-reference," Chase said.

"What do you mean?" Dolores said.

"How about places that both the daughter *and* the mom visited," he said. "Start with those."

"Sounds good," Dolores said.

"Strap yourselves in," Kiley said and she began typing.

Chapter Forty-Four

Teschal was still in the briefing room, Richards hovering by the door, Jennings and Gabriel long gone. She'd spread the photographs of the murder scenes, corpses, furniture, drapes, everything, on the table before her and was studying each in turn, looking for some overlooked factor, but finding nothing.

The first murder, the Mckenna girl, raped, stabbed, her throat cut nearly to the bone, found on the banks of the West Wickham River. The second murder, D-Block Raccine, the main suspect, found in an alleyway between two run-down apartment buildings in the troublesome south end of the city. Burned, torn to shreds, his head attached by a few fleshy threads of muscle and some skin. Also battered and broken by the apparent fall from the third-floor window of one of the buildings, broken glass everywhere. The rookie cop found in a similar state at the bottom of an empty elevator shaft in an abandoned mill on Quarry Street. The prostitute and the porn director in a run-down apartment at the bottom of Warren Street—she'd been beaten, her throat cut, he'd been torn apart and burned alive. The Irish girl, torn up and burned in her third-floor apartment on lower Anawan Street just east of Mitre Square, barely a mile from the abandoned mill on Quarry Street.

Evidence suggested that the Flynn girl had been standing near the door when it burst open. The wood had been splintered, scorched, the hinges torn lose. She'd apparently run to the bedroom in an attempt to escape, maybe through the window and down the fire escape. But the assailant had followed her. She never managed to close the door. She'd apparently been struggling with it when the killer caught up with her. And that's where she met her end.

"You can stare at those all night long," Richards said, his finger flipping through his mobile phone, his eyes scanning the screen. "I think our best bet would have been the video, but there's not much there."

Teschal looked up, nodding.

"Four murder scenes," she said, almost thinking out loud. "The officer in the old mill—easy access point there. He'd gotten in through an open door at the loading dock. The killer may have already been inside or simply followed him. But Raccine in a locked apartment, door bolted from the inside? No possible means of access there. The porn director—fairly easy access point, *if* the killer used the door. But what about the broken window? And the Flynn girl—the door was bashed in. And the wood was scorched."

She gathered up the photographs, slipped them into the folder.

"Oh, I spoke with the Mckenna woman tonight," she said.

"That's a dead end. I can see the correlation with the first murder, but it occurred the second she returned from abroad. The officer, well, she had no way of knowing what happened to damage the chain of evidence or who was responsible for the mistake. It was a rookie blunder. And the others...?" Richards shrugged. "Does she have something against criminals in general?"

"That's our job," Teschal said. "I did notice a lot of news clippings lying around her apartment, all dealing with crime."

"You know as well as I do that when someone goes through what *she's* gone through, loses a loved one to violence, accompanying trauma...well, more vigilantes have been born from those circumstances than any other.

But she's not Charles Bronson stalking criminals in parks after dark with a gun. What is happening to these people, well she couldn't pull it off. Certainly not by herself. Hell, I can't imagine who *could* pull it off."

"You are correct. Not by herself. So if she *is* our perp, then she has at least one accomplice."

Richards sighed. "I'm heading home."

"See you in the a.m.," Teschal said with a sigh.

She glanced back at the empty table. No ideas left there worth considering. She listened to Richards' footsteps echoing as he moved down the hall. Then she shut the light and headed for her office.

Chapter Forty-Five

Chase was returning from the sixth-floor bathroom of the Connell Library when he heard a sound. He paused, frowning, glancing about and then leaning over the gallery rail. A deep gloom had settled over the floor below, the sofas and chairs had become crooked shadows. If he didn't know better, he'd swear that the place was closed for the night. He waited, listening, but heard only the faint sound of rain striking glass and the rustling of leaves and the sighing of branches as the wind moved through the ancient oaks that guarded the old library.

He checked his watch—nearly eleven. He proceeded along the carpeted walkway, turning into the small alcove that housed room number twelve to find Kiley and Dolores still huddled around the computer terminal, fully engrossed. The overhead light was set on its lowest setting and the glow of the terminal gave their faces a ghostly pall. A scattering of thick old books lay sprawled across a narrow table against the inner wall, a single reading lamp spilling its soft glow across old yellowing pages.

"Thought you got lost," Dolores said, glancing at him and flashing a smile.

"Don't think I didn't try. It wouldn't be hard to do with all those corridors and book shelves. It's like a maze out there. And it's dark downstairs. What time does this place close?"

"Midnight," Kiley said pausing to raise her glasses and rub her eyes. "It stays open twenty-four hours during finals, but spring semester just ended and the first summer session hasn't started yet. Mostly grad students this time of year."

She lowered her glasses and started in again. "So, we've found plenty of questionable organizations. Many ancient, some contemporary."

"Organizations? How long was I in the bathroom?"

"Long enough," Dolores said consulting the notebook Kiley had brought in her knapsack. "We were searching for organizations centered on revenge when we stumbled upon listings that concerned supernatural entities."

"Demons and familiars and such," Kiley said. "And of course there is no shortage of cults associated with everything from Satanism to alien abduction, not to mention an endless assortment of sects that worship some aspect of nature or nature as a whole."

"Hey, the burned bodies," Chase said. "That *does* reek of Satanism."

"We've covered some of that, Sherlock," Dolores said. "That's why we've been checking histories of some of the places Allison and Elise visited, looking into myths, legends regarding Satan, demons, witchcraft, what have you. If we can find a demon that is called upon to burn up an enemy or seek revenge, then we can start looking into cults that might be *associated* with that demon. *Capisce?*"

Chase nodded. "That actually makes sense."

"But we've been striking out. We can't find any cults that fully meet the criteria. Another issue is finding a connection between the victims. Male, female, varying age groups, law abiding citizens, criminals…" She shrugged and tapped a pen on her thigh."

"Well, there's the Mckenna girl," Chase said. "Then we have the rookie cop, and of course the 'wrong place, wrong time' prostitute. But the others are, well, scum bags. A rapist-murderer and a porn director shooting a snuff film, fleeing some bad business out west. And the Irish girl who was acquitted of a murder everyone is certain she committed." Chase shrugged. "Maybe Wyatt Earp's ghost is the killer. I mean it looks as if someone is trying to clean up the streets of Gevaudan."

***

Teschal was sitting at her desk in her office. She'd written something on a pad of paper, something she'd drawn several lines under, the word *cult*. Something about the word rang a bell. It was clear that most of the victims had been less than stellar citizens. Even detestable. All but the police officer and of course Elise Mckenna. But her murder had been a separate event, a catalyst of sorts. Maybe. And the prostitute. There are certainly no shortage of hazards associated with *that* particular profession.

The connection between the first, second, and third murders was still nagging her though. There seemed to be too much coincidence there, too much smoke not to suspect a fire. And Teschal kept thinking about Allison Mckenna and her morbid news clippings and late-night murder-scene sojourn. Growing obsession there.

Teschal sat back in her chair, stretched. Her mobile phone rang. She checked the number, didn't recognize it.

"Hello," she said.

"Detective Teschal," a young sounding male voice said. "This is Special Agent Vickers, FBI Forensics Lab. Detective Jennings suggested that I contact you regarding our analysis of the audio samples she submitted."

"Of course."

"Well, Detective, we fed the sounds on the track through our computer system and tried to match them to various animal cries. But, aside from the static and distortion, which *was* extensive, the harmonics, well…think of it this way, human hearing can detect sounds ranging from 300 Hz to around 3400 Hz. Any sounds above or below those levels are usually undetectable to the human ear. Like a bass drum kick at a concert or a dog whistle, they'd likely be more felt than heard, if at all. The low end is called infrasonic and exposure to it can bring on symptoms ranging from chills to sheer panic. The high end is called ultrasonic and extensive exposure can cause hearing loss."

Teschal heard Agent Vickers shuffling papers.

"Now, the sounds on the audio samples you sent us are quite unusual in so much as they extend into both extremes, well beyond the range of human hearing. That suggests that not only were the sounds on the tape *not* those of any feral or domesticated animal, but they were also definitely *not* made by a human being. As a matter of fact we couldn't match them up with *any* living creature in our data base, and our library is extensive."

"What are you saying?"

"Well, the best we can determine is that the first sound was some sort of an electronic impulse. Certainly not animal or human, something manufactured in a recording studio maybe."

Teschal felt her heart begin to race wondering what Captain Donovan would think of all this. Or her mum.

"And the second sound?"

"The second sound bore a considerable resemblance to audio we have of an F-5 tornado. A massive displacement of air; like the noise in a very powerful wind tunnel. Imagine opening a door during a severe storm. But the computer squashed that notion as well. It too was most likely some sort of electronic impulse. Sustained, but manufactured just like the first sound."

"I don't follow, how is this possible?"

"We're still working on it," Vickers said after a moment of hesitation. "But it's a safe bet that neither of those sounds were made by the killer."

"I understand," Teschal said softly.

"I'm sorry we couldn't be of more help, but, as I said, we'll keep searching for a match. It's just possible that we missed something. But I'd say that whoever committed your murders was a good deal more substantial than an electronic impulse."

Teschal thanked Agent Vickers and ended the call. She sat back in her chair, closed her eyes. A grim silence settled over her office. She could hear a clock ticking someplace. No living creature had made the sounds. Something electronic, something completely *unknown*. Like a door opening—

Teschal's mobile phone rang again, severing her line of thought. She opened her eyes and scooped up the thing. She recognized the number immediately.

"Mum?" she said, leaning forward, resting her elbows on the desk. "Are you all right?"

"Ay," Vadoma Teschal said in her finest Scottish brogue. "I was worried about you, daughter."

One of her *spooky* moods tonight, Teschal thought. She could tell by the thicker than usual accent.

"You shouldn't be up this late," Teschal said, rubbing her eyes, the breath of fear she'd felt on the back of her neck when she'd seen the number fading into the air. "No need to worry about me."

"I'll always worry about you, my *chey*," the elder Teschal said. "Besides, I couldn't sleep. I was playing bridge earlier. I did well. You'd have been proud of me. New fellow, Mr. Reed. Not a Romany, but a real Scot and they are rare. Kept talking about golf—but I see potential there. Still has most of his hair."

"That's great Mum," Teschal said, smiling a wry smile. "Your social life is better than mine."

"Stop that dear. You work too hard. No man wants a woman who doesn't know when to come home."

Teschal pursed her lips. "You may be right."

She paused, leaned forward, the chair creaking.

"Mum," she began, "I'm doing some research about that case I'm involved with, and I was wondering if you could recall any more stories from your time in Scotland with the *Romanichal* in your RV."

"Caravan dear," Vadoma said.

"Caravan," Teschal agreed.

"What sort of stories dear?"

"Stories about, oh, religious rituals involving people being burned."

"Wicker men? Like the Celts and Druids? No, nothing like that," she said. "Unless it was a *Martiya*."

"*Martiya*?"

"A familiar. Oh, your grandfather told me about them once when I'd been into his home-made shiny. Told me the *Martiya* would come in the night to take me away as it did all the bad children, take me to hell and leave me there to burn slowly. Scared the Bejesus out of me. I never got into the shiny again, but the headache the stuff gave me was enough to discourage me. The story of a demon carrying me off to hell, well that was sheer overkill."

"The *Martiya*," Teschal whispered.

"Yes. There were others too, all dreamed up to scare children, keep them in line. Best to let it be. Be a *drabarni* my dear. Like your grandfather."

"Mum, you should go to sleep," she said.

"*Besh, besh*, my *chey*. I will. I just had a feeling you might be in danger."

"I'm fine Mum. Promise."

"All right daughter. Good night and pay no mind to the *Martiya*. They died out with the old ways. Oh, but I'd dozed off earlier and I did have a dream about you—not really about you, but I think you were there."

"Dream?" Teschal said.

"A woman was standing alone in a dark place. I think the woman was you. There were creeping shadows. And then there was a sound that came from a long way off.

Like something drifting down from a craggy tor on a chill wind."

"What sort of sound?"

"It was a cat crying," Vadoma Teschal said. "At least I *think* it was a cat. In the dream my ears told me one thing, but my heart told me something *very* different." She sighed heavily into the phone. "Then I woke up."

"That's good Mum. Thanks for calling."

"Just be careful dear. I'll pray for you."

Teschal told her mother not to worry and to sleep well and hung up. She studied the phone for a moment and tucked it into her jacket pocket.

"Enough," she said and she pushed her chair back and got to her feet. She went to the door, shut the light and closed and locked her office. She slipped the keys into her jacket pocket and started down the corridor, the stillness of the old building wrapping itself around her like a dusty shroud. She'd gone ten feet when a sound crept up behind her stopping her dead.

Teschal spun around, her hand moving instinctively to her service revolver. The corridor was empty. Shadows seemed to be everywhere, the lights not as bright and antiseptic as usual. No wonder, she thought, a bank of lights was out at the far end of the hall, past her office. The glass panes in the office doors lining the hall were likewise darkened, adding to the somber mood.

She strained to see into the gloom. The sound came again, closer. A baby cooing or…a cat crying.

Teschal felt herself frowning. The air seemed to grow cold around her. There was something eerie about the sound, something *ethereal*. She thought of her mother's dream and waited, a deep chill spreading across her shoulders. It was the sound from the tape, the electronic impulse of which Special Agent Vickers had spoken.

Not made by anything living, he'd said. Not made by anything of this world, he'd implied.

"Is someone there?"

Silence. Something, some primordial instinct told Teschal to turn around and walk away. Fast. And if there was one thing her mum had taught her, it was to trust her instincts.

Teschal considered the elevator, thought better of it and took the stairs.

The staircase was thick with shadows and her footsteps echoed on the concrete and steel steps. She paused on the second-floor landing, craning her neck to gaze up through the balusters, her hand gripping her holstered service revolver. Had a shadow flitted past the fourth-floor landing?

The gut feeling told her to hurry. She obeyed, bursting forth into the lobby where two uniformed officers were talking with Richards by the main exit.

"Hello Detective."

Teschal looked to the dispatch station, to the source of the Creole accent.

"Hello, Eloise."

"You okay Detective? You look a little…shaken."

"Slipped," Teschal said. "Late hours limit the spinning time at the gym. Stairs are a poor substitute."

Eloise smiled. It was a broad genuine smile.

There was more there, more with Eloise, than most knew about, Teschal thought. It was the bayou Cajun in her. The Haitian. That *old world* knowledge was evident even though the woman clearly tried to play down her heritage. Not unlike the way Teschal tried to play down her own.

"Good night," she said, glancing back at the stairwell door one last time, just in case.

"Night detective," Eloise said.

Teschal waved to Richards, made her way to her car, let herself in and started it up. She felt her gaze being reluctantly drawn to the window to her office. Surrendering to the urge, she looked up and felt the breath flee her lungs as, for a sliver of a second, she thought she saw some shadowy form standing at the window watching her. But the lights to the office were off and the door was locked, and so that would have been impossible.

She shivered, wiping moisture from her eyes and struggling to compose herself. After a moment she slipped the big SUV into gear and headed home through the drizzle and gathering fog.

Chapter Forty-Six

A tone sounded over the Connell Library public announcement system and a female voice announced that the library would be closing in twenty minutes.

"All right," Dolores said. "Let's review what we've found."

"Okay," Kiley said, running her fingers through her short dark hair. "Most of the places Elise Mckenna visited were in the United Kingdom or Ireland. She was into Alfred Watkins' ley lines, which he discussed in his book The Old Straight Track back in the nineteen-twenties."

"That book was on Elise's desk," Chase pointed out.

"Yes, it was," Dolores agreed, nodding. She consulted the notebook in her lap. "Invisible energy lines traversing west Europe. Religious sites from as far back as the Iron Age and perhaps earlier were established along these lines, burial mounds, ancient forts, now replaced with—"

"—Christian churches and cemeteries," Kiley finished. "Also associated with underground streams, blind springs as they were often called. Sources of spectral energy."

"Divining rods were used to find these springs," Dolores said, nodding and checking off a note and turning the page. "Diviners were apparently very sought after in ancient times."

"Okay, ancient energies," Kiley said. "On to places she visited. Templar churches: Temple Church in Bristol England, Denny Abbey, Clontarf Castle in Ireland, Rosslyn Chapel in Scotland. St. Michael's Chapel in Wales atop the

Skirrid Fawr, a holy mountain that supposedly split open the moment Christ was crucified. Skara Brae, a four-and-a-half-thousand-year-old fort in Scotland. Orkney. Maeshowe, also in Scotland, where there is a burial chamber where Vikings left graffiti back in the twelfth century. Fountains Abbey. Fingal's Cave in Scotland. The Stone of Destiny, also known as the Stone of Scone in Ireland, which originated in Egypt and is associated with both Jacob and Moses. The Speckled Mountain, Breac Sliabh, with its burial mounds, the site of the earliest known Neolithic village in Ireland. Stonehenge, which may actually have originated in Wales, and a host of lesser standing stone sites."

"Newgrange," Chase said, chiming in. "I thought that place was interesting because the sunlight shines in through its entrance for only seventeen minutes each day at dawn."

"A lot of the builders of these sites were clearly fascinated with astronomy," Dolores said.

"And the dead," Kiley added.

"And Elise visited all of them," Chase said.

"She also visited several places associated with St. Patrick," Dolores said. "There was Croagh Patrick, his holy mountain."

"The Blarney Stone at Blarney Castle," Kiley continued. "The Rock of Cashel in Muenster where the old boy supposedly used a three-leaf clover to explain the Holy Trinity to the local king. Apparently the Rock originated twenty miles away in the middle of a mountain range called the Devil's Bit where St. Patrick supposedly banished Satan."

"And of course Glastonbury," Kiley said with an exhausted sigh. "Supposedly the last resting place of King Arthur and maybe even the Holy Grail not to mention a great concert venue."

"That's a lot of material to sift through," Dolores said.

"And don't forget the Bridgton Triangle," Kiley said.

"The Bridgton Triangle?" Dolores repeated. "That's just a local legend isn't it?"

"Well," Kiley began, seemingly determined to enlighten Dolores on the subject, "the Triangle stretches as far south as Gevaudan's northern tip and as far north as North Wickham centered around Holy Hill Swamp on the west side of Bridgton, not too far from where we are right now. The train tracks on the far side of the commuter lot we parked in run along the swamp's eastern border."

"I didn't think it was so near," Dolores said.

"Most people don't realize how many tributaries there are to the Holy Hill Swamp," Kiley continued. "A lot of weird stuff has happened in the Triangle over the years. I wrote a paper on it for an anthropology class; Joseph Campbell would have loved it. There were Indian massacres from the earliest Indian wars in the late 1600s, massacres where entire families in isolated cabins were murdered by local war parties, followed by the equally bloody reprisals by British troops. Plenty of ghostly sightings remain as testament to all those gruesome events.

"Then, beginning in the 1960s, things *really* got weird. There were reported big foot sightings, ghostly camp fires, mysterious hooded figures, UFO sightings, and even cult-like incidents occurring in the 70s and 80s— slaughtered animals in the woods, pentagram carvings on stones, tombs and graves disturbed. Tombstones turned over, even bodies removed from coffins, bones missing. A lot of weird things have happened in this area." Kiley shook her head slowly. "Maybe this place is cursed or simply a magnet for weird occurrences."

"That's just lovely," Dolores said, flipping the notebook shut. "I *would* like to get some sleep tonight, thank you."

"You've never heard about the Triangle?" Kiley asked with a twinge of incredulity.

"I'm from East Boston. Our ghosts are associated with the Revolution. And I was *never* into the occult."

"You don't know what you've been missing," Kiley said. "Many of the Bridgton Triangle cases are still unsolved. And that motorcycle gang, the Ghosts, hang out at Jones Beach on Bell Rock Pond at the southern tip of the old Indian reservation near Old Dominion Road. So you see this area is not without its own skeletons in the closet. I suppose it's possible that these trips to ancient sites by the Mckenna women have nothing to do with these bizarre events. Maybe local supernatural forces are responsible. Or at least local individuals who value those legends and want to capitalize on them for their own warped reasons."

"You mean cults," Dolores said.

"We keep coming back to that word, don't we?" Chase said in a sing-song voice.

"I wonder if the police have reached the same conclusion," Kiley said.

"I don't see *any* conclusion," Dolores said. "We may be dealing with a cult, but those other incidents involved grave robbery and vandalism, not murder."

"Maybe the cult, if it *is* a cult, has stepped up its agenda?" Kiley said. "Maybe they've switched from animal killings to *people* killings? Or maybe it's a new, completely different cult?"

"Can we finish with Europe before we start in on America?" Chase said.

"Agreed," Dolores said.

"Oh, wait," Kiley said. "There's something on this webpage I found about our old friend St. Patrick that struck me as odd." She took the notebook from Dolores and flipped through it. "Caorthannach," she said.

"What the hell is that?" Chase said.

"Well, we know that Elise was spending a lot of time at sites in Ireland associated with St. Patrick, right?"

"Yes." Dolores leaned in closer.

"St. Patrick is credited with ridding the Emerald Isle of snakes, right?"

Chase and Dolores nodded in unison.

"Well, that's probably symbolic for his driving Paganism out of Ireland and ushering in Christianity, but there was this legend about this demon that St. Patrick found on his holy mountain, a demon that refused to leave. But old Pat got a horse, chased the thing down and cast it into the sea."

"Snakes," Dolores said. "Another word for villains? Criminals?"

Chase nodded. "Could be. Kiley, what sort of demon was this Caor…"

"Caorthannach," Kiley said. "It was a fire demon."

A strange hush fell over the room. The sound of wind through distant branches was the only noise.

"Could some group be following St. Patrick's lead?" Dolores said, breaking the stillness, her voice low. "Driving the snakes out of Gevaudan, using this fire demon as inspiration?"

"If that's true, what about the other cases?" Chase asked. "Greece and Ireland?"

"Well, Ireland fits right in," Kiley said. "Place of origin and all. Greece *could* be a copycat…"

"Maybe this is an international cult," Dolores said.

"Oh God," Kiley said softly, pulling her hands away from the keyboard as if something might leap from the computer at any moment and bite her fingers. "What the hell are we into here?"

"Okay," Chase said, raising his hands as if in surrender. "It's late and we're all tired. The cult angle is an interesting one and worth looking into, but for now let's call it a night."

"Agreed," Dolores said, considering the stack of books she and Chase had pulled from the shelves.

"Do we need to re-shelve those?" she asked.

"No, the staff checks these rooms every morning," Kiley said.

Dolores nodded and handed Kiley the numerous copies she'd made.

"I've always liked research." Kiley tucked the sheets of paper into her knapsack. "You learn things."

"I'm a researcher by trade," Dolores said sighing and shaking her head slowly, "but this was a bit of overkill."

"All right," Kiley began, "summing up, we've researched every demon from Abaddon and Abraxas to Kali as well as witches from Ancient Greece to Salem. We've checked into the history of cults and sects including the Templar Knights and their purported descendants the Freemasons, as well as the Branch Davidians, the Ku Klux Klan, Jim Jones' People's Temple, the so-called Illuminati, Charles Manson's Family, and even Scientology. Not to mention ancient cults that worshiped everything from serpents to the fine art of cannibalism, Indian cults of assassins, the Thuggees—"

"Like in that Indiana Jones movie," Chase added, enthusiastically.

"You must forgive him," Dolores said. "Chase gets all his information from old movies and pop culture."

"Bronze Age cults in Judea associated with Baal," Kiley resumed. "The assassins that tried twice to kill Saladin…it just goes on forever. We've also looked into various forms of human sacrifice and cultures throughout history that participated in such rituals. The Carthaginians who sacrificed babies to appease the gods, ancient Israelites who purportedly sacrificed children to a Canaanite God called Moloch.

"Next we have the Etruscans. Then the Chinese, who committed ritual sacrifices, particularly during the Shang Dynasty. Then we have the Celts and the Druids and their Wicker man sacrifices. The ancient Hawaiians also got into the act, sacrificing enemy chiefs to feed their God of War, Ku. The Mesopotamians used poison, the Aztecs sacrificed volunteers to feed their sun god.

"And don't forget the Egyptians and the Incas," Kiley continued, undaunted. "But most of these cultures either sacrificed prisoners, servants, or specially chosen, well-treated victims. In many cultures being sacrificed was an honor. And *nowhere* is there any mention of people being *both* ritualistically burned alive and mangled as if by an animal."

Dolores rubbed her temples. "I have a headache."

"And we've just scratched the surface. If this *is* a cult committing these ritualistic killings, they may be derivative, using different elements from past cultures as well as some aspects that they've dreamed up to carry out these murders."

"Maybe we've missed something."

"I'll do some research on my own," Kiley said.

"Good idea," Chase said, stretching. "Let's get the hell out of Dodge before they lock us in for the night. I…" He frowned, his eyes straying to the open webpage.

"Kiley, what's that symbol mean?" he said.

"Oh this," she said, pointing to a pentagram that occupied one corner of the page. "That's a Wiccan symbol for protection against evil."

"No," Chase said, leaning closer, "*that* one." He pointed to a circular tangle of lines in the lower left corner of the page.

"That's like the medallion that was hanging on Elise Mckenna's bedroom door," Dolores said.

"It's a Celtic shield," Kiley said.

"A good luck charm?" Chase said.

"In a way, I suppose," Kiley said. "Its original purpose was to ward off evil, profound evil."

***

Allison Mckenna was sitting on the balcony of her expensive apartment, nursing three fingers of an equally expensive Scotch, watching the crescent moon emerge from the clouds. She'd been awakened by the latest in an unending string of nightmares, nightmares that usually began with her standing by watching helplessly as some dark, shadowy entity tore her daughter to shreds and ending with her doing the same thing to someone she'd known only from an image, an image she'd seen only briefly on television or in a newspaper. And once on a surveillance video. And once in person. This time she'd dreamed of Detective Teschal. Little wonder after the woman's unexpected visit, and the attitude she'd seen fit to drag along with her. In the dream Mckenna had been watching Teschal as she walked down a shadowy corridor, alone. And as she rushed toward her, Teschal had abruptly turned and called out.

And then Mckenna had awakened, bathed in sweat, sobbing, doubled over, her body pulsing with an unimaginable terror. It was always the same—*almost* always. Tonight she hadn't caught up with Teschal. And for that she was grateful.

She glanced at her watch. It was late, and she was still dressed, sort of. Sweats and sneakers had become the norm as of late. And occasionally a bath robe. But who cared? And in spite of the late hour, she was desperate. She needed air, even if it was stale and humid air. A drive would do her some good, maybe clear her head. And the dream had filled her with an almost frantic need for human companionship and the counsel of the one human being on Earth who might appreciate her predicament and even empathize with her. Maybe, just maybe, if he would agree to see her at this hour, she could find a little solace. She only hoped he would understand.

She considered the horns of the moon, silently pleading for the dreams to leave her in peace, for sanity to visit her one last time before she died.

The moon looked down, cold, complacent, uncaring. And thunder rumbled in the west.

Before the sound faded, Mckenna had gathered her purse and her keys and donned a trench coat she kept hanging in a closet by the door, and set out into the night.

Chapter Forty-Seven

It was much too late for visitors, or so Father Jean Rousseau was thinking as he made his way downstairs to answer the bell to the vicarage door. Maybe someone from the previous night's visage had come to speak with him, thank him for holding the vigil on church property. But that seemed unlikely. Fortunately, instead of being in bed Rousseau had been watching a Seinfeld re-run. *Tres amusant!*

But awake or not, the knocking at this hour was enough to shatter any jovial mood. "*Que'est-ce que ca peut ben faire?*" he thought aloud. "What the hell?"

Rousseau reached the doorway to the kitchen, which was thick with the sort of deep shadowy silence that seemed to thrive in old buildings. The bars of moonlight streaming in through the big windows above the double-sink were glinting off the hanging pots and pans and gathering on the spotless checkerboard floor. Mrs. Cote, the vicarage cook and housekeeper, was long gone.

He moved through the kitchen, flipped on the front hall light and went to the door. He peered through the narrow windows at the sides of the heavy wood door, but even with the porch light on, all he could see were shadows. Kids no doubt he thought, playing *ding-dong ditch* as he and his friends had while growing up on the north side of Montreal.

"Who is it?" he asked.

"Father Rousseau," a woman called. Her voice was raw, distressed.

Rousseau carefully unlocked the door, pried it open a few inches and peered through. Gevaudan was a city with many bad actors and one couldn't be too careful. And he was not young anymore. He'd never been a boxer, he'd managed to avoid that particular cliché, but he had played Lacrosse and some rugby and had been more than capable of handling himself in any scrum be it on-field or off. Not that there was much worth stealing in the vicarage. The Catholic Church, like many religious institutions, was in decline. There was no gold for the taking, no Templar treasure hidden beneath the floorboards. Just a few trinkets of his late mother's tucked away, and of course the old building's fixtures.

But his job was to assist those in need, and the wretched face that presented itself was that of someone in *dire* need.

"Father," the woman said.

Rousseau needed a moment to put a name to the distraught face. When he finally did, his first thought was, *My God, what has happened?*

The woman was a parishioner, though not a regular as of late. She was terribly disheveled, her hair mussed, her clothes wrinkled. But that was understandable, considering the ordeal he knew she'd been through. The porch light was hardly flattering, but it was honest. Rousseau considered the deep dark circles beneath her eyes, the gaunt cheeks. She was the very image of death warmed up. *Mort.*

"Mrs. Mckenna," he said, the name coming back to him like a lost dog. "Good God, come inside."

***

Chase was standing on Dolores' veranda watching the clouds consume the stars and the sliver of moon. Dolores was in the kitchen making a pot of late night coffee.

"What'cha doing?" she called playfully.

"Looking at the stars," he said, his hands on the cool damp railing, "before they disappear again."

"More things in heaven and earth," she said as she stepped out onto the veranda with two mugs of steaming coffee.

Chase took one and Dolores nestled up beside him. He wrapped his arm around her.

"Here comes the rain again," she said.

"Eurhythmics," Chase said. "Always liked the video. Ethereal. Very Hound of the Baskervillish. The moors of Dartmoor, a fitting place for dark and mysterious things."

Dolores sipped some coffee. "I feel cold and raw. I can't seem to warm up."

He drew her closer. A long silent moment passed between them—there was no discomfort.

"What are you thinking?" she asked.

"The same thing you are. I'm wondering what's going on here? I'm wondering if Teschal is doing the same sort of research we're doing, or if we've just gone 'round the bend? Overactive imaginations. Ghosts, witches, and demons, oh my."

"A non-believer?"

"Let's just say the jury is still out. You?"

"Same. But something did happen once, a long time ago. I was a senior in high school," she began, her eyes filling with moonlight. "My friends and I managed to sneak into a dorm party at Bridgton. It was still a college then, not as big as it is now. Rolled up the sidewalks before 10 p.m. No metal detectors at the dorm doors. It was a snowy night. My mother thought I was staying at a friend's. She rarely asked or cared. My girlfriends and I decided it best to find someplace to crash for the night instead of risking the ride home.

"Anyway, we found ourselves in the room of the older sister of one of my friends. There were maybe a half dozen of us, not exactly drunk but feeling little pain. This was in a big corner room on the top floor of Woodridge

Hall, the oldest building on campus. Creaky old place, lots of nooks and crannies. Shadows where there shouldn't be any shadows. Well, one of the girls brought out this Ouija board she'd found in a closet at the beginning of the year."

Dolores held the coffee against her chest as if trying to absorb its warmth.

"We decided to play. I sat down cross-legged on one side of a small coffee table and my girlfriend did the same opposite me. There was one woman lying in bed beside us, and another woman sitting behind me. My other friend had gone prowling the halls looking for a date. And then there was my friend Jeff, the guy who got us into the party to begin with, sitting beside us on the floor between these two windows. I remember the wind howling, the quad filling up with the white stuff. You could hear the windows shuddering in their old frames.

"Anyway, we started asking questions, stupid questions at first, questions that we couldn't verify at the time, questions young girls tend to ask like, 'Will I get married,' and such. Jeff chimed in and asked a question I'll never forget. He asked the board what the initials of his parents' second child were. Well that planchete thing moved across the board with no hesitation at all. It picked three letters. JRR. The woman opposite me, Karen was her name, frowned and turned to Jeff. 'You're the oldest', she said. 'I thought your younger brother's name was Robert?' I didn't even know Jeff *had* a brother. Or *sister* for that matter. But when I looked up at him his face was bone white. He was shaking, and he was a big physical guy, a rugby player, not the type to get rattled."

Dolores drew in a long breath as if summoning a degree of courage in order to finish the story.

"I remember his words to this day. He said, 'I forgot,' his voice faltering, 'my parents' second child was John Ronald Robillard. But he died at birth.'"

"Is that true?"

Dolores nodded solemnly.

"I never told anybody that story," she said, her voice a hoarse whisper. "But it happened. Needless to say that was the end of our Ouija boarding for the night. I didn't sleep a wink, I just kept listening to the wind moaning outside and the old wood windows rattling like bones. So maybe Hamlet was right about there being more things in heaven and earth. Maybe, just maybe, there's something really strange going on here. And maybe we're not prepared for what we may find. And realizing that scares the hell out of me."

***

Allison Mckenna was sitting in the vicarage kitchen at the long table sipping tea, Father Rousseau across from her trying to read her eyes through the dark circles that seemed ready to consume them. They'd been blue once, or so he thought. A priest was not supposed to notice the color of a woman's eyes. But Mckenna's eyes had been striking. Alive. Vivid. But tonight they seemed to be looking out from the face of a corpse, the whites reddened and the life seemingly ebbing from them.

"This is a bit unusual," he said, hesitantly, almost wincing, "but when I realized that it was you—"

"I'm sorry. I couldn't sleep and I've been having terrible dreams."

"About Elise?"

"Yes, some," she said, her eyes studying the mug of tea. "But mostly about the man who killed her, the man on the video from the nightclub."

"Have you spoken with the counselor the police recommended?"

Mckenna shook her head slowly. She brought the teacup to her lips but did not sip it. The steam rose before her eyes like fog.

"I haven't seen you at the Survivors' Group either."

Again she shook her head.

"That man who killed your daughter is *dead*," Rousseau said. "God intervened. And justice was served."

"I don't know if God intervened," she said softly. "I don't know *anything*."

"We can't know such things. That's the mystery of faith. Think of it this way if it helps—if God did *not* provide justice, then fate or the universe did. You had *nothing* to do with that man's death."

"Then why did I dream it?"

"You saw it on the news." Rousseau took her hand. It was impossibly cold. "The images got into your subconscious. And you were completely overwrought."

Mckenna raised her eyes. They were dark, bottomless.

"What is it?" Rousseau said, sensing a chill. A branch scratched at the window pane.

"I dreamed it the night it happened," she said softly. "*Before* I saw it on the news."

A shadow crossed Rousseau's craggy face. "But..." he began, not knowing how to proceed. "You must be mistaken—"

"I woke up screaming, because in my dream *I* was killing that man."

"That's not possible." Rousseau released Mckenna's icy fingers. "Your dream was perfectly normal under the circumstances. You shouldn't feel guilty about being human, about being a mother. I assure you, God understands. *And* forgives you."

"Does he?"

"God forgives *all* who ask for forgiveness."

"But I saw the flames and the blood." She breathed a heavy sigh and a strange sliver of a smile touched her lips. "And this is the part that bothers me the most—I *liked* it."

***

Teschal was sitting in her living room, nursing some white wine, bathed in the glow of a large candle and some Elgar playing softly on the CD player on the mantle above the fireplace, thinking. She'd tried to sleep, but decidedly unwelcome things kept creeping into her mind, things concerning the case. Things like the dead eyes of Anthony Lee Carver gazing at her through the slits of his black leather mask, the flaming skull on the back of Lyle Chisholm's vest, strange ethereal sounds drifting down darkened corridors, the foul pungent smell of sulfur. And then the events of the previous summer came calling, adding to the mix, gruesome events that had transpired in nearby Wickham, events that had culminated late one night in a darkened ICU at Mercy General Hospital with the smell of burnt offerings hanging in the summer air, and the smoke shrouding the fiery face of the blue thunder moon. It was a night she would always remember, a night no human being could ever forget. And some dark voice in her head was telling her that this case was heading in the same direction, was somehow carved from the same ancient rune.

And so she had gotten out of bed, gone to the kitchen and poured herself some wine and turned on the Elgar, one of her mother's favorites. Now, bathed in the flickering glow, hoping perhaps to channel Vadoma Teschal, to channel her *own* shamanistic abilities, her thoughts turned back to the case. There were things here that were impossibly wrong. Her mother had told her as a girl that the universe was so much bigger than anyone knew, and so much more mysterious than could be imagined. And it was in this nether-region, this dimension lying between realities, where answers were often found, realizations achieved. It was like walking into a dark room and trying to find a penny and finding it on the first try.

Teschal believed that there *was* magic in the universe, though it rarely showed itself. And she believed that there was evil as well, evil so deep and dark and profound that it reeked of…of brimstone.

Yet nothing tangible presented itself. But something in her mind *did* click. It was like a key turning a tumbler. And whatever *it* was that had jolted her, *it* was telling her clearly that answers were not to be found in the phrases of Elgar or in the safety of her candle-lit living room. These were her mother's trappings, not hers. The jolt she'd felt was Eve Isla Teschal finally coming to terms with *her gypsyhood, her romipen,* realizing that *her* trappings, *her* signs, came from a different place than her mother's, her *diya's.* Eve Teschal's trappings, her inspirations, were out there in the night waiting for her to find them.

Teschal set the wine glass down on the coffee table, blew out the candle, picked up the remote and silenced Elgar. She went to the bedroom closet where she retrieved her gun from the locked safe in the back corner. She loaded it, slipped it into its holster and fastened it around her shoulder. Then she slipped into a thin leather jacket and headed out. She would simply drive around for an hour or so, thinking, looking for the magic hiding in the seams of the universe. And the evil.

"It will find you," Vadoma Teschal had said.

And Eve Teschal thought, *Ma-sha-llah*; as God, as Del, wills it.

***

Father Rousseau watched from the second-floor hall window of the vicarage as Mckenna drove off in her Volvo. He'd listened to her sad vague ramblings, walked her to her car and waited until she'd started the engine before letting himself back into the vicarage. He felt uncomfortable. Not just because Mckenna was a woman, a single woman no less, visiting him at this hour, but because she was a *disturbed* woman, a woman consumed by grief and perhaps something else. And there was anger and hatred, hatred of the dead man responsible for her daughter's death, hatred of herself for not intervening when it had been humanly possible. Maybe even hatred of God for letting it all happen. And Father Rousseau knew that he hadn't helped her one bit. She was beyond his help. Allison Mckenna needed divine intervention to save her drowning soul. Maybe even a psychiatrist and a place where she'd be safe from herself.

But she was an adult and he was not a family member and therefore unable to contact the authorities and request a Section Twelve. And she had committed no crime, had not endangered herself or others and therefore was free to come and go as she pleased. He'd recommended therapy, had even seen her at one of Jennifer Tinsley's Survivors' Group meetings. But she'd failed to return for a second visit. And so there was little he could do but make recommendations and be a shoulder for her to cry on when needed. In the end Mckenna was alone with her grief. And her hatred.

Yet there was something else, something unseen clinging to her, like a parasite. Rousseau could sense *it*, whatever *it* was, hiding there in her soul, behind her eyes watching. He'd glimpsed it tonight when she'd told him how she'd relished her dream about killing the man who'd murdered her daughter. And he was suddenly afraid for her. *Spiritually* afraid.

But it was late and he was aching for a good night's sleep, but very much doubting he'd find one this night. He turned to look back through the window at his church across the street one last time before turning in. It was something he did every night. It was a habit that granted him a degree of solace. The old gray stones could be oddly comforting at all the right times and in all the right ways. But tonight something caught his eye, something near the side door of Saint Genevieve's, something strange and disquieting.

He spread the curtains, straining to see clearly.
"What the—"

***

Eloise hit the switch for line seven which caused the blinking light to become steady.

"Gevaudan Police Department, this call is being recorded." Listening to the caller she nodded slowly, a frown growing on her dark face.

"Yes sir, uh, Father, I'll send someone right over. Saint Genevieve's church. I'd advise you to wait until a cruiser arrives at the scene. I'm going to put you on hold while I speak with the nearest patrol unit. Please stay on the line."

Eloise hit the hold button, glanced around the silent lobby and picked up her mobile phone. She punched in some numbers and waited as the line began to ring.

***

Chase picked up his mobile phone and said hello.

Dolores looked up from her side of the bed. They'd dozed off while studying Kiley's notes which were spread across the bed.

"It's your associate," Eloise said. "I don't know if your stringing ass is interested, but this one was a little weird so I figured I'd call."

"Sure, I'm open to suggestions."

"Well, there's a call from a priest about a possible break in at a church, Saint Genevieve's."

"Not exactly a plane crash on Route 495, but it could prove interesting," Chase said.

"Well, you said to keep my ear to the rail for weird calls and a burglary at a church is pretty weird, but if you're not—"

"I'm interested. I guess only a real weirdo would want to break into a church."

"Or someone in desperate need of redemption," Eloise said. "Hint, hint. I hope the place doesn't burst into flames when *you* get there. Or maybe that should be the other way around."

"What's going on?" Dolores said, rolling closer.

Chase covered the mouthpiece. "Little job, no big deal. I won't be..." Chase paused, reached over and took Dolores by the hand. "Hey, want to take another ride?"

"I don't know. I haven't recovered from the *last* ride."

"Don't worry," he said grinning. "This one's no problem, just a little prowler, that's all. Probably nothing."

"Sure. There ain't no Indians down there General Custer."

"Huh?"

"Famous last words."

Chapter Forty-Eight

Father Rousseau considered the phone in his hand and the elevator music emanating from it. He put the thing to his ear and looked out the window. The side door to the church and the small courtyard that it opened into were lost to the shadows cast by the numerous pine trees lining the adjacent street and the nearest buttress. The figure he thought he'd seen was gone, the strange glow as well. Had the prowler gained access to the church somehow? Rousseau wondered if he'd forgotten to lock the side door. It certainly wouldn't be the first time. Or most likely the last.

He studied the phone. He'd actually called the police. Damn. Hasty? Perhaps. Better safe than sorry though. Or so he'd heard.

He set the receiver in its cradle and cursed aloud. It was hardly the Christian thing to do, but he'd called the police without checking things himself. Well, better late than never.

He went downstairs, shrugged a light-weight runner's jacket on and opened the door. He stepped out into the cool night—the breeze was refreshing. Summer was approaching. The days were still tolerable though, the typical New England humidity not yet taking hold.

Rousseau looked to his left, toward the intersection as a spattering of cars drove past, then over his right shoulder at the small colonial cemetery beside the vicarage with its slender leaning tombstones and wrought iron fence. No movement there. He sniffed the sir, smelled a wood stove. He raised his eyes heavenward. The drizzle had eased and some stars and the crescent moon were visible through the broken cloud cover.

The sound of the vicarage telephone jangling in its cradle found him—the police calling back because he'd hung up. Standard operating procedure. He paused, wondering whether he should go back, answer the thing and wait for the police to arrive like some sort of frightened invalid. But this was *his* church, *his* responsibility, and to wait would be feeble and pathetic. And feeling feeble was something he'd never been able to tolerate. Time may have claimed his youth, but it had not touched his pride. Or his stubborn streak.

And so Rousseau closed the door on the persistent ringing and started down the cobbled path. He reached the deserted street, looked both ways out of habit, crossed, and started up the walkway that led to the side door of Saint Genevieve's.

He noticed a light in the nun's quarters across the street, on the other side of the square nestled between the funeral home and the big stony bones of Saint Genevieve's Catholic School. Ground floor. The library. Yes. That young nun, what's her name, Benedict, something-or-other, reading again. Well, there was nothing wrong with that. Youth; they never seemed to sleep.

Rousseau continued up the path, drawing the key from his pocket as he took hold of the big door's wrought iron handle. It felt oddly warm. He frowned, looked around. There was a gentle breeze stirring the shrubs and the trees. A cat cried out, its voice ethereal, haunting, caught up on the wind. Nothing unusual about that, Gevaudan was a city and there were strays everywhere.

He slipped the big key into the lock and turned it. The latch clicked. The door had been locked all along. No harm in checking though.

He pushed open the heavy wood door, stepped inside. The darkness was palpable, only some dim light seeping through the stained-glass windows set into the opposite wall of the church, which ran parallel to Church

Green Road. He was greeted by the familiar sense of the church's cavernous innards, the arched ceiling rising into dark oblivion above him. And there was the sensation of air moving through the rafters, the building breathing.

Rousseau had experienced this many times while sitting at his desk in the office in the back hall. He'd even gone so far as to peek into the hall and once or twice into the church itself when he was certain he'd heard something, only to find that he was completely alone. It was simply a familiar peculiarity the building possessed, as if the stones were alive. But tonight the sensation was stronger, less ethereal. More *real*.

The cat cried out again, piercing the stillness.

"Damn," Rousseau said aloud, regretting his indiscretion immediately. "Forgive me," he said softly.

Had he heard someone laughing?

He felt a chill, fought it back. *Damn*, he thought. This was *his* church, *his* home. But that was vain, Saint Genevieve's was in fact *God's* home, one of many. But he was its custodian and his job was clear.

Gathering his wits, he set out for the vestry and the bank of light switches. He could see the outline of the altar to his right and the vast array of pews to his left, his eyes slowly adjusting to the folds of blackness. He could make out the massive columns lining the great space and the stained-glass windows featuring the stations-of-the-cross.

The sound came again, louder. Less cat-like. And it had *definitely* come from *inside* the church.

Something snagged Rousseau's eye. A light. No, a glow coming from the chancel beyond the altar.

Dear God, he thought, there *was* an intruder in his church, an intruder who had brought a terrible chill along with him, a strangely familiar chill. It was a sensation that he had felt only once before while on an archaeological dig in Great Britain when he was a curate chasing Iron Age ghosts. But that had been many moons ago; this was happening tonight!

The glow began to creep closer, growing brighter as it approached, moving out in front of the altar, down the steps and toward the head of the aisle, moving toward *him*. The cat sound came again, louder, different somehow. Not a cat at all. Not anything of this earth.

"Oh God—" he heard himself say. And then the flames were consuming him. And through the flames he saw the face, if that's what it could be called. And then the searing pain was inside him and his hair was burning. He raised his hands. They were smoldering and the flesh was falling away in blackened, bubbling clumps and he felt something tear at his stomach.

***

"So this is how it works," Dolores said. "This woman calls you and you try to beat the cops to the scene, get some video, a few pictures, and then rush them to your friend, Connie, who you shag, oh, for the hell of it."

They were driving along Church Green Road toward Saint Genevieve's Square, Chase at the wheel.

"That part bothers you," Chase said.

"No, no. Well, *yes*, it bothers me. I'm not quite *that* progressive a thinker."

Chase grinned.

"You like me being jealous," Dolores said, punching his arm.

"Yes," he confirmed. "It's good for my ego."

"Oh yeah?" Dolores retrieved her mobile phone from her purse. "I wonder what Connie would have to say about this? Maybe I should just make a call? What do you think of that?"

"Yes, call right now."

"Really? I should—"

"—call the fire department, fast. 911."

"What?"

"That's Saint Genevieve's up ahead," Chase said. "And that light in the window, those are flames."

"Christ," Dolores said punching in the numbers.

Chase veered sharply up onto the curb, slammed the SUV into park and rolled out the driver's side. He was suddenly operating on some semblance of auto-pilot, scrambling along the sidewalk and then crossing onto the lawn, losing his footing on the wet grass, mounting the few steps to the huge main doors, trying the big wrought iron handles, finding the doors to be locked, and running around to the side door.

He reached the smaller door, seized the handles and hauled it open. The heavy door slammed against the outer wall with a resounding thud. But before Chase could enter, a flaming apparition appeared before him, knocking him aside, bathing him briefly in an intense wave of heat and light. He fell sideways, landing hard on the stone flags inside the foyer. He raised his eyes, choking back the cloud of acrid smoke swirling around him, and saw, for a fleeting instant, a ghastly, glowing apparition hovering near the far end of the altar. He watched, dazed, as the image flickered, faded and vanished leaving only a twisting column of smoke in its wake. And the pungent smell of hydrogen sulfide. Then there came the sound of a cat howling at the darkness somewhere within the church walls. Chase was on his hands and knees, scampering through the slowly closing door, then running, half stumbling toward the smoldering heap writhing on the lawn.

He tore off his sweat shirt and fell beside the blistering shape, wrapping his shirt around the squirming pile of charred flesh, extinguishing what remained of the flames, which had clearly and horribly burned away most of the clothing the person had been wearing as well as a good portion of the skin. The melted face turned to Chase, its one remaining eye locking on his. Then a shriveled, charred claw of a hand grabbed him by the collar and pulled him close with the inhuman strength of a dying man.

Chase fell forward, nearly landing on top of the figure his eyes inches from the bubbling mass that had recently been a face. The man craned his neck, pressed what was left of his lips to Chase's ear and hissed a series of words, a phrase perhaps.

"Ambulance is coming," was all Chase could think to say. His voice was little more than a harsh whisper. His stomach was churning with what remained of his last meal.

Then the fingers loosened and the hand fell away, flopping down onto the lawn. And the rest of the grisly molten shape slowly crumpled in upon itself.

Chapter Forty-Nine

Chase was seated on the curb, a hooded beach shirt he'd kept in the way back of his SUV clinging to his sweat-bathed body, his other shirt ruined, taken into evidence by forensics for chemical analysis. The taste of death was on his lips, the terrible odor of burned flesh and sulfur filling his being. It was a smell he'd never forget, no matter how hard he'd try. And the image of what he'd seen was seared forever into his brain.

He raised his eyes before the pulsing glow of emergency vehicle LEDs: police cruisers, fire engines, ambulances (one of the stripped-down versions from the Medical Examiner's office and one fully functioning one that had been called for him, until he'd managed to explain that there was no need). He had simply been part of an attempted rescue that had gone terribly wrong, his physical wounds were minimal. His psychological ones were another matter.

He sensed an arm draped across his shoulders. Dolores was sitting beside him, gazing into the confusion. She turned to him, forced a sad smile and squeezed his shoulder.

"I think I'm falling in love with you," she said.

Chase simply nodded, smiled weakly. He'd wanted to say more, would have given *anything* to have said more, but a grim little smile was all he could muster at that moment. He felt his gaze being drawn to Bonner's Funeral Home, which was perched on a grassy incline across the street from the church. Beside it stood the convent where the nuns of Saint Genevieve's Order lived. Adjacent to this stood the Catholic school of the same name where they taught. His gaze drifted past the building, across the clogged intersection, past Dolores and the mild look of dejection gracing her lovely face, to the vicarage with its lighted windows now bustling with unholy activity.

"Where's Teschal?" he said, his throat smoke-raw.

"I tell you that I'm falling in love with you, and that's what you think to ask?"

"I love you too," he said, meaning it, or perhaps just putting her off. He was still drifting outside his body and in no state of mind for such a declaration.

"She's across the street talking with the sisters. Are you all right?"

"Swell. Listen, why don't you go over there, see what you can hear."

"Always the stringer. You're sure you're okay?"

Chase nodded. "Sure. Under the circumstances."

Dolores nodded, kissed his cheek and brushed a few strands of his hair aside. "I accept your apology, under the circumstances."

She offered him a wan smile, got to her feet and started up the sidewalk. She reached the rear of the church and started across the street, weaving amongst the clutch of near-motionless cars, her eyes set on the gathering of nuns at the door to the convent building. And Teschal.

***

"This is Sister Benevides," the woman in the dark colored robe said. "She was in the study reading when the fire broke out."

A young sister wearing a sweat suit approached Teschal slowly, meekly. Her pale face was stained with tears. In one hand was a tattered old book. The other hand was clutching a silver crucifix that hung about her neck.

"It's all right, Sister," the older nun said. Her hair was silver, her eyes warm. She gently took the young woman's hand and urged her closer.

"Sister Benevides," Teschal began. "Can you tell me what happened?"

Richards was by Teschal's side, notebook and pen at the ready. Officers were moving among the many onlookers asking questions, searching the shadows by the funeral home, probing the shrubs dotting the landscape of the busy square with flashlights. Shadowy figures armed with flashlights were also moving through the schoolyard of the adjoining Catholic school. The windows of the school were completely alight as if the place were alive with some late-night activity, a parents' association meeting or school pageant. However the shadowy figures moving past the big glowing windows were not proud grinning parents but rather grim-faced uniformed police officers searching for a killer.

"I was reading in the study." Sister Benevides pointed to a lighted first-floor window in the stone and brick structure behind her. "There was a breeze so I'd opened the window. I've smelled smoke before at night. Wood stoves are common, even when it's warm. And fire pits. We have a wood stove, though it wasn't in use tonight. I was looking out the window. I like to watch the cars go by, see their lights moving through the square, think about where they might be going. And I like to look at the church. It's a solid, friendly place. Used to…"

Her lips moved silently before her voice returned.

"I didn't grow up in a very stable home. This is the best home I've ever known."

"And what made you call the fire department?" Teschal asked, her voice surprisingly soft.

"I saw a glow through the stained-glass window." Her eyes turned reluctantly toward Saint Genevieve's stone edifice. "Just there." She pointed a trembling finger. "Closest to the altar—the seventh sign of the cross—the first six are on the other side."

Teschal nodded slowly, realizing that the young woman was referring to the design cut into that particular stained-glass window.

"I got up so fast I dropped my book. I have it now," she added, holding the tattered copy of *To Kill a Mockingbird* out to show the detective, before letting her hand drop to her side.

"I've read it every summer since I was a little girl," she said softly. "I went to the window and I just knew that it was a fire. Oh God." Sister Benevides suddenly gasped into her palm.

The older nun took the young woman in her arms and held her as she struggled to regain her composure. After a moment Sister Benevides nodded, wiped her eyes with a tissue the older nun provided. The book slipped from her hands and landed on the walkway. Teschal stooped down, picked it up and handed it back to the sister, who offered the detective a frightened little smile.

"Sister," Teschal prompted, "did you see anything unusual tonight, maybe someone near the church? A strange car perhaps?"

"Well," she said, glancing warily at the older nun as if wondering if she should continue. "Father Rousseau *did* have a visitor."

"A visitor?"

"You must be mistaken," the older nun chimed in. "She's overwrought—"

Teschal raised her hand to silence the woman and Richards leaned in closer.

"When was this?" Teschal asked.

Sister Benevides shrugged. "Past eleven I think."

"What exactly did you see?"

"I saw her leave," the young sister said softly, her eyes moving nervously between Teschal and the older nun.

"Father Rousseau would not have a visitor at this hour," the older nun insisted. "Certainly *not* a woman."

"Did you see a car? Maybe a license plate?" Teschal prompted, ignoring the older nun's protestations.

"Yes, I saw a car. But I didn't need to see the license plate, I knew who owned it. I'd seen her there before, several times. Father Rousseau was counseling her, the girl's mother. She used to go to mass at Saint G's, Saint Genevieve's I mean, Saturday evenings, she and her daughter. I'd seen Father Rousseau speaking to them on the church steps. The girl was studying about old religious buildings…but she died."

Teschal felt her gut tighten and she glanced at Richards who'd set his jaw and was nodding slowly.

"It was Ms. Mckenna who stopped in to see Father Rousseau. Allison Mckenna."

"You're sure?" Teschal prompted.

Sister Benevides nodded. "Positive."

"How long after Ms. Mckenna left before you saw the glow?"

"Oh, not more than a half hour or so. And then…" The woman's voice cracked and the older nun stepped forward and wrapped her arm around her waist.

"Who'll offer communion," the young sister said, her lips quivering, sobs growing in her throat.

Sister Benevides seemed to slump down into the older nun's arms. Two other nuns moved in to shore her up.

"Thank you," Teschal said. She glanced at Richards, nodded and turned and walked quickly toward the street, her eyes scanning the crowd until they settled on Chase sitting on the curb by the church.

***

Dolores had been hovering by the shrubs that ran between the convent and the funeral home, mingling with curious onlookers, eavesdropping as best she could. Now she was watching Teschal as she headed for the street. She waited a beat and then broke from the onlookers, moving toward the funeral home, pacing Teschal.

Dolores proceeded down the walkway from Bonner's Funeral Parlor, glancing briefly at the people who'd congregated on Bonner's big wrap-around porch, crossing the sidewalk just as Teschal did and stepping off the curb, moving faster now, bobbing between the creeping cars, ignoring the blaring horns and disgruntled shouts emanating from the motorists who'd clearly lost their patience with the traffic jam. When she reached the opposite curb, she walked toward the heart of the square, reaching Chase at nearly the same instant as Teschal.

"I was wondering where you'd gotten to," Teschal said as Dolores appeared. "Hear all you needed to hear?"

"What can I do for you Detective?" Chase said, pulling Teschal's stern glare from Dolores.

"I was just wondering how you managed to end up here at the right moment?" she said curtly.

"Insomnia. Dolores is my neighbor."

"I couldn't sleep either," Dolores volunteered. "We decided to go for a drive. We happened to be passing by when…"

Teschal sighed deeply, turned to consider Dolores, who managed to meet her gaze. Then she turned to Chase.

"Your efforts to help were admirable," she said, her tone genuine. "Perhaps my opinion of you was not entirely accurate." Her eyes held Chase. "But I suppose time will tell."

She considered the long line of cars attempting to traverse Saint Genevieve's Square as two uniformed officers desperately tried to keep the flow civilized.

"Did you see anything strange, anyone running away?" she asked. "Driving away, maybe?"

Chase shook his head. "I saw the glow in the window as we were driving past. I told Dolores to call 911. I parked, sort of, got out and ran to the main doors, but they were locked. Then I went around to the side door. When I opened it the priest ran past me, knocking me down, and...well, just for an instant I looked into the church wondering where the source of the fire was..."

He struggled to dredge up the terrible memory.

"Yes," Teschal prompted.

"And when I looked inside," he managed, "I saw something."

"Some*thing*?"

"Like a fire I guess. At first I thought it was a person. Then it faded. But there was so much smoke."

"Show me."

Dolores helped Chase to his feet and Teschal led the way to an inconspicuous side door near the back of the church a few yards from Chase's parked SUV. Two firefighters emerged from the door in full gear as they arrived, axes in hand. With grim faces they trudged off toward a fire engine with flashing red LEDs that was parked several yards behind Chase's SUV.

"We can't go in," Teschal said, "but if you could point."

Two uniformed police officers were standing just inside the doorway. The main aisle of the church was lined with bulky fire hoses that trailed off toward the door through which Chase had gained access. Two firefighters were moving about inside.

A haze of smoke hung in the air making the statues of a crucified Christ and Mary appear ominous. And the stench of hydrogen sulfide was everywhere.

Teschal stepped into the small foyer, Dolores and Chase by her side.

"There," Chase said pointing toward the near-side of the altar.

"All right. Now, since you've declined medical treatment, you can go home. I'll find you if I need you," Teschal said and Dolores led Chase toward the SUV.

"Oh, there was something else," he said, turning back. He'd been uncertain of what he'd heard the priest say, unsure if he'd actually heard *anything*, but he figured he should tell Teschal everything.

She cocked her head.

"The priest said something to me when we were on the ground and I was putting out the fire."

"What did he say?"

"He said *cri du chat*. Or something like that."

Teschal frowned. "This is a French Parish. Father Rousseau was French, originally from Montreal."

"I speak a little French, Detective," Dolores volunteered. "I took it in high school. That's a common expression. *Cri du chat*—"

"It means cry of the cat," Teschal said.

"Cry of the cat," Dolores affirmed.

"I took French too."

Richards arrived, flanking Teschal.

"Take him home," was all Teschal said and Dolores led Chase toward the car.

Once inside the SUV, Chase on the passenger side, Dolores at the wheel, she turned to him.

"Are you sure that's what he said?"

Chase nodded. "Pretty sure." The flashing LEDs were filling the car with glowing phantoms.

"*Cri du chat* is a medical condition that afflicts some babies," she said. "Superstition insists that cats caused *Cri du chat*. Old wives' tale. The condition leads to physical deformities, extensive medical issues. And when children suffering from *Cri du chat* cry they sound like cats."

"I heard a cat," Chase said. "In the church. And the other night, in the empty house where Derek, the tech at KTX, saw the face in my video. The sound is on the audio of the video I shot."

"Jesus, are you sure?"

"Yeah," Chase said zipping the sweat shirt, "*very sure.*"

Dolores nodded, started the car.

"First thing in the morning we should talk to Kiley. She may be able to dig something up, some cult factoid associated with crying cats that might make sense," he said. "And I should let Connie know what's going on."

"I was wondering when you'd mention her," she said, roughly jamming the SUV into gear and driving down off the curb, slowly merging with the other cars, horns blaring, a rain-coated police officer waving her onward.

The traffic was thinning, beginning to move more quickly now, and as she cleared the square Dolores glanced into the rearview mirror at the church and the numerous emergency vehicles with their flashing LEDs. News trucks were arriving, reporters emerging from vans with camera men armed with video units. She remembered Chase's equipment lying on the floor in the back seat, all but forgotten. He'd ceased to be a stringer tonight—tonight he'd become part of the story, rejoining the human race, so to speak. And there in the rearview mirror was Teschal, standing by the church door with the other detective, watching it all unfold, watching *them.*

***

Teschal's eyes followed Chase's SUV as it merged with the traffic.

"What are the odds?" Richards said as he moved up beside her.

"Of those two being here at the right moment?" Teschal said. "Astronomical I'd say."

"You know who his contact is?"

"I do," Teschal said flatly. "I do. But it pains me a little."

"What are you going to do about it?"

"Nothing at this point. It would be difficult to prove whether anything illegal has occurred. Indiscretion? Certainly. Criminal?" She shrugged. "I'd need warrants to get the proof, cell phone records at the very least. And maybe a burner phone was used, which would make things more difficult." Teschal sighed. "And at least the stringer *did* try to intervene tonight. His equipment never made it out of his car. And he may actually prove helpful before this is all over. Besides, just now we have infinitely more important things with which to concern ourselves."

***

Allison Mckenna opened her eyes with a start, looked up to see the windshield of her car and the cinder block wall of her apartment building's underground garage on the other side of the glass.

"Oh God," she hissed. "No!"

She fumbled with the car key, which was still in the ignition. Turned off. She'd shut the car, closed her eyes for a second and…and fallen asleep!

"Dear Jesus, no!" she screeched, wrenching the keys free and stumbling out the door. Slamming the door, she crossed the dimly lit garage, moving awkwardly past the shadowy shapes of other tenants' cars, BMWs, Audis, a Range Rover, heading for the elevator at the far end her feet unsure and her heart thudding against her ribs.

She reached the elevator, slammed her palm into the call button, nearly dropping her purse. Somewhere in the shadowy garage something that sounded like a cat cried out.

Mckenna spun around, backing into the door, a deep chill gripping her guts.

"Go away," she whispered. "Please go away."

The elevator door pinged, opening abruptly, and she fell backward into the well-appointed compartment, catching the brass railing within, managing to remain on her feet, hauling herself over to the control panel and punching the button marked with the numeral four.

"C'mon," she pleaded, tears staining her cheeks, her eyes desperately probing the shrinking darkness between the elevator doors. Then she was rising through the elevator shaft. The lights flickered and the elevator stopped. The doors pinged open and she stumbled out into the corridor, glanced warily around, and headed for her apartment. She fished her keys from her purse, dropped them, cursed, scooped them up and awkwardly slipped them into the lock. She turned the knob, leaned into the door and practically fell into her darkened apartment.

She tossed her purse and keys in the general direction of a nearby table, missed her aim and listened to them both fall to the floor as she closed and secured the door. She rushed to the bedroom, gathered up a fist full of television remotes from the night stand and flicked each on in turn until the television screens adorning the wall opposite the foot of the bed were glowing with technological life. Then she gathered up an armful of clippings from the night table and scattered them across the bed.

She began leafing through the clippings, scanning the photos, breezing through the headings with trembling fingers, sobbing into the shadows until an image on the largest of the television screens caught her tearful gaze. The image was that of a well-dressed woman holding a microphone standing in front of a church.

"No," Mckenna whispered and the remaining clippings fell from her hands and floated to the floor like dying moths. She picked up one remote then another until she found the correct one and raised the volume on the largest of the screens.

"—as horrible as anything imaginable," the reporter said as the television volume grew. "A priest here at Saint

Genevieve's has been killed in a bizarre and terrible accident, having apparently been burned alive—"

Mckenna sank to her knees in front of the televisions as the tears liberally slid down her pale cheeks. She raised her hands, planted them between the flat screens and closed her swelling eyes, pressing her forehead against the Plexiglas screen, her lips muttering the word "no" over and over, the volume building and building until a gut-wrenching scream broke from her throat, tearing blood vessels lining her windpipe to shreds and piercing the gloom of her apartment like a dagger, blocking out all other sounds except that of a cat crying someplace out in the night.

Chapter Fifty

Allison Mckenna opened her blood-rimmed eyes. Time had passed, though how much she could not tell. All she knew was that she was heart sick. She wiped dried tears from her face, sniffed the stale air. She looked at the drawn curtains—no indication of bright sunlight, only a vague glow. Sunset? Sunrise? Perhaps nothing more than the street lamp on the corner. Or a lingering late spring dusk. She thought about a cup of tea, but remembered the one Father Rousseau had shared with her and the notion, like a sliver of glass, slipped from her mind, leaving bloody shreds of gray matter in its wake. She might never drink tea again.

She rolled onto her side, squinted at the alarm clock. Less than an hour had passed since she'd seen the news. She flopped down into the nest of pillows she'd called home for God only knew how long. Her eyes found the flickering array of televisions on the wall opposite her king-sized bed, a bed that was far too large for her small frame. The bed had become a desert as of late, a reminder of just how alone she really was in all that was happening, how utterly alone. And she realized with grim certainty that the time had come to set her plan in motion, to implement her own *final solution*. If only she'd had the courage to carry out her plan a few hours earlier…

She let her thoughts turn to the bottle of pills she kept in the top drawer of her nightstand. She found herself reaching for them, actually going so far as to open the drawer, when a fearful face filling the largest of the television screens gave her pause.

The image was that of a man or at least something masquerading as a man. Dark eyes, dark greasy hair, unshaven. *Evil* etched into every crevice, filling every hair follicle, brimming forth from the eyes with a twisted hint of a smile.

Mckenna felt something hitch in her chest like a suture ripping open prematurely. She scooped up the remote on the nightstand, the one to the fifty inch, and raised the volume.

"—lead in the North Side Strangler Case may be at hand," a female reporter was saying, "as police release this photograph of a man wanted in connection with the child murders. Police are not calling Joseph Griece a suspect, but rather a person of interest. But police warn that he *is* a registered sex offender and has been missing for several days. If you see him, please contact police at once. Do not approach him as he is presumed to be dangerous."

Mckenna had heard enough. She closed the drawer to the nightstand and sat up. *Yes*, she thought, her gaze searing into the terrible face on the screen, her heart beginning to race. *Oh, yes.* Perhaps there was some redemption to be found for her this night, perhaps some crescent moon-sliver of redemption. And after it was done, after she'd finished her work, then she could finally leave everything behind and join her beloved Elise.

Chapter Fifty-One

Joseph Griece, oblivious to his newly acquired fame, stood staring at the filthy bathroom door, his ears straining to hear the tiny sound coming from the other side. The sound made his heart race, as it always had. This one was special, so little, so ripe.

"Fuck," Joe said softly, his voice surprisingly shrill, surprisingly innocent. "Savor it," he told himself, grinning and closing his eyes. "Put it off. Yes. Later is better."

Opening his eyes and stepping out of his slithering mind, he went to a small counter in the corner of the dank room where he'd placed the bags of food he'd bought at a neighborhood supermarket. He'd driven the car he'd stolen into the woods by way of a disused fire road and left it hidden behind some fallen foliage. Joe was nothing if not resourceful.

He thought of that fucking probation officer with his neat tie and glasses looking so smug and condescending. That fucker was singing a different tune now. No one would find him here. This had been his home away from home long ago, his refuge. And he knew it well. They'd come searching, but they'd failed to find the secret door and gone away. Joe had listened as they'd fumbled about, laughing to himself. Fools. All he had to do was keep the teenagers away, the ones who came to fuck and shoot up. Oh the irony of it all.

He tore open the bags, tossing the paper into a big barrel he'd found nearby, and began loading the groceries into the coolers he'd gotten at Walmart. He'd purchased the ice at a local 7-Eleven. Couldn't be too careful—spread the wealth, while it lasted. Don't shop nearby. Easy rules to follow. Someday Joe figured the urge would fade, maybe even disappear. Then he could move to Florida, Key West maybe, bask in the sun and swim in the sea. But not just yet. He still had work to do. There were no voices whispering to him in the night, never had been. No psycho-babble, only an unrelenting urge, much like that of his mother. She'd taught him well.

Joe Griece finished loading the groceries, covered the coolers and went to the hidden door. Unlocking it, he stepped out onto the passenger loading ramp. He looked around. He'd always admired the construction, especially the hidden door which sat flush with the curved wood facade. Imperceptible. All to maintain the illusion for the crowds.

South Coast Star Land Amusement Park or what was left of it. Griece had worked here as a teenager, actually running some of the rides, and knew all the secret passages, forgotten doors. This had been the House of Horrors ride. Painted cars on rails bearing images and carvings of serpents, dragons, and skeletons had once carried park visitors into the dark dungeon-like maze of tunnels and plaster-of-Paris monsters lit by strobes and colored lenses as ghastly sounds crackled from hidden speakers.

Griece let his eyes roam across the cracked and buckled asphalt that had once been a bustling midway. There was a fog rolling in, making the other dilapidated buildings, the dance hall, the roller rink, the arcades, the massive Shore Dining Hall, look like things out of an old western ghost town.

Griece considered the skeletal remains of a roller coaster rising out of the mist like a spiny serpent breeching a desolate sea. Once the beloved Shooting Star, the coaster had been reduced to a tangle of vine-riddled wood pierced sporadically by small trees like probing fingers reaching into tight wet places.

A sick little grin split Joe Griece's razor thin lips. He turned to go back inside, catch some zzzz's on the mattress someone had set out for trash pick-up (it had been a 'bitch' to roll the thing up and cram it into the back seat of the car but it had been worth the struggle). Besides, the little one wasn't going anywhere. Griece had all the time in the world.

He started for the door, but paused, his fingers brushing the rusted metal. He turned, listened. It was a cat crying somewhere out in the gloom. A brother of the night, Joe Griece thought.

"Good night," he whispered. And then he went inside, closed and locked the door. In a moment he was asleep on the mattress. And somewhere in the forgotten midway the cat cried out again. Louder. Closer.

Chapter Fifty-Two

Chase stood under the shower in his apartment for so long the water began to cool and still the odor of scorched flesh and hair remained. After he towel dried and put on sweats, he went down the hall to Dolores' place. She'd made eggs and bacon. He hardly touched them, just stared off into space, the droning of some late-night talk show playing on the television in the living room. Outside the rain had returned.

"You're human," she said, breaking the silence.

"I've spent all this time, all these years videotaping and photographing tragedies and it never occurred to me that there was emotion on the other side of the lens." He bit his lip, frowning. "Well, that's not exactly true. I guess I always knew. I suppose I just didn't care."

"That's harsh. No one's perfect."

"You're kind Dolores," he said. "And I know that I don't deserve it but thank you, though it forces me to face a few things about my divorce, things I need to come to terms with."

"Then it wasn't a total loss." Dolores grinned and squeezed his hand. "Maybe nothing ever is."

***

Teschal was sitting in her SUV outside Allison Mckenna's apartment building, huddled over her laptop, the glow of the screen filling her steel blue eyes. She'd been doing her own research, even going so far as to send a few emails to her mother's friends back in the UK, posing questions to relatives whose names her mother had mentioned, told stories about over the decades. She hardly anticipated getting any answers, she wasn't even sure that the addresses were active. Besides, her mother had alluded to the fact that those same relatives blamed her for remaining in America on the existence of her daughter. And perhaps there was some truth to that allegation.

But Teschal understood that her mother had sought every opportunity for her daughter, and that included dual citizenship. It was of course ridiculous for the family to blame the daughter for the mother's behavior. But gypsies were nothing if not eccentric. And vindictive—always looking for an argument, searching for 'drama' in times of peace. But there was something very wrong here and Teschal was willing to welcome help from any source.

Richards, on the other hand, had made up his mind, had practically suggested Teschal arrest Mckenna, charge her with obstruction of justice, or at least get a warrant to tap her phone, have her followed. Things were getting desperate. But between Mckenna's money and the fact that judges and local politicians were known to take great pains to be empathetic when it came to grieving mothers and widows, of which the Mckenna woman was both, such efforts would doubtless prove fruitless. Not to mention the fact that there was simply no evidence to suggest she'd done anything illegal.

And so Teschal refused to consider such rash measures, at least at this point, though she did agree that Mckenna had some explaining to do. But there was more here than met the eye, so much more. And haste made waste. And she couldn't risk Richards or anyone else getting wind of her unusual inquiries.

But strange ailments often called for strange cures. And things in and around Gevaudan had been very strange as of late. So strange that Teschal's captain had sent her an email. He wanted to meet with her in the morning, first thing. No pleasantries expected there.

But Abasi Donovan was not your typical police captain; he knew the score all too well, knew that this case was exceptional in many ways. And he knew *her*, Eve Teschal, knew her history, her *family* history. And he appreciated it all. That was after all why she'd been assigned to the case. This sort of thing fell within her area of expertise if it could be said that there *were* any experts in such areas.

But neither the police chief nor the mayor cared about such things. Neither did the city council. Progress was progress and results were results. And none of those political bastards really wanted to know all the details. All they wanted was for the case to be put to bed.

A cult was what Donovan was suggesting—she'd read it between the lines of his email. But that was only logical, and possibly true. But if a cult *was* responsible for these killings why was no one on the street talking? All indications pointed to one or two culprits, in spite of the bizarre MO. Organized individuals using some strange chemicals to burn their victims easily transported and easily applied. Maybe the victims were unconscious when the chemicals were applied. Brimstone? Sulfur? And the lacerations. No trace of metal in the wounds. DNA was still inconclusive.

Teschal was well aware of the incidents that had transpired in and around the local reservation years earlier, the mysterious activities of the so-called Bridgton Triangle Cult. Mostly legend there. Rural myth. A scattering of occurrences over decades involving evidence of strange ceremonies being performed, disturbed graves, slaughtered animals. And these things had taken place back in the sixties and seventies; the perpetrators, if they were still alive, would be geriatrics. Her gut told her that there was no viable connection. But then her unusual ability to *sense* things, to see beyond the hard facts, was why she was here.

Shamanistic abilities was the term Vadoma Teschal used. Her daughter the *drabarni*. And perhaps she'd be right.

Teschal sighed as her mind sifted through the facts and notions. Bad people were being brutally murdered. The Mckenna girl had been the catalyst. And the foreign murders? Copycat killings? Hardly, because the details of these killings had been kept as much under wraps as was possible. The killer was the only one who knew all the details. But there could always be leaks, like the leak providing the stringer with his leads. Even the prostitute's murder could be explained. But the dead rookie cop was the outlier, the piece to the puzzle that simply did not fit. And now this priest.

She had checked the cop out as thoroughly as possible, searching for any hint of impropriety, corruption, any hidden criminal past. There was nothing. She'd even listened to his last call-in, the one he'd made the night of his murder, the one where he'd spoken of going into the old mill where he thought he'd seen a strange light. He hadn't asked for back-up, but it had been sent nonetheless. Routine.

The responding officer had found the abandoned cruiser, smelled the smoke, gone in through the open loading bay door. And he'd found the young rookie's body lying crumpled and smoldering at the bottom of an open elevator shaft in the sub-basement.

But it was getting late. Forensics was tearing Saint Genevieve's church and its surrounding buildings apart. She'd done all she could there, at least for tonight. She'd be back there at first light. Besides, she was exhausted. Not thinking clearly. Asking superstitious gypsies in the 'Old Country' for help in solving the case, in finding…in finding *what*? Ghosts? Monsters? A medieval cult with international agents killing off bad people around the world? And of course Captain Donovan would be waiting in the morning to complete the picture.

She sat back, looked up at Allison Mckenna's balcony. There was a strange glow coming from behind the sliders. A vivid glow. Much brighter than a television screen. But then again, Mckenna had several televisions in her apartment.

Teschale frowned, cocked her head to one side. The television screens, most of them, were in the bedroom, not the living room.

She leaned forward, straining to see through the falling rain. But the light had faded and the apartment had fallen into darkness.

She sighed, closed the laptop and set it on the passenger seat. Then she started the SUV and drove off, toward home. The rain was easing, but the sky was a dark shroud. Dawn was still a long way off. She was about to shut the police radio when a ripple of static broke through. Wrong channel, she thought. Emergency, fire.

This, *whatever* it was, was for a change not her problem. She was not thinking clearly and she needed some peace.

Teschal shut the radio, silencing the dispatcher's voice. But there *was* one more thing she needed to do before she slept. There was one more person with whom she needed to speak in spite of the late hour. And that would be a surprise for both of them.

***

Dolores had dozed off, but the telephone woke her with a start. It was actually a good thing, she'd been having a nightmare. She'd been locked in the Bridgton library after closing and there was something chasing her, some unseen thing that sounded like a cat.

"Yeah," Chase said as he sat perched at the edge of the bed with the receiver in his hand. "Eloise, I don't think I could make it just now, it's—"

Eloise; Chase's source in the Gevaudan Police Department. Dolores couldn't imagine what might be going on to warrant her calling Chase after what he'd been through.

"Jesus," he whispered, glancing back at Dolores. He reached out, squeezed her thigh. She sat up, pushing hair from her tired eyes. "All right." He hung up, ran his fingers through his hair.

"You don't have to come if you don't want to," he said.

"Your job sucks," she said, reaching out and rubbing his back. "What is it this time? Cat up a tree?"

"Fire." He looked around for his keys.

"Another?"

"Eloise says that the cops are heading out in force—rumors are flying. Could be related to our cult. Or the North Side Strangler."

"Christ," Dolores said. "Where?"

"South Coast Star Land," he said slipping his sweat shirt over his head.

"Star Land? The old amusement park? That place has been closed for at least ten years." Dolores gathered up her purse. "Just a lot of old rotting buildings."

"Yeah, it's probably some homeless guy with a trash barrel that got out of hand."

"Should I bring S'mores?"

"Something about that sounds a little twisted."

***

Connie woke to the sound of her telephone ringing.

"What the fuck?" she complained, swinging her feet off the sofa in her office where she'd dozed off. She went to her desk, picked up the phone, growled "hello" into the mouthpiece, first noting the caller ID. California? Who the hell did she know in California?

"Ms. Moncrief?"

An unfamiliar woman's voice on the line.

"Who is this? Do you know what time—?"

"You've been calling *me*," the woman said. "Some woman named Kyle Ross or something leaving this number and your name."

"Who are you?"

"Carly Reynolds. My fiancé was Justin Ledeux."

The rookie cop who was killed.

"Ms. Reynolds, I thought that you were living in Texas."

"Justin's family lives in Texas; mine is in San Francisco," she said. "We'd met there in college. Now, I figure the best way to tell you to stop calling me, since my *not* responding isn't getting the message across, is to call you and tell you myself. Believe me, I was angrier when I punched in your number, but I'm tired and haven't slept much."

"It is late," Connie said.

"It's three hours earlier here," Carly said.

"Please, Ms. Reynolds, I just want to ask you a few questions about your fiancé, about the night he died."

"There's not much to tell," she said, her voice still sounding raw after all this time. "He worked the graveyard shift. One night he headed out to work the same as always, around ten-thirty. He always liked to make roll call. I was a teacher, first grade. I was in bed. I woke up to tell him to have a safe night and walked him to the door. That was our routine.

"I remember trying to sleep, but I couldn't. Then I got the call. He'd apparently stopped to investigate something suspicious at one of those old abandoned mills. He'd called it in, been advised to wait for back-up because it's a popular place for heroin addicts to shoot up and gangs to gather. Damn things should all be torn down."

Connie heard Carly struggling to compose herself.

"That's it," Carly managed. "He was found at the bottom of an open elevator shaft by the responding back-up unit. They saw his empty vehicle, smelled the smoke, found an open door."

Connie closed her eyes tight. "I'm sorry," was all she could think to say.

"Well, I hope you're happy now," Carly said, "so I don't expect to hear from you again."

Connie felt herself nodding slowly. "You won't."

"I'll never forget that night. I still have nightmares about it. In my mind I see Justin walking into that old mill. I can smell the smoke in my dreams. Hell, I even hear the Goddamned cat that kept me awake all night."

Connie felt her eyes open wide. "Cat? You owned a cat?"

"No. Outside. It must have been an alley cat, some stray. I'd never heard it before, but you know how that sort of thing is, they come and they go. All sorts of things are out there in the night. All sorts of things."

Chapter Fifty-Three

Vadoma Teschal stirred, her eyes fluttered open. Gradually the shadows in her room fell away and the woman standing by the window came into focus.

"*Drabarni*," she said softly, a small grin touching her lips.

"You knew I was here," Teschal said softly.

Her mother nodded slowly.

"Always impressive," Teschal said.

"You're my *rat*, my blood. I always know when you're near." She squinted at the clock on the night table. "How did you manage to get past those *bengalo* nurses at this hour?"

"I waved my badge at those *devilish imps*, as you call them," Teschal said mirthlessly. "It still opens some doors."

"My *chey*, the police officer." There was a twinge of derision in the old woman's voice, but there was also a sense of pride mixed in as well. Teschal would probably be the only person who could detect it though. She was starting to realize that this *family blood* thing worked both ways.

"Well, at least you never called me a *musker*," Teschal said.

"*Muskers* harass *Romanies*. You are *not* a *musker*. But you did have to run the gauntlet of *sun-downers* lining the corridors, even at this hour. Always grabbing at visitors, asking them to take them home with them, putting them off, making them think twice about visiting their family members, their loved ones. Such *dili* behavior, it's pathetic."

"I survived. You're worth it. And they're not crazy, just sad and lonely."

"So, here you are, twice in one week. The *case* must certainly be getting under your skin. The universe works in mysterious ways."

Teschal sighed. "I'm sorry to bother you at this hour."

"You should be—my schedule *is* a pressing one," she said wagging a lean digit at her daughter, feigning anger. "But you *did* interrupt my dreams. And those are *so* very precious. They are what remains."

"What were you dreaming about?"

"Oh, sometimes I dream of the future, but tonight I was dreaming of the past. Northern skies, cool and vivid blue with those big fluffy clouds, fog in the morning, sudden rain, my caravan overlooking the River Ness. Your father." A mischievous smile flitted across her lips. "But you don't need to hear about him."

"No," she whispered. "I suppose that I don't."

Vadoma chuckled knowingly.

Teschal knew little of her father. He'd supposedly died back in Scotland before she was born, but that may have been little more than convenient myth. But this was hardly the time for a lesson in family history.

"It's odd. I can remember schoolyard fights as if they'd just happened, but I can't always remember what I had for supper. And sometimes the words play hide and seek with my tongue."

"I'm sorry," Teschal said, remembering how sharp her mother had been in years gone by. Always one step ahead, always aware. The inevitable slide was painful to watch.

But things had been relatively good today, there had been no struggling with words, no speaking in tongues. Today her mother had been mostly on her game. Understanding that Vadoma Teschal would most likely never leave Long Pond was a profoundly sobering thought though.

"So then, to what do I owe this visit?"

"Your dream," Teschal said. "The one we spoke of earlier."

Vadoma's eyes widened. "It came true," she whispered.

Teschal nodded.

"You're all right though?"

Again Teschal nodded.

Vadoma closed her eyes and Teschal watched the old woman's lips move around what appeared to be a silent prayer of thanks. She looked away, feeling uncomfortable, sensing that she was somehow interrupting a very private moment or an embarrassing one. She found herself gazing through the big windows overlooking the pond. The crescent moon was slicing through the dark clouds, its glow glinting off the turbid water below. Drops of rain struck the glass.

"The rain is returning," she whispered. *The moonlight will fade*, she thought.

"Sleeping *shon*," Vadoma said, grinning. "Sleeping moon."

"Stop it Mum," Teschal said, closing her eyes, sensing her mother in her head.

"It's a gift from *Del*, from God, not the other."

"*Beng*."

"The Devil." Vadoma grinned. "I'm glad you remember some things. Maybe if you remembered more, didn't treat it all, your heritage, as if it were something to be ashamed of, something to be hidden away like a deranged relative, maybe then you could answer your own questions."

Teschal stirred, as if planning to leave.

"*Besh, besh*. Sit, please," Vadoma said. "I'll be good."

Teschal settled back into the chair.

"The sound in your dream," she said.

"The cat's cry," Vadoma confirmed. "Not a cat at all."

"No," Teschal agreed. "Not a cat at all. But something is out there, Mum, *killing* people."

"*Something*. That's a big word."

"I know." Teschal sighed.

"Your grandfather would be able to explain. He was a *Magus*, a clever man who could talk with ghosts, appease them. And demons. A *marturo*, a prophet. What some might call *cunning*. *He* would know if there was a *martiya* out there, a spirit of the night."

"A demon? Mum, how do you appease demons?"

"With sacrifices my dear," Vadoma said in a harsh whisper. She opened her mouth to say more, but a high-pitched sound pierced the stillness, a squeaky wheel, probably on a med cart being pushed along the smooth beige linoleum on its nightly mission to deliver peace and sleep to those in need.

"Mum," Teschal began, "why do gypsies see these *things*, know of these things? Things no one else sees?"

"*Romani*," Vadoma corrected. "Not *gypsy*. *Gypsy* came from the word *Egyptians*, a name the Europeans gave to us."

"*Why* Mum?" She leaned forward, resting her elbows on her knees and lacing her fingers. "Why do *we* see?"

"Because, *Kishan I Romani, Adoi san' I chov'hani.*"

"Wherever gypsies go, there the witches are, we know."

"Good my dear," Vadoma said, cackling, "you remembered."

"You drilled it all into my head, whether I wanted you to or not."

"But to your question my dear," Vadoma said. She forced herself up onto her elbows, slid back against the pillows so that she was sitting up, her mane of silver hair fanning out against the pillow, making Teschal think of an angel's halo.

"*Bhut*," Vadoma said, her eyes glistening in the shadowy room.

"*Bhut*," Teschal repeated.

"A malignant spirit, a demon. The *Romani* know these things because we live part of our lives in *their* world, in the places *between* the worlds. *We* know *them*, see them in our dreams and recognize them when we see them in reality, in all their forms. And they know us. The *Gadjos* don't see. Their minds are like locked doors."

"These *things* Mum, where do they come from?" Teschal wrung her hands slowly, desperation and frustration seeping into her voice.

"The sky," Vadoma said pointing toward the ceiling with a bony finger. She let her hand drop into her lap. "Deep within the earth. Some come from the dark places between dreams and reality. Some come from within ourselves. Some…" She shrugged.

Teschal sighed. Her mother was slipping back into the *haze*, the lucidity of the past few days fading.

"When I was a child I heard a story about a girl from a nearby village who'd found a *friend*," Vadoma began. "No one ever saw this *friend*. Some folks said it was the ghost of her mother who'd died giving life to the girl. Some said the girl was simply lonely or perhaps daft.

"It went on for a while. Then things began to change. It was evident that someone was hurting the girl. Welts, bruises, cuts. Burns. People began to suspect the father. Then one day the little girl set fire to the tiny cottage she lived in as she sat in her dead mother's rocking chair. People in the village who'd run to help said that she could be heard singing as the flames consumed the thatch above her. The girl's father rushed home from the fields to find the smoldering remains of his home and what was left of his daughter lying in the ruins."

Vadoma's voice faltered. She cleared her throat. "Sacrifice," she whispered.

Teschal's mouth had gone bone dry.

"Just one of those unsolved things in the end," Vadoma said. "Everyone in the village understood what had happened. It seems that cottage where the girl lived had a history, a dark history. And something had come calling and the little girl had been there to answer the knock at the door. Because she was innocent, sensitive, receptive. But of course the local constabulary couldn't put any of that in their reports.

"You see the *Romani* believe that there are places where so much bad has happened, sometimes over centuries, that these places simply go on attracting bad energy like magnets. And we can sense such places, and the things drawn to them. It's all part of our *romipen*, our *gypsyhood*. A lot had happened in the woods surrounding that village where the little girl lived.

"And a lot has happened around *this* place, Gevaudan. The history books are full of the stories. Red Indian wars. Unsolved murders. *Bhuts. Martiyas.* Maybe worse."

"How do I find *this* one Mum?"

Vadoma lay back in bed, closed her eyes and sighed deeply. "It will find you."

Teschal grimaced. "And how do I get rid of it?"

"Become a *Magus*." Vadoma settled into her pillow. "Listen. Feel. Your heart will guide you, will lead you to where you must go. And remember, a sacrifice is needed."

Teschal opened her mouth to speak, but her mobile phone chimed.

Vadoma closed her eyes.

Teschal scooped up the phone, put it to her ear.

"Yes?" she said. She listened, turned her gaze to her mother and in a cold flat voice she spoke into the phone. "I'm on my way."

Chapter Fifty-Four

Eve Teschal guided her SUV through the drizzle, fog, and thickening late night summer traffic, toward the ghostly flashing blue and red lights atop the hill in the distance, her own vehicle's pulsing blue LEDs signaling all to move aside.

Old Dominion Road had once served as the only major route running between the South Coast of Massachusetts and Cape Cod. These days it was used mostly by truckers seeking to avoid the clutter of Routes 195, 3, and 495 and the quaintly named Old Cape Highway, which was neither old nor quaint. But tonight Teschal's police radio reported that there was a six car pile-up in the east-bound lane of the Old Cape Highway resulting in traffic being re-routed onto Old Dominion, thus creating near grid-lock conditions, limitless energies converging in a hazy stream of idling engines and glaring headlights.

The stream of traffic looked completely out of place creeping between the weed-riddled shoulders of Old Dominion. The only evidences of civilization along the road's tattered edges were a spattering of dilapidated buildings and a few arcane streetlights. Gone were the numerous fast food joints, the early burger stops like the Star Drive-In, the fried seafood shacks like Macrae's, and the drive-in theaters, relegated to history. Old Dominion, an aged artery surrounded by Indian Reservation land that comprised the southern tip of what locals referred to as the Bridgton Triangle, a notorious region where crumbling graffiti-rich walls of granite and brick that had once been bustling mill complexes rose up out of the dense foliage like the petrified bones of extinct monsters.

Old Dominion, an all-but-forgotten stretch of road separating two large dark bodies of water, the Massasoit Reservoir to the north, from which Gevaudan drew its drinking water, and its twin, Bell Rock Pond to the south, where fishing and boating were allowed. This southerly pond also featured a patchwork of overgrown hiking trails, countless disused campsites, and a short spit of sand known as Jones Beach, stomping ground to the infamous Ghosts motorcycle club and, most recently, the epicenter of the so-called North Side Strangler case, where the lifeless bodies of no fewer than four small children had been discovered.

Teschal considered each of these facts in turn as she proceeded, chiding herself for not paying attention to the fire emergency call she'd heard on her scanner while parked outside Allison Mckenna's apartment building. But she'd been tired, distracted. It had been a mistake that she would not repeat.

She finally arrived at what remained of South Coast Star Land, which lay beneath the dark sky in a state of dilapidation behind a sturdy ten-foot-high chain link fence which also served as trellis to an assortment of climbing vines and weeds.

Abandoned, left to rot, the place had once been a popular destination for summer outings. The long extinct dance hall had once hosted such acts as Glenn Miller, Cab Calloway, and the great drummer, Gene Krupa. There'd been All-Star Wrestling bouts and nationally acclaimed boxing matches. Aerosmith had even played there in the early seventies, before they'd come to be called Aerosmith.

Teschal had only lived in Gevaudan for seven years, so she had never experienced the place, but she was well aware of its reputation. Star Land was legend.

Tonight, the old amusement park was alive with more activity than it had seen in well over a decade. But tragically the commotion was not of a celebratory sort. Tonight, the pall of chaos and death hung over the place like the caul of a sickly newborn.

The main entrance to the parking lot, which had been blocked by a huge metal swing-gate secured by concrete abutments and firmly locked in place with rusted chains and padlocks, had been opened and pushed aside and the cracked and weed-infested lot beyond was now filled with an extensive collection of emergency vehicles.

Teschal's pulse began to race as she pulled up to the entrance where she was promptly halted by two burly uniforms, one of whom wasted no time in approaching the driver's side window.

"Where the hell—" the man began, but Teschal offered the officer her ID and, after studying it briefly, he nodded and handed it back.

"Who's in charge?" Teschal asked.

"Detective Collins. You can't miss him."

She drove onward, through the lot, winding her way between the few remaining light poles, toward the main entrance, which stood beneath the last vestige of what must once have been a massive rocket ship. Another officer, a blonde woman standing beside a local cruiser with flashing blue LEDs, signaled for Teschal to stop and in an instant was alongside the SUV.

"Detective," the woman said, immediately recognizing Teschal.

"What happened?"

"Gevaudan FD thought it was just vandals or homeless people, but hell, Detective, they didn't think that for too long. Word is that it's the North Side Strangler."

Teschal felt herself nodding grimly.

"Detective Collins is in charge, Captain Donovan is on his way."

"You have a suspect?" Teschal said.

"What's left of a suspect. You should speak with Detective Collins."

Teschal thanked the woman and drove toward the clutch of emergency vehicles gathered at the entrance to the midway, the countless LEDs charging the murky air with surrealistic energy. She pulled up beside one of the ambulances, killed the engine and climbed out into the misty drizzle. She crossed to the ambulance as two EMTs were loading a gurney into the bay. One of the techs, a rugged man with a Fu Manchu moustache and a shaved head, glared suspiciously at Teschal. Lying on the gurney was a small Asian girl, perhaps seven or eight years of age. The child glanced warily at Teschal—her dark eyes were literally brimming with a bottomless primordial fear.

"Eve," a male voice called.

Teschal turned to see Collins standing at the foot of the rocket ship's remaining stabilizer.

"What happened?" she said, joining him.

"Joseph Griece," Collins said. "You remember, the sex offender we wanted to question."

"How could I forget?"

"We've had an APB out on him ever since. Tonight, the responding officer at this scene gave me a call," Collins said. "They found the fucker in the House of Horrors. He'd made himself a little apartment there, coolers, bathroom, groceries, even a hot plate. Wouldn't be much in the winter, but it was pretty fucking cozy for the summer time."

"He's dead?"

"That's why you're here—same MO as your murders. The son of a bitch was torn to shreds and burned to a crisp. There'd been a good blaze going when the first call came in, a truck driver passing by saw the smoke. Mostly smoldering now. But in buildings this old, hot spots are a concern. Fire can live in forgotten hollow spaces for a long time without anyone knowing. Gevaudan FD had a hell of a time finding the door to Griece's layer, for lack of a better word—it was built into the wall like some secret fucking passage."

"If the door was hidden, how'd the perp get to Griece?"

Collins shook his head. "We're searching the building, but so far we can't find any other access point."

"Any witnesses?"

"One. You just saw her. Seven years old. She was tied up in the bathroom."

"Jesus." Teschal put her fingers to her lips. She turned to consider the ambulance with its precious cargo.

"She's fine," Collins said. "A little dehydrated, a little smoke inhalation, shock. She was taken from a housing project late this afternoon—John Farias Corners over on Lane Avenue behind the Stop and Shop. Mom's being taken to Mercy General in Wickham. That's where they'll take the girl. It's the closest. Dad's in Cassandra Junction for another forty days, B and E. Numerous. I have a psychologist heading to the hospital to help with the statement."

Teschal turned to the second ambulance, which was sitting at the back of a large building to the immediate left of the midway entrance. A big loading door set into the building had been raised and several police officers were gathered there.

"What did she see?" Teschal asked.

She turned back to the first ambulance as the tech with the shaved head hopped down from the bay, closed the doors and ran to the cab. He climbed in, cranked the siren and drove toward the exit.

"Nothing," Collins said. "She was locked in the bathroom. We found items from two of the other victims in the room with this son of a bitch. He was our man, there's no question about that."

Teschal shook her head. "Anything else?"

"Nah. We asked the girl who did it, but she just kept saying the same thing over and over. I don't know what we'll be able to get out of her. Trauma. That fucker—" Collins shook his head angrily.

"What did she say?"

Collins sighed, shook his head. "She just kept saying that the cat killed the man. It was the cat."

Teschal felt an icy chill crawl up her spine.

"I guess this is your case too, now," Collins said. "C'mon. I'll give you the tour." He strode toward the main entrance.

Teschal scooped up her mobile phone and punched in some numbers.

Realizing that she was not following, Collins paused by a bank of rusted-out turn-styles, glanced impatiently at his watch.

"Richards?" Teschal said into her phone. "Get out to South Coast Star Land on Old Dominion Road. We've got another one."

She shut the phone, started toward the turn-styles, but paused when she saw two technicians from the ME's office wheeling what remained of the late Joseph Griece out the big loading door toward the ME's retrofitted ambulance. She signaled for Collins to wait and jogged over to the vehicle. She could smell the hydrogen sulfide as she approached the gurney. Brimstone.

"Hold up," she said, waving her badge at the technicians.

Frowning, they paused to consider her identification.

"It's okay," Collins shouted from beside the turn-styles.

A female tech with short-cropped blonde hair glanced at her partner and then moved around the gurney and unzipped the body bag. Her partner, a lean silver-haired man with a gaunt face, grabbed the other half of the bag and peeled it open turning deliberately away to avoid the terrible stench, effectively revealing what remained of the late Joseph Griece.

Teschal moved closer, forcing her eyes to study the smoldering remains. This was the worst one yet. The face of the man on the gurney had been torn open by some powerful weapon. The left eye had been eviscerated and now resembled a blackened smashed grape dangling from the socket. Bits of bone were visible poking out of the charred flesh. Chunks of splintered cartilage were protruding from the bloody gash that had once been his throat. A cheekbone was visible. Most of the nose was gone. Several huge gashes were visible running diagonally across the dead man's abdomen, the jagged edges of the wounds were singed and blackened. The splintered points of a few broken ribs were jutting out of the flesh here and there. The left arm was clearly detached from the shoulder joint and was lying beside the body wrapped in a clear plastic bag. The charred body was also partly layered in a thin layer of yellowish powder, sulfur, Teschal concluded.

She nodded and the technicians sealed up the bag and wheeled its occupant toward the waiting ambulance.

Feeling nauseated, Teschal turned toward the ghostly midway. She spied what remained of a Ferris Wheel rising from the mist like the fossilized ribs of a dinosaur. In the distance were the tangled bones of an old wooden roller coaster. This was indeed a place for the dead. But it was where she was supposed to be. Her mother had been right about that. Answers would never find her while sitting on her sofa nursing glasses of wine. Eve Teschal's answers would always come from dark places far from any comfort she'd ever known. It seemed the old witch was right about a lot of things.

"It needs a sacrifice," Vadoma Teschal said from some deep crevice of her daughter's mind.

Sacrifice, Teschal thought, her mind racing. What sort of sacrifice? Not Griece? He was just another victim. Then who?

She wiped her mouth with her sleeve. The cool damp air had succeeded in driving the nausea back and she set off toward the main entrance where Collins was talking on his mobile phone, waiting impatiently to show her what her instincts had brought her to see.

Chapter Fifty-Five

"There," Chase said, pointing at the clutch of emergency vehicles with their flashing LEDs. "They've got the right lane shut down."

"Drive past," Dolores said. "I have an idea."

He obeyed, moving along with the thickening traffic, creeping past the flares that were burning in the right lane, the drizzle pelting the windshield, the wipers making a squeaky sound as they swept across the greasy glass. Two officers wearing vivid yellow and flat black rain-coats were standing beside the flares, directing traffic, a state police cruiser parked just ahead of them, its own LEDs flickering blue in the dismal air.

"There's an abandoned gas station just beyond," Dolores said. "It's been there forever. We used to sneak in through the fence at the back of the lot. It's one of the first local secrets I learned when I moved down from East Boston. We'd come out in the beer garden just outside that dining hall that looks like a huge Quonset hut."

"How come I never heard of this? *I'm* the local."

"I guess I just fell in with a bad crowd. There," she prompted and Chase abandoned the traffic and veered into the derelict service station. He drove past the skeletal remains of gasoline pumps and parked beside the big chain link fence at the side of the dilapidated building. He killed the engine and climbed out into the drizzle.

"Let's shoot some footage through the fence," he said. "If we try to bring the video unit in there, we won't get ten feet."

Dolores agreed, handing the video recorder to Chase, who moved up to the rusted fence and began tearing strips of vegetation away from one section. Once he'd cleared a spot, he aimed the lens through one of the gaps, switching the unit on and slowly zooming in on the partly boarded-up entrance to the Horror House, which was clearly the crux of the activity.

Dolores joined him, lacing her fingers through the fence and peering into the ruined midway. She could see Teschal standing on the loading ramp of the Horror House talking with a man wearing a trench coat who looked as if he should be stalking the streets of Victorian London.

"Who's that?" she said.

Chase shifted the lens. "I think his name is Collins. He's the one working the Strangler case."

"Those little kids," Dolores whispered.

"My friend Eloise has a good nose for news," Chase said. He lowered the video unit. "All right, where's your secret passage?"

***

"Gevaudan FD found the guy lying dead on an old mattress when they broke in," Collins said as he and Teschal climbed the ramp to the Horror House entrance. "Burned pretty badly. His head was hanging by a cord. One arm was on the other side of the room."

Teschal absorbed these facts silently, nodding. Then, as if hearing a sound, her gaze shifted to the adjoining lot and her eyes lit on Chase's SUV through a portion of fence that the climbing weeds hadn't completely claimed.

"Son of a bitch."

"What is it?" Collins said.

Teschal gestured with her jaw. "The press is here."

"So long as they stay out of our way."

***

Chase set the video unit on the back seat of his car and followed Dolores toward the back portion of the service station where the trees and weeds had practically consumed what remained of the forsaken building's garage. The windows were partly boarded up, and the framed portions that were still exposed were filled with broken shards of glass and fathomless shadows.

"Here," she said, pointing to a section of chain link fence that had evidently been cut with bolt cutters and partly rolled aside. The weeds and small trees were so thick it would have proved impossible to find unless someone knew exactly where to look.

"Follow me," Dolores said and she squeezed through the gap, pushing the rolled-up fence aside in the process. Chase glanced warily around and followed.

***

The air filling the room in the front left corner of the Horror House was still smoky and the walls had been blackened, partly by the fire and partly by years of mold infestation. There were dusty yellow streaks like flaming plumes on the back wall beneath which lay a badly burned mattress.

"Cozy," Teschal said, moving carefully around the charred mattress. The floor creaked beneath her weight. The plastic police-issue booties she'd slipped on over her boots made soft rustling sounds on the old warped wood floor. A trickle of dust fell from the scorched ceiling. She sniffed the rancid air.

"Did he take all the kids here?"

"Probably," Collins said panning a flashlight around the room. "Jones Beach is just up the road. This was the ride operator's office," he said, pointing to a partially collapsed desk in the corner. "The magic carpet was through there." He pointed to a padlocked door in the rear corner of the room.

"Magic carpet?" Teschal said.

"I grew up in Bridgton. Spent a lot of summer nights here. Most of the ride you'd be moving along on tracks in these little cars painted like monsters. They'd carry you up to the second level and back down again and let you off back there and you'd follow these glow-in-the-dark foot prints to the magic carpet. A scary voice would tell you to sit on a bench and the thing would drop out from under you. You'd fall a couple of feet landing on this big conveyer belt that would carry you down to the exit. You had to walk through a rotating barrel to get out to the midway."

Teschal nodded. "Quaint. I doubt the kids who've been here lately would remember it with such fond nostalgia. If they'd lived."

"One did," Collins said.

Teschal nodded grimly as she squatted down beside the scorched mattress. There were straps nailed into the wall at the two upper corners of the make-shift bed. She felt her teeth grind together and her stomach tightened.

"Fucker won't be using this place anymore," Collins said.

Teschal felt herself nodding.

"Circuits are long dead. Griece used these." He pointed to a tripod topped by two battery operated work lights that had grown dim from overuse.

"The bathroom door was locked?"

It was Collins' turn to nod. "The firefighters heard the girl screaming, kicked it in. She was tied to the toilet." He aimed the flashlight into the bathroom.

Teschal stood up, crossed to the bathroom doorway, peered inside. The toilet bowl was black with grime, the ceiling layered in dark water stains. The floor was concrete. There was a bucket of dirty water in the corner.

"Maybe he tried to tidy up a little," Collins said.

"How thoughtful."

Teschal turned back to the main room.

"This place needs to be torn down," she said softly.

"Kids still come here to have sex, shoot up." Collins sniffed. "The company that owns it is based in Florida."

"Out of sight, out of mind I suppose," she said.

A shadow fell across the floor and a board creaked. Teschal turned toward the sound. A man was standing in the doorway that led to the midway. He was dark skinned, stocky, African-American, with hawk-like features, a hook nose, intense eyes, thinning silver hair.

"Captain," Collins said.

"My two favorite detectives working together— how touching." Donovan's voice was deep, possessing the slightest hint of a West African accent. He raised his dark eyes, studied the room.

"This place was something back in the day I hear. Since then…" His voice trailed off.

"I don't need to tell you both how this works," Donovan said. "The mayor has been calling me hourly. The governor daily. The chief is on oxygen. The FBI has one foot in the door. A few members of the city council would just love the Feds to step in, discredit the current administration, mostly to satisfy a few not-so-secret political agendas. And now I can tell them all to relax, at least on one front."

He walked over to the mattress, considered it.

"I assume you checked this place out at some point," Donovan said, his eyes moving across the scorched bedding.

"Yes, but most of the buildings, including this one, were buttoned up tight as a drum," Collins said. "And this door was concealed, made to look like a wall. Hide the behind-the-scenes magic from the park visitors I suppose."

"Our boy was smart," Donovan said. "His type often is. He would have been sure to keep things looking deserted. He must have known this place pretty well, though. Frequent flyer maybe. Old employee even. No extant records I presume."

"Social Security maybe," Teschal said.

"Long time ago," Collins said.

"But worth a look," Donovan said.

Collins nodded briskly, looking perhaps a little sheepish to Teschal. She realized he'd searched the place, would have done so without question due to its proximity to Jones Beach if for no other reason. But he hadn't searched nearly as well as he should have. And Jack Collins was just now coming to terms with that fact. He would think about that point for a long time to come, especially during those late-night hours while lying in bed as the clock counted the minutes. She did not envy him. No cop would.

"Collins, your people need you," Donovan said, his eyes returning to the burned-out mattress. "They found a car out by the fire road, the VIN matches one reported stolen three days ago from a garage in Wickham. Our boy's abandoned car was found near the same garage."

Collins looked to the door and the midway beyond.

"Some guidance is needed out there," Donovan said.

Collins nodded, understanding the polite way in which Donovan was telling him to get out. He glanced at Teschal, telling her with his eyes, "your turn," before leaving.

The echo of Collins' exiting footsteps had faded completely before Donovan spoke again.

"You know why you're on this case, Eve," the captain said. "I've been in touch with the Irish and Greek authorities regarding the similar cases they're investigating, but they've been reluctant to share information thus far.

And I've called in a few international favors as well, but everyone's stumped. The spotlight's on us."

Donovan cocked his head, switching gears. "How's your mother?"

"Holding her own I suppose."

Donovan nodded, sighed.

"We both know that there's more to your case then a determined hit man. But some very bad people are no longer with us. The rookie, the priest, and of course the Mckenna girl—those are the real tragedies. But the rest…when you tell John Q taxpayer that some drug dealer or pedophile was torn to shreds and burned to a crisp in the process, well, they actually think about it for a minute before half-heartedly condemning the perpetrator's behavior. If at all. On the record, the elected officials are worried that a vigilante may be out there. Off the record they're counting the votes they might be losing each second this bastard remains at large. With the Strangler case coming to a close all eyes will be turning your way."

Teschal nodded slowly, her stomach growing cold. It was not altogether unusual for a typical citizen who was sick and tired of political expedience to side with the occasional vigilante, to support and cheer for the Bonnies and Clydes who bucked a system that simply didn't seem to be working.

"But vigilantes don't carry out murders in this fashion," Donovan observed. "Vigilantes carry guns. They do what they do quickly and efficiently. Unless the act itself has meaning." Donovan raised his eyes, turned them on Teschal; they were the very definition of intense.

"I can't find any ties with ancient rituals and I've researched it as thoroughly as possible," she said. "But I still suspect that something old is…" Her words trailed off into nothingness.

"Something old," Donovan echoed.

She nodded.

"I swear I'd suspect that Mckenna woman, but there are too many holes in that theory," he added. "But I understand what you mean about *something old* being at work here. That's why I assigned you to the case, but you already knew that. There are other good detectives available, but they all share what you and I might call a *limited perspective*."

"I'm thinking that there's a cult behind it all."

"I tend to agree," Donovan said. "I suppose the Mckenna woman's involvement could simply be coincidental. I just can't picture her being involved in such a thing, at least not directly or of her own accord. So, how close *are* you?"

"Closer than I know, I suspect," she said, finally looking Donovan in the eyes. They were impossibly dark.

"Well, wrap it up fast. Both our asses are on the line. Keep me in the loop."

Donovan nodded, turned and headed out the door.

Teschal paused, glanced around one last time, mouthed the word "fuck" and followed.

***

Chase and Dolores had crept along the fence, moving through the tall brush and overgrown trees, until they reached the rotted walls of the beer garden where several rotting picnic tables sagged beneath folds of mist. To the left was the yawning maw of the South Shore Dining Hall where bands had once played to crowds being served lobster rolls, cooked crab, clam boils, clam cakes, and clam chowder. The once bustling hall had been reduced to a huge hollow cavern steeped with shadows, its asphalt floor lined with trash, its rafters thick with roosting pigeons. Once brightly painted picnic tables were stacked high in the recesses of the festering gloom. Two uniformed officers were standing just outside, talking, one smoking. Dolores and Chase crouched down to listen.

"This weather sucks," the younger of the two complained as he removed his cap and scratched his shaved head.

"It's good for my lawn," the older officer said as he studied the screen of his smart phone. "Won't see a drop come July."

"I rent. Jesus, those poor kids. That fucker got what he deserved."

"I have two kids," the older officer said closing out his phone. "He sure as hell did."

"Who the hell do you figure wasted him?"

"What makes you think it wasn't some sort of accident? Maybe he had a propane grill in there. Maybe it blew up in his face. Not much left of his face from what I hear."

The young man winced, took a drag on his cigarette.

"The guys are saying that the bastard's head was nearly torn off," the older officer continued. "And one arm was on the other side of the fucking room. And he was burned up along with the mattress and some of the room. An exploding propane tank could do that I figure."

Dolores glanced at Chase who was nodding slowly.

"You'll learn," the older man said.

"Learn what?"

"The dicks don't tell us shit unless it suits 'em. You have to listen to the rank and file to get the facts."

"Yeah, sure," the younger officer said. "So what do we do now?"

"Search the place."

"Looking for what? The kid was locked in the bathroom when the fucker bought it. I mean, someone musta' hated this guy a lot if it wasn't an accident. And that means that they're long gone."

"Yeah," the older man said, "but you never know. If someone *did* kill this guy, they might still be here. Some of these crazy fuckers like to hang around and watch the fireworks."

"And what's all this shit about a cat?"

Chase felt a frown slip over his face. Dolores turned and glared at him.

"That's just talk," the older cop said. "One of the guys heard the kid say she heard a cat outside the room she was locked in just before all hell broke loose. Poor kid was probably scared shitless."

The young man nodded, finished his butt and tossed it aside.

"Don't let Collins see you do that," the older man said. "Or that fucking Teschal. She'll chew you a new asshole herself and you won't enjoy it one bit no matter *how* nice her own ass is. Contaminating a crime scene with your own DNA, not too fucking bright."

The young man laughed. A beat passed and his face went grim. Then he stooped down, scooped up the spent butt, glanced around warily and tucked it into his pocket.

"Got your flashlight?" the older man said.

His associate nodded.

"Let's start in here. At least we'll stay sort of dry."

The two officers produced their flashlights, switched them on and headed into the massive South Shore Dining Hall.

"What was this place?" the younger man asked panning his light around.

"Used to be a place for kids to have fun. Eat seafood, watch bands play. Saw the Jack D' Johns here once."

"They a punk band?" his partner asked, his voice echoing in the cavernous space.

Dolores sat back on her haunches, the leafy branches settling around her shoulders like a shawl, their dampness working into her clothes.

"Well?" she said.

"I think it's time we have a very serious conversation with Allison Mckenna," Chase said. "Before something else happens."

"Do you *really* think she's involved with a cult of some sort?"

Chase had begun moving back toward the gap in the fence through which they'd entered, Dolores on his heels.

"If she *isn't*," he said, holding the rolled-up portion of fence aside so she could squeeze through, "then maybe she can tell us who is, and where we can find them. In any event, I'm convinced that she knows a lot more than she's told anybody, Teschal included. Who knows, maybe we'll get lucky and be the ones to find out what's *really* going on here."

"I'm not sure that would qualify as luck," Dolores said softly.

***

The drizzle had increased by the time Teschal emerged from the Horror House. Richards was standing at the base of the entrance ramp leaning against the rusted hand rail talking with Collins.

"I don't get paid enough for this shit," he was saying.

"None of us do," Collins agreed his finger swiping across his mobile phone screen.

"If it wasn't for my blue light I'd still be sitting in that traffic." Richards raised his eyes when he spied Teschal on the ramp.

Teschal had stopped at the top of the entrance ramp to study the dead midway, her eyes pausing to consider each of the closed-up partially collapsed vending booths with their faded and chipped paint and the rusted remains of the many rides.

She thought of her mother at Long Pond watching the waves break against the rocky shore where no beach had ever been. She shook her head, struggling to fight off a headache born of stress and sleep deprivation that was growing behind her eyes. She glanced at the fence where she'd glimpsed Chase's SUV. There was nothing there now.

"Where's the stringer?" she asked.

Collins raised his eyes, glanced toward the fence. "Guess he got what he was after," he said dismissively.

"Fuck," Teschal muttered. She made her way to the bottom of the ramp, pointing at the midway as she did.

"Make sure they search every inch of this place," she said to Richards.

"What?"

Teschal paused at the bottom of the ramp, spun on Richards—her face was stone. "*Every* inch!"

"Where—" he began before realizing the futility of the question. "Great," he mumbled. But Teschal was gone, jogging through the drizzle toward the parking lot, the lingering mist and smoke parting before her like insubstantial doors and just as quickly closing in behind her, turning her receding form to shadow.

Chapter Fifty-Six

Connie hung up the phone, Chase was not answering his mobile. She called for Dale. The young woman appeared in the doorway, as chipper as ever in spite of the hour. The story was heating up and all hands were on deck putting together a special edition of Dark Side dedicated exclusively to the Night Stalker case.

"Ms. Moncrief?"

"You and Derek mind the fort dear," Connie said.

"You're going out? But we just got some footage from Mr. Christian about the fire at the old amusement park—"

"Why's he out there?" she shot back, annoyed. "He should learn to focus."

"Well, his text said that they've found a body and there was a little girl—"

"What?"

Dale stepped back into the hall as if she'd been slapped. "It's on the police scanner too. And Channel Seven interrupted the usual programming to say that they may have caught the North Side Strangler."

"Mother fucker," Connie's eyes swept about her office before growing abruptly grim and locking on Dale. "And Chase is there?" A beat passed and then she grabbed up her purse. "How does that son of a bitch do it?" she said to herself.

"We just got the video. Derek is setting it up."

"Tell Derek to edit the piece himself and if anyone calls for me, take a message."

Dale watched as Connie headed for the back door.

"But what if Mr. Christian wants to talk about his footage? The editing? You know how he can be."

"I wouldn't worry about it dear. I have a funny feeling that I'll be talking with him before you do," Connie said as she pushed through the back door and out into the worsening rain.

"I'm not sure if he's still at the scene, but—"

"I said don't worry about it." Then, speaking softly to herself Connie added, "I'm going to talk with someone entirely different. Chase is on his own."

"But—" Dale pleaded.

"Don't wait up," Connie called as the door closed behind her.

Chapter Fifty-Seven

Connie pulled up to the curb a hundred feet or so before the entrance to the Daniker building. She killed the engine and looked out through the rain at the gated underground garage entrance and ornate green awning-covered walkway that led to the main door. No doorman was evident, but the place was high-end nonetheless. Probably a buzzer system to gain access. That presented a problem.

She sat back pursing her lips. This was still technically Gevaudan, a city of nearly two-hundred-thousand people, most of whom were up and out at the crack of dawn in a vain attempt to eke out a living in a country where the division between wealthy and poor was growing by leaps and bounds. And here was this quiet little bastion of opulence, a haven for the idle rich, perched high atop a hill in the northwest corner of the city where some of the most notorious mill barons had once lived in their near-palatial mansions.

Connie had never been the opinionated type at least so far as wealth was concerned. But remembering how a good portion of Gevaudan was comprised of tenements, housing projects, Section Eight apartments, and small raised ranches, the Daniker Building with its sleek facade and private parking seemed noticeably out of place.

And yet Allison Mckenna, for all her money, was a sad woman, at least according to Chase and his newly acquired *other half*. Connie was determined to see for herself, reach her own conclusions. She'd always been a solo act when it came to reporting. Good instincts. And if Chase wanted out of the picture, well, so be it. But she had to wonder whether jealousy was her chief motivating factor. It was possible, she had to admit that. Damn. When had she turned into a sap? When had the hard-boiled news person grown a woman's heart? And why the hell had it happened now?

But first things first. The question before her was how to approach Mckenna, that is, if the woman was even at home. But then of course she *would* be at home wouldn't she? The hour was late and Chase's description of the woman had been that of a shut-in, a woman wallowing in a bottomless pit of despair and grief brought on by her daughter's murder.

Connie felt her resolve fading. After all, who was *she* to barge in on this pathetic woman armed with painful probing questions, hoping desperately to somehow prove her worth to a divorced man who considered her to be little more than some fringe benefit? Just because she'd never gotten close enough to *anyone* to need them or want them this much gave her no right to become the proverbial cold, heartless bitch she'd always been fitted up to be.

"Shit."

Connie took hold of the key in the ignition, started to turn it. But Chase's SUV appeared in her rearview mirror at that moment, and her fate was sealed.

***

"Do you think she'll talk to us?" Dolores said, craning her neck to study Mckenna's empty balcony. "She *was* the last person to see that priest who died in your arms alive. Maybe she *does* have something to hide?"

"Maybe," Chase said, pulling into a parking space across from the main entrance to the Daniker building, well beyond Connie's car, which his preoccupied brain failed to notice. "But this may be her only chance to tell her story before Teschal puts two and two together. She deserves that much. So I'm bringing the video unit."

"Don't you think Teschal's got her hands full out at the amusement park?"

"She'll know what that little girl said and she'll piece it all together quickly," Chase said pocketing the keys and inspecting the video camera. "And she'll realize just as quickly that none of us can fully comprehend what's been happening. The cat's cry, *Cri du chat*. It's what I heard. It's what the priest heard. I don't know what it was or what it means, but it's the proverbial *one thing*, the unifying factor in all that's been happening. But not the only unifying factor—Allison Mckenna is the other constant in the equation. And we all know that the culprit or culprits are still out there somewhere, and Mckenna may be the only living person who can fill in the gaps. Teschal simply can't risk her disappearing or turning up dead."

"I hope you're right," Dolores said, climbing out of the SUV.

So do I, Chase thought as he stepped out into the rain and led the way toward the Daniker Building's main entrance.

***

Connie watched as the couple passed beneath the green awning. They stopped when they reached the door and Connie felt her pulse freeze when Chase glanced her way. She ducked down below the dashboard and remained hidden for a few minutes, the only sounds that of her racing pulse and the thrumming of the rain on the car roof. By the time she sat back up, Chase and the Dolores woman were nowhere in sight. The only movement near the building was that of a man wearing a blue and white shirt jogging up the block, desperately trying to dodge the rain drops, looking as if he'd just made a delivery. There'd been no sign of him a moment earlier, so Connie assumed that he must have exited the building. Definitely not Chase. He and the Dolores woman *must* have entered as the delivery man was exiting, beating the buzzer system.

"Damn." The bastard was nothing if not lucky.

Connie waited, watching closely, trying to imagine another way inside. The underground garage was gated. She could see the kiosk where a card would need to be swiped in order to gain access.

Then she noticed that the delivery man who'd started walking up the street had stopped at a van parked by the curb. Even from this distance she recognized the big ornate 'W' insignia of the Waterfront Cafe on the side of the vehicle. The man had opened the side door and retrieved a large white bag.

"Late for delivery men," she whispered to herself, consulting her watch. But wealth did have its privileges, and the Waterfront *was* known for catering to just such wealth and at all hours.

She watched as the man closed the side door to the van, turned and headed back toward the building. This was her chance.

"A little luck to go around Mr. Christian," she whispered to herself. "Looks as if fate is on my side tonight."

Connie pocketed her car keys, tucked her purse under the dashboard and climbed out of her car.

***

Allison Mckenna heard the knocking through a thin veil of sleep and opened her eyes. She hadn't had a decent night's sleep in weeks—her first thought was that she'd dreamed it. Then it came again, persistent. She glanced up at the clock. Well past midnight.

She slipped out of bed and got to her feet, hesitant. She'd dozed off with her sweat suit on again. She looked to the numerous television screens adorning the bedroom wall. Each was alive with flickering images, news shows from all over the world, everything from the BBC to TNN to Al Jazeera by way of a special very expensive feed that had raised a few eyebrows at the cable station (and perhaps Homeland Security).

The knocking came again. The sound made her feel better, relieved even. Maybe tonight had been enough, maybe *it* had gone for good. But she'd heard something in the parking garage. And she had dreamed of a ruined roller coaster and faded, mold-ridden Hollywood monsters painted on rotting plywood walls. No, it had not gone anywhere. It was only a matter of time before it came to tell her all about it, seek her approval. She'd better get rid of whoever this was before *it* arrived.

***

Chase looked at Dolores who shook her head, the sound of his knuckles rapping against the expensive wood door still echoing through the fourth-floor foyer.

Dolores had been prepared to ring each bell in turn until someone answered, but while deliberating luck had presented itself in the form of a man wearing a shirt bearing the Waterfront Cafe emblem who was in the middle of making a large late-night delivery. He'd actually held the door open for them. It seemed even God's chosen got take-out, albeit take-out from a high-end establishment like the Waterfront that was renowned for keeping most unusual hours and specializing in what many might call eccentric appetites.

"Fate hath intervened," she heard herself say as they'd crossed the lobby, her heart thudding wildly from someplace within the confines of her throat.

"That sounds ominous," Chase had said before the elevator doors pinged open.

They'd ridden up in silence, the sound of the wind moving through the elevator shaft around them and the dull distant insistent thrumming of the rain the only sounds. The door had opened with a ping and a whoosh and, as it had, the air seemed to flow suddenly from the elevator into the fourth-floor lobby as if being sucked into a vacuum. The flowers on the tables lining the foyer had fluttered and Dolores would have sworn that the expensive wall sconces' bulbs had flickered. But Chase never seemed to notice any of it. Or if he had, he'd neither commented nor reacted.

Chase knocked on the expensive looking wood again. The sound of the knocking had barely faded when the door opened a crack and Mckenna's pale face appeared.

Dolores felt a twinge of horror and actually clutched at her own throat like some Hollywood starlet in a 1940s melodrama. The woman looked dead, her eyes red and swollen, still rimmed with tears and dark circles that spoke of countless nights spent gazing up at the ceiling or at one of the many television screens that occupied her bedroom wall.

"Hmmm," Mckenna managed. But instead of demanding an explanation for the intrusion, or slamming the door in their faces, she simply melted into her darkened apartment, allowing the heavy door to slowly creak open.

Dolores glanced at Chase and he gently nudged the thing open. Mckenna's shadow was visible moving toward the den, her refuge. Chase and Dolores followed hesitantly, an impossible sense of dread folding giant bat-like wings around them.

They found Mckenna sitting, once again, in the recliner amidst a freshly cut scattering of newspaper clippings. Dolores noticed a pair of scissors lying on the floor next to the recliner and several mangled pages of newspaper stacked beside it.

"I'm not going to ask how you got in," she said, her dark moist eyes glistening. "And I'm too tired to tell you to leave."

Chase hefted the video camera, but Mckenna shook her head.

"Put that out in the other room," she said.

"This may be your only chance to tell your story," Dolores said.

"I'll tell *you* first then we'll talk about *that*," Mckenna said, her bony spectral finger protruding from the gloom like that of a Dickensian phantom.

Chase went to the dining room and set the video unit on the table. But he found his fingers were reluctant to release the instrument's handle. His stringer's brain brightened at that moment and he carefully maneuvered the unit so that it was aimed at the den doorway where the tiny screen registered the shadowy image of Allison Mckenna sitting in the recliner in the corner. He switched the thing on, hit the record button and flipped the tiny screen shut. He considered his handiwork and returned to the den.

Mckenna gestured toward the sofa and Chase and Dolores settled into it just as they had during their previous visit. The rain was a torrential wall against the window behind them, it was thrumming like a massive beating heart, the vague glow from a streetlight beyond passing through the cascading rivulets, making the shadows on the walls look as if they were melting.

"What exactly brings you here at this hour?" Mckenna said.

"A priest died in my arms tonight," Chase said, struggling to discern Mckenna's drained nearly lifeless face from the darkness. It was the face of someone at the end of their life, a face ripe with some deadly disease that was slowly consuming its owner.

"You were seen leaving the rectory shortly before it happened," Dolores said, her voice a harsh whisper.

"I'm so sorry," Mckenna said. "Father Rousseau was a good man." Her voice was devoid of emotion. "I had no idea that you were there."

Chase glanced at Dolores. "We were," he grimly affirmed.

"My daughter, Elise, and I used to go to Saturday night mass there." Mckenna's voice was suddenly hoarse, worn to the bone. "She used to tell me about the history of the church, about the history of churches in general, mostly the famous ones, but she also knew about the local ones. Saint Genevieve's, a very old French Saint. We used to attend St. Brigid's in Wickham before my husband died. Elise liked Brigid. She was controversial, a female saint whose essence may have been derived from a Celtic Goddess. Genevieve was tame compared to Brigid, but the church was closer to this new address. And of course, Genevieve was my daughter's middle name."

"Of course," Dolores said softly, glancing at Chase.

"I have some French ancestry. I always liked the name, even before I knew Genevieve was a saint." Mckenna managed a slight smile.

The shadows suddenly throbbed like a pulsing vein as a streak of lighting burned the sky, a rumble of thunder in tow.

"My Elise knew all the stories," Mckenna said, her voice brightening a bit, sounding somewhat renewed. "I told you how she loved religious history, knew about all the sites from Stonehenge to Notre Dame and every Iron Age cemetery and ritualistic site in the UK, Ireland. She knew all about blind springs, dowsing rods, standing stones, Alfred Watkins ley lines, a frightened pope's efforts to eliminate the Knights Templar on one dark Friday the thirteenth. She understood how contemporary religious sites had been built on ancient ones to make the transition from an old religion to a new religion easier." Mckenna sighed. "But I suspect that I went over much of this the last time you were here. I forget a lot lately. I haven't slept well in some time."

"Why did you go back to those places after...?" Chase said, having heard the explanation already, but hoping the video unit's mic might capture at least some of it for the official record.

"After Elise was killed? I think we covered this."

Dolores began to speak, but Mckenna raised a lean finger.

"I wasn't sure of that myself," she began, "at least at first. I guess I felt that, somehow, if I visited the places she'd visited, and went on to some of those that she hadn't lived to see, well, I guess I thought that somehow I'd recapture her...*essence* I suppose."

Mckenna choked back a sob. It was the first genuine sign of emotion Dolores had seen since she and Chase had arrived.

"Does that make sense?"

"But you didn't find her," Dolores said.

Mckenna shook her head slowly.

"Did you find *anything*?" Chase said.

"Not even a trace of her," Mckenna said with a sad grin. "I just wandered the globe with this open wound searching for Elise's ghost and finding nothing."

She paused, cocked her head to one side.

"But that isn't exactly true, is it?" she said. "Open wounds attract bacteria don't they? Open wounds tend to get infected. Is that what you meant when you asked if I'd found *anything*?"

Chase remained silent. He was staring intently at the dark spot where he knew Mckenna's face to be.

More thunder sounded, louder, closer.

"He meant—" Dolores began, feeling the need to say something.

"Do you feel it?" Mckenna said suddenly, interrupting Dolores, her voice thicker, more resonant somehow, flowing from the shadowy corner like a river of mud. She leaned forward, her eyes glowing with intensity.

"Feel what?" Dolores said.

"*It*," was all Mckenna said.

Dolores frowned, inched closer to Chase, whose mouth was hanging open as if he'd planned to say something, but had thought better of it. The air had grown cold in spite of the humid rain falling past the partly open window behind them.

"It comes to me in my dreams." Mckenna reached over to the end table with spider-leg fingers, quietly scooping up a pill bottle that had been hiding behind the brass base of what might have been a Tiffany lamp with a lead-glass hummingbird shade.

"*What* comes to you in your dreams?" Chase asked, hoping to God that the video camera mic was picking all this up.

"Something old. Something *very* old, older than us, older than *anything*."

"What does *it* look like?" Dolores said.

Mckenna seemed to perk up.

"You've seen it. At least a shadow of it, its residual energy, like a ghost, a shade of its passing. Not the *real* thing. You wouldn't be here if you'd seen the *real* thing."

"We saw something on a video I shot," Chase said.

Mckenna's face grew impossibly grim, fearful.

"Have you sensed it following you?" she said.

"It sounds like a cat, doesn't it?" Chase said.

Mckenna nodded slowly. "It can sound like many things, *look* like many things. Look like nothing. But it doesn't make noise as we understand it. The sound you heard, the cat's cry, I think of it as a rusty hinge on a door closing. Or opening."

Rain pelted the window. Chase shifted his position. The leather sofa creaked.

"Don't worry, it will find you," she said, sensing his discomfort and poking at it sardonically.

"Why?" Chase said, his throat feeling suddenly as if it were stuffed full of old bones.

"Because you've seen it. It doesn't like to be seen."

"So why is it killing people?" Dolores said, taking note of the suddenly pale sheen on Chase's face.

"Because that's what it does. I believe someone woke it up a long time ago and it was just waiting for someone to need it again, waiting on the other side of a door. And it found me. Or maybe I found it. I think it sensed my heartbreak. And it's been with me ever since, like an infection. It killed the man who murdered my daughter and then the police officer who mishandled the evidence. I heard all about it in my time going in and out of that precinct. Looking at those pictures and the video of my daughter leaving the club with that son of a bitch right behind her, watching her, thinking about how it would feel to—"

A sob gurgled past Mckenna's lips. She covered her mouth with the hand holding the pill bottle.

Chase caught a glimpse of the bottle's label. Dilaudid, he thought. A full bottle.

"Where did you get those?" Dolores asked.

"I've had some kidney stones," Mckenna managed, composing herself. "These are good for the pain. And I have some friends in the medical profession. My husband *was* a doctor."

"You're going to take those, aren't you?" Chase said.

"All good things must come to an end," Mckenna said, laughing wryly. It was a terrible sound.

"And the others?" Dolores thought to ask. "The other people who were murdered?"

"It would go after the last person I looked at."

"Does it go out every night?" Dolores said.

"No. I never know when it's going to go out. It's like living on the edge of a razor, waiting, hoping that it won't...so I can't take any chances. That's why I have all the photographs, the televisions, so there won't be any chance of..." Her voice trailed off into nothingness.

"And Father Rousseau?" Chase said. The words seemed to cut through the thick dark air like a blade.

"I fell asleep in my car after visiting him," Mckenna said, her voice growing cold. "He'd tried to help. I went to him to...seek forgiveness, maybe."

"But you can't control it," Dolores said.

"No one can. It killed that bastard that murdered my daughter. It also killed the officer. I'd seen the video at the station, that detective, Teschal, she showed me, and then I'd seen the officer because he *apologized* to me before I left. Do you *fucking* believe that? I never would have known anything about him or what had happened with the evidence if he hadn't come up to me in the lobby of the precinct and told me how sorry he was, assuring me that they'd find my daughter's killer!"

"And the others?" Dolores said, feeling suddenly breathless and insubstantial.

"The others," Mckenna said. "I'd seen them on television or read about them in newspapers, the internet, MSN. BBC. CNN. Done research when it was needed."

"And Greece and Ireland?" Chase said.

"I get a lot of television stations—Greece, Ireland, Japan, the UK, Pakistan...there are a *lot* of bad people out there. This fucking planet is just *drowning* in bad people. *Evil* people. There have been countless Elise's. Far too many. And countless D-Block Raccines."

There was a sound and Mckenna lifted her head.

"Was that a—?"

"I think someone knocked on the door," Dolores said starting to get to her feet.

"I'll go," Chase said. "It must be Teschal."

"Be sure," Mckenna said, leaning forward, her face like a bleached skull rising from a dark sea.

Chase paused, offered Dolores a worried glance and headed for the door.

"Who do you think is at the door?" Dolores said.

"It always stops by after each…incident, to tell me, in its way." Mckenna settled back into the recliner, the leather making a sound like skin being tightly stretched over bone.

"That explains the heavy-duty door…"

"The door to Genevieve's room is made of oak. Oak is old and special. Respected. An unspoken pact. A mutually agreed upon stop sign, though not binding. No, not binding by any means. Some things know no bounds."

"And the medallion? Not exactly a good luck emblem is it?"

"Celtic protection. Another unstated agreement of sorts."

"Have you seen this thing?"

"I never look. I cover my eyes and face. It's blinding to see, to look at, the light. Every color, so bright…and I scream into my palms until it leaves. And I dream that I'm there with it when it strikes. And I wake up screaming."

"How did you know about the porn director?" Dolores said.

"There was a special on television about the pornographic industry a couple of weeks ago," Mckenna said with a sliver of disgust in her voice. "I didn't mean to keep watching, but it was like seeing a train wreck, I just couldn't look away. It exposed the darker side of the industry, AIDS, other STDs. John Holmes. One segment dealt with *snuff* films. Carver was mentioned. The narrator explained that he was suspected of being involved with at least one *snuff* film and had disappeared. They showed him being interviewed years earlier. One of the most evil looking people I've ever seen. He'd explained how violent S and M films were becoming very popular *and* lucrative. The story was that he'd been commissioned privately to create that film. Rich bastards with too much money, too much free time, and no souls. He even tried on his trademark black leather mask for the camera. I'll never forget the sight of his terrible eyes looking out through the slits."

"That man tonight," Dolores said, "at the amusement park, the—"

"The *North Side Strangler*?"

"How could you know about him?"

"His photograph has been all over the local television stations. Just like the Irish girl who'd been acquitted of a murder everyone knew she'd committed. And that man tonight was a registered sex offender who'd disappeared, jumped probation. The reporter on television said that the police considered him to be a 'person of interest' in the Strangler case. Do you believe that? A 'person of interest!' That's politician-talk for fucking child killer."

Dolores started to speak, but no words came.

"You need to leave, soon," Mckenna said, her voice suddenly hushed. "It will be coming to tell me what it did. And it won't be happy to see you here. I don't think that it likes strangers, especially those that it's been following." A terrible grin split Mckenna's lips. Her teeth shone from the shadows like fangs.

Dolores felt her breath catch in her throat.

"And after it leaves, I'm going to take these." Mckenna shook the pill bottle, it sounded like a child's rattle.

"How do you know that will make it go away?" Dolores said.

"I don't," she said flatly. "But one can hope. At least it won't be my burden anymore."

***

Chase paused to check the video unit, found it to be running smoothly, and then went to the door. He paused, his hand inches from the knob, a sliver of fear slipping into his heart like a splinter. The thing knew him, had been following him. It had been with him in that darkened old house. Watching.

Chase felt impossibly cold.

"Fuck."

Then it struck him like a dowsing of ice cold water to the face. This whole thing was ridiculous. *Beyond* ridiculous.

He glanced back toward the den. It was so simple, so predictably obvious. He and Dolores were being manipulated by a mentally ill woman. That was it. She was even manipulating the police. Hell, when had he become such a fool? Allison Mckenna was either completely mad or simply playing crazy in order to cover up for her friends, friends who were committing murders in cult-like fashion for some unknown reason. It was all just that simple, yet so undeniably clever. Even Teschal seemed to be falling for the woman's scheme.

Damn, he thought angrily. It all stops here. He was smarter. And he would not be fooled anymore.

The knock came again, startling him. He touched the knob, twisted it and opened the door.

"Well, well, well," Connie said. "Isn't this cozy. *Menage e tois* anyone?"

Chapter Fifty-Eight

Teschal wove through the traffic that had been pumped into Old Dominion Road like blood into a weak artery, greasy rain pelting her windshield, thunder booming, lightning skipping along the horizon like stones across a pond. Her mind was brimming with ideas, bursting with possible solutions. But try as she might, she just couldn't paint Allison Mckenna as the killer. But it seemed blatantly apparent that the woman knew more than she was telling.

There just *had* to be a murderous cult operating in and around Gevaudan, all indications pointed to it. The only things missing were pentagrams drawn in blood on the walls at the various murder scenes and black candles laced with human fat smoldering on makeshift altars. This was all the work of some ancient sect resurrected for some demented purpose by determined individuals with whom Mckenna had somehow fallen in league.

But if there *was* a cult at work, where were its members holding their rituals, planning their murders? In one of the countless abandoned mills peppering the city's landscape? In some secluded grove in the nearby Indian Reservation where other cultish activity had taken place decades earlier? Perhaps by means of the internet? Hell, maybe even deep within the Bridgton Triangle.

It occurred to Teschal, not for the first time, that the motorcycle gang the Ghosts were likely suspects, in spite of the fact that the North Side Strangler victims had turned up on Jones Beach, a place they frequented. Jack Collins' interview with Lyle Chisholm, the leader of the Ghosts, had, perhaps, been an enlightening one after all. Many of the Ghosts had criminal records and were known to carry a wide assortment of weapons. They were also known to be quite vicious in their dealings with rival gangs as well as anyone who crossed them.

Perhaps it had all started just that way, with the dead children. Maybe the Ghosts were having their revenge against Joe Griece, the North Side Strangler, a previously unknown entity who'd tried to implicate them in the child murders. Griece may have been the original target, though an anonymous, elusive target. Maybe the Ghosts had been working systematically down their own list of suspects, starting with D-Block Raccine, then Anthony Carver and Corrister Flynn before finally hitting the right candidate.

The Ghosts had, on occasion, been chased out of Star Land, having been caught partying and sleeping in the abandoned buildings, just as they'd been chased out of some of the old mills in Gevaudan and in the nearby towns of Bridgton, North Bridgton, and Wickham, even turning up at the defunct State psychiatric facility in Wickham from time to time. And the murdered rookie cop, the outlier in the equation, might simply have been the victim of a 'wrong time, wrong place' incident. Perhaps he'd stumbled upon the Ghosts partying in the old mill on Quarry Street and the confrontation had turned deadly.

But the MO was the biggest problem. The complex and strange method by which the murders were being committed presented issues. The Ghosts were neither clever nor methodical, murder in their circles often resulted from fights, bar room brawls. And the few murders they were likely to plan would have involved knives or guns. And the possibility that they had gone after the likes of Corrister Flynn or a West Coast porn director hiding out in Gevaudan seemed implausible.

Then a truly bizarre and disturbing thought drove itself like a sewing needle into Teschal's brain and she asked herself, what sort of person might hold a serious enough grudge against the criminal element in Gevaudan to take cold calculated action by murdering the worst of that lot in the most gruesome fashion imaginable? The name Jennifer Kinsley immediately presented itself. She and the members of her Survivors' Group fit the vigilante mold perfectly. They possessed motive, opportunity to meet regularly, organizational skills. And several members of the group carried firearms, mostly as a response to their shared experiences with violence. Two members of the group were actually police officers from neighboring towns. One member was even a retired FBI agent. And another member, Chet Mosely, owned a garage on lower Warren Street, a mere stone's throw from the porn director murder scene. And auto repair shops were known to house plenty of corrosive chemicals and acetylene torches.

Teschal's gut grew cold. Was it possible? Was Kinsley lying about Allison Mckenna's refusal to join the group? Or had Mckenna declined to participate in the group meetings because she'd come to suspect what Kinsley and the other members were *really* involved in and had simply been too frightened to relay those suspicions to the police? Was fear the driving emotion behind Mckenna's strange behavior as opposed to grief?

Jennifer Kinsley had nonchalantly explained to Teschal from her office doorway how each member of the group would have been more than capable of murder at some point. Revenge was a powerful motive.

It seemed impossible, insane even. But Joe Griece's mangled burned body was not a figment of Teschal's imagination. Something horrific had happened in that room in the old Horror House at South Coast Star Land. And an unfathomable hatred for a child killer would certainly explain a lot. The other victims were criminals too. A man creating a snuff film, his second no less, who'd already cut the throat of the woman he'd hired to unwittingly appear in it. And then there was Corrister Flynn who'd beaten a murder rap though she was clearly as guilty as sin. And the man who'd raped and murdered a promising young woman as well as sold drugs to hundreds of addicts and casual users in and around Gevaudan. Each victim symbolic in their detestability. Each worthy of a terrible death. Allison Kinsley and her Survivors' Group ridding the city of its monsters, one at a time.

But what about the rookie cop? Could the group possibly have come to hate that man enough due to his failure to help secure justice for Elise Mckenna to kill him? Was it possible that the Survivor's Group was that determined, that murderous? That inhuman? Or had he simply had the bad luck to walk in on them in the Quarry Street mill where they'd been secretly meeting, plotting their next murder? The group would probably have had their 'killing arsenal' on hand and used it on the intruder. Another burned and mangled body, this one lying crumpled at the bottom of an elevator shaft.

And to add to the scenario, Teschal knew that the group met at Saint Genevieve's Catholic School every Thursday night. But they'd been meeting in the church basement community room for the past few weeks because the room they'd been using at the school had been partly flooded by a burst pipe. Teschal had stopped in two weeks earlier to speak with Jennifer Kinsley and stayed for coffee, talking with some of the members *and* Father Rousseau, who she understood stopped in frequently to visit with the group. And the late priest had reported an intruder lurking around the church just before he'd been killed. Was it possible that a member or members of the group had been seen by Rousseau while breaking into the church to retrieve some incriminating evidence they'd left behind? Then, when Rousseau stumbled upon the scene, they'd been forced to kill him?

But the fact that Rousseau had been killed in the same manner as the others suggested that his murder had been planned. Perhaps he'd come across something incriminating and simply had not fully understood its ramifications and some group members had gone to the church expressly to kill him before he'd reported his discovery to the proper authorities.

And the last person Rousseau had spoken with before his death was Allison Mckenna, the woman who seemed to be at the dark heart of all that was happening.

Teschal was suddenly very concerned for Mckenna's safety, as well as any pertinent information she might possess. If Mckenna were to wind up murdered, that information would die with her.

A very pointed discussion with Ms. Mckenna was suddenly imperative. Even if the woman knew nothing, even if this outlandish theory that had abruptly formed in Teschal's fevered brain proved baseless, it was definitely long past time to stop being polite with her.

Things were reaching critical mass in Gevaudan this night. Teschal felt it in her gut, sensed it unfolding all around her, just as her mother had told her. *Drabarni.* Witch. Psychic. All those names she'd come to hate, to deny. All coming together tonight, just like that night last summer when she'd paid a midnight visit to Mercy General Hospital in Wickham to discover what had been happening with a couple named Graves. Teschal had a sick cold feeling that what awaited her this night was no less terrifying than what she'd encountered in that darkened ICU. She'd need to be ready for anything.

Teschal picked up the radio mic, called into the station. Eloise answered the call.

"I need a unit sent to the Daniker Building on Tremont Street," Teschal said.

"Yes, detective," Eloise said. "Should they—"

"Just tell them to stand by and report to me if they see anything they might consider suspicious. *Anything.* I'm heading there as we speak."

"I'm calling it in," Eloise said before signing off.

Teschal cradled the mic, gritted her teeth. Eloise, she thought. Chase Christian's suspected source in the Gevaudan PD. But there was nothing she could do about that now. The cosmic tumblers were falling into place quickly. Dealing with Eloise would have to wait. Eve Teschal was listening to her instincts now, embracing her intuition as Vadoma Teschal had insisted. She only hoped she wasn't too late.

A uniformed officer wearing a neon yellow and black raincoat saw the flashing blue LEDs in her SUV's grill, stepped out suddenly into the creeping stream of cars, forcing it to a halt and waving Teschal through.

Teschal waved to the man, veered out of traffic, maneuvering up onto the sloping shoulder of the road and then back into the line of cars, slipping around a pickup truck, the driver of which looked as if he could have killed her just then. Then, as the traffic parted, she sped off toward the glistening lights of Gevaudan. And Allison Mckenna.

Chapter Fifty-Nine

Chase let Connie into Mckenna's apartment and stepped out into the foyer. He glanced around. Had he heard something? The only sound he could detect was that of the rain. Frowning, he closed the door and turned to consider Connie, who was standing off to one side glaring at him, her lips pursed, her arms crossed.

"This way," he said softly and he led her through the living room and the dining room, past the video unit (which was humming along dutifully atop the table, recording everything transpiring in the den, the doorframe between the two rooms functioning as a makeshift frame to the evolving scene).

Chase's mobile phone began vibrating in his pocket. He drew it out into the dim light. Eloise. Bad timing. For once, he would not be able to take her call. What was happening was just too important. And the very unstable Allison Mckenna might consider the call to be some form of betrayal and throw them out. He hit the 'dismiss' button. Then he rejoined the others, hovering inside the den doorway, careful not to block the shot.

Dolores turned to consider the new arrival.

Mckenna raised her red-rimmed eyes and studied Connie with an odd detachment.

"This is Connie Moncrief," Chase said, awkwardly. "She produces a spot on the late-night news for KTX."

"I know who she is," Mckenna said softly. "Welcome to the Dark Side. Accidents, shootings, stabbings."

"It pays the bills," Connie said, snippily.

Chase recognized the raw edge of anger in Connie's voice—he'd heard it many times before.

Don't fuck this up, Connie, he thought.

Connie took up position in the den doorway, inadvertently blocking part of the shot, standing inches from Chase as if making a statement to Dolores that she had no intention whatsoever of going gently into Dylan Thomas' 'good night.' She offered Dolores a desultory glance, moved on to Mckenna's worn face, finally letting her eyes settle upon a stack of CDs on the table by the door. She reached down and picked up the topmost disk.

"*Bat out of Hell*," she said, studying the blood-red image of a man on a motorcycle bursting from a grave and the huge bat squatting atop a tombstone, wings spread, teeth bared in mid shriek. "Meat Loaf."

She set the CD down and the stack spilled across the table.

Dolores noticed Mckenna wince.

"Black Sabbath," Connie said, lifting another CD.

She set the Sabbath CD down and let her fingers stray to another.

"Mmmph," she said, picking up this third disk. "Nazareth. You just don't look like the hard rock type to me."

"My daughter enjoyed all sorts of music," Mckenna said, impatience and perhaps a touch of contempt growing in her voice. "These were her latest discoveries."

Connie flipped the CD around, holding the cover up so that the others could see the lavender-tinted image of a three-headed hound with bat-wings perched on a mound of human skulls in a dismal hellish swamp.

"Cerberus," Connie said, ragged scorn piercing her voice. "The three-headed hound that guards the gates of hell, unless I'm mistaken." Connie set the CD down.

"What do you *want* you rude woman?" Mckenna said, anger twisting into her tone like a fishhook.

"Well, seeing that no one else has asked the questions that need to be asked," she said curtly, "and as I'm trying to get to the bottom of this and not drag it out, I'll ask those questions if nobody minds. And please forgive my lack of tact, but time *is* wasting."

"You put it so diplomatically."

"What about these killings?" Connie said, cutting to the bone.

"Connie!" Dolores said, her voice riddled with incredulity as she attempted to intervene on Mckenna's behalf. "You don't understand—"

"Oh, I think I do Del. If you and Chase here are playing house, so be it. But it's clouding his judgment."

"Connie—" Chase tried, but the woman was having none of it.

"Is there something I'm missing here?" Connie said, her eyes burning with growing fury. And scorn.

"You're jealous," Mckenna said, a small revelatory grin spreading across her darkening face.

Connie turned on her. "Listen, I have nothing but sympathy for you and what you've been through, but people are dying—"

"Do you miss Lysander?" Mckenna said, her voice barely a whisper. "She *was* your friend, *more* than a friend really."

Connie went rigid, her hand straying to the scar on her forearm.

"How—?"

"She misses you," Mckenna said. "She doesn't blame you. You didn't have that much to drink, just enough to lose control of the...BMW was it?"

"Fucking cunt," Connie growled. "Just *who* the hell do you think you are?" Then, in a hoarse whisper, "*What* the hell are you?"

Chase stepped in front of Connie in an attempt to contain her. She was shaking with rage, tears starting in her eyes. She'd been reduced to a raw nerve and Chase knew he was partly to blame.

"I'm just the messenger," Mckenna said.

"What?" Chase said, turning, genuinely puzzled.

"Ms. Mckenna," Dolores said, "I think you need to seek some help."

"You think I'm crazy?"

"I mean, the things you've told us—"

"I've told you the truth," Mckenna said, her voice once again flat, devoid of emotion.

"There's *nothing* following you," Dolores said quietly but firmly. "There's *nothing* killing these people for you. It's just other people. Why don't you tell us who they are, where they are, and why they're doing these things."

Chase turned to Connie, who was still seething.

"This is some sort of cult killing bad people, isn't it?" Dolores pressed. She moved to the edge of the sofa, leaned in toward Mckenna, reached out for her.

"Is that what you think?" Mckenna shook her head and laughed a sad little laugh. Then her right hand, which had been lying placidly in her lap, shot out and seized Dolores' wrist.

"I—" Dolores complained, shock lacerating her voice like a scalpel.

"Wait with me," Mckenna said, cutting Dolores off, tightening her grip around the woman's wrist, drawing her close, her impossibly sick breath filling Dolores' senses. "It's coming. And that detective, Teschal, she's coming too. One happy family."

"Ms. Mckenna—" Chase managed, when he saw Dolores' terrified eyes. He took a step toward the two women, but stopped dead when the sound of a cat crying pierced the gloom.

Mckenna's lips twisted into a wry smile and she released Dolores' reddened wrist.

Dolores fell back into the sofa, clutching her wrist and shrinking away to the far end of the sofa.

"It's here," Mckenna said, her eyes swelling with tears. She considered the bottle of pills in her other hand, let out a shrill little laugh and let them slip from her fingers. They landed on the carpet and rolled away. "Too late for those now."

"Fuck this," Connie said and she turned and headed for the door.

"Wait!" Dolores called, still cradling her reddened wrist and getting to her feet.

Chase was on Connie's heels as she moved past the dining room table and into the living room. Overtaking her, he grabbed her arm and spun her around. He opened his mouth to speak, but the broiling emotion he saw in her eyes jammed the words back into his throat.

"What?" Connie hissed.

"Connie, you need to stay here," he managed.

"Fuck *her* Chase," Connie growled, her pathetic eyes locking on his. "And fuck *you*!"

She twisted, pulled free of his grasp and went to the door. Her fingers touched the knob just as the cat cried out again, the sound coming from everywhere and nowhere all at once. She pulled her hand back. The door knob felt hot. She swallowed hard, her pride falling to pieces at her feet. And that was too much for Connie Moncrief.

"Fuck all of you," she whispered and she tore open the door.

"No—" Chase managed.

The cry came again as the door opened, revealing the empty foyer beyond.

"Nothing," Connie managed, glancing around and turning back to Chase, shaking her head slowly. "Nothing," she whispered, a profound sadness in her voice.

She opened her mouth to speak again, but the words died in her throat. She squeezed her eyes shut expelling a single tear which trickled down her cheek.

Chase had never seen her cry. He reached out for her, but froze when his gaze was suddenly drawn to something in the foyer behind Connie, above her left shoulder.

The dimly lit foyer with its well-appointed wood wainscoting and crystal sconces was quivering like a reflection in a puddle into which someone had dropped a pebble. The quiver became a ripple, spreading across the entire foyer, lapping at the edges of the doorway like an undulating sea striking the shoreline. And then the foyer melted away completely and a blinding white field of searing heat replaced it. And from the scalding new landscape came a terrible sound rushing through the doorway like a freight train careening through a tunnel, its whistle shrieking like a dying animal.

Connie saw the terror in Chase's eyes before she felt the searing heat at her back or heard the tornado sound in her ears, and instinctively she turned toward the terrible white void. Her scream rose to an impossible pitch as her face exploded in a glut of blood. Her dying brain told her that she was being thrown backward through the air, propelled by an invisible force, her clothes bursting into flame, her scream turning to molten plasma in her throat.

A horrible heat blasted its way through the room, tearing pictures from the wall, flipping chairs and furniture, hurling knick-knacks in every direction. Chase was thrown backward, landing hard on the rug, his head rebounding off the dining room half-wall. He forced himself up onto his elbows as a terrible wave of blistering heat washed over him, singeing the hair on his forearms and draining the moisture from his eyes.

Dolores screamed, gripped the door frame to the den for support, intense waves of heat wafting past her like impossible heat phantoms, her flesh beginning to burn. She opened her eyes for a split second before being forced to close them again, but in that instant she saw the doorway alive with white fire, rippling waves of intense heat flowing into Mckenna's expensive apartment, igniting anything flammable, consuming the carpet, causing anything it touched to smolder and melt. And in the scorching heart of it all was a horribly misshapen entity that was somehow growing *out of* the door jamb as if its very being was somehow passing between the molecules of the wood and wall-board. The horrible thing was using Mckenna's apartment like the rung of a ladder, pulling itself from its world into Dolores' world like an immense sea monster emerging from some hellish sea. Behind it, the foyer had ceased to exist. The expensive wood, carpet, and brass fixtures had been replaced by an endless void of blinding white light rippling with waves of unimaginable heat.

And there at its heart was the twisted face Dolores had seen in the shadows of Chase's video from the empty house, only magnified a thousand times. Thick knobby limbs reached around the doorframe, digging into the wood and plaster, crimson-colored veins throbbing beneath the mottled glowing skin. And behind it that terrible sea of molten white heat like the guts of an impossible blast furnace, with burning writhing shapes rising up out of the white-hot muck and then sinking back into the void like burning children drowning in lava, and glowing blue-colored rivulets of liquid fire creeping like tentacles across the carpeting toward her bringing with them the undeniable stench of burning sulfur.

Dolores squeezed her aching eyes shut and fell away from the door frame, landing on her hands and knees. But the light pierced her eyelids and in that light she saw that the horrible apparition in the doorway had been replaced by the terrible familiar shape of a man wearing old jeans and a torn sweatshirt, a man with a harsh unshaven face, fly unzipped, leering dark eyes, stained teeth, razor thin lips twisted into a crooked smile, with bulbous fingers twitching convulsively at his sides. In Dolores' mind the terrible noise had stopped and a deafening silence had taken its place. The scalding air continued to pour through the doorway in spite of the weird calm that seemed to surround the man and it caused the man's gray hair to wave like kelp at the bottom of a terrible sea.

"Hello Dolores," the man said, his voice a harsh echoing whisper. "I've missed my little girl."

Dolores buried her face in her hands, tried to scream, but her throat had gone bone dry. She was dying, they all were. The hellish screeching resumed, gushing through the door to the foyer like a raging river. She forced her eyes open and, amidst the chaos, smoke, and impossible heat, she saw Allison Mckenna standing before her, eyes closed, face placid in spite of the horror erupting around her.

Dolores tried to shout at her, to tell her to get down before the encroaching flames reached her, but the relentless cacophony drowned out her shouts and the heat forced her to cover her watering burning eyes with her hands again. In a desperate bid she dared to open her eyes for one brief instant, hoping to grab for Mckenna and drag her to the floor where the air was tolerable. But Mckenna was gone. In her place were bits of debris, dancing momentarily in the turbid air and then falling through space like shooting stars, crystallizing in mid-air and finally bouncing off the rug and furniture like transparent embers.

***

Teschal sensed something, a ripple in reality, a tear in the fabric of the universe, like a punch to her gut seconds before she rounded the corner and glimpsed Mckenna's building with the black smoke billowing from the windows. And she saw the vivid blinding shafts of white light piercing the glass sliders and windows, reaching into the dismal night like laser beams. And as she watched, one large window exploded. But instead of flames bursting forth, a human form appeared, shards of glass like the crystalline tail of a kite trailing obediently behind the body as it fell to earth, tearing through the green awning and finally landing with what must have been a sickening thud on the walkway beneath.

Teschal threw her shock aside, jammed her foot down onto the brake, skidding to a halt across the street in front of one of the expensive brownstones from which people were spilling out onto the sidewalk, pointing.

Screams and shouts filled the night as Teschal tumbled out of her SUV. She scrambled across the street, racing toward the body on the walkway, realizing in an instant that the broken bloody heap had once been Allison Mckenna. And then she was racing for the door just as several choking panicking people in tee shirts and sweat pants and nightgowns began to emerge, guided by a shocked young man in a police officer's uniform.

"It's the fourth-floor corner apartment," the officer shouted. "I just got here. I called in the alarm as soon as—" was the last thing Teschal heard as she burst through the open door into the smoky lobby and broke for the stairs.

***

Dolores saw the approaching flames, creeping up the sides of the den doorway, clawing at the ceiling. The light was gone as was the thing in the doorway, having faded in a terrible deafening shriek of nothingness an instant after Mckenna crashed through the window above the sofa, taking with it the blank blazing hot-white landscape that had flooded the fourth floor foyer. But the apartment itself was ablaze, the flames were consuming whatever they touched, ribbons of fire climbing the walls, crawling across the rug, thick rolling smoke everywhere.

"Chase!" she screamed into the carnage. No response. What had she learned so long ago in elementary school? Stay below the smoke.

She began to crawl toward the den doorway.

"Chase!" she hollered again, her vocal cords raw as hamburger. Then she saw him, in the dining room, on his hands and knees. She hurried toward him, smoke and noxious fumes clogging her throat, grabbing for her like charcoal-gray tentacles.

She reached him, grabbed his hand, felt the burned flesh. He was shouting something unintelligible, Connie's scorched body inches from his face.

"We've got to go!" Dolores shouted.

Chase turned to her, his face bloody, clumps of hair burned away, the flesh scorched where the edge of his hair-line had been.

"Now!" Dolores tightened her grip. Then her eyes fell on what remained of Connie and she felt her insides roll over. She turned away, swallowed hard and, with every ounce of strength she could muster, she wrapped her arms around Chase's chest and dragged him away from the smoldering bloody remains of Connie Moncrief. Finally coming to terms with what was happening Chase turned to Dolores, nodded briskly and followed her on hands and knees toward the door.

Dolores reached the door, turned to make certain that Chase was still with her, glimpsed the stacks of images Mckenna had gathered of criminals and sex offenders sailing into the smoky air like flaming sparrows trapped in a burning barn. She turned back to the open doorway just as a shape broke from the wall of smoke.

"Is there anyone else?" Teschal shouted.

"No," Dolores managed. "Connie's dead."

"Get out," Teschal shouted above the crackling din.

Dolores and Chase crawled into the hall where the last of the tenants were scrambling for safety, avoiding the elevator and cascading down the stairs, fire alarms raging, emergency beacons flashing strobe-like from every corner of the hall.

Teschal watched Chase and Dolores until the swirling smoke had consumed them, and then she crawled into the fire storm, moving toward the dark shape lying on the floor at the edge of the dining room. She found Connie, felt her insides cramp up, moved close to what remained of her face, quickly assessing the situation, studying the spots where bone was poking through the yellow-black char that had once been flesh. She instinctively felt for a pulse, but the smoldering skin fell away like overcooked meat beneath her fingertips. She spun around, crawling back toward the door, gasping and choking. There was nothing to be done. It was not safe for her to remain any longer. The flames were consuming everything. Burning drapes were falling to the floor and dark noxious smoke was rising from the smoldering carpeting, gathering in dark roiling nimbus clouds near the ceiling.

Teschal reached the hall, tumbled down the first few stairs, climbed down the rest and emerged into the rainy night just as the first fire engines were pulling up, their sirens wailing, their red LEDs flashing like heat lightning. She leaned into the hedges, coughing, evacuated the contents of her stomach and stumbled toward the street, wiping her lips with her sleeve, collapsing at the edge of the lawn beside Dolores and Chase.

Blurred figures that must have been firefighters were moving past her. Hoses were being unrolled and stretched out across the well-tailored lawn and walkway behind them. She heard crashing glass as the ornate doors to the Daniker Building were reduced to rubble as first responders muscled their way into the lobby.

Teschal ignored it all, looked up, found Dolores' reddened eyes, then leaned forward and closed hers.

Chapter Sixty

The sky over St. Brigid's Cemetery was slate gray as a small contingent of people gathered around Constance Ophelia Moncrief's grave. The drizzle had, thankfully, ceased, but the air was still raw. It might very well have been the dead of winter instead of late spring.

Less than two dozen mourners had turned out for the funeral and a handful more for the wake. Chase stood with Dolores on a slight rise beside a large twisted oak tree. His forehead and right hand were bandaged; the burned skin beneath the wrappings still ached. But he'd been lucky. Connie had once said that he should be thankful for her—one day she'd come between him and tragedy. She'd been right. If he'd been the one to open Allison Mckenna's door that fateful night…

He studied the gathering of mourners. Several of the young technicians and trainees from KTX were huddled in a knot off to one side. Dale, Derek, and of course Kiley, who was looking somber in black, among them. Several of the station big-wigs had stopped by to pay a cursory visit to the grave site. They were easy to spot—perfectly coifed hair, expensive looking suits and black dresses. There seemed to be no family anywhere Chase could detect. Alone. Connie had been alone. Chase felt sick in his heart. Was this what awaited him, a cold lonely death beneath a bone-chilling sky?

Dolores sensed his pain, squeezed his hand. He turned to study her lovely eyes, noticed tears there. And a bit of a smile. The day was suddenly not so bleak and raw.

Chase let his gaze return to the scene, suddenly conscious of the priest speaking from the graveside. For a fleeting second he envisioned the horribly burned face of Father Rousseau speaking to the small contingent from above the dog collar, heard the words *cri du chat* move past his ears, but a wispy tendril of mist and a gust of raw wind carried the horrid illusion away.

Chase's gaze was drawn to two figures standing on a small hill some yards beyond the open grave—Teschal and the other detective, Richards. She'd apparently been watching Chase. When she realized he'd seen her, she nodded slightly. Chase did likewise. They shared something now, he and Teschal. They'd both been there at the end, when…when what?

The answer was an inconceivable one, yet an undeniable one. The fact is they'd both been there when some*thing* from another world tried to enter this world, ultimately failing thanks to the sacrifice of a profoundly sad, ultimately doomed woman, leaving a blazing inferno in its wake. And Chase realized that as time passed, what he'd seen would become less substantial, the images less definitive, distorted. Like any memory, the incident would soften and blur and his mind would inevitably seek a rational explanation for the horror he'd witnessed. And he also realized that the questions would linger like ghosts trapped in an old house that could never be completely exorcized.

Yet here he was, alive. Dolores too. And Teschal. But the losses were great. Connie was gone leaving a strange hole in his heart that he suspected would remain empty for some time. And brave grieving Allison Mckenna as well, gone to meet her daughter and husband in some far-off land. Her funeral was on hold. Her death had been ruled a suicide, but extenuating circumstances made a quick burial impossible. And distant relatives, perhaps smelling the sudden availability of an unclaimed inheritance, wanted to be in attendance for the proceedings.

In the end nothing unusual would turn up except maybe some brimstone. Perhaps some things were best left unsolved. Chase and Dolores would attend that one as well. They owed that much to Elise Genevieve Mckenna's deceased mother. In the end, they may have been the ones who understood her better than anybody. And that fact was fodder for a lifetime of nightmares.

"We should go," Dolores said. "I need to change your bandages. And we could both use some coffee, this cold air isn't good for anyone."

Chase agreed and the couple turned to leave. He glanced back one last time at the gun-metal-colored coffin with the pale lilies draped across it. There was so much he'd wanted to say to Connie, so much he owed her. But in the end it would all have to wait until he saw her again. And for the first time in his life, Chase actually believed that he *would* see her again someday, somewhere. And that notion brought him some degree of solace. Apologies and unspoken sentiments would have to keep for the time being. They could, in fact, last a lifetime. And perhaps beyond.

"Ready?" Dolores said.

He nodded and together they walked off into the brightening day.

Chapter Sixty-One

Chase was sitting in Dolores' recliner staring out at the lights of Gevaudan, listening to U2 performing *Bad* on the radio in the bedroom. He could make out the distant Bridgton University water tower perched atop Prospect Hill on the steep slopes that rose up behind Clemson Dormitory, its distinctive airplane warning lights blinking red.

"Here you go," Dolores said, entering from the kitchen with a cup of chicken broth, which she set on the TV tray beside Chase. He touched the cup with his bandaged hand, abruptly drew it back.

"Hot," he said.

"Sorry." Dolores picked up the mug of tepid broth and blew on it. Since that night in Allison Mckenna's apartment, Chase had sought out cooler things, and he was still reluctant to sit in the sun, not that there had been much lately. But who could blame him?

"Time to change the bandages," Dolores said, setting the broth aside and moving closer.

Chase had lost a patch of hair by his left temple. The doctors said it might grow back, but there was a second degree burn in that spot and it was uncomfortable. And his right hand had been burned, not terribly, but enough to warrant bandages and antibiotic cream as well as a watchful eye. Connie had taken the full brunt of whatever force had swept through Mckenna's apartment that dark rainy night. The building had been saved. No one else had been hurt. Dolores had come away from it all with a sunburned face. Her eyes had needed some hydration and her throat had been sore for a few days afterward, but otherwise she was fine. *Physically* fine.

Dolores leaned over Chase and began gingerly peeling away the bandage.

"There we go," she said softly, tossing the dressing into a nearby trash barrel and studying the wrinkled pink flesh. "Coming along."

"When do I see the doctor again?"

"Ralston or Cheever?"

"Not the one who keeps talking about physical therapy—my hand is fine. The one who is going to tell me if I need to get a toupee."

"Ralston. Monday." She applied a dab of silver sulfadiazine cream from a tube lying on the tray and then cut a fresh section of steri-strip and gently taped it into place.

"You'll be as good as new," she said setting her first aid kit, the one she'd thrown together after several trips to Walgreen's after Chase got home from the hospital, on the tray. Lucky was how the ER doctor had categorized Chase. An inch or so more to the right and he might have suffered some damage to his eye. No flames, just intense heat. Heat that had no business existing outside a volcanic vent, as the ER doctor, a woman named Carling, had suggested.

"Don't you worry," Dolores said checking the broth. It was nearly cold, just the way Chase liked it these days. That too was not unusual. Many burn victims, even those with relatively minor burns like him, often reported being unable or unwilling to touch hot things or spend any significant time in the sun, even long after they'd healed. "You'll be playing piano again in no time," she said.

"That's good," he said. "Because I couldn't play before," they added in unison, managing matching smiles.

"Your other girlfriend, Eve, called earlier, to check on you."

Chase snorted. "That's a good one. I guess she finally believes our story."

"Not much choice I gather, that is once her people finished sifting through what remained of Mckenna's apartment."

"Very forthcoming on her part."

"I think she's still in shock," Dolores said. "It won't last though, she'll be her tight-lipped ice queen self soon enough. Her type never really changes."

"I don't know about that. Maybe she's just misunderstood."

"Like anybody we may know?" Dolores carefully moved the TV tray with the broth aside and climbed up into Chase's lap. She snuggled close, sniffing the silver nitrate cream.

"You smell like a lifeguard," she said.

"I'll give you mouth to mouth later on."

"Can't hardly wait."

Chase wrapped his arms around her, drawing her close.

"Teschal still has the video unit," Dolores said, her eyes following the lighted wing tip of a passing plane. "Says she may have it for some time."

"She can keep it. There was too much heat for anything usable to have survived. Besides, I don't want to see whatever may be on it."

She nodded. "Agreed."

Chase sighed.

"What is it?"

"You know. I keep dreaming about Connie reaching for that doorknob. And after—"

"Shhh," Dolores whispered kissing him on the temple. "Don't think about it."

"But you saw it too."

She nodded solemnly. "I saw it. Whatever *it* was. And I was reaching out for Mckenna when she crashed through that window and fell four stories head first. And I saw what was left of her when we got down to the street."

"Now *you* stop thinking," Chase said, drawing her closer. He kissed her gently and she smiled, wiping away the start of a tear.

"Kiley called. I guess they want Derek to take Connie's old job, at least until they find a permanent replacement. They all wished you well."

"Good for Derek."

"You know what bothers me though?"

"What's that?"

"I heard the police questioning some of the other tenants in Mckenna's building that night. I guess I'm getting pretty good at this reporter thing, eavesdropping at every opportunity. Anyway, the neighbors, well, they all said the same thing. They heard us shouting, smelled the smoke. But they never heard the horrible tornado sound coming from the hall, or the cat sound, and they only saw a glimmer of that vivid white light, just a glow. But the light *we* saw was blinding. And the noise, it was deafening. How was all that possible?"

"It wasn't. But they weren't lying. I think what we saw in the hall behind that *thing* was some other place. And I think we were the only ones meant to see it if that makes sense."

"Like another dimension?"

Chase shrugged. "My grandfather was what locals called a real *christer*. The kind of guy who was always giving out advice or telling a story. He used to say that there were cracks in the universe, places where old things slept, like Jim Morrison talking about the doors between things. I always thought my grandfather was just trying to sound cool, talking like Morrison. But now, thinking back on it all, I suspect he actually believed that stuff. To some degree at least."

"Shakespeare's 'more things in heaven and earth?'"

"I think Mckenna's traveling to all those ancient places, carrying all that grief and anger with her, all that hatred for whoever killed her daughter, aching for revenge, well, I think it was like your Ouija board experience," Chase said. "I think she invited something in, some dark thing sleeping in one of the cracks my grandfather was talking about, something lurking behind one of Jim Morrison's doors. A hitchhiker. I think it fed off her grief, her anger, lived off her like a parasite. And maybe, deep down in some dark place, Mckenna *wanted* it around. Perhaps, once she realized what the arrangement was, she even thought she was doing some good. Maybe the terms of the arrangement were the sticking point. And in the end she couldn't live with it. She was, after all, only human. And she'd been stricken with something that thing we saw in the doorway never had, a conscience."

Chase sighed heavily.

"Jesus, I don't know if any of this makes sense. But not much about this whole thing *does* make sense."

"Maybe we weren't so far off the mark when we suspected that a cult was behind all this," Dolores said. "Maybe the idea transcends dimensions. But…"

"But?"

"Well, for a second, when I turned away from that thing in the doorway and closed my eyes, I saw…" Dolores bit her lip.

"Saw what?"

"I saw my father."

"Jesus," Chase whispered.

"But I think I understand it now. It means that he's dead. It means that he's with that thing on the other side. And he can't hurt me from there." She managed a weak little smile.

Chase felt himself nodding slowly. He saw a fresh tear at the corner of her eye, watched it trace a line down her cheek. He reached out and gently brushed it away.

Dolores' smile grew stronger.

A moment passed and Chase turned toward the table by the sofa. He gestured with his jaw.

"Where should we hang that?"

Dolores reached over and lifted a small cardboard box that was lying there and handed it to Chase. He lifted a folded fuchsia-colored sheet of paper from the box, unfolded it and took out the object that had been wrapped within. He turned the six-inch-long item over in his hand before handing it to Dolores.

The object was in the shape of a cross, but it had been carved from wood and hand painted. It featured an image of the crucified Christ in its center. Each extension featured an image Dolores' research had told them was symbolic of Jesus' suffering during the crucifixion in the form of terrible experiences the Haitian people had endured. One suggested the harsh treatment of women and another the deforestation of the island itself. Another symbolized hunger, and the fourth, a tiny painting of a crying child, apparently a reference to the harsh conditions experienced by infants.

"It belongs in a place of honor," Dolores said.

Chase nodded while re-reading the note that had accompanied the cross for the dozenth time.

He had been unable to reach Eloise after she'd come to see him one day after he'd been seen medically. She'd been quiet, sullen, almost guilt ridden. She'd actually apologized for having put him in harm's way.

"Don't blame yourself," Chase had said. "I'm a big boy."

But though Eloise had not argued, he knew she'd been having none of it. That the last time they'd spoken. Efforts to reach her a few days later had produced nothing but a steady ring and eventually a mechanical message from Verizon stating that the number was no longer in service. Dolores had been dispatched to investigate and found only an empty apartment and a landlord with a small package for one Chase Christian, freelance stringer.

Within the package was the small cross, which was meant to bring its owner luck and perhaps a little faith. The note had simply read:

Chase, this is a Haitian good luck charm, a Haitian Cross. You may need it. I've decided to go back to New Orleans. I'd forgotten why I'd moved away in the first place. I miss the Quarter and the ghosts there are friendlier. Bonswa, El

"Well, one good thing *did* come out of this," Dolores said, taking the note, cross, and box from Chase and gently setting them on the TV tray, and then leaning in and kissing him on the lips. "*One* thing makes sense."

Chase felt a smile touch his lips and he kissed her in return.

"I have absolutely no idea what you're talking about," he said and together they laughed.

Chapter Sixty-Two

Captain Donovan was seated across the table from Teschal in the conference room, Richards a few chairs away. At the head of the big table was a flat screen television on a metal cart. Wired to the set was a DVD player.

"Let it rip," Donovan said and Richards raised the remote, aimed it at the player and pushed a switch.

The unit hummed to life. The screen lit up with bug fights, static poured from the speakers.

Teschal leaned forward, lacing her fingers atop the table. Donovan was typically stone-faced.

The static parted, and a grainy scene unfolded. The vague image of a woman sitting in a recliner grew from the deep shadows. The video was apparently shot from approximately fifteen feet away, through a doorway to a small room. The video unit had clearly been positioned outside the room on a table perhaps, based on the height and angle, in order to capture as much of the unfolding scene as was possible. The woman in the recliner was evidently Allison Mckenna. She was speaking, but her voice was barely audible.

Richards slid several sheets of stapled papers across the table to Donovan, who picked them up, donned a pair of glasses he retrieved from his suit jacket pocket, and perused them.

"These are the names and addresses of all the people in the video," Richards said. "Plus any data we have right down to speeding tickets. There's nothing worth noting. We did let a lip reader have a crack at the video, but the room proved too dimly lit to get anything substantial."

Donovan nodded, lowered his glasses. "Who's she talking with?"

"Dolores Kane," Teschal said. "She's sitting on a sofa to the left, hidden by the door frame. She's an associate of Chase Christian, the stringer. She does research for a few lawyers in Gevaudan, one in Bridgton. A few local private investigators have also used her services over the years. One or two insurance companies. Under the table mostly. SSI recipient. Some sexual abuse in her past. I'd say she's one of the good guys."

Donovan nodded slowly. "We can leave most of that information in this room."

Static devoured some of the image and when it resumed another woman became visible, standing in the doorway with Chase, who glanced knowingly back at the video unit as if checking its functionality.

"Constance Moncrief," Teschal said. "Former producer of a late-night news show called the Dark Side based at KTX's satellite studio over on Ridgton Road. The show specialized in car crashes, shootings. She perished in the fire."

In the video, Connie picked up an object from a table positioned just inside the doorway, a CD from the looks of it. She set the item down then lifted another. She seemed to be talking with the Mckenna woman, perhaps even arguing with her, gesturing with her free hand, pointing at the woman. Then she held a third CD out for the others to see, before setting it down, speaking continually.

Connie and Chase turned, nearly in unison, as if they'd heard a sound. Even in the dim lighting it was evident that there was great anger etched into the Moncrief woman's face. She turned back to Mckenna, shaking with growing fury, before turning abruptly and storming out of the small room, past the video camera, bumping the table, causing the unit to shift slightly, Chase on her heals.

Teschal shifted in her seat. She'd seen this part too many times already.

Donovan leaned closer. His chair creaked softly.

The woman identified as Dolores Kane appeared in the doorway, calling after Chase and Connie. And then all hell broke loose.

Dolores raised her hands as if to ward off a dull shimmery light that seemed to be coming from someplace behind the video unit. She hunched down suddenly as if struggling to keep her position in a gale-force wind, her hair whipping out behind her. She screamed for Chase. But there was no other sound, no blinding light, just the dull shimmery glow and the silent wind. She was gripping the doorframe now, struggling to remain standing. And then there was a flash and the video unit tumbled off the table and fell to the floor, landing on its side, but still recording in spite of nearly continuous waves of visual and auditory static.

Dolores was crouching down now, desperately clutching the doorframe. Flames were visible, creeping into the frame, blowing across the scene, lapping at the walls, smoke filling the room. Dolores was screaming and coughing. She turned toward Mckenna, who had slowly gotten to her feet and was standing calmly behind her, raised her hand and reached up for her. A wave of static tore across the quivering scene and when the image stabilized, Mckenna was gone from view and glistening bits of debris were raining down on Dolores.

Dolores suddenly spun around and crawled on hands and knees past the video unit, clearly colliding with the mechanism, swinging it around until it was pointing in the direction of the door to the foyer through the legs of the dining room table and chairs. More static, like bolts of lightning, tore through the frame. Then, for a fleeting instant, there was a writhing shadowy form crammed into the doorway to the foyer, some twisted hulking shape with long crooked limbs, framed by blinding white beams of light that pierced the spaces between this horrific entity and the surrounding door frame. And lying between the lens and the thing in the doorway was a sea of blue flame that was hungrily consuming everything in its path. And then the film melted away and the bug fights resumed.

Richards hit the remote, silencing the static and putting an end to the bug war.

Donovan leaned forward, removed his glasses and laced his thick fingers.

"Would you excuse us detective?" Donovan said and Richards, looking mildly stunned, glanced at Teschal, set the remote on the table and got to his feet.

"Close the door please."

Richards complied.

Donovan rapped his fingers on the table.

"He won't appreciate that," Teschal said.

"He'll get over it." Donovan pursed his lips, hung his head, a stance that made him look more hawk-like than ever.

"Eve, you and I have seen things that most people would never dream about. We come from places where, let's say, the minds are more receptive to certain ideas, to certain *phenomena*. And we also know that not everyone understands such things."

Teschal nodded slowly as her eyes studied the wood grain of the table.

Donovan got to his feet. He walked slowly to the door, touched the handle, but did not open it. He glanced back over his shoulder.

"I'd say this one remains unsolved," he said. "I'll handle the chief and the mayor. Over time the press and the public will figure our killer simply stopped killing, finished whatever he'd started, or just moved on to greener pastures. Maybe he died in the fire and we're just covering it up. Maybe Joe Griece was responsible. Two birds, one stone.

In the end they'll wind up thinking just what they want to think. And maybe, this time, that will be for the best." Donovan opened the door.

"That'll be a hard sell," Teschal said.

Donovan sighed. "You let me worry about that."

Teschal felt herself nodding slowly.

"Good work detective. Oh, you might want to bury that DVD in the evidence room along with any copies you may have. Some *forgotten corner* of the evidence room where it can sleep peacefully."

Teschal watched Donovan leave, listened to his footfalls fading into the distance. She remained, her eyes staring into space. And she thought of her mother. *Drabarni*, she thought. Witch.

After a long moment she got to her feet, went to the video unit and ejected the DVD. She studied it for a long moment and slipped it into its case, shut the television and left the room.

Home

Chase and Dolores were perched on stools at the Night Owl Diner counter, plates of Coney Island hot dogs set before them, coffee cabinets in glasses resting in steel-handled tumblers beside these. A crimson summer sunset was streaming in through the surrounding windows, glinting off the aluminum trim, the rain long gone. Tom Petty and the Heartbreakers were singing *Even the Losers (Get Lucky Sometime)* from the guts of an ancient jukebox squatting in the corner. The black and white checker-board floor looked freshly washed and waxed, the smell of cooking burgers and Coney Island meat sauce filled the air. There were slices of pie under glass. Silver napkin dispensers. All the trappings of contentment squeezed into one small corner of the universe.

"I've never had one of these before," Dolores said as she finished her first 'dog.' "Always thought they were fattening. I suppose they are, but what the hell, they taste so fucking great. Were they really invented at Coney Island?"

"I thought I heard that they were actually named by owners of a place in Chicago who'd first *found* them at Coney Island or something like that, but the facts are a little muddled. The truth is lost to gastronomical history I guess."

"Well, in any event, they're great."

"I'm glad you approve," Chase said watching Dolores bite into another hot dog. He was slowly coming to terms with the fact that he was falling in love with her. He had never felt this way before, certainly not about Julie or about *any* woman for that matter. But then again he and Dolores had been through something that no one else on earth had ever experienced. And he'd always heard that it was in such moments of pure traumatic terror that the truth came spilling forth. And that was just fine with him.

But Chase was no fool. The road of life had its bumps. And the road that a relationship followed was perhaps the bumpiest of all. But some things were worth a jolt or two. This much he understood, perhaps at long last.

"How we doing?" the fry cook asked, wiping his hands on his apron.

"Great," Chase said.

"You know, I remember when this guy would come in here with his granddad," the man said in his deep baritone voice. "They'd order just what you've got there, dogs with the works and coffee cabs. Plenty of folks did that over the years, but I remember those two for some reason." The man shrugged. "I guess some things never change."

The man laughed his rumbling laugh, shook his big head and walked back to the grill where he scooped up his spatula and resumed flipping burgers.

Chase looked down at his empty plate. He could not remember Coney Island dogs having ever tasted as good as they had with Dolores by his side. All was right with the world.

A beat passed and in that instant he realized that something was amiss. He scanned the diner. The people sitting in the booths and at the counter seemed oddly familiar. There was a man in a postal uniform sitting by the door reading a newspaper. Some teenagers were crammed into a booth at the end of the counter flipping through the menus. Two mechanics with dark blue coveralls were seated at the counter near the bathrooms. But the clothes the patrons were wearing were somehow out of place, the hair-do on the waitress at the far end of the diner talking to a couple sitting in a booth looked wrong somehow.

Chase's gaze was suddenly drawn to the far end of the diner. There he saw a man sitting in a corner booth opposite a boy of perhaps twelve, whose back was to him. The man raised his eyes, spied Chase and smiled a warm familiar smile.

Chase returned the grin and turned to consider the big man at the grill, the man who'd just spoken to him. He was not the man Chase had seen working at the Night Owl as of late. That man was black, and his name was Charlie. Yet Chase knew *this* man nonetheless. *This* man was Ernie and he had been the Night Owl short-order cook when Chase would visit the Night Owl as a boy with his grandfather.

Chase turned to look back at the man in the booth and everything fell into place. *God*, he thought.

He turned back to Dolores, who had finished her food and was drinking her coffee cab. At that moment Chase realized that he was dreaming, and his dream had taken him and Dolores to a place he actually loved, a place he'd never visited with Julie, mostly because she'd never *wanted* to go there. This was a place he'd only visited by himself ever since his grandfather had died, a grandfather who was now sitting in the booth in the corner with a twelve-year-old Chase Christian dining on Coney Island dogs and coffee cabinets.

He turned to Dolores. She was grinning broadly.

"I love you," she whispered.

And then Chase woke up. He'd dozed off in Dolores' recliner, Dolores in his arms, asleep, safe and warm. Tom Petty had finished up, Enya had replaced him, the ethereal sound of *Even in the Shadows* drifting from the radio in the bedroom. Outside, the moon had risen.

Chase's eyes sought out the baseball sitting in its clear plastic case on the table by the sofa, no longer lacking 'Big Papi's' signature. When Dolores had presented the ball to Chase and shown him the third autograph he'd smiled broadly.

"How…"

She had simply grinned mischievously. "Friends in low places," she'd said softly.

The memory made Chase smile, probably always would. He touched his bandaged forehead. It was actually feeling better. He closed his eyes. And, as he began to settle back into his warm blanket of sleep, he thought he heard a sound, a cat crying someplace off in the night. He opened his eyes with a start, his gut tightening. His gaze was immediately drawn to a shadowy shape. Dolores' cat, Midnight, was lying stretched out on the back of the sofa, silhouetted against the window, considering him with tranquil, green eyes.

Chase felt himself grinning with relief, almost laughing.

"Good night cat," he heard himself say.

Midnight blinked once and turned his feline attention to the lighted cityscape beyond the glass.

Sighing, Chase melted back into Dolores' arms. He could still smell the Coney Island hot dogs from his dream. A moment later he found himself, once again, with Dolores, dining on Coney Island dogs and coffee cabs at the Night Owl Diner.

About Kevin Bouchard

Kevin Bouchard lives in south coast Massachusetts with his wife Robin and their Lhasa Apso Scarlett. He has earned a Bachelor of Arts degree in Theater and a Master's degree in Education, both from Bridgewater State University. He has worked as a Special Needs teacher in various settings for more than three decades. He has also worked as a professional musician playing drums with cover and original rock bands in and around Boston. **Cry of the Cat** is his second novel. His first novel, **Blue Moon**, which was the first novel to feature Detective Eve Teschal, is also available from Solstice Publishing.

Social Media

Website: www.kbouchard.com

Acknowledgements

There are many people who deserve my deepest thanks for the assistance they provided with the evolution of this tale. With regard to the character Eloise's history, I need to thank Marc Manigat, MD for relating some of his personal experiences with the infamous Ton Ton Macoute while he was growing up in Haiti. It's good to know that he got the better of the situation and is here to tell of it. Another individual I need to thank, (though he was an unwitting contributor and therefore will remain nameless), is a former student who enlightened me as to his time spent as a child soldier in a heretofore unnamed West African nation; the stories he related were indeed grim and perhaps the real horror story here. This information helped flesh out the character of Captain Donovan.

Chase Christian's profession as video 'stringer' is a somewhat familiar one; I briefly worked as a journalistic 'stringer' covering school committee meetings and such for local newspapers, typing up copy well into the wee hours. I also need to thank a friend from years gone by, Ted Gartland who, when we weren't playing rock and roll in clubs in Boston and he wasn't winning a Pulitzer Prize for photo-journalism, took the time to show me how a big city photographer made his living sometimes crossing the proverbial 'yellow police tape' to get the 'shot'.

Detective Eve Teschal's enigmatic history as it pertains to the Romany gypsies is a matter of my own curiosity and research. Her dementia-stricken mother's experiences are loosely based on my own mother's journey, (they say you should write about what you know, even if it is painful). And along those lines I must thank the kind and gracious staff at the various hospitals, geriatric rehabs, and skilled nursing facilities who I have met along the way. The information they have provided was much appreciated and the care they give to those in need is priceless.

I also owe thanks to many school-based police officers who have provided me with invaluable information pertaining to police procedure.

I am, as always indebted to my amazing wife Robin; a medical professional for nearly four decades she as well as her various associates proved an invaluable resource with regard to the medical elements of the story.

Gevaudan is a place that was born in my mind, though it is based on any number of countless mill cities and towns that pepper the New England landscape, (a few of which I have actually called home). Other places in the story, (the Bridgton Triangle, Bridgton University, South Coast

Starland) though loosely based upon real locales I have either visited or read about, are in the end aspects of my imagination. Chase's bad dream about the tenement entryway is my own; it has stayed with me since my childhood and is still scary and I would not part with it for anything. The Ouija Board story is mine as well; I still cannot explain it away.

Some of the tales relayed by characters in the story meant to enlighten or warn are derived from ancient ones that have been kicking around the planet in one form or another for decades, perhaps centuries. Others are products of my own imagination.

Midnight the Cat is from my childhood. The Night Owl Diner stands on the corner of a busy intersection in one of those mill cities I referred to as well as on a corner in my mind where its denizens will forever be preparing and dining on Coney Island hot dogs and coffee cabs in the glow of a perpetual summer evening.

www.ingramcontent.com/pod-product-compliance
Lightning Source LLC
Chambersburg PA
CBHW070308040726
47501CB00018B/387